VEILED THREATS

SECONDS

VEILED THREATS

FRANK SIMON

CROSSWAY BOOKS • WHEATON, ILLINOIS
A DIVISION OF GOOD NEWS PUBLISHERS

Veiled Threats

Copyright © 1996 by Frank Simon.

Published by Crossway Books
        a division of Good News Publishers
        1300 Crescent Street
        Wheaton, Illinois 60187

Cover Design: Cindy Kiple

First printing, 1996

Printed in the United States of America

Library of Congress Cataloging-in-Publication Data
Simon, Frank, 1943–
     Veiled threats / Frank Simon.
        p.   cm.
     ISBN 0-89107-880-0
      I. Title.
PS3569.I4816V45 1996
813' .54—dc20   96-10577

05	04	03	02	01	00	99	98	97	96
15	14	13	12	11	10	9	8	7	6	5	4	3	2	1

FOR MY DARLING LAVERNE

CONTENTS

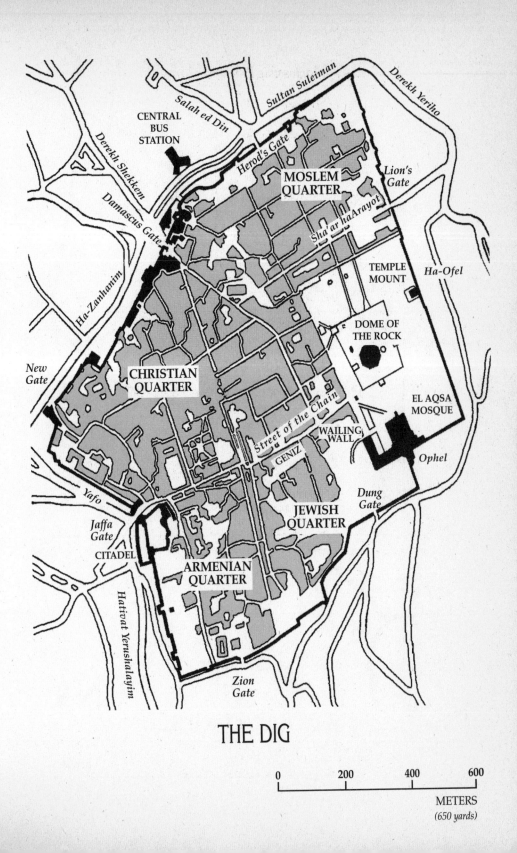

CENTRAL
BUS
STATION

Salah ed Din

Sultan Suleiman

Derekh Yeriho

Derekh Shekkem

Damascus Gate

Herod's Gate

Lion's
Gate

MOSLEM
QUARTER

Sha'ar haArayot

TEMPLE
MOUNT

Ha-Ofel

Ha-Zanhanim

New
Gate

DOME OF
THE ROCK

CHRISTIAN
QUARTER

EL AQSA
MOSQUE

Street of the Chain

WAILING
WALL

Ophel

GENIZ

Yafo

JEWISH
QUARTER

Dung
Gate

Jaffa
Gate

CITADEL

ARMENIAN
QUARTER

Hativat Yerushalayim

Zion
Gate

THE DIG

0   200   400   600

METERS
(650 yards)

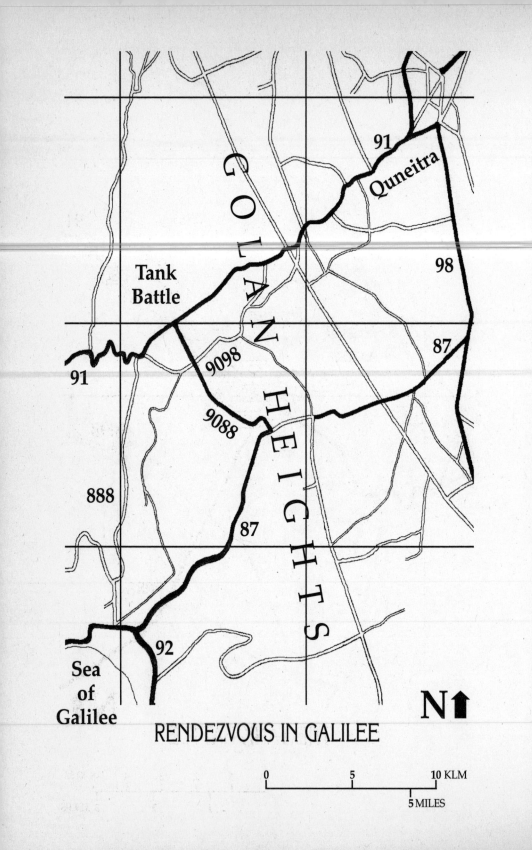

GOLAN HEIGHTS

91

Quneitra

98

Tank
Battle

91

9098

87

9088

888

87

Sea
of
Galilee

92

RENDEZVOUS IN GALILEE

N

0   5   10 KLM

5 MILES

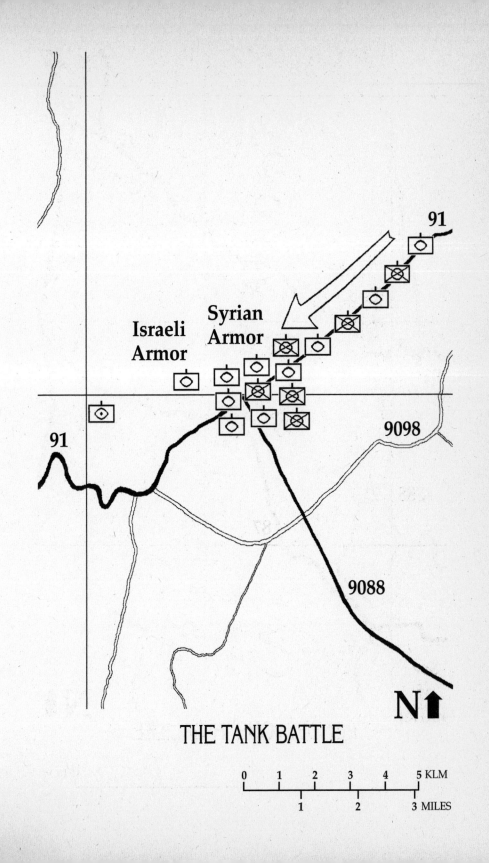

91

**Israeli
Armor**

**Syrian
Armor**

9098

91

9088

N

THE TANK BATTLE

0 1 2 3 4 5 KLM

1 2 3 MILES

1

ATTACK ON THE DOME OF THE ROCK

Captain Ya'acov Isaacson resisted the urge to look at his watch. It had been a little over an hour since the anonymous tip had come in, requiring quicker action than he was used to. Sweat popped out on his brow despite the cool, late-spring day.

He tried, unsuccessfully, to convince himself that he was inconspicuous. He shifted uneasily in his robes and looked up self-consciously at the fringe of his white, checkered *keffieh*. He knew his Arab clothing was quite authentic. With the makeup and his Semitic features, he looked like a follower of Mohammed. But he wasn't, and some of the real Arabs around him seemed to suspect it, although so far no one had approached him.

That he was on the Haram esh-Sharif, otherwise known as the Temple Mount, was bad enough. Orthodox Jews were forbidden to walk upon the Mount for fear of accidentally treading on the location of the Holy of Holies in the ancient Temples. This in itself didn't bother Ya'acov since he wasn't observant of the Law, let alone Orthodox. But this was uncontested Arab territory, and that did bother him. To complete his discomfort, he and one of his men were inside the third holiest shrine in Islam, after Mecca and Medina—the Dome of the Rock.

His uneasiness brought the earlier anger back with full force. He had asked Colonel David Kruger for twenty-five men but had been given only five—all regular Israel Defense Forces, not Military Intelligence like himself. The colonel had explained that any more would surely give them away and result in an Arab riot—not the best way to counter an alleged terrorist plot. But what could Ya'acov do with five men?

To add to his worries, Ya'acov felt he was not prepared to lead the operation. He had studied infantry tactics and counterterrorist operations during officer training but had no experience in either. The only army work he knew was intelligence, although he was very good at that. He knew the numbers: who had what, and what Israel and the various Arab forces could do. But he had never led men into combat. The colonel had emphasized, as only he could, that this was an Intelligence matter—it had to be led in-house. It took someone who understood the big picture.

That was Colonel Kruger's story anyway. Ya'acov had consulted his sergeant, an IDF regular by the name of Jerry Izenberg. He had asked the man for his recommendation to interdict a terrorist group trying to blow up the Dome of the Rock. Izenberg knew his stuff. What Ya'acov lacked in infantry knowledge, he made up for in judgment of character and good common sense. If he didn't know how to do something, he found someone who did.

Now Sergeant Izenberg waited outside with three of his men, forming something a little too tenuous to call a perimeter. And if that was the perimeter, Ya'acov and the man with him were either the reserves or the defenders of the inner ward. Ya'acov almost snorted at the thought.

◆

Abdul Suleiman glanced nervously toward Avraham Abbas as the two men waited near the entrance to the El Aqsa Mosque. The colonnaded entrance stood at their back, while before them stretched an improbable green belt that ended at the raised platform upon which the Dome of the Rock was built.

Abdul was distressed but knew better than to question the plan further. He had done that once and still painfully recalled his rebuke. All of their previous operations had made sense. But to blow up the Dome of the Rock . . .

Years ago Avraham had named the group the Palestinian

Revolutionary Force, or PRF. The Israeli Intelligence groups knew very little about the group, and most associated it with the PLO. Actually, all the PRF had in common with the PLO was ethnic identity.

Avraham turned his head as if he had heard Abdul's thoughts. Abdul shivered even though it was quite warm. He turned back toward the men. They were spread out, he noted with pleasure. He had trained them well.

"It's time," Avraham whispered.

Abdul nodded and started walking toward the east side of the Temple platform. He was to enter the Dome on the north side while Avraham led the nine men through the south. Abdul would enter first and, if anything looked wrong, walk through without stopping. Avraham watched Abdul ascend the southeast stairs. He counted slowly to himself. Then he walked slowly toward the southern stairs. His men spread out and followed him at irregular intervals.

◆

"Captain, we may have something." Sergeant Izenberg's voice sounded loud in the radio earphone.

"What is it?" Ya'acov whispered, hoping the tiny mike hidden in his robes would pick up his voice.

"Eight or ten Arabs trying hard to look like they're not together. They're coming up the steps now. And I don't think they've got praying on their minds."

"You sure?"

"They're up to something. What are your orders, sir?"

"You know what to do, Sergeant. Force their hand. If they're the ones, nail 'em. You need us out there?"

"No, sir. There might be a leaker or two."

Great, Ya'acov thought. What he and the man with him would do about leakers getting past the sergeant he had no idea. He felt the reassuring bulk of his Uzi submachine gun, wondering if he would be able to pull it out of his robes if he had to.

Ya'acov continued to divide his attention between the doors to the south and west, trusting that his man on the other side of the "holy rock" was watching the north and east.

Ya'acov's pulse had been rapid before, partly from adrenaline and partly from being out of shape. But now the waiting pushed his heart to the point of bursting. It seemed ages since his sergeant had issued the warning. He wondered if his radio had gone out, but that was unlikely, verging on impossible. Besides, he wouldn't need the radio to tell him the fight had begun.

"It's them!" his earphone shrieked.

The rapid rattle of Uzis sounded strange, part of the sound coming through the Dome's doors and part from Ya'acov's earphone. Fragments of orders and warning shouts punctuated the gunfire. Ya'acov listened in fascination as he heard Izenberg grunt with sudden exertion, the rustle of his clothing almost as loud as the guns. The sergeant shouted a quick curse, followed immediately by a startled gasp. Then all Ya'acov could hear was a choking sound and moments later a sharp crack as if the mike had hit something hard.

"Sergeant?" Ya'acov whispered.

There was no answer, although Ya'acov could still hear the sounds of struggles. He looked cautiously around the Dome interior. The Arabs were all heading for the north door. Ya'acov started edging back, staying close to the Rock while keeping his eyes on the southern entrance. When he was far enough back, he glanced quickly to the side, looking between the pillars and the Rock. There, in his direct line of vision, lay a crumpled wad of clothing with two sandals protruding at an odd angle. Ya'acov's fear was replaced with something colder and more final as he stared at the remains of his man.

Ya'acov jerked the Uzi out of his robes and thumbed the safety off. He spun around, his eyes taking in the arabesque kaleidoscope surrounding him. The only sounds, other than his own, came from outside, indistinct and quite irrelevant. Whoever was inside the Dome was being extremely cautious. Ya'acov tried to convince himself that the attacker had fled but knew it wasn't so.

Four large columns surrounded the Rock like sentinels, with three smaller columns between each. Eight more large columns made a circuit of the outer ambulatory interspersed with sixteen smaller ones. These and the massive Rock itself offered ample hiding places. Ya'acov crept to a large column near the Rock and peered around the edge toward the north entrance, the so-called Door to Paradise. He thought he heard a rustling noise near the door but couldn't be sure. He pondered this for only a moment—he knew what the man had to be doing.

Two large columns bracketed the north entrance. Ya'acov glanced at the nearer and dashed toward the other, cursing under his breath at the noise he was making. The terrorist could certainly hear him. Ya'acov locked his feet and skidded past the column, turning as he slid. A startled Arab on his knees looked up from a small package on which he had been working. He jumped to his feet as his hand darted, viper-like, into his robe. Ya'acov was bringing his Uzi around when his right sandal struck a crack in the floor. His leg caved in, and he started tumbling forward.

Ya'acov was conscious of falling, unable to stop. The Arab's gun, also an Uzi, was out and swinging toward him. Ya'acov pulled his trigger, stitching a jagged line of holes in the column just above the Arab's head. The man ducked as Ya'acov continued his graceless fall. Ya'acov hit the floor in a heap, gasping painfully as the hard stone pounded the air out of his lungs. His right hand flew open, and the Uzi skittered across the stone flags making a horrible clattering noise.

A wicked grin curled upward on the Arab's face. He extended his arm until his submachine gun was almost in Ya'acov's face, relishing the sweet revenge he was about to take. Ya'acov looked past the man toward the center of the Dome.

"Sergeant! For heaven's sake *shoot* him!" he roared.

When the Arab glanced quickly over his shoulder, Ya'acov kicked with both feet, hitting his opponent's shins. The man's sandals went out from under him, and he toppled as awkwardly as Ya'acov had. The IDF officer wheezed as he moved more quickly than he had thought possible. He landed on his enemy and reached for the man's gun hand with both of his own. The Arab glared up at him, furious that he had been fooled. His free hand shot toward Ya'acov's face. Ya'acov grabbed it with his right hand.

The Arab's face changed in a horrible way—from a mask of hate to one of triumph. He was far stronger than Ya'acov and more adept at close-in fighting. Ya'acov held his opponent's gun hand with all the strength in his left hand, but it wasn't enough. Slowly the muzzle came around.

Ya'acov glanced to the side.

"Over here!" he shouted. "Hurry!"

Ya'acov felt the pressure waver. He pushed as hard as he could, but the gun moved only an inch. There it stopped as if backed up by solid rock. The Arab's momentary fear was gone. He would not be fooled again. The muzzle regained its lost ground and continued its inexorable transit. Ya'acov could see the rifling in the barrel. At the bottom was a waiting bullet. And when it left the barrel, dozens more would follow, quicker than any eye could see.

Ya'acov glimpsed a large hand as it flashed past his peripheral vision. It slammed against the barrel and pushed it away. The Arab started to turn, a shocked expression erasing his triumph. A fist smashed into his face, knocking his head back on the stone floor with a loud crack. Ya'acov looked up, his mouth hanging open. The IDF soldier, one of his men, held out his hand.

Ya'acov ignored the help and crawled quickly to the package at the base of the column. It was, as he had thought, several pounds of C-4 plastic explosive rigged with a timer and detonator. Ya'acov deftly turned the timer off, trying not to shake. The slender black hand rested on the three-second mark. Ya'acov carefully removed the detonator. Sure that the bomb was safe, he looked up.

"Where did you come from?" Ya'acov asked as the soldier helped him to his feet.

The man looked surprised. "You called me over, Captain."

"I had no idea anyone was in here with us. It was an act of desperation. I thought I was a goner."

"You nearly were, sir."

Ya'acov couldn't help a weak smile.

"Meaning, I didn't know what I was doing," Ya'acov said, watching the man closely.

"I didn't say that," the man blurted.

"You didn't have to. Not to worry. I *didn't* know what I was doing."

Ya'acov watched the man struggle for a diplomatic reply.

"What about this man, sir?" The soldier said, changing the subject. He patted Abdul down and pulled him roughly to his feet.

"Take him away. I'll get the bomb and the guns." Ya'acov hesitated, suspecting he wasn't going to like the answer to his next question. "How did it go outside?"

The man looked down. "Not good, sir. They got Sergeant Izenberg and Ben Allen."

"They got Uri Kesar also," Ya'acov added, pointing to the shapeless heap near the Rock. "This one must have done it, but I didn't hear a sound."

"Some of these guys are quiet as cats. We did get two of them. Must have been about a dozen. We weren't able to capture any alive. It was a miracle any of us survived when they opened up. Then we almost had a riot going before the Border Police arrived. They brought some Arab muck-a-mucks along. It appears things are going to settle down now."

"Until the next time," Ya'acov said.

"You sure you're all right, sir?"

"Yeah, I'm fine. Let's go. Keep an eye on our friend there."

2

THE
LONGHORN

Anne McAdams pushed through the door of the American Colony Hotel and walked to the curb. She was rather short and had an unremarkable appearance—well-tended brown hair, cut close, and eyes that were green or gray, depending on the light. Her large round glasses flashed in the sun as she turned her head.

At her nod, a taxi swerved up to the curb. Anne got in, glancing at the Arab driver and wondering if he could speak English.

"Hebrew University," she said.

"Givat Ram or Mount Scopus?" the driver asked.

"What?"

"Two locations. One north of the city, the other near the Knesset."

"Oh. The one north of the city."

She gave the driver the name of the building where Moshe Stein had his office and sat back to enjoy the ride. In the two days she had been in Israel, she had not gotten used to the way Middle-Eastern cities were laid out. Very few of the Jerusalem streets met at right angles, and she decided that the best word for the city layout was "meandering."

The driver pulled briskly away from the curb, eliciting an angry honk as he cut off an Egged bus. He continued north on Derekh Shekhem for several blocks, where he slowed abruptly, downshifted, and made a tire-screeching right turn onto Derekh Har Ha'Zetim. They were traveling east, Anne noted, pleased with her sense of direction.

But then the street curved around to the north before making a final twist back to the northeast. The driver made a hard right turn moments later, followed almost immediately by a left turn, then bore right at a Y intersection. The road continued to twist and turn as it made its leisurely way up the side of Mount Scopus. By this time, Anne had no idea which direction they were going, except she assumed the American Colony was somewhere behind her. They rushed past signs in Hebrew and Arabic and many that also added English.

The driver turned right into a large parking lot and swept in beside the modern buildings of the University, pulling up in front of one in something barely less than a panic stop. He pointed a much-used finger at the nearest building.

"There," he said.

Anne paid him and got out. A glance at her watch told her she was on time, assuming, of course, she had no trouble finding Professor Stein's office.

She rushed inside, almost colliding with a young man with books to his chin. She apologized and asked where Dr. Moshe Stein's office was. He nodded to the stairwell, giving her a number on the second floor. Anne found the office and knocked.

A deep "Come" sounded from within.

She pushed open the door. Inside was a medium-height man with a bushy black beard that reminded Anne of her image of the patriarchs. His dark brown eyes peered at her over narrow reading glasses, as if deciding whether she was friend or foe. Black eyebrows resembling thatch provided awnings for the eyes. Anne found the sight fascinating.

"May I be of assistance?" he asked.

He had almost no accent—not at all what she expected.

"Excuse me, Doctor Stein," Anne said, feeling like an undergraduate. "I'm Anne McAdams. I have an appointment with you at 9 o'clock."

The brown eyes continued to regard her as he assimilated her words. She began to wonder if she was in the right office.

"Yes!" he declared, almost shouting as he broke into a broad smile. "Sit down, sit down."

He pushed a tottering stack of books to one side and jerked his

appointment book out. He turned a few pages, then ran his blunt fore-
finger down the entries.

"There," he said, as if the last mystery of the universe had been
solved. "Doctor D. A. McAdams. The A is for Anne? What is the D?"

"I go by Anne," she replied.

"I see." The arched eyebrows indicated the opposite. "And I am
Moshe." The smile came out again as he rummaged in the center
drawer of his desk. He pulled out a pair of bifocals and exchanged them
for his reading glasses.

"McAdams," he said, an intent look on his face. "Irish, a few generations back. And an Irish given name starting with D—something
inferior to Anne."

"Not Irish," she said.

"McAdams?"

"The D."

Moshe smiled. "I will find out," he said as if speaking to someone
else. "So, post-doc work in archaeology. No need to look any further.
You're in the archaeologists' paradise. The only problem is *where* to dig."

"That's why I was so glad you said you would help us. I've read
your work."

"Thank you. And the Hebrew University is acquainted with the
University of Texas Department of Archaeology. It is our pleasure to
assist colleagues in any way we can. Have you some preferences?"

"I was thinking about Caesarea."

"A good choice," he replied but not with enthusiasm.

"Is there a problem?" she asked.

"No. Caesarea is an excellent choice. It's a fascinating site. Still
much work to do there. But . . . would you perhaps consider a suggestion?"

"Why, yes, of course."

"This is only a suggestion. I'm sure the Caesarea site would be very
rewarding, and if that's what you would like, we will set it up. But have
you studied any of the work we've been doing in the Jewish Quarter in
the Old City?"

"Some," she admitted. "But I'm not as familiar with it as other
sites."

Moshe described the devastation the Jewish Quarter had sustained in 1948 and in subsequent wars. He spread out large black-and-white glossies on his cluttered desktop as he pointed out city walls and houses from the time of King David, towers and buildings Herod the Great had built, as well as later Roman and Crusader ruins. Anne was amazed at the density and preservation of the finds—a Herodian wall cutting through a pre-Exilic house; the Roman Cardo Maximus forming a central north-south line in the Old City, running unbroken for hundreds of feet.

"There are more archaeological finds packed into the Old City than any other site I know of. And it's a *living* city, not some dead tell. Now, along with the good must come the bad, am I right? Unfortunately. The Jewish Quarter Reconstruction and Development Company, affectionately known as 'the Company,' is waiting to build on every available square meter of the Old City. And patience is not one of their virtues. But they also pay for much of our excavations. And we have enough supervision to last until Messiah comes. Our work is coordinated by the Institute of Archaeology at the Hebrew University, *and* the Department of Antiquities and Museums of the Ministry of Education and Culture, *and* the Israel Exploration Society. But the Company—always in such a rush."

Anne shifted uncomfortably in her chair. "How can you work under those conditions?" she asked, unable to conceal her distaste.

Moshe laughed, appearing not at all concerned. "We hurry. That's not good, but it's the way it is. There's always a project waiting to build as soon as we put our shovels down. That means we have to use machines—backhoes, even bulldozers."

That earned him a sharp glance undiminished by her glasses.

"Not to worry," he continued. "It really doesn't cause as much damage as you might think. And look—have you ever seen such sites?"

Anne gazed at the pictures, imagining what it would have been like to be on those expeditions. She had planned on roughing it; not that she especially wanted to, but it was usually required. To dig down thousands of years within walking distance of your lodging . . .

"You've sold me," she said at last. "I presume you are prepared to make your suggestion a little more specific."

"Of course." He smiled. "There's a new site I would like to investigate that is between the Jewish and Moslem Quarters. I would be honored if you would be the codirector."

"I would be glad to," she said with a nod. "What's the site like?"

Moshe paused before answering. "Several months ago a building blew up on the north side of the Street of the Chain near where it runs into the Wailing Wall."

"Blew up?" Anne asked, her voice rising.

"Terrorists, we think. Whether they did it on purpose or a bomb went off accidentally, we don't know."

"Did anyone claim responsibility?"

"Not in this case, so it probably was an accident. Anyhow, that building and the one next to it were scheduled for demolition to make way for a new hotel. So we have to get in there before the construction crews."

Moshe eyed her speculatively. "You're frowning. Anything the matter?"

"Something I heard on my way out of the hotel—a fragment about the Dome of the Rock. This site reminded me of it."

"Oh, that."

Moshe looked down at his desk. He squared up a tower of books that looked on the verge of collapse. "There's an old Jewish proverb," he said. "'May you live in interesting times.'"

"I've never heard that one."

"Actually, it's not exactly a proverb. It's a curse. But it's certainly true for today. Some crazies tried to blow up the Dome of the Rock yesterday. The IDF were there. How? Don't ask me. And there was a firefight. Two of the terrorists and three soldiers were killed. They captured one of the guys as he was planting his bomb inside the Dome. The rest got away in the confusion. Almost had a riot before it was over."

"Arabs were trying to blow up the Dome of the Rock?"

"Actually the paper didn't say who it was. Might not have been Arabs."

Anne refrained from asking the obvious.

His smile returned briefly. "Could be a Jewish extremist group, as you are thinking but are too polite to suggest. At least the Arabs think so. The PLO are screaming about it; what else?"

"What do you think?" Anne asked.

"I really don't know. I can't imagine an Arab group trying to blow up the Dome."

"What about the man they captured?"

"Paper says they haven't been able to identify him or the dead men. Maybe we'll learn more later. Meantime, I suppose we should get back to your business."

Anne struggled with her feelings. What was it like to live in a place where this sort of thing was normal? Like most Americans, Anne was used to the relative peace enjoyed in the United States. She knew many places in the world were not so blessed, but coming more or less face-to-face with terrorism made it personal.

"Yes, I guess we should," she said, trying to focus on archaeology. "Your suggestion sounds fine to me. What are the chances of finding something?"

"You never know. But in the Old City it's very likely. Anyway, I'm glad you want to join us. I've got my usual quota of slave labor—students. But I really can use an experienced archaeologist as codirector of the dig."

"Speaking of students," Anne said, remembering her other task, "I've got one coming in tomorrow on an El Al flight from New York."

"Another longhorn?" Moshe grinned.

Anne laughed. "I suppose you're disappointed I didn't come in here with my cowboy boots and spurs. No, the guy's name is Mars Enderly. He's not from the University. He's from Southern Methodist University in Dallas. I've never met him. He's working toward his Ph.D. His department at SMU arranged it with UT. So I will supervise his work."

"Mars. What an interesting name. How is he getting here from the airport?"

"I'm going down to Tel Aviv to get him."

"Lod."

"What?"

"Ben Gurion is in Lod, which is east of Tel Aviv," Moshe said with a smile. "But we'll use my vehicle. I must take care of my help. It's too hard to come by. Where are you staying?"

"The American Colony, which brings up another point. I booked us for only four days. I don't know about Mars, but I can't afford to stay there the entire time I'm in Israel."

"I've already taken care of that," Moshe assured her. "By Monday afternoon you'll have rooms at the Albright Institute hostel."

"You thought it likely we'd need some place to stay in Jerusalem?"

"Of course I could not know for sure, but I had to assume that my colleague, whom I had not met, would be intelligent enough to seize the wonderful opportunity offered her."

"As I recall, I don't believe the Albright Institute is connected with the Hebrew University," Anne said.

"You are correct. The Institute is run by the American School of Archaeology. But I have ways to get things done."

"Thank you," she said, trying to hide her amusement.

"You are most welcome. Now, what time is the flight?"

◆

Captain Ya'acov Isaacson pulled open the top right-hand drawer of his desk and grabbed the Nestle's candy bar as if it might get away. He pushed the drawer shut, propped his feet up on the desktop, and peeled the wrapper. Just as he took a healthy bite, the phone rang. He chewed rapidly, picked up the phone, and gulped the wad down.

"Hello," he rasped as some of the chocolate went down the wrong way.

"Ya'acov?" said the caller. It was Lieutenant Colonel David Kruger, his boss.

The captain was tempted to ask who else would be answering the phone but caught himself. "Yes, sir."

"I need to see you."

"I'm on my way."

"No—I'll come by your office. See you in a minute."

Ya'acov looked at the receiver as if it had sprouted legs, then slowly replaced it in the cradle.

He had barely removed his feet from the desk when a sharp rap sounded on the door, and David Kruger rushed in without waiting for an answer.

"Come in," Ya'acov said as his boss sat down in a side chair. The look he got let him know that lieutenant colonels expected more deference from captains.

"We're not feeding you enough?" David commented, spying the candy wrapper.

"Have to keep my strength up. Something happening, sir?" Ya'acov was well aware of his weight problem, which was officially noted in his Israel Defense Forces medical records. It was something he had to deal with soon, but he wanted to put it off as long as possible.

"You could say so. The Prime Minister wants intelligence on the Temple Mount incident."

"I'll send out for some."

"Isaacson!"

"Yes, sir?"

"I didn't come in here to get your opinion on the government. You were there. What's going on?"

"Sorry, sir. But they've been after us ever since it happened. We don't know much. Do they want us to make up something?"

"Of course not. The whole Arab world is screaming for our heads, and the PM needs to feed the media. The Dome's only the third most holy shrine in Islam."

"It's still there."

"But it nearly wasn't. Without that tip, it would have been all over."

David leaned back and massaged his forehead. "All right, let's review it again," he said with his eyes closed.

Ya'acov sighed. "We received the tip from a thirteen-year-old computer hacker around twelve-thirty hours. It seems some of the ultra-Orthodox encourage their children to learn to use computers, as long as they don't do it on Sabbath. The kid hacked his way into one of the new Jerusalem central office switches and was amusing himself by looking up auth codes and credit card numbers. When that got boring, he found he could patch into the telephone lines and listen in. That's when he heard these two Arabs talking about blowing up the Dome of the Rock."

"This Jewish boy speaks Arabic?" David asked.

"Yes, he does—we've verified that. But is he telling us the truth? Could be he's covering up what his parents are involved in."

"I could point out that the parents are ultra-Orthodox, but I get your point. Continue."

Ya'acov shifted uncomfortably in his chair. "I guess the real question is, doesn't this smell more like an ultra-haredi plot? Oh, and one more thing. The kid tipped the *Jerusalem Post*. So most of the papers, with the exception of the *Post*, are gently suggesting, with the highest journalistic ethics, that we have an ultra-haredi gang on the loose."

David opened his eyes. "Jews blowing up the Dome of the Rock? Well, given the circumstances, I could believe that."

"Perhaps, sir." Ya'acov's tone said the opposite.

"Carry on," David said.

"After some difficulty, we managed to convince the Arab religious authorities of the plot, and they agreed to let us take a squad up on the platform. Just as Sergeant Izenberg got the men set up, in came the Arabs. One leaked through and killed the man inside the Dome with me. The sergeant forced a fight outside that routed the terrorists, killing two at a cost of two more of our men. I attacked the leaker and almost got myself killed. I defused the charge, several pounds of C-4, and we were all done. Three for two and one captured. Not so good."

"Anything on the prisoner?" David asked.

"He's smart and tough. He won't talk. We're trying to trace him by fingerprints and mug shots, but no luck so far. TV coverage mirrors the press, with CNN out in front and the rest struggling to catch up. They've analyzed the attack to death and are telling the public what they should think: *The Jews done it!*"

"You have a way with words," David said dryly.

"Yes, sir. There is one small bright spot. The *Jerusalem Post* thinks it's that new terrorist group we've begun to hear about—the Palestinian Revolutionary Force. How they heard about them I have no idea. But that won't cut much ice with the rest of the media. What would they expect a Jewish rag to say?

"The Arab citizens are screaming in their usual incoherent style. Iraq and Iran are foaming at the mouth, which is certainly not unusual for them. Syria is a little more subdued, but not much. The Saudis are grumbling in their beards as they look around to see how the other Arab states are reacting. And Egypt is relatively quiet, for now.

"I caught a Syrian newscast off the satellite about a half hour ago. The announcer described it as a plot by the religious Jews aided by American Zionists. Said it was the latest in a long series of attempts to destroy the Dome so we could start building the Temple. Once again we're on our way to the Mediterranean without a boat."

"What do you make of the Syrian situation?" David asked with deceptive calmness.

"As the colonel knows, the Syrians are not content with our common border. They would like all of northern Galilee, in my opinion. The only thing that's been stopping them is how embarrassed they get every time they attack us."

"So they're bluffing?"

Ya'acov considered before answering. "No, I don't think so. Not many in Intelligence agree with me, but I think they want a go at it. And this incident could provide the excuse they want, regardless of who really did it."

"Hmm. You may be right. I sure hope you're wrong, but this whole thing has a bad smell about it. Anything else?"

"Not at this time."

"So, who do *you* think did it?" David asked, his eyes boring into Ya'acov's.

"It could be the work of one of the PLO factions, or any one of dozens of splinter Arab groups. It's sheer guesswork at this point. If I had to guess, I'd plump for the PRF. The *Post* could be right on this. But we really don't know."

"General Levy wants more than this. The PM, I gather, was quite specific."

"That's all there is right now. We're working on it as hard as we can. Maybe something will turn up."

"I'm sure the general will appreciate it."

"I hope so, sir."

Ya'acov was glad that seeing General Levy was his boss's job. David rushed out.

Ya'acov waited a few moments, then replaced his feet on the desktop. He grabbed the remains of his candy bar and finished his interrupted snack.

3

A SURPRISE FOR MARS

Mars Enderly had had better days. First his flight into JFK from Dallas had been delayed by weather. That this reduced his long layover he conveniently forgot. Then he found that the only way to get to the International Terminal was by bus. The rain caught him full force as he staggered up the bus steps holding a large suitcase and a canvas tote bag.

"Where's the International Terminal?" he asked, unable to see the driver clearly through his rain-streaked glasses.

"I'll announce it," a New York accent answered. "Move to the back."

Mars swallowed his retort. He tried to do as the man said, but the bus was crammed. The rain continued to pour down, making a hollow drumming noise on the top of the bus. The humidity completed the job of fogging his glasses. He set down his bags and wiped his glasses on his shirt. It didn't help much.

After several stops, the driver announced the International Terminal. Mars thought for a moment he would be trapped on the bus, as no one appeared willing or able to let him out. Finally he squeezed past and stumbled out the rear doors. The bus immediately started off, the large rear wheels splashing him.

"Welcome to New York," Mars grumbled as he avoided the skycap and rushed into the terminal. The cool air conditioning fogged his glasses completely. He stepped to the side to keep from being run over and removed the glasses for serious cleaning. He pulled his shirttails out and polished the lenses until they were dry. Satisfied, he put his glasses back on and tucked in his shirt.

He had over two hours to wait. He made a trip to the restroom to work on his appearance but decided there wasn't much he could do.

He was surprised to see a moneychanging booth when he returned to the main terminal. Although he hadn't planned to, he decided to get some Israeli currency. He countersigned two fifty dollar traveler's checks and gave them to the teller along with his passport. She counted out the currency and shoved it and the passport back through the slot.

Mars's next decision was not as easy. He had time to call his father in Dallas, but he really didn't want to. He knew the elder Enderly would give some "fatherly advice." Still, Mars felt he should talk to his dad before leaving the country.

He walked to the bank of pay phones, let the machine examine his calling card, then punched in the number.

Moments later he heard, "Hello."

"Dad, this is Mars. I'm in New York waiting on my flight to Tel Aviv."

"Mars," came the faraway voice, obviously relieved. "Glad you called. Didn't know if I'd hear from you."

"Yeah—didn't have time to call you from D/FW," he lied. "Had to rush to catch my flight. You wouldn't believe how crowded the terminal was."

"That's okay. I'm glad you had time in New York. How's the Big Apple?"

Mars glanced out the big glass windows.

"Right now it's raining—about what you'd expect for the last day of May, I guess. But it's supposed to clear up. It's two hours until the flight. I changed a few traveler's checks into Israeli money—had to show my passport to get it. Thought about getting a snack but decided to see what they've got on the plane. Want anything from New Yock?"

Joe Enderly laughed. It was genuine, Mars knew, and almost as charming on Mars as it was on his father's business associates. Joe

Enderly wasn't worth millions because of ignorance and bad breath. "How are you flying out?"

"You are kidding, of course. Who would go to the Holy Land but by El Al?" Mars's Jewish accent was recognizable but not very good.

"I suspect the price was right and the flight direct."

Mars winced and struggled to contain his irritation. "Yeah, I guess that's it. And speaking of direct, I see that old Dad has applied his business acumen to analyzing my decisions again."

There was silence at the other end of the line. Then, "That wasn't my intention, Mars. Since you mentioned my business, it's not something I'm ashamed of, any more than I am of my tour in the Navy. You know how I feel about my work."

"Yes, I know. Enderly and Son. Dad, we've been through this too many times. I want to be an archaeologist. I don't want to join you in your counting house." Mars fell silent, strongly tempted to slam down the receiver. Why did his talks with his dad always end up like this? All he had wanted to do was say good-bye.

"Mars?"

"Yes, Dad?"

"I'm sorry."

"Yeah. Me too."

"I appreciate you calling. I know I'm a pain to you, but I really don't mean to be. I love you, Son. More than I think you realize."

"I love you too, Dad. That doesn't have anything to do with the other."

"Yes, I know. Mars?"

"Yes?"

"If you need anything, call me."

"What could I possibly need?"

Joe laughed. "I don't know. I only want you to know I'm here. Please call me from Israel. I'd like to hear how you're doing. Reverse the charges."

"Okay, I'll call, and it probably will be collect. I'm not loaded with shekels right now."

"Son, I remember my school days. Call me."

"Thanks, Dad. I will. Bye."

"Bye."

Joe waited until he heard the phone click and the dial tone came. He slowly replaced the handset in the cradle.

◆

True to El Al's schedule, Flight 002 boarded on time. With a little help from the attendants, Mars found his way to his window seat in the forward part of the coach section. He sat down, fastened his seat belt, and rummaged in the seatback pocket.

Soon he glanced furtively from the pages of the airline magazine to watch a middle-aged man settle down in the next seat. The man had on a black suit and broad-brimmed hat. Round wire-rimmed glasses and a bushy black beard with long side locks completed the rather forbidding appearance. He paid no attention to Mars.

The huge, blue 747 was pushed away from the boarding ramp right on time. The rain had stopped, and now the afternoon sun struggled through a few holes in the gray clouds.

The delay for takeoff lasted only a half hour. The big jet lumbered down the runway with surprising acceleration and lifted off, assuming an almost uncomfortable angle for the departure climb. The pilot banked slightly as they crossed over the coast and headed out over the gray, choppy Atlantic. The view disappeared abruptly as the plane entered the base of the clouds.

At cruising altitude, the attendants marched down the double aisles with their aluminum juggernauts, defying anyone to get past them. Mars took a bourbon and Coke to occupy his time until dinner. He made a hurried trip to a cramped cubicle that called itself a lavatory. He returned to his seat to find that the carts were back with dinner.

Mars suspected he would not be offered pork chops, and he was right. He selected the lamb roll entree. The man next to him said something in Hebrew. The attendant replied in kind and handed him his tray. Mars watched in fascination as the man sat back for a long prayer before starting his dinner. Mars didn't know what the food was, but it certainly smelled good.

Mars decided his own dinner was the best he had ever had on an airplane. He chose music over the movie and flipped to the classical channel. The first selection was Pachelbel's *Canon in D*, one of his favorite pieces. He felt himself drifting off to sleep somewhere over the Atlantic.

◆

Not long after breakfast, the pilot pulled the power back on the four high-bypass fanjets, and the blue 747 began a gentle descent toward the coast of Israel. Mars watched line after line of white breakers marching across the turquoise Mediterranean toward a coast that was just coming into view. A high-pitched whine sounded as the flaps started down, followed moments later by the disconcerting bump of the wheels extending. Over the coast, Mars saw the city of Tel Aviv with its many low-lying buildings, punctuated by a few tall ones sprawled below. Off to the south was the old city of Jaffa, looking ancient and peaceful nestled among its date palms.

The pilot made one final turn and settled into his final approach. The tires chirped loudly as the 747 touched down at Lod's Ben-Gurion International Airport. The plane pulled up to the gate and stopped, the engines winding down after the long flight.

Mars shuffled out of the cabin with the rest of the passengers, feeling like part of a cattle drive. He picked up his suitcase and tote bag and started toward the main terminal. He stopped before the imposing Customs sign and read what he could legally bring into Israel. Deciding he wasn't in any trouble with the State, he walked down the green concourse. The Israeli agent stamped his passport with a solemn thump, and Mars was officially in the land of Abraham.

"Shalom," the agent said. "Enjoy your stay in Israel."

Mars murmured a reply and struggled past with his weighty load, wondering how he would find Dr. D. A. McAdams, since he had never met the man.

"Mr. Enderly?" a man with a black beard asked.

"Dr. McAdams?" Mars asked, evaluating the solidly built man and the short woman standing with him.

"No. I am Moshe Stein with the Hebrew University. This young lady is Dr. McAdams."

"*You* are Dr. McAdams?" Mars asked, unable to keep the surprise out of his voice.

"Careful," Anne cautioned with a smile, "your chauvinism is showing."

Mars felt a flush of embarrassment, which made him mad. Why did he have to make a fool of himself the very first thing?

"No, it's not that at all," he said. "The only way I've ever seen your name is D. A. McAdams. I had no idea. I apologize, Dr. McAdams."

"Mr. Enderly, I think you have the wrong idea about me," Anne said. "I'm not an ultra-feminist." She was smiling, the twinkling green eyes open and friendly.

He relaxed a little, and a trace of a smile turned the corners of his lips. "My name's Mars."

"Please call me Anne. We're going to be working side by side, so formality is out."

"Yes, ma'am."

Anne paused for a moment.

"I started to call you Mars, but . . ."

"But knew it couldn't possibly be my real name," he finished for her.

"She has an interesting name too," Moshe observed, looking pointedly at Anne.

"Now that you mention it," Mars replied. "The A, I take it, stands for Anne. What's the D for?"

Anne glanced at Moshe, only to see his studied innocence.

"Do you have more luggage, Mars?" Anne asked.

"She won't tell me either," Moshe volunteered. "If I find out, I'll tell you. And you must do the same for me."

Anne gave them both a look that seemed capable of giving them sunburn.

"Shall we go?" she asked. "I could ask where you got the name Mars."

"Yes, I guess you could."

She waited.

"Are we ready to go?" Mars asked.

Moshe laughed and led the two out of the terminal and up to what he called his vehicle—a 1961 Volkswagen bus that had had a somewhat checkered career. It sported the original paint job, blue—what there was left of it. It had more dents and outright bashes than could be counted—

something like the grains of sand on the shore. The passenger-side door was minus the window and had to be held shut with a piece of wire. The back was crammed with disorganized archaeology paraphernalia. A few aluminum folding chairs were included in case more than the driver and one passenger would be riding.

Mars lofted his luggage into the back and climbed inside, wending his way forward. Moshe assisted Anne up into her seat and wired the door shut.

"Be careful of the folding chairs," Moshe advised Mars. "They're not in real good shape."

Mars felt something give under him and hoped he would not fall through.

"Thanks for the warning," he said as Moshe climbed up into the driver's seat. "Your vehicle appears, ah, very functional."

"Meaning a piece of junk," Moshe translated.

He jammed down the clutch and engaged the starter. The associated mechanicals did not seem happy at being called into service, and Mars began to wonder if the engine would start. After a few cranks, an explosion sounded from the back, and the engine roared to life, a blue cloud obscuring the rear view. Mars could tell it had been some time since the bus had had a muffler.

They climbed steadily as they traveled the short distance from Lod into the Judean Hills and finally to Jerusalem, or, as Moshe informed them, Yerushalayim. They entered the city on Sederot Weizmann.

"Up ahead is the War of Independence Memorial," Moshe said as they proceeded down Yafo toward Ha Nevi'im. "A few more turns and we'll be there."

Moshe pulled up in front of the American Colony Hotel and switched off the engine. Mars shook his head, wondering if the ringing in his ears was from the flight or the drive.

Moshe turned in his seat. "I imagine you'll need to get your internal clock adjusted. I'll help you in with your bags."

"Thanks—I can get them."

"Very well. I'll be back for you two tomorrow."

"That's Saturday," Mars objected.

"You mean Sabbath?" Moshe asked with mock surprise. "Doesn't affect me, but don't quote me. As long as we stay away from the

Orthodox neighborhoods we'll be all right. Normally we don't work on Saturday or Sunday, but we're holding up a construction crew that's waiting to build a new hotel. It can't start until we check the site."

"What is the site?" Mars asked.

"Tomorrow," Moshe promised.

"Thank you, Moshe," Anne said. "I'll help Mars get settled. We'll see you in the morning."

"Good. I'll join you for breakfast here at the hotel, if that's agreeable."

"Fine," Anne replied.

Moshe drove off, trailing a plume of blue smoke behind him.

"Let's get you checked in," Anne said. "I imagine jet lag's about to get you."

"Naw, us SMU Mustangs are tough."

In the lobby, Mars avoided the bell captain and set his bags down at the registration desk. During the check-in ritual, Mars produced his passport and showed the prepayment voucher for his stay. The clerk extended her "Shalom," and Mars graciously turned down the offer of a bellhop's assistance to the room.

"That's done," he said to Anne. "What say we look around a little since we don't have anything to do until tomorrow?"

"Are you up to it?"

"Why, sure. I had a double dose of Geritol today . . . this morning . . . er, yesterday—whatever."

Anne laughed. "Why not? I'll wait for you in the lobby."

The room, he noted, wasn't smooth and shiny like a Hyatt, but rather comfortable and neat—the way he liked it. He put the bags next to the bed and hurried back downstairs. He paused in the stairwell. Anne was looking through the lobby doors. In a moment she turned and saw Mars. She smiled. After a short pause he returned it. Not only was his professor not a man, she was not a stuffy academician either. This was not at all what he had expected.

"That didn't take long," Anne remarked. "Thought you'd want to freshen up."

"Nope. Rarin' to go."

"The Old City is less than a half mile away. Want to walk?"

"Sounds good to me. Lead on, McAdams."

They walked down Derekh Shekhem, past St. George Cathedral and St. Stephen's Church to arrive at the Damascus Gate to the Old City. They crossed Sultan Suleiman and stood looking at the crenellated towers guarding the ancient stone ward.

"Built when?" Anne asked.

He stole a quick glance at her. "Why, Professor McAdams, pop quiz already? I thought we had the day off."

"You don't know," Anne said, playing his game.

"It's called the Damascus Gate by Christendom, Sichem Gate by the Jews, and Gate of the Pillar by the Moslems. Contrary to popular opinion, it does not date from the time of Christ. It was built around 1540 by Suleiman the Magnificent, as the Arabic inscription on the arch lintel states. And we *know* he was magnificent 'cause he said so. Do I pass?"

"A plus," Anne said. "I'll bet you're a terror to your profs."

"Not me."

"Want to see the Dome of the Rock?"

"Yes, I do."

They made their way through the jumble of ancient buildings in the Moslem Quarter of the Old City. Most of the streets were too narrow for cars. Except for a few large churches or mosques, most of the buildings were small houses, apartments, or shops. But one's eye naturally gravitated to the octagonal blue structure with the golden dome, the third holiest site in Islam.

Mars and Anne stopped at the kiosk outside the Bab en-Nazir gate to the Temple Mount and bought tickets to see the Dome of the Rock and the El Aqsa Mosque. They walked through the gate and up the steps to the Dome's platform, marveling at the perfect geometrical symmetry of the octagonal walls and the round drum supporting the gleaming dome. The arabesque, blue faience tiles were breathtaking in their detail.

"They sure did a good job refurbing it," Mars said, referring to the restoration done in 1963.

"It's exquisite," she agreed.

They joined a tour group and entered the building. Inside were two concentric circles of columns, arranged in geometric perfection. In the very center was a large golden-yellow rock jutting through the floor. The guide informed the tourists that this was the pinnacle of Mount

Moriah, where, according to Moslem tradition, the prophet Mohammed, mounted on his charger, left earth for heaven. Part of the rock, the guide said, broke away and tried to follow Mohammed and had to be pushed back into place by the archangel Gabriel. He indicated the horse's hoof marks and the archangel's fingerprints.

"Heavy duty," Mars whispered with mock awe.

"Hush. You'll get us thrown out."

Back outside, they walked to the east side of the platform and gazed at the Golden Gate.

"Really looks beautiful in the afternoon sun, doesn't it?" Anne asked.

"Yes, it does."

They took the southern steps down from the platform and strolled to El Aqsa Mosque, impressive in size and architecture but without the symmetry of the Dome. Oriental rugs covered the floor of the cool interior. Some of the columns, dazzlingly white, made of Carrara marble, had been presented by Mussolini. The ceiling overhead had been a gift from Egypt's King Farouk.

"I wonder what kind of fairy tales the guide has for us this time," Mars whispered.

"Shush."

It was early afternoon when they finished the tour. Anne glanced at Mars. Bravado or not, she could tell he was getting tired. She found herself liking him, even if he was a little brash. But, she had to admit, she had probably been a little brash herself as a postgraduate.

"Say, it's past lunchtime, isn't it?" Mars asked.

"Yes, I suppose it is. What do you suggest?"

"We have two choices, I guess. We can stop at one of these street vendors and get some roast camel hump . . ."

"Ugh!"

"When in Rome . . ." he argued. "Or we can look for a McDonald's."

"Are there any here?"

"I wouldn't be surprised."

They settled for an outdoor cafe. Mars plopped heavily into his chair.

"Getting tired?" Anne asked innocently after they ordered sandwiches and iced tea.

"Not a bit," he insisted. "Say, are there any, you know, shows in Jerusalem?"

"If you mean what I think you mean, no. There are some genteel night clubs but nothing raunchy."

"You misjudge me, madam. Genteel is what I meant."

"I'll bet. Why don't we go back to the American Colony and get some rest. Later we can have an early dinner. I suspect tomorrow will be a long day."

"To the hotel it is."

◆

Captain Ya'acov Isaacson sat down at the table, turned the writing pad slightly, and pulled a pen out of his pocket. He paused for a moment, then started making a list. He longed for a candy bar and a soft drink, but he knew these would not fit the image of a ruthless interrogator. This was an aspect of his job he did not enjoy and did not feel qualified for, although his boss said he was good at it. *Probably because he doesn't want to do it*, Ya'acov thought with irritation. He nodded to the guard standing by the door. The soldier opened the door and called outside. In a moment the prisoner came in, flanked by two other guards.

"Leave us," Ya'acov said. The three soldiers hurried out. Ya'acov wrote one further line, then put the pen down. He looked up at the man. The captive stared over Ya'acov's head as if he were alone in the room.

"You don't know who you're dealing with," Ya'acov began in passable Arabic. "I know what you are thinking: this is Israel and we'll be turning you over to our judicial system and you'll take your chances there. Who knows, the judge might even give you a medal. Forget it! I'm with Military Intelligence, not the regular IDF. The Mossad we're not, but I can *still* keep you here as long as I want—and do whatever I want."

Abdul Suleiman glanced down at his questioner. His expression did not change.

Ya'acov tried to read the prisoner's eyes. If there was a reaction there, he couldn't see it.

"We'll start with your name." He waited five full minutes for an answer. Finally he retracted the ballpoint pen and put it back in his pocket. "Guards."

The three soldiers returned as quickly as they had left. Two escorted the prisoner out while the third remained.

"It's not good for prisoners to get too much rest," Ya'acov said.

The other nodded and left the interrogation room. Ya'acov got up and walked out the only other door. He felt in his pocket for change as he headed for the canteen.

◆

Anne stepped off the elevator. Not seeing Mars, she took her time walking across the lobby to join the line at the door to the restaurant. She stood behind a heavy-set man struggling to keep a large portfolio tucked under his arm.

"Hi," Mars said, coming up suddenly.

Anne whirled around, striking the man's portfolio with her purse. The oversized envelope fell to the floor, scattering its drawings and photos.

"Oh, I'm sorry," she said, stooping down.

The man got down on his knees, careless of his well-tailored suit, wheezing a little with the effort of regathering his material.

"I feel like such a klutz when I do something like that," Anne told him as she helped gather some black-and-white photos.

"What you feel and what you are are not always the same," the man said with a New York Jewish accent. "A klutz? I think not. I can actually drop these all by myself. I've done it."

"There's one more over there." Anne retrieved a large photo hiding behind a potted plant. She paused, looking at the picture before handing it back.

"That's a beautiful picture of Haram esh-Sharif," she said.

"Yes, it is, isn't it? There's more history tied up in that little mountain than any other place on earth."

"Yeah, some Arab guy gave us an earful a little while ago," Mars observed.

"Ah, a skeptic," the man beamed. "How wonderful. It does pay to examine the merchandise."

Anne watched the picture disappear into the envelope. "I have to ask—what are you doing with those pictures?"

"Forgive me. I should have introduced myself. I am Zuba Rosenberg."

"Pleased to meet you. My name's Anne McAdams, and this is my colleague Mars Enderly."

"Shalom to you both. As to what I do, my enemies say all manner of unkind things, but I am actually a tour guide. I run a little organization in Greenwich Village, and from time to time I bring tours to the Middle East. These pictures will be used in one of my talks on Jerusalem."

"Rosenberg," came a voice from the door.

"My table's ready," Zuba said. He took a step, then paused. "Would you two care to join me?"

Anne looked at Mars.

"I would deem it an honor," Zuba added. "I can see we are interested in the same things, but I haven't found out why yet."

"We would be delighted," Anne said, though *curious* was closer to the truth.

"Fine." Zuba headed for the maitre d'.

Their table was set for four. The maitre d' seated Anne as the men fended for themselves. Zuba parked the portfolio in the vacant chair.

"You will forgive me if I observe that the average American wouldn't know Haram esh-Sharif from a parking lot, except they'd wonder where the stripes were."

"The Ugly American," Mars said.

"No, ignorant and proud of it."

Anne laughed.

"So?" Zuba eyed his companions.

"Well, Mr. Rosenberg . . ." Anne started.

"Zuba please."

"Zuba, Mars and I are archaeologists. We're here in Jerusalem on a dig. In the Old City."

"Wonderful. Are you working with anyone?"

"Yes. Moshe Stein with the Hebrew University."

"Moshe. How is the old rascal?"

"You know him?"

"For years. His methods are somewhat eccentric, but he knows his stuff."

The waiter appeared at Zuba's elbow, pencil poised over his pad.

"Ah, starvation has been narrowly averted. What will you two have?"

"I think I'll try the Saint Peter fish," Anne said. "Sounds interesting."

Mars turned his menu to the fish entrees. "I was going to have a hamburger, but I guess I'll have the fish also."

"I will make it unanimous," Zuba said.

The waiter wrote rapidly, closed the pad, and left with a nod.

"Probably the last we'll see of him," Mars said.

"I doubt that," Zuba said. "You picked a good hotel. The food's good, and so is the service."

"How did you get to know Moshe?" Anne asked.

"Oh, it was years ago. I was exploring the Old City and came upon a particular dig. It was a tremendous hole in the ground with a pre-Herodian tower base at the bottom. And there was this long, rickety ladder going down into it. It was raining that day, so I wondered, what is that noise coming from the hole? I leaned over the barrier, and there was this guy holding an umbrella in one hand while he scraped away with the other—with a spade, of course. I asked him what he was doing. He tilted the umbrella back and invited me to come and see. That didn't sound terribly appealing. The ladder didn't look all that sturdy, and my frame is somewhat robust. But I accepted. I was glad when I got down, but more so when I got out. I made a good friend that day."

"Do you see him often?" Mars asked.

"Every chance I get. But tell me, what are you two looking for?"

"We don't know yet," Anne replied. "Moshe knows of a promising site near the Western Wall—a bombed-out building."

"I think I've heard of it. Right off the Street of the Chain."

"That's it. We've got to see if something's there before a construction crew comes in. Sounds like we'll be rushed."

"Moshe's had quite a few digs go that way. Don't worry, he'll still do it right."

"Are you sure you're not an archaeologist?" Anne asked.

"Only a tour guide," Zuba replied. "But such tours!"

"Are you conducting one now?" Mars asked.

"As a matter of fact I am. I will give a talk at the King David Hotel tonight, then we're off for two weeks. We start at Jerusalem and go to Bethlehem, Hebron, Tel Aviv, Haifa, Nazareth, Tiberias, Massada, and Jericho."

"Bunch of little old ladies?" Mars wanted to know.

"No. It's a group of Christians from Topeka, Kansas. They want to see their roots."

"*Their* roots?" Anne asked.

"This is the land of Jesus."

"Doesn't that bother you?"

Zuba frowned as he looked at Anne. Then he understood. "Oh, I see what you're thinking. The New York Jew vs. the Midwest Bible-beaters. It makes sense, I guess. But a lot of what makes sense doesn't make sense if you look at it closely. I'm afraid I'm traveling under slightly different colors than you suppose. You see, I too believe Jesus is God's Son."

Anne was dumbfounded, and Mars's jaw dropped.

"It's not as extraordinary as it seems," Zuba continued. "The Orthodox Jew says he doesn't know Messiah's name. I say I do. Jesus. Or more properly, Yeshua. What about you two?"

Their silence gave Zuba his answer.

"That's all right," he said. "I was there one time myself."

He grabbed his portfolio and fished inside for two small books with black covers.

"Here," he said, extending one to Anne and the other to Mars. "It's the New Testament and Psalms. Very interesting, and guaranteed not to hurt you. And as archaeologists you should note that it's the most accurate ancient book in the world."

"Is Moshe a Christian?" Anne asked.

"Moshe does not share my views on this. But we are still friends. And he may change his mind someday."

Anne didn't know if she was relieved or not. For the briefest moment she had the ghastly thought that Moshe was a Christian too. But then she knew it couldn't be. Moshe was not a fool to be taken in by myths. However, Zuba was a puzzle. The man was obviously educated—he certainly knew archaeology, for a layman. How can a person be intelligent in one area of life and a fool in another?

"I see," Anne said at last. She fingered the textured cover of the Bible.

"Perhaps one day," Zuba said.

Mars shoved his Bible back toward Zuba.

"Now look," he said, his face flushing in anger, "you can . . ."

Anne grabbed Mars by the hand.

"But . . ."

"Please," Zuba said. "I am sorry, my friends. I meant no offense, I assure you. It's just that I care. From the bottom of my heart, shalom."

"Here comes our dinner," Anne said quickly as the waiter approached with their tray.

"You are a lifesaver," Zuba told the man, who looked puzzled for a moment, then began serving them.

"Enjoy," Zuba said.

Anne sampled her fish. She was somewhat surprised to find it was quite good. She liked fish well enough but had learned that "fresh" was usually a synonym for "frozen."

She watched Zuba. The man appeared at ease on the surface, but she sensed a hidden turmoil—though clearly it did not affect his eating.

When the waiter brought the dessert trolley, Zuba said with authority, "Everything there is wonderful, but the chocolate mousse is the most wonderful of all."

"None for me," Anne said.

Mars declined also, obviously not having found his good humor again.

"Coffee?" Zuba asked.

Both shook their heads.

"You must excuse me," Zuba said. "I must be off or I'll be late for my lecture." He spoke to the waiter in Hebrew, and the man nodded. Zuba gathered up his portfolio. "The dinner is on me," he told his companions.

"Oh, no," Anne said quickly. "You needn't do that."

"It's done," Zuba said with a smile. "You won't see the waiter again." With that he departed.

Anne and Mars were left alone at the table.

"We're going to be at it early tomorrow," she said.

"Guess so. Damper's already been put on the evening."

"Mars, please. He's a nice man."

Mars didn't try to hide his irritation. "Sure. Okay." He obviously didn't mean it.

For a moment Anne's mind went back to the last visit to her West Texas home. Her mother had been so excited about the trip to Israel. This had pleased Anne until she learned that her mother's interest was in the land of Jesus. Now comes this Messianic Jew who loves archaeology but also believes in Jesus—Yeshua. Anne felt a cold knot form in her stomach. Something unseen seemed to threaten her peace of mind.

She pushed back from the table, then stopped. With the barest hesitation, Anne slipped the New Testament into her purse. Mars stood up, leaving his on the table. He walked her to her room on the second floor and said good night. He then returned to his room, threw himself into bed, and went to sleep.

4

THE DIG BEGINS

Mars walked out his door at quarter to seven. Anne had said they were to meet Moshe for breakfast on the hour. He considered knocking on her door to see if she was ready to go down but decided not to.

He entered the dining room and was surprised to see Anne already seated, sipping a cup of coffee. A ray of the morning sun shone through her full hair. The golden glow fascinated him as his eyes traced the details, finally ending up on her face. He flushed as she looked up and caught his gaze.

"Good morning, Mars," Anne said. Her smile was open and sincere.

"Um, hi," he mumbled as he sat down. The waitress poured him some coffee, then left them to look over their menus. Mars took an incautious sip, wincing as it burned all the way down.

"Wow! What a way to wake up." He tried valiantly to smile but was not successful.

"Am I interrupting?" came a voice from behind Mars.

"Moshe, sit down," Anne said, looking up. "We're having some coffee. Ready for breakfast?"

"Look at me," Moshe said in mock distress, running his large hands over his bulging shirt. "Does this give you a clue?"

He sat heavily, placing his *Jerusalem Post* on a corner of the table.

"Where is the waitress?" he asked.

"Shalom," she said, coming up behind him.

Moshe jumped.

"Get around here where I can see you," he said over his shoulder. "I would teach you some Hebrew idioms if it weren't for my American friends."

"You might learn a few yourself," she replied.

"What will you have?" she asked, turning to Anne.

Anne ordered cereal and toast. Mars had the same, while Moshe ordered poached eggs, two bagels, and a grapefruit. The waitress finished writing and left for the kitchen.

"One of my students earlier this year," Moshe said. "Smart."

"Archaeology major?" Anne asked.

"No. Economics. She took an introductory archaeology course as an elective. Mark my words—she'll be Finance Minister someday. I eat here a lot since it's handy to the Old City. But she has no respect for her elders."

However, the service was excellent, and the absence of conversation testified to the quality of the food. Anne finished her coffee and looked at the front-page picture in the newspaper.

"The Dome of the Rock," she announced.

Moshe slowly unfolded the paper. "Yes. The Arabs are continuing to scream about the situation. They say it's a Jewish plot so we can rebuild the Temple. The Prime Minister is wringing his hands. He really hasn't said anything, except that we would never do such a thing. The *Post* seems a little unsure, even though earlier they were speculating about some new terrorist group—the Palestinian Revolutionary Force."

"Anything new?" Mars asked.

"No, thank goodness. That's all we need is to have something happen to their precious Dome."

Moshe looked down at his watch.

"Almost 8," he said. "We need to be on our way."

◆

Moshe pulled up within the barricades blocking part of the Street of the Chain and shut off the engine, leaving the bus in gear to keep it from rolling away.

"Emergency brake doesn't work," he explained as he jumped out.

"Ben," Moshe said as a man wearing disintegrating blue jeans and a baggy cotton shirt walked up.

"I want you to meet Dr. Anne McAdams and Mars Enderly." Moshe turned to the Americans. "This is Benjamin Navon—goes by Ben. Best equipment operator I've got. The more levers and pedals the machine's got, the better he likes it."

Ben gave both a firm handshake with work-hardened hands.

"That's instead of decent pay," Ben said in heavily accented English.

"Enough pleasantries," Moshe said. "Someone here is paid by the hour. Don't I hear your machine calling you?"

Ben smiled, then loped off to his backhoe. He climbed up on the machine and cranked the engine. It came to life with a roar and settled down to an uneven idle. He lowered the front bucket and started scraping away the hard-packed soil from within the foundations of the demolished buildings.

"I wish we didn't have to use that," Anne said.

"Can't be helped," Moshe replied. "We're holding up an expensive construction crew."

"Anyone else working on the site?" Anne asked.

"Unless we find something, we won't need anyone else."

"Let's hope it's *until* we find something," she said.

"Of course."

Ben worked his machine with considerable artistry, wheeling it about with precision as well as speed. He often lifted the front wheels off the ground as he bore down on the rocky subsoil to scoop away the rubble of centuries. The pile of debris grew rapidly.

About an hour later Moshe motioned for Ben to stop. "We need to check the foundation."

"Why?" Mars asked.

"The building might have been built on ancient footings. It happens more often than you'd think."

Moshe took picks and shovels out of the bus and handed them around. The four spread out and started digging down to expose the foundation stones. Despite his age and seeming lack of fitness, Moshe kept up with the others as he dug down into the dry, rocky soil.

Finally he stopped and cleaned away the clinging dirt from the bottom stones. He looked at the stones, then climbed out and looked in the other holes.

Moshe shook his head. "This foundation was laid down when the building was erected. And so far we haven't seen any shards or anything to indicate an ancient site."

"Does that mean nothing's here?" Mars asked.

"Too soon to tell."

Moshe pointed to a spot about ten feet from the front of the foundation. "Ben, let's move back from the foundation a little."

Ben climbed up on his backhoe and started digging a trench about fifteen feet wide parallel to the street. Moshe examined each bucket load as it was dumped. "This is unusual. Most of the time we see ancient detritus in the subsoil even if we don't find any structures. But so far, nothing. Of course, we'll sift the soil later to be sure."

The excavation soon became monotonous as the backhoe dumped load after load. Ben pursued his work as if it were the most important thing on earth, right up to the point Moshe signaled him to stop.

Moshe hauled a large blue cooler from the back of the bus. He carried it in his arms since the handles were broken off.

"Mars," he said, "please get us some chairs out of the bus."

They lined the chairs up near the trench. Moshe and Ben picked what they wanted and sat down. Anne and Mars dug around trying to find out what all was in the cooler.

"It's all good," Moshe announced. "Everything delicious and guaranteed kosher."

He took a healthy bite from his sandwich with obvious relish. Anne picked the nearest thing to hand and sat down. Mars grabbed something too and poured some coffee for Anne and himself.

Anne had to admit the sandwich was good, even if she didn't know what it was. It was spicy, but not as spicy as Mexican food.

"This is wonderful," she said. "What is it?"

"Enjoy," Moshe replied.

When they were done, Moshe packed the assorted wrappings back in the cooler and returned it to the van. He then instructed Ben to dig a new trench about fifteen feet deeper into the building site. They spent the rest of the afternoon just like the morning. They shut down near dusk, and Moshe drove Anne and Mars back to the hotel.

Moshe turned to Anne. "Tomorrow it's the hostel. Ready to leave your luxury accommodations?"

Mars groaned from the back.

"That sounded like a discouraging word," Anne observed.

"And the skies are not cloudy all day," Mars finished for her. "But we're not home on the range, folks. I'm going to miss the Colony."

Anne laughed, as Mars hoped she would. "These students from SMU are all alike, Moshe. Next time I'll bring another longhorn."

Moshe toyed with the gearshift lever. "Something I've always wondered . . ."

"What's that?" Anne asked cautiously.

"How did the University of Texas get such a mascot?"

"They got last choice," Mars said in a rush.

Moshe started to laugh, but Anne's expression stopped him at a wide grin.

Anne turned sideways in the seat and gave Mars her undivided attention.

"Hi," he said sweetly.

"I almost forgot," Moshe said before Anne could take up the gauntlet. "I'm having a couple over to my apartment tonight, Dan and Rebecca Adov. Dan's a reporter for the *Jerusalem Post*. Would you two like to join us? If you don't want to, say so. Probably not much fun for young folks."

Anne looked back at Mars. He nodded, then gingerly made his way through the junk to the bus's rear door.

"We'd love to," Anne said.

"Good. I won't be able to come after you, I'm afraid. My apartment needs a touch here and there to make it presentable."

"Is it anything like your office?" Anne couldn't help asking.

"There are some similarities," Moshe admitted.

"We'll get a taxi. What time should we come?"

"Make it 7:30. Here. I'll write the address down."

"Thank you, Moshe," Anne said, taking the note. "We'll see you then."

Mars untwisted the wire, pulled open the door, and held out his hand. She took it and stepped down to the curb. His eyes followed her as she drifted past. A few seconds later Mars heard a discreet cough.

Moshe was grinning at him. "I make better speed with that door closed."

Mars felt as awkward as a teenager as he shut the door and fumbled with the wire. Moshe nodded and drove off, turning left at the next corner.

"Guess that leaves us time to get packed before going over," Anne said.

"How thrilling," Mars grumbled as he watched the blue cloud slowly dissipate.

◆

"This is nice," Mars said, looking up at the mass of stone towering above them.

The taxi had delivered them to an apartment complex on French Hill. It was a series of stair-step stone homes, marching up the hill as if they were buttressing the summit. A lone minaret stood in the distance, providing a cultural counterpoint. It was convenient to Mount Scopus to the west and the Old City to the south.

"Looks like the perfect place for an archaeologist," Anne agreed. "Convenient to the University, too."

They took the stairs up to the second floor. Mars knocked on the door. After a few moments they heard footsteps, and the door swung wide.

"Come in, come in." Moshe led them into the combination living room and dining room. The furnishings were utilitarian and well-worn—a couch, three mismatched chairs, and a small coffee table. Large bookcases were crammed with books, but there was nothing on the walls except one framed photograph. It was a black-and-white 8 x 10 obviously photographed from a smaller print that had not been very good in the first place. It was a picture of a young woman and two small boys.

The couple on the couch got to their feet. The man was rather slim and had well-trimmed black hair with a little silver. The lady's hair was all one shade, and she had an expression that indicated she liked having things her own way.

"Anne, Mars, I want you to meet Dan and Rebecca Adov, friends of mine for longer than I can remember. Dan, Rebecca—Anne McAdams and Mars Enderly."

Dan's handshake was firm and friendly, Mars noted with approval.

"Mars—that's an interesting name," Dan said, his eyes glinting behind round, wire-rimmed glasses.

"Speaking of interesting names," Moshe interjected, "Anne's full name is actually D. Anne McAdams."

"Thank you, Moshe," she said.

"My pleasure. Now, you people get acquainted while I put the finishing touches on dinner."

"What does the D stand for?" Rebecca asked.

Mars made a steeple of his hands and rested his chin on the apex. He smiled at Anne. Anne struggled not to return it but couldn't keep a straight face.

"Devious," came a voice from the kitchen.

They all laughed, breaking the tension.

"Delovely," Mars said. Anne watched as a line of red crept past his collar and flushed his face. She didn't know whether to be embarrassed for him or pleased at the compliment—if it was a compliment.

"That comes from a song older than you are," Dan said. "My compliments to your musical knowledge. And I believe your observation is correct."

"Fair warning," Moshe said. "I'm putting on the finishing touches."

"Shall we powder our noses?" Rebecca asked Anne. They left the room.

Dan waited until he heard the door close.

"This will be interesting," he said.

"What?"

"Rebecca is dying to know your lady's name. And she is extremely adept at extracting secrets."

"Anne and I are not . . . I mean, she's not my lady."

"You have no interest in her?" Dan asked.

"Ah, I didn't say that," Mars replied after a long pause.

"I didn't think you did," Dan said.

"Your wife won't find out," Mars said.

Dan looked doubtful. "Rebecca's—how shall I put it? Formidable. The French do so much better with that word."

"You don't know Anne," Mars said.

Dan managed to keep a straight face. "As a reporter, you know what my next question will be."

Fortunately, just then the bathroom door opened, and the women passed by on their way to the table.

Dan glanced at his wife and lowered his voice. "She didn't find out," he admitted.

Moshe seated his guests and then brought out the first course, expertly serving each person.

"You may have missed your calling," Dan observed.

"What do you know? You spend all day with your beak in a typewriter."

"Word processor."

"Whatever. I think we're ready." He sat down at the head of the table. "For our American friends, this is *humus* with pita bread. Enjoy."

The *humus* was followed by *shashlik*, grilled sliced lamb. Anne was momentarily suspicious; she halfway expected steamed entrails a la something unpronounceable, but was pleasantly surprised. The conversation languished as the food disappeared from the plates.

"I hope everyone saved room for dessert," Moshe said as he pushed away from the table. Four sets of utensils landed on the plates in anticipation. Moshe clattered around in the kitchen, opened the refrigerator, and pulled something out. There was a long pause and some strange noises before their host returned. Moshe brought in a metal tray and placed a large crystal parfait glass at each place, mounded with chocolate mousse wreathed with whipped cream and topped with a cherry. Accompanying each dessert was coffee in delicate china cups.

"Moshe," Rebecca said, "that looks heavenly."

"It is," he agreed. "It required constant checking while I was making it."

The cherries disappeared in a hurry, followed soon by the whipped cream. The mousse went more slowly as they savored the rich chocolate.

"The portions are sure generous," Mars observed.

Moshe snorted. "I can't stand those restaurants that serve desserts in those dinky little cups. A waiter once brought me a tiny scoop of ice cream and told me to enjoy my dessert. I told him I would if he'd bring it out."

"Did you really?" Anne asked.

"Of course I did. He took it away and brought me a large bowl. Good thing he did, too. Reinstated his tip."

Anne laughed.

"He really did," Dan said. "I was there. Rebecca fortunately was not; she hates scenes. I tried to act like I didn't know him."

"That's the trouble today," Moshe grumbled. "We let those who serve act like the guest. It's not right, and we shouldn't let them get away with it."

"Take the soapbox away before he gets up on it," Dan said.

"This is the best dessert I've ever had," Mars commented. "And I'm not just saying that."

Anne nodded in agreement. "My uncle has a favorite saying: 'That's so good you'd slap your mother for another one.'"

They finished the dessert. The Turkish coffee was strong and hot and brought the dinner to the excellent ending that few meals ever have.

There were no complaints when Moshe suggested they retire to the living room. Anne picked the narrow sofa, and Mars, after a moment's thought, sat there also. He wasn't sitting next to her, but he wasn't sitting at the other end of the couch either. Dan and Rebecca took side chairs at one end of the couch, while Moshe threw himself into a well-worn chair that had to be his private preserve.

"Now that we are all comfortable . . ." he said.

"That was really excellent," Dan remarked with a sigh.

"Thank you. Coming from you, I consider it a real compliment. Now as I recall, when I left you people to get acquainted, you got sidetracked—on what I can't remember. Dan, you and Rebecca have our American friends at something of a disadvantage since I told you some of their background before they got here. All they know is that Dan works for the *Jerusalem Post*."

"We certainly must improve on that," Dan said. "I am a reporter for the *Post*. Rebecca helps me on some of my assignments, but she's mainly the executive director of our household."

"Dan, dear," Rebecca interrupted, "I thought we weren't going to joke about that anymore."

"Hmm. Sorry. Not much more to tell. Being a reporter may sound exciting, but it's plain, hard work around a lot of unpleasant people."

"He means politicians," Moshe interpreted.

"And a certain archaeologist." Dan glanced at Moshe. "You didn't get us here to spring something on me, did you?"

"Me? Would I do such a thing?"

"You have. And more than once. Have you found something?"

Moshe waved a hand. "No, my friend. At least not yet. Anne and Mars are helping me excavate a site in the Old City, but we've barely started. But if we do find something, you will be the first to know."

"What sort of things do you write about?" Anne asked.

"Whatever I'm assigned. The latest squabble between the Likud and Labor, incidents at the Western Wall, and quite often archaeological finds. I have been involved in several of Moshe's, and not quite by accident, I'm sure."

"Are you accusing me of using the press?"

"Yes."

"*That* was certainly direct."

"You didn't deny it."

"Here I serve you a wonderful dinner, and this is the way you repay me."

"You old raconteur—you're setting up your account so you can call it in later."

"How embarrassing," Moshe rumbled. "What must our guests think?"

Dan glanced at Mars and Anne. "They think we are close friends," he said in a softer tone of voice.

This appeared to fluster Moshe.

"Moshe told us your schools, but not where you were from," Dan said, changing the subject.

Anne decided it was "ladies first." "I'm from the high plains of Texas, a little town called Lorenzo, about twenty miles from Lubbock. My dad's name is Bob, and my mom's is Florence. Dad's a cotton farmer—not the easiest way to make a living in that part of Texas. I'm an only child. When it came time to go to school, it was either Texas

Tech or the University of Texas. My parents wanted me to go to Tech because it's close. But I've always wanted to be an archaeologist, so I talked Dad into the University."

"You *are* effective in convincing people," Moshe observed. "Now, what about Mars?"

Mars cleared his throat uncomfortably. "I'm from Highland Park, an incorporated town surrounded by the city of Dallas. My dad's name is Joe. My mother died five years ago. Her name was Elizabeth. After high school I went to Southern Methodist University, where I received my Master's degree in archaeology. I'm working on my doctorate as we speak."

"Would your father be the president of Dallas Heuristics?" Dan asked.

"Why, yes. How did you know?"

Dan smiled. "I am a reporter. Your dad's company is heavily involved with Israel Aircraft Industries."

Anne could tell Mars was ready for the conversation focus to shift. "How long have you known Moshe?" she asked Dan.

"A long time," he answered.

"Since Kibbutz Dan," Moshe added.

A silence fell. Anne looked at Moshe and then Dan.

"Where is that?" she asked cautiously.

"It's in the Hula Valley north of Galilee, under the Golan Heights. We all arrived there before the '67 war. Dan and Rebecca were aliya from America." Moshe paused and looked down at the floor. "I grew up there, and that's where I met Sarah. After I got my Bachelor's degree, we married and lived there, in between my service in the IDF. That's where David and little Jonathan were born."

"Moshe . . ." Dan said softly.

"It's all right." Moshe's expression was an odd mixture of sadness and peace. "I had such a dear family—until August 12, 1963. I was away on reserve duty.

"Kibbutzniks have this thing about using all the land there is. We had this sorry field that was over a ridge on the Golan side, quite remote from the rest of the kibbutz. Sarah was out there with the boys hoeing weeds.

"We had been having trouble with Arab terrorists infiltrating from

Golan for quite a while. Sometimes they shelled or shot rockets at us. But this time it was personal. I wish I could say it was quick and merciful, but it wasn't. Sarah was apparently repeatedly raped in front of my sons, then they mutilated the boys. I don't know how long the torture would have gone on if Rebecca hadn't come looking for Sarah. She ran back to the kibbutz for help, but it was too late. The terrorists finished Sarah and the boys off with knives and escaped across the border. They were never caught."

No one said anything for over a minute. Anne couldn't take her eyes off Moshe. How could people do such things? And how was Moshe able to deal with it?

"Moshe, that's horrible," she said, knowing it couldn't express what she felt.

"Yes, it is. It's a long time ago now, but I'll never get over it. I'll never forget my Sarah. I love her as much now as I ever did. I miss her so. And my boys."

Mars cleared his throat. "You never . . . ?"

Moshe shook his head. "No, I never remarried. Mars, my friend, there was only one woman meant for me. I miss her. I'll always miss her. And no one can take her place."

"I'm sorry," Anne said.

"For what?"

"For bringing it up."

"Why? It brought back good memories as well as bad. Besides, you didn't bring it up—I did."

Everyone tried to keep the evening going, but it wasn't possible. Moshe tried his best to be the perfect host, but it was a weak effort. The embarrassing silences were punctuated by well-meaning gambits, but nothing worked. Finally Rebecca announced that she had a terrible headache, and the Adovs excused themselves.

"Moshe, we'd better be going too," Anne said.

Moshe looked at her but said nothing.

"I am sorry about what happened," she said. "I care, but I feel totally helpless."

"You are very sweet," Moshe said. "Feeling helpless is something you get used to in Israel. We bustle about, and we've accomplished a lot. But one thing we can never forget. Forget the peace initiatives—

we're surrounded on three sides by people who hate us and would like nothing better than to drive us into the sea. You know, it's odd . . ."

"What's that?" Mars asked.

"This is the Holy Land."

There was a long pause.

"We'll see you tomorrow," Anne said finally.

"Yes," Moshe said. "Thank you for coming."

Moshe turned to Mars, and some of the old charm returned. "Look after our lady."

"Oh, yes," Mars replied with obvious embarrassment. "I will."

"I know you will. See you two tomorrow."

5

RAIDING THE
PRF

The loose metal shade rattled in the wind as the naked bulb cast a yellow pool of light over the entrance to number 7 Sha'ar haArayot in old East Jerusalem. The Moslem Quarter was quiet, which was not surprising since it was 3 o'clock in the morning.

Inside, the scene was not so peaceful. An innocent question during a long-delayed meal had begun a chain reaction and suddenly all thoughts of eating were forgotten.

Avraham Abbas glared at Mustapha Kabran, who was seated across the table wishing he was anywhere else. Mustapha had become the group's acting chief of operations, the job Abdul Suleiman had done so well. Abdul had been an excellent leader and tactician, and he was one of the few men who could get along with Avraham, at least most of the time.

"Are the bombs ready or not?" Avraham had demanded.

"Not quite, but we're working on them." Mustapha rubbed his bulbous, pock-marked nose to cover his exasperation. He knew better than to lie. Avraham could always tell. Besides, he never took anyone's word for anything.

"I left you clear instructions before I left today. What's the holdup?"

"It's because of the change of plans. If we're going to hide the bombs in cardboard boxes, I have to break down the satchel charges and divide the C-4 among the boxes. And I'll need some more plastic.

Also, there's a special explosive I'd like to get that looks like paper or cardboard. We can build boxes with it and even put some sheets in the boxes. It will take a lot of work, if we're really going to get as many boxes as you said."

Mustapha knew he was in trouble before he finished speaking, but he couldn't stop in time. His bushy black eyebrows arched upwards as he waited for the blast.

"*You* are questioning *me*?" Avraham thundered.

"No, certainly not. That did not come out as I wished."

"*When* can I have my bombs? We have to strike fast to take advantage of the Dome of the Rock coup."

For now the attack's premature ending was conveniently forgotten. All that mattered was the intense public reaction.

"A few days, if I can get the other stuff I need. I'll send some men to our base in Jericho to get the C-4. I don't know what to do about the explosive papers."

"I want the bombs by tomorrow evening."

"But . . ."

"No buts! I will have those boxes of photographs with me when I return from Tel Aviv."

"What if the Jew was lying?"

Mustapha half-expected Avraham to give him another blast, but the man only looked at him. That was worse than a tongue-lashing. "The Jew was not lying. I went to Tel Aviv today. Dan Braun *does* have a cousin named Naomi Braun. Whether she is a survivor of Auschwitz or not, I don't know. But that's not the point, my dear Mustapha. I was busy getting things done today. I wasn't looking for excuses. Do you see?"

"Yes," Mustapha lied.

All Mustapha knew about Dan Braun was what Abdul had told him before the Dome attack. Avraham was proud of the fact that he could pass for a Jew, complete with an excellent forgery of an Israeli identity card. Several weeks ago he had been "Rabbi Avraham Horowitz" and had met Dan Braun at an outdoor cafe in the Old City. Avraham had charmed the other man. Braun had this old photograph of his cousin, Naomi, taken before World War II in Poland. And she had boxes of old photos in her house in Tel Aviv. Avraham had even managed to talk Dan out of his cousin's picture.

The phone rang.

Mustapha jumped. He hesitated, then picked up the receiver.

"Hello," he said cautiously.

"This is Daoud!" a voice said. "Get out! I think the IDF is on their way over there."

"Who is it?" Avraham demanded.

Mustapha put his hand over the mouthpiece. "It's Daoud!" He took his hand away and spoke rapidly. "How do you know? Tell me!"

Avraham reached toward the phone. "He knows better than to call on that line! Let me have that!"

Mustapha scooted his chair away from the table and waved the PRF leader away.

"I saw the officer point toward our building from the corner," Daoud spilled out. "Then he led his squad one block north. They're coming down the street behind you now!"

"I understand. Get out of there." Mustapha slammed the phone down.

"Well, what did he say?" Avraham growled.

"An IDF squad is on its way here. They're on the next street over at this moment."

"What?"

"That's all he said."

"First the IDF surprises us at the Dome of the Rock. Now this. What's going on? No one knows about this headquarters."

"Maybe Abdul's been broken."

Avraham slammed his fist down on the table, causing the telephone to jump. "Mustapha, can't you think, even a little bit? Abdul is a good man. He will not break. They'd kill him before he would tell them anything."

"What do we do?" Mustapha asked.

Avraham was silent for so long, Mustapha began to wonder if he had heard.

"We have no choice," Avraham said finally. "Take the men to the Jericho camp."

"But what about our equipment?"

"Leave it! There isn't any time."

"But . . ."

"Do as I say! Move!"

Mustapha jumped back from the table, his chair crashing to the floor. He gave the necessary orders. Men erupted out of the back room grabbing their weapons.

"Leave the rifles, you idiots!" Mustapha thundered at them. "Take the pistols and knives, and make sure they're hidden. Wait for me. I'll be right down."

The first man opened the door and peered outside. He then scampered down the stairs. The others followed, making a lot more noise than Mustapha would have wished. Mustapha waited a moment. Avraham seemed unaware of him. Mustapha shrugged and rushed down the stairs.

Avraham looked slowly around the room until he came to the package containing "Rabbi Horowitz's" clothes. He picked up the package and walked out, carefully closing the door. He reached the street and walked out under the entrance light. It was quiet. Then he started walking east toward the Temple Mount. His plan would continue. It would succeed. It had to.

◆

Lieutenant Yehuda Baum looked down the steep, dimly lit stairs as a rather rumpled looking individual rushed up from the street entrance.

"Lieutenant Baum?" Ya'acov Isaacson asked as he reached the top.

"Yes, sir," Yehuda replied as he saluted.

"I'm Ya'acov Isaacson, Intelligence. Where is he?"

"Gone."

"Gone? What happened."

"Don't know. We thought he was an ordinary informer—you know, favors, money. He came up to one of our patrols and said he had seen some suspicious activity here—people coming and going at odd hours. Said he saw a man drop a rolled-up rug once. Inside was an AK-47."

"This Arab was a gun expert?"

"Just telling you what he said. He led us here and pointed out the entrance. The lighting outside is quite bad, and the next thing I knew, he was gone. He wasn't under arrest."

"Obviously," Ya'acov said.

The two men entered the dimly lit room, their boots crunching on the filthy floor. Maps and pictures were tacked to three of the walls, while a Palestinian flag hung on the fourth. A half-eaten meal was on the table. One of the chairs was lying on its back.

"Left in a hurry," Ya'acov observed. "They see you coming?"

"Don't think so. Because of the circumstances, we kicked the door down without warning. We did a quick search. No hand weapons, but we did find some rifles and explosives in a back room—both raw and made-up—satchel charges and quite a few smaller bombs."

"I bet I know what *those* look like," Ya'acov grumbled.

"What's that, sir?" Yehuda asked.

Ya'acov half-turned and looked out the door.

"I believe the PM will be interested in this," he said with a sour grimace the lieutenant could not see.

"Is *he* coming here?"

Under other circumstances Ya'acov would have been tempted to laugh. Instead he glanced at his watch. "Not at 4 in the morning. Perhaps after breakfast."

"What's going on?"

"This is an Intelligence matter."

The lieutenant hid his irritation very poorly and started clomping about the room, kicking debris aside.

"Don't do that," Ya'acov ordered.

"Yes, sir," Yehuda replied. He turned and left the room.

Ya'acov walked into the back room. A bare bulb hung from its cord, shedding a glaring light on the crude bomb factory. Crude but effective. And among the larger charges were exact duplicates of the bomb he had disarmed at the Dome of the Rock.

"Ya'acov?" came a voice from outside.

"In here, sir."

David Kruger came through the door as if just ahead of something dangerous.

"Where is the Arab?"

"Lieutenant Baum let him get away."

"Ya'acov!"

"Colonel, he's ordinary IDF. He doesn't know what we're working on. I suppose we could hope for a little more talent, but . . ."

Ya'acov glanced at his boss and decided it was best not to pursue the subject. "Sir, I came here as soon as I got the call. I told the duty officer to send a team over as soon as he could round one up. Should be here soon. But it looks like this was the headquarters for our group, or at least one of their hideouts. The larger charges match the ones at the Dome."

"So who are they?"

"Palestinians, for sure. Could be a PLO splinter group. Everything we've found is consistent with that conclusion. But I still think they're part of the Palestinian Revolutionary Force. I wish we knew more. They're either quite small or very secure."

"Well, so far that makes you and the *Post* versus the rest of the media, which are busy screaming that Israel did it. Fairly and impartially, of course." David paused as he struggled to keep his temper. "For what it's worth, I agree with you."

"Colonel?"

"Yes?"

"Will this information be leaving Military Intelligence?"

"Ya'acov, I could tell you it's none of your business. But for your information, I'm scheduled to brief General Levy in the morning. And after that, he'll brief the PM."

"Perhaps not a good idea."

"I suppose you're going to tell me why."

"Colonel, since you asked me, our Arab friends are still plenty beaked off at us. The Dome of the Rock almost gets blown up and those dastardly Jews *have* to be the culprits, case closed. We could catch Mohammed himself doing the job and they'd *still* swear we did it. Only trouble is, they won't stop at swearing."

"Where's all this going?" David asked impatiently.

"Sir, I know our Prime Minister isn't one to seek publicity, but if he kind of accidentally let slip that he thought the PLO or the PRF were behind this . . . Arabs blowing up the Dome of the Rock doesn't quite compute."

"But here's the evidence."

"Yes, but how do we prove it? The Arabs will claim that we faked it. And there's something else . . ."

"Okay, Ya'acov, assuming I won't regret it, what else?"

"Sir, I'm afraid that any publicity about this will only fan Arab hatred, no matter how good the proof. The reports are bad all over. But the ones from Syria are especially ominous. They're getting ready for their armored exercise. Or at least that's what they're calling it."

Ya'acov glanced at his boss and decided it was time to stop.

"Thank you for your help," David grumbled.

"Only doing my job, sir."

"Yes, I know that. But I have to brief the general and he will tell the PM. And, yes, I'm quite aware of what the PM is likely to do with it. I'm not entirely dense."

"Yes, sir."

"And it will probably have the effect you predict."

"Yes, sir."

"But there's not a blasted thing you or I can do about it, so let's not waste any more time arguing."

"Yes, sir."

They both turned at a sound from the entrance.

"Sounds like our team's here," Ya'acov said, grateful for the diversion.

"Good. Be sure they do a good job."

"Yes, sir."

"And the report's to be on my desk at zero eight hundred."

"You will have it."

"Very well. Good evening."

David stalked out, his ill humor trailing behind him.

Ya'acov peered outside. "Ah, Lieutenant Jacovy, how nice of you to come out. I trust you are ready to tackle this opportunity we have for you."

The lieutenant gave him a grim smile.

"Yes, I see you are," Ya'acov continued. "Hop to it. I need all the facts no later than zero seven hundred. And you can help me put it together for the old man."

Ya'acov paused and saw the response he expected.

"There, I knew you'd like it. See you back at the shop."

◆

Avraham Abbas scowled as he pondered his setbacks. He put the men in Jericho out of his mind as he tried to decide what he should do.

He adjusted the package under his arm as he looked east over the city walls toward the Mount of Olives. It was still quite dark on the Temple Mount, but Olivet was surrounded by a bright red halo. Then a brilliant ray of orange light flashed out as a tiny sliver of the sun peeked above the mountain. The taller structures seemed almost on fire as the rose-colored Jerusalem limestone reflected the sun's light.

The exquisite beauty was lost on the PRF leader. He trudged past the Dome of the Rock and down the steps. He left the Old City by Herod's Gate and made his way to the Central Bus Station. A quick trip to the public toilet and he returned as "Rabbi Avraham Horowitz," looking only slightly rumpled. He purchased a ticket for the next bus to Tel Aviv.

6

NAOMI'S LEGACY

Anne had forgotten about the long stretches of boredom that go with all archaeological digs. She, Mars, and Moshe had little to do but try to stay out of Ben's way. Slowly the mound of dirt grew out on the street.

They had lunch out of the blue cooler and continued work until late in the afternoon. Then Moshe dropped them off at the American Colony.

"Are you two ready to move to the hostel?" Moshe asked.

"I don't know about Anne, but I'm not looking forward to it," Mars said.

"Actually I think you'll like it, from what I've heard. The rooms are nice. You have to prepare your own food, but what can I say? It sure beats sleeping in a wadi and going weeks without a bath. And it's reasonable. Besides, there'll be other archaeologists around. What could be better for a couple of young scholars?"

"Sounds like a sales job to me," Mars observed.

"Would I do that?"

"Yes," Anne answered for him.

"Well, if that's the way I'm to be treated, I must be off. Want to move your stuff over there first thing in the morning?"

"That will be fine," Anne answered. "Will our being late to the site cause any problems?"

"Not a bit. Ben will appreciate a reprieve from having my nose poked in his business. See you around 8."

The battered bus lurched off and disappeared around the corner.

◆

The Eldan truck had been ready for him as promised. The rental people couldn't have been more helpful as they provided "Rabbi Horowitz" with a city map and gave him the directions he requested. And the drive to the dilapidated house in an older section of Tel Aviv had not taken long.

He brooded as he scanned the weed-choked yard. The house was badly in need of paint, and the second-story guttering looked on the verge of total collapse. Overgrown shrubs surrounded the house, as if to protect it, framing a narrow passageway up to the forbidding front door. The door had three dingy glass panes high up, suggesting after-thought rather than plan.

It was time to act. Normally a thoughtful man, Avraham had been given much to think about, more than he cared for. He pushed his recent reversals to the back of his mind as he thought over what he would say.

Avraham wasn't worried about his appearance. He could thank his Jewish mother for that and her attempts to bring him up correctly. Attempts that stopped abruptly when she found another man, one who definitely did not want to have a little boy around. Rather, the problem now was, would his plan work?

He walked up the steps and knocked firmly on the door, causing the glass panes to rattle. The house was silent. He waited impatiently as the minutes crept by. He began to wonder if anyone was home, feeling a curious mixture of irritation and relief. Then he heard a muffled sound and steps approaching. A few moments later the door opened a little, and an old lady peered out suspiciously.

"Good morning," Avraham said hesitantly. "I am Rabbi Horowitz. Avraham Horowitz."

"Yes?" the lady replied.

"Would you be Naomi Braun?"

Her eyes narrowed, and the door closed slightly.

"Why do you want to know?"

"I believe you are a survivor of Auschwitz."

The blood drained from her ancient face. Her skin looked like parchment.

"How do you know that? No one in Tel Aviv knows that. Now, what do you want?"

"Forgive me, dear lady. I did not mean to upset you. I would not have come except my mission is of extreme importance. I am on an Executive Committee associated with Yad Vashem. In my research I came across a photograph with the name 'Naomi Braun' on the back. I was empowered to try and find you to see if there are other pictures you could share with us. As to how I found you—there was no address on the photograph; only the name. Tel Aviv seemed a likely place to look. The phone directory gave your address."

"I see."

Avraham could see she was struggling with the information and emotions half-buried in her unfortunate past.

"You must know how important our work at Yad Vashem is," Avraham continued. "We have people coming to us by the thousands from all over the world. Can we help them find out what happened to their relatives, they want to know. We do what we can, of course, but as extensive as our archives are, we know more photographs and documents exist. We're talking about a national treasure."

"Won't you come in," she said finally, making her decision.

She led Avraham to a sparsely furnished sitting room. The three chairs and the single wooden table were old and coming apart. But everything was clean. Avraham sat down in the offered chair and tried to be comfortable on the bunched-up stuffing that was peeking out through holes in the faded fabric.

"I think I know the photograph you're talking about," Naomi said. "I made the mistake of giving it to my cousin several years ago. Actually he's my first cousin once removed, but not removed far enough. His name makes no difference. I shouldn't have trusted him, but what can I say? He saw the photograph on one of his infrequent visits to see me, mostly to ask for money. Said he wanted it because I was so dear to him. Should have known right then. But no . . . I gave him the photograph, but no money. He's no good."

"That I do not know," Avraham said.

"Well, I do," she assured him. An odd animation came into her eyes. "The past is very painful to me. A young man like you can't understand that. My parents were killed before my eyes—shot dead because my father was trying to protect my mother, and the ones who did it laughed as I ran to him. He put his arm around me moments before he died."

"I am sorry," Avraham said. "But you know that's why Yad Vashem is so important—so this will never be forgotten—what happened to you and millions of others—and to help those who want to know what happened to their loved ones. As a rabbi, I see so much of this."

"Yes, I know it's important. And I *have* thought about what I have here. I always planned to give my estate to Yad Vashem, but even thinking about it is more painful than I can bear."

"Yes, dear lady. And I would be the last one to bring you grief. Only an overriding cause could bring me here. Please forgive me."

"You did not cause my problems. God brought you here, no doubt, and I must go along with it. So I must tell you how all this happened. My father's parents came to Poland from Germany after they were married. They settled in Warsaw, where my father and his brothers and sisters were born. Other than the stigma of living in the ghetto, we did fairly well. Grandfather was a photographer, the best in all Warsaw. Naturally families came to him for weddings, bar mitzvahs, and on high holy days. Over the years he accumulated thousands and thousands of photographs, along with notes on who the people were, the occasion of the photograph, and so on.

"Now, Father was the oldest, so it was decided that he would take over the business. His brother Viktor helped out in the shop as he tried to decide what he wanted to do in life. Mostly he involved himself in the many problems people had in the ghetto. He would have made a fine rabbi, I suppose. He kept a lot of records in the shop as he helped people with their legal and social problems."

"What have you got here?" Avraham asked.

"What you came for, I'm sure," she said with a wave of her hand. "But you have to know why. What we heard from Germany, as Hitler came to power, sickened us. At first we didn't think we were in any danger in Poland; but as time went on it looked very bad. Our relatives in Germany wrote us letters. We knew what was going on.

"My father knew the ghetto would be a dangerous place if Hitler invaded. How dangerous all of Poland would be we couldn't imagine. Finally Father decided to sell the shop and move to the countryside. And we had just moved when the invasion came. There we were in Szydtowiec with our belongings in boxes. The Nazis got our whole family before we could even think of escape. Of us all, I only know what happened to Mother and Father and my Uncle Viktor and his son Johann.

"He and Johann survived Auschwitz, as I did. When the liberation came, we went back to Szydtowiec. The boxes of photographs and records were still there—a Gentile family had taken our house and had saved them.

"There's not much more to tell. We left the boxes with them and got on one of the illegal boats—we were one of the ones to get through to Tel Aviv. After the War of Independence, we had the boxes shipped. I've been here ever since, although Uncle Viktor passed away a few years ago. Johann married Golda Melkovsky here in Israel."

A strange look came over her face as she remembered the past. "I haven't thought of them for years. They were quite nice actually, unlike their only son, who will remain nameless."

Avraham pursed his lips as he tried to hide his impatience. "Would it be possible to see what you have?" he asked finally.

She was silent for so long, Avraham was sure she would refuse. "I guess you must," she said.

She led him to the back of the house, to a large door with a massive padlock. Her hand slipped into a pocket and produced the key. With a heavy click it was open. She opened the door wide and flipped on the light. And there, in a large windowless room, were row upon row of boxes stacked nearly to the ceiling.

"How many are there?"

"Oh, a hundred or so. Most haven't been touched since Poland. Several have pictures and records of our family—those boxes nearest the door. I have been in them from time to time, but not very often. It brings back too many memories."

"I'm sure it does. But what a treasure for Zionism."

"Yes," she said slowly. "I suppose it is. And I guess I am glad you have come. I am an old lady now. My heart . . . My doctors—what do they know? They say I will not live much longer. I do want these to go to Yad Vashem, but after I'm gone."

"Surely. I understand. All that is necessary is to move the boxes out with the understanding that they will not be opened until, God forbid, that day comes."

"No! They are not to leave my house until then."

Avraham was taken aback and had trouble regaining his composure. With effort he restored his unctuous smile.

"Whatever you wish. What would you like to do? Your will perhaps?"

"I had not thought of that. Yes. That would be acceptable. I will have one drawn up."

"May I be of assistance? I could have a lawyer come by."

Naomi thought this over. It was clear she considered her privacy invaded. "Yes, I suppose that would be best. And you will have to be my executor."

"I would be honored," he said, trying to hide his irritation.

This was not at all what he wanted, but he could see no alternative. They agreed on 5 P.M. the following day, and Avraham took his leave. He had no intention of waiting until she died but hoped to keep her from doing something else with the documents, now that she was stirred up.

Avraham drove toward the beach and pulled up at a pay phone. He looked up and down the street as he composed what he wanted to say. No one was within earshot. He picked up the receiver and inserted the tokens. He punched the number and waited impatiently as it rang.

"Hello," came the answer. Avraham recognized Mustapha's voice.

"I must remain in Tel Aviv another day. Then I will come to see you."

"I understand."

"Is the date harvest going well?"

"Considering the labor shortage, quite well."

"I'm depending on it."

Avraham heard the phone click dead. Slowly he replaced the receiver and got back in his truck.

◆

The move to the hostel went smoothly. Anne could tell that Moshe had taken care of the details with his usual thoroughness, although he had said nothing about it. She was beginning to understand that what seemed to be signs of disorganization disguised a genuine Israeli spirit of getting things done right. And, she had to admit, the hostel *would* serve them nicely. It was rather spartan, but it was clean and functional.

Anne was not able to tell if Ben was grateful for their tardiness. He worked away in what seemed like a replay of the day before, with the same results. She knew they had to be making progress, but it seemed as if the dirt within the foundations was not dropping any lower. And still no finds.

Moshe dropped them off at the hostel. If he was concerned about the dig, he gave no indication.

◆

Shlomo Beker looked into the glaring television lights like a trapped animal. As Prime Minister of Israel, he felt it his duty to be on top of every situation. There were plenty of men in opposition parties, not to mention his own, who were eager to suggest otherwise. And political power was an ephemeral thing. Let it get away and someone else would pick it up.

"Mr. Prime Minister," his press secretary announced, "fifteen seconds."

Shlomo put the typewritten pages on the lectern and tried to keep from fidgeting as the seconds ticked off. He felt a new jolt of adrenaline as he saw the red light go on.

"Good evening. I come to you today with peace foremost in my mind. A few days ago an attack was made on the Dome of the Rock in the heart of Jerusalem. I cannot find words to describe how bad this was. I can only be thankful that our Israel Defense Forces were able to stop the terrorists before any serious damage was done.

"As is well known, Israel respects the religious beliefs of all peoples and is utterly committed to religious freedom and mutual respect within our borders. Had the attack on the Dome succeeded, it would have been a disaster of unparalleled proportion—a tragedy to all peoples—a tragedy we are very grateful we were able to avert, even at the cost of three Israeli dead.

"The world cries for justice, and so it should. And I, speaking for Israel, cry for justice also. Two days ago Intelligence personnel discovered the headquarters of the terrorist group responsible for this horrible crime. Let there be no mistake. We found bombs identical to the one the IDF disarmed at the Dome. And although the terrorists fled before our soldiers got there, we did discover their identity. Evidence at their headquarters positively identifies them as being part of the Palestinian Revolutionary Force."

Shlomo proceeded to narrate a series of photographs and video clips covering the headquarters investigation. By the time he concluded and the ominous red light went off, he was dripping with sweat and appeared pale and on the verge of collapse.

He looked at his press secretary. "What do you think?"

"You have told the truth," the man said in a soft voice. "Israel could not ask for more from her Prime Minister."

"What about the Arabs?"

The press secretary looked at his shoes rather than answering.

◆

Avraham smiled to himself as he made the final turn onto Naomi Braun's street. Locating a lawyer had been no problem. A quick search in the telephone directory and a single call had been all that was necessary. David Rubinstein had been only too happy to draw up a standard will for the testatrix, designating Yad Vashem as her sole beneficiary. All that remained was to execute it.

Avraham pulled up in front of Naomi's house and glanced down at his watch. They were right on time. They got out of the van and walked to Naomi's front door. Avraham rang the bell. After a few moments they heard footsteps in the entrance hall.

Naomi opened the door and looked out. She recognized Avraham, then looked at the lawyer.

"Madame Braun, may I present David Rubinstein. Mr. Rubinstein has drawn up a will according to your wishes."

"Yes, please come in," Naomi replied with obvious reluctance.

She led them to her sitting room, where they found a middle-aged man seated on one of the three chairs. He stood immediately. Avraham almost gave himself away in his shock. It was Dan Braun.

"Rabbi Horowitz! What are you doing here?" he demanded.

"You've met my cousin?" Naomi asked, turning to Avraham.

"Yes, dear lady, I have. I met Dan in Jerusalem, oh, about a month ago."

"But yesterday—you didn't tell me you knew him."

Avraham held up his hands as he struggled to come up with a plausible explanation.

"Peace, my friends. I didn't *know* I knew him. Braun is a common name. You didn't tell me your cousin's name yesterday—first or last. Maybe I should have asked, but it didn't occur to me."

"I see," Naomi replied as she thought it over. "You two are friends?" she asked suspiciously.

"I have no enemies," Avraham said. "I met Dan one time at a cafe in Jerusalem. We talked about this and that."

"Wait a minute! Something's going on here," Dan said.

"Dan, behave yourself or get out of my house."

"I want to know what's going on, Naomi."

"Well, you can ask nicely."

"Please allow me," Avraham said smoothly. "Dan, this is David Rubinstein. We are here at your cousin's invitation."

"Why have you come?"

"Dan, shut up! I'm sorry, Rabbi, this was unexpected. My charming cousin has decided to pay me a visit. Perhaps to ask for money—who can say?"

"Naomi, I came to see you."

"And ask for money. You hadn't gotten around to it before my guests arrived."

"What are they here for?"

"If it's any of your business, which it isn't, they're here to help me do my will. I'm giving my things to Yad Vashem."

"Naomi, what are you doing?"

"Take the cotton out of your ears. I just told you."

"But why didn't you tell me first? I'm your next of kin. Tell them to go. We need to talk this over."

"There's nothing to talk over. I know what I have to do, and I'm going to do it."

Dan glared at Avraham.

"I forbid it!" he roared.

"Get out of my house!" Naomi pointed to the door. "Get out this instant, and don't come back! Ever!"

Dan looked around as if for help.

"But, Naomi, I'm your cousin."

"Get out or I'll call the police!"

Dan knew he had gone too far. And he knew his cousin was capable of doing what she threatened. He spun on his heel and stormed out, slamming the door behind him.

"Utterly worthless," Naomi observed.

"I am sorry if we have caused you trouble," Avraham said.

"It was not of your causing. Let's sit down and get this over with. I'm not feeling well."

This Avraham was only too willing to do. The only problem they had was in finding witnesses. Avraham had to try three houses before he found two people who were willing to witness the will. Naomi refused the lawyer's offer to file the will in his office, saying she preferred to keep it in her writing desk. Avraham thanked her profusely, and he and the lawyer bowed themselves out as quickly and gracefully as they could.

Avraham dropped the lawyer off at his office. Then he paused for a few moments as he looked down the street at the beach a few blocks away. The blue Mediterranean was beautiful in the late afternoon sun. He thought about getting in the van and driving to Jericho right then but decided against it. He would remain in the modest Tel Aviv hotel, then return to Jericho in the morning. Then he would see what Mustapha had accomplished.

◆

Ya'acov Isaacson looked up as his friend Ari Jacovy came into the video room. Ya'acov shoved a cassette into the VCR and pressed the Play button.

"Sit down," he said, waving toward a chair. "Thought you'd like to see this."

"Which is?"

"It's sort of an Arab 'how do I love thee, let me count the ways.'"

"Oh. Replies to the Prime Minister."

"Exactly. Watch."

The first clip showed a frenzied demonstration of thousands of Iranians in Teheran marching and screaming slogans. Many held posters showing Shlomo Beker hanging from a gallows or decapitated by large, curved swords.

"Ah, our articulate friends to the east," Ari said. "I'm not up on my Farsi. What do the good Iranians have to say?"

"Arabic I know, but not Farsi. But the transcript is pretty graphic, as you might expect. They claim the Prime Minister is covering up a Jewish plot to blow up the Dome and build the Temple. To put it mildly: if they were on our border, they'd probably invade. The fundamentalists—and who in Iran isn't?—are beyond mad. I haven't seen them this worked up since the Shah fell."

Ya'acov punched the Fast Forward button and stopped the tape a few seconds later.

"And here is a clip from Damascus," he said. "Not quite the ambience of Teheran, but the feeling's the same. Hey, these guys want to rip our guts out."

"So what's new about that?"

Ya'acov hit the Stop button. He sat looking at the TV screen for a few moments before replying. "In a way it's not new, of course. But in a way it is. The Arab world has traditionally been at our throats. But the level of hate is way up. Islamic fundamentalism is scary, but the military situation is what has me worried. We're not talking about Nasser and tanks that go better in reverse than they do forward. We're talking chemical warfare, rockets, and greater numbers in whatever category you want to look at. And in my opinion the Syrians at least are dead serious. They're going to do something."

"I sure hope you're wrong."

"So do I. But I'm not. Not many of the spooks agree, but it's clear enough to me."

"You report this to the old man?"

"We've discussed it. I don't know if he's convinced, but he's thinking about it."

"So, what's going to happen?"

"You think I'm right?" Ya'acov asked with a wry smile.

"We'll see. Now, about my question . . ."

"Northern Galilee. I think we had better watch the Syrians."

Ya'acov rewound the tape and started viewing it again. This time he and Ari made notes.

◆

Avraham drove toward the sunrise, streaming a cloud of dust behind the heavy van. An orderly line of palm trees paralleled the left side of the road, their tops a rich green in the rosy light of dawn. He had passed the last IDF patrol fifteen minutes ago—not that he had been overly concerned about it. But the closer he got to Jericho, the more he longed to get out of the black suit and hat. Already he was attracting a lot of the wrong attention from the local Arabs.

He twisted the wheel and guided the lurching truck through a curve in a barely controlled slide. He stood on the brakes as he saw the house, still not familiar with exactly where it was. The truck shuddered to a stop, allowing the trailing dust cloud to catch up. Avraham shoved the gear shift into reverse with a loud *crunch* and backed up. He looked alternately out the side mirrors as he quickly backed the van into the narrow space between two houses. He killed the engine, jumped down, and ran for the door, which opened before he got there. He rushed inside as the door swung shut again, leaving the room in almost total darkness. A light clicked on.

"Did you have any trouble?" Mustapha Kabran asked.

Avraham glanced around. They were alone. "None. Why should I have?"

"Your clothing."

"Nothing I can't handle," he said as he threw off the hat and tossed his coat on a chair. "But I'll be glad to get out of them. Are the rest here? Have you got all the stuff?"

Mustapha shifted uneasily. He was still not used to being the acting chief of operations in addition to his preferred role of chief of security. He was coming to understand what a fine job Abdul had done. It had always looked so easy. But the reality was quite different, very difficult and detailed.

"Everyone is here. I dispersed them around town as you instructed. We're working on the bombs. Considering what we've been through, the work is going quite well."

"Good. She wouldn't let me have the photos, but she did will them to Yad Vashem."

"What do we do now?"

"We go and get them."

"So the plan to bomb Yad Vashem is still on?" Mustapha asked, unable to keep the concern out of his voice.

"Are you questioning me?"

"No. Most assuredly not."

"Good. *This* will get their attention."

Mustapha could not think of a safe reply, so he remained silent.

"When will the bombs be ready?" Avraham asked.

"Some are ready now. But we'll need more for the number of boxes we're getting. And I haven't got that explosive paper I told you about. It wasn't until late yesterday that I located some in Ramallah. We need it to make the boxes and to stuff them with enough incendiaries to get a good fire started. The bombs alone won't do the amount of damage you want."

"I know that! Now for the last time, how long?"

Mustapha couldn't put it off any longer. "Two weeks, maybe three," he said.

"Two or three *weeks*?" Avraham thundered. "You have a week."

"But we just got here. I've got to go to Ramallah to get the stuff. Then we've got to make more bombs and the boxes. And I've got a thousand other things to take care of . . ."

"You sound like a woman in a bazaar. Abdul never chattered at me like this. Abdul did what I said. You want me to do your work for you?"

Mustapha was tempted to tell him yes. He looked away as he tried to control his temper. A sudden chill came over him as he remembered the rumors about Avraham. People who disagreed with him usually disappeared.

"Answer me!" Avraham thundered.

"It will be as you say," Mustapha replied, swallowing a sour taste at the back of his throat. "I will prepare the men and then leave for Ramallah. We'll work around the clock." He paused and looked cautiously at Avraham.

"What is it now?" Avraham demanded.

"What about Abdul?"

"I'm working on that. But first we must execute Operation Twilight."

"Have you got us a way in?"

Avraham laughed, throwing his head back with an outward show of good humor that had Mustapha smiling in spite of himself. "I will talk our way in, and they will never even suspect."

"What?"

"This surprises you? I know these people. You watch. It will go as I say."

Avraham watched his second in command. Mustapha looked away as he weighed what he should say.

"Finding the photos is most fortunate," he said finally. "How do we exploit this?"

"You are learning," Avraham observed. "There will be no problems. My appearance is quite authentic, and my Hebrew is very good. And I know enough Yiddish to get by."

"What's our plan?"

"Let's go to the table. Get some paper and pens."

7

THE FIND

Mars and Anne sat down in the overstuffed chairs in the hostel lounge as they waited for Moshe to arrive.

"Let's see, it's been five days now," Mars said.

"And nothing to show for it," Anne finished for him.

"Except that bodacious big pile of dirt we keep shoving in the street. Which is then mysteriously carted off from time to time."

"Perhaps we should write a paper on that," Anne said. "Would you care to coauthor?"

"Why, Dr. McAdams, I would be thrilled." Mars paused and looked at her. The background sounds seemed to vanish as his thoughts drifted in an unexpected direction. "Actually I would be quite honored to write a paper with you."

Anne glanced at him to see if he was engaging in one of his leg-pulling exercises. He wasn't. "Why, thank you, Mars. I would like that too."

Mars was about to reply when a familiar sound caught their attention. They looked out the window in time see a blue Volkswagen pull up and lurch to a stop. A door slammed, and moments later Moshe came into the lounge, his bearded face beaming at them.

"Good morning," he said. "We have a special treat today—breakfast in the Jewish Quarter."

"When you said you were going to have breakfast with us, I thought you meant here," Anne said.

"Did I say that?"

Anne glanced at Mars, who only shrugged.

"Shall we be off?" Moshe asked.

He spun on his heel as if there could be no question of his judgment. Mars helped Anne up into the front seat and wired the door shut. He then hurried around to the back and climbed in.

Moshe gave them a quick review of the kinds of foods they could have—the differences between the European cuisine and that of the Middle East, all this while driving with his normal style of abandon.

He parked at the excavation and led his associates deep into the Jewish Quarter through narrow but neat streets. Soon Mars and Anne were thoroughly lost as they twisted and turned every few blocks. And the blocks, if you could call them that, were short and the streets crooked. Small shops were everywhere, some in small stone buildings or arcades and some in the open under colorful awnings. Brilliant brassware jostled fresh fruit and beautiful fabrics. And permeating everything were the smells—subtle smells of leathers and sandalwoods, and stronger ones from small cafes.

"We'll eat here," Moshe said as he led them to a small table. "They serve wonderful breakfasts. No bacon and eggs, though. Strictly kosher."

Moshe ordered for them in Hebrew. A few minutes later the waiter placed a tray of pumpernickel bagels, cream cheese, and thin slices of a white fish on the table. Mars looked at Moshe.

"Lox and bagels, what else?"

The bagels were not a problem. Mars tried the lox gingerly. He smiled when he found it quite good.

"Glad it meets with your approval," Moshe muttered.

Anne made a delicate choking sound as she saw Mars color at the remark.

"I didn't know what it was," Mars grumbled.

"That didn't bother Anne," Moshe said.

Too late Mars realized that he had been twitted. A smile gradually came to his face as his sense of humor returned from where it had been hiding.

They were finishing when a man came down the street with what looked like a silver bagpipe. It was actually a large, ornate coffeepot from which hung several small cups.

"What is that?" Mars whispered to Moshe as the man approached.

"Turkish coffee. Want some?"

Mars started to say no when he saw Anne's amused expression.

"Of course," he said.

He motioned to the vendor. The man gave him a huge smile through a bushy black mustache. Some of his teeth were missing, and most of the others looked as if they were not far behind. He quickly unhooked a cup and put it under the long, graceful spout, tilting his whole body to pour the tar-like substance.

Mars took the cup as the vendor watched. Mars looked at Moshe and Anne, who smiled and nodded to him. Mars considered taking a tiny sip but decided that wouldn't do. He swigged down a healthy shot.

"How is it?" Anne asked immediately, her chin on her hands, a Cheshire smile perched on her face.

Mars cleared his throat with effort. "Fine," he said. "Want some? My treat."

"How sweet. I think I will."

Mars looked at her in surprise, then turned to the vendor. The man was already pouring another cup. He set the drink delicately before Anne. Three pairs of eyes were on her as she took a drink.

"How is it?" Mars asked.

"Just like my grandmother used to make."

"You must have had some grandmother," Moshe said with obvious admiration.

"Yes, she was quite a lady. Granddad liked his coffee strong. He worked long days on their farm and needed something to keep him going. She'd put about a cup of grounds in the bottom of a coffeepot and boil it—no filter. It was black and about half caffeine. Even so, this stuff does it one better."

"Good," Moshe said, nodding to the vendor. "I'm sure our friend would be horrified to know he had been beaten by a little old lady from Texas."

"His reputation is secure."

Anne finished her cup, then waited for Mars. Mars looked up at the vendor with a weak grin. The man nodded his encouragement. Mars downed the rest and handed the cup back along with Anne's. The vendor said something Mars didn't understand, but the meaning was clear enough. Mars shook his head. One cup was plenty. He paid the man, and the latter walked off in search of his next victim.

"The stuff you get in a cafe is a little better," Moshe said. "But a cafe doesn't have the atmosphere."

"I'm sure," Mars agreed. "You could roof buildings with that stuff."

"It is rather robust."

Mars downed the rest of his water before getting up to follow the others back to the site.

Ben was waiting for them. He cranked up the backhoe as the archaeologists walked up. It was a continuation of all the previous days. The mound of dirt grew rapidly. Ben dumped a load, then wheeled about and went charging back into the trench, lowering the bucket as he went. The blade bit into the soil, and the engine groaned as it forced the backhoe forward. The bucket lurched upward with a sound like a crude bell being struck. Ben backed slowly out of the hole and shut off the engine.

"That sounded interesting," Moshe said. "Could be a large boulder—or maybe something else."

They walked down into the pit with Moshe in the lead. He got down on his hands and knees and ran a hand trowel down the bucket's last impression until he found the object. He dug around it for several minutes as he cleared away dirt from the top and sides. He looked up, beaming. "It's a column drum."

He ran his hand down about four inches of the vertical surface as he tried to estimate the diameter. "Definitely monumental. Looks to be about four or five feet in diameter. And something else . . ."

"What?" Anne asked.

"I think it's marble, and that would make it unique. All the other drums we've found have been made of local limestone."

"Herodian?"

"Could hardly be anything else. Not pre-Exilic. Not Hasmonean, I think. Definitely not from a time later than 70 C.E."

Moshe smiled up at the others like a child who has found a lost toy. "Well, boys and girls, looks like we have some work to do. And we're going to need help. Anne . . . you, Mars, and Ben start digging this drum out while I organize some work details."

Moshe strode back to the bus and departed in a cloud of blue smoke.

"Let's get to it," Anne said.

"Do you want to use the backhoe?" Ben asked. "I can get some of the dirt away without touching the column. It will save some time."

Anne agreed.

Ben dug down carefully about four feet on all sides of the drum.

♦

Ben parked the backhoe's rear scoop and retracted the stabilizing pads. He moved the tractor away from the holes and shut it down. He stepped down as a familiar blue bus returned. Moshe trudged across the rocky soil with another middle-aged man at his side.

"Anne, Mars, this is Michael Shapiro. He'll direct our work force and generally keep us on track. He's so valuable, I don't have a job title for him."

"Bondslave," Michael volunteered.

"How many times do I have to tell you—not in front of our guests."

Moshe examined the column pit. "I see you had Ben dig down with the backhoe. Good. That will save time. This may be junk left over after a building was razed. Then again, it may be a fabulous find. Anne, Mars, would you two like to do the honors? Get in two of those holes and start getting the rubble away from the drum. Let's see if it's sitting on something."

Anne jumped into one of the holes, and Mars took an adjacent one. They first took down the thin wall of dirt separating the two holes, then started removing the dirt from the column. The marble was remarkably smooth and only a little stained by the surrounding earth. Even after lifting out the loose dirt, the bottom of the drum was not exposed.

"That's the tallest drum I've seen in Jerusalem," Moshe said. "Most are about four feet tall. This one certainly surpasses that."

"Help has arrived," Michael said.

"Good," Moshe replied. "Get them started on the column."

Michael singled out three men and started them enlarging the hole.

The others watched from the rim. It took almost two hours to dig down less than two feet.

"Look at that," Moshe said. "The drum's still on the base—perfectly centered too." He pointed to the thin line separating the two pieces.

"Could be another drum," Michael said.

"No. Grade level can't be that low. It's got to be the base. Be careful now. You're going to find a floor under that. We don't want to damage it."

The men continued down with hand trowels, scooping the dirt aside. A few minutes later a trowel point pinged off something hard. The man enlarged the hole's bottom and opened up an area about a foot square. He looked up and said something in rapid Arabic. Moshe got down in the hole and peered at the stone on hands and knees.

"Paving stones," he said at last. "And it looks like white marble." Moshe took Michael's hand and pulled himself out. "We're getting ten more men in about an hour. And a bulldozer."

Michael started to protest.

"You know the rules. I hate to use the machines as much as you do, but we have to. The Company thinks they're going to start on their hotel in a few days. We have to hurry."

"But this is a fabulous find!"

"One step at a time. First we have to prove it. I'm meeting with Kretzmer in half an hour. I'll tell him we must have another week."

"Not enough!"

"Patience. First we get a week. The Company won't like it, but they'll accept it. Later we'll get another extension, assuming we keep finding things. You know the drill."

Michael's expression showed what he thought of architects and builders, but he could see that Moshe was right.

"So," Moshe continued, "get the work organized. Get the dozer in there to remove the overburden. Anne and Mars will be in charge while I'm gone."

◆

"When can I move my crews in?" Samuel Kretzmer asked. He was one of the Jewish Quarter Reconstruction and Development Company's planning directors. He had encountered Moshe several times before, and none of the meetings had worked out as expected.

"Is that a model of the hotel?" Moshe asked as he walked over to examine it.

"Yes. And it is costing me a fortune every day I have to delay."

"Beautiful design. The stonework will blend in very well. You do excellent work."

"I could comment on the fact that you didn't answer my question."

"Oh, you are much too polite for that. It's something I like very much about you."

"Moshe—when can I have it?"

"The site?"

"No, your rattletrap bus. *Yes*, the site. You know we cooperate with you, but this is important. It's not some dinky apartment building. It's going to be the most famous hotel in Jerusalem—not the biggest, but the best. This is costing a ton of money."

"I am sorry to inconvenience you," Moshe said softly.

"You haven't found something, have you?"

"I am afraid we have."

"Oh great! I'm going to have to twiddle my thumbs while you scrape around some stupid rock wall looking for busted pots."

"Not a wall. At least not yet. Could be anything."

"Don't tell me that. How long?"

"A week or so."

"Will you keep me posted?"

"You know I will. And I *am* sorry. We'll do our work as quickly as possible. I have a large crew working on it right now."

◆

The blue bus lurched to a stop. Moshe climbed down and closed the door. He walked over to Mars and Anne.

"Did you get the extension?" Anne asked.

"Some. Found anything else?"

"We're hauling a lot of dirt out. For all of Michael's grumbling, it didn't take him long to put the bulldozer to work. We're trying to get close to floor level before we start with the hand work. We ran into one of the capitals a short distance from the drum. It's Corinthian. Also a few potsherds. Definitely Herodian. The place positively reeks of Herod."

"Reeks is right," Moshe said. "I don't know who was worse, Herod the Great or the Romans."

By early afternoon the bulldozer had excavated the site around the drum to within a foot of the floor. Finally Michael signaled the driver to withdraw. Moshe, Mars, and Anne went down into the depression along with the rest of the workers.

"Time for exercise," Michael said, looking at Moshe.

"Surely you don't expect archaeologists . . ."

"Surely I do."

"Well, I never," Moshe said. But his hands said that he did.

"Come, children," he said to Mars and Anne. "Let me see if this slavedriver has some shovels that fit your hands."

Moshe examined the pile of shovels carefully, then pulled out two.

"What luck," he said with a grin. "Perfect." He gave one to Mars and the other to Anne. He grabbed one for himself with a little less care. "There are some gloves over there if you want them. I'd recommend it."

Moshe picked a spot near the center of the pit and started digging. Mars started digging a few feet from Moshe, and Anne a little further on. Little mounds of dirt grew steadily as each hole started inching down. It was slow going as the rocks kept turning the blades aside. Mars was the first to reach something.

"I think I have the floor," he said.

He got down on his hands and knees and scooped dirt away from the bottom.

"Looks like black marble."

"It was white at the column."

"Yeah, but this is black."

"Fire?" Moshe asked.

Mars rubbed the stone hard and looked at it again.

"No. It's black marble. Looks like it's in beautiful shape."

"Great. Let's uncover the rest of it."

Slowly the beauty of the ancient floor began to emerge, like some immense photograph being developed. The tiles were set at forty-five degrees to the baseline of the floor in alternating squares of black and white marble. The tiles were in surprisingly good condition, although some sections were crushed by tumbled wall ashlars.

"Let's stop here," Moshe said, glancing at his watch.

"When are you going to ask Samuel for even more time?" Michael asked.

"Let's see what else we find first. Is the guard set for tonight?"

"'Is the guard set for tonight?' No, I thought I'd let all the thieves take what they want."

"I knew I could rely on you. Your efficiency is only surpassed by your charm."

Michael grumped at this as he called the workers over to brief them about the next day's work.

The talk on the way to the hostel centered on what the find was. Moshe admitted that he had no idea—only that he was sure it dated from the time of Herod and that he suspected it was an official building. And that the marble column and floor made the site unique.

"See you children in the morning," he said as they arrived.

8

STOLEN
PICTURES

A re they still watching the truck?" Mustapha Kabran asked.
Avraham turned away from the window.

"They're gone, fortunately for them."

"You can't really blame them. They're young. They see the yellow Israeli license plates, and they think we're either Jews or collaborators."

"You are not to tell me what to do!"

Mustapha turned away.

"These young stone-throwers had best stay away," Avraham continued. "If they don't, they will regret it for a short time and their parents longer. Now, besides you, I will require one other."

"Who would you like?"

"You are my chief of operations," Avraham said, as if reminding himself of a fact he regretted.

"Majid Jaha."

"Call him."

Avraham checked over his black suit, making sure that "Rabbi Horowitz" was ready for travel. Majid came in from the back room. He said nothing, and his expression gave no indication of his feelings, if he had any. Majid was a complete mystery to Avraham. No one knew anything about his background, and he would say nothing about it even when questioned. But he always did what he was told, with no grumbling.

"Are you ready to go?" Avraham asked him.

There might have been a nod.

"Good," Avraham said. "Quickly now. I will go out first and open the back of the truck. When you hear the doors open, run out and get in."

Avraham rushed out and unlocked the back doors. He twisted the handle and pulled the door open. Majid rushed into the dark interior, followed immediately by Mustapha. Avraham slammed the door and locked it. He ran for the driver's door, unlocked it, wrenched the door open, and jumped inside. He stomped on the clutch and engaged the starter in the same instant. The engine ground for a moment, then caught.

Avraham engaged first gear just as a teenage boy appeared between the houses across the street. The boy threw a stone as hard as he could. Avraham drew back as the stone barely missed the windshield, striking the metal trim below the driver's side wiper. Three more boys appeared, and all were scrabbling around looking for stones.

Avraham stomped on the throttle and let out the clutch. The truck shuddered as the back tires spun in the dirt. Avraham twisted the wheel sharply and aimed for the gap between the houses on the other side of the street. The boys dropped their rocks and began running. Avraham smiled as he saw the terror in their eyes. There was no way the nearest ones could get out of the way in time. He swung the wheel hard to the left and jammed on the brakes. The van slew around and slid sideways until it was inches from the nearest house. Avraham looked out of the passenger-side window. Half a dozen faces stared at him, rock throwing forgotten for a moment. He laughed and drove off.

There were two ways to get to Tel Aviv, but Avraham knew there was only one way for a good rabbi—through Jerusalem. He turned south onto 90, traveling roughly in the direction of the Dead Sea, parallel to the Jordan River a little over five miles away. A few miles outside Jericho he turned to the west as he joined Road 1 and began the steep ascent up to Jerusalem.

He made fairly good time until he passed the 458 intersection. Then up ahead he saw that westbound traffic was stopped. Avraham slowed down and came to a reluctant stop. In spite of his confidence, he felt mild anxiety as he saw an IDF patrol checking all vehicles.

After a half-hour of creeping along, Avraham saw the car ahead of him start off toward Jerusalem. Now it was his turn. He rolled down the window and pulled up to the officer in charge.

"Shalom," he said, smiling down at the man. "I am Rabbi Avraham Horowitz. What seems to be the problem?"

"Shalom, Rabbi Horowitz," the officer responded. "That's not something I'm supposed to discuss, but we're about to break up the roadblock anyway. We had a report that some terrorists would be traveling from Jericho to Ramallah."

"But this is not the direct route."

"Sometimes it's smart not to go direct. And this isn't the only roadblock. Now, I'm sorry, Rabbi, but I will have to search the back of your truck. There can be no exceptions."

Avraham felt his stomach go ice-cold. He had been so sure of himself that he had not brought any weapons—not that he would have stood a chance against a fully armed IDF patrol anyway. He toyed with the idea of running the roadblock and abandoning the truck up the road, but he knew he wouldn't even make the first mile. He was at this Jew's mercy, and there wasn't a thing he could do about it.

He turned off the engine and set the emergency brake. He got out and accompanied the officer to the back doors. Wondering what Mustapha and Majid would do, he inserted the key and unlocked the door. Just as Avraham gripped the handle, a soldier ran up.

"Lieutenant, Headquarters on the horn. We are to pack up and return to base."

The officer turned back to Avraham.

"We will not have to trouble you further, Rabbi. Enjoy your trip. Shalom."

"Shalom," Avraham replied in a daze.

He tried to stop his hands from shaking as he relocked the back door. He then walked back to the cab.

Other than heavy traffic around Jerusalem and again near Tel Aviv, the rest of the trip went smoothly. Avraham parked down the street from Naomi Braun's house a little after 2 P.M., close to his original plan.

Avraham stepped down from the cab with studied indifference. He glanced cautiously up and down the street, then proceeded to the back of the van. He unlocked the doors and pulled open the right-hand one.

"Hurry," he said, peering into the truck's interior darkness. "No one's around."

Avraham led the two across the street. As he started up the steps, the door opened, and Naomi walked out.

She froze the moment she saw Avraham. "Rabbi Horowitz, what are you doing here?"

"Forgive me, dear lady, but I forgot something when I was here earlier this week. Would it be convenient for me to talk with you for a moment?"

Naomi hesitated as she looked past Avraham at his companions. "Who are these men? I don't understand."

"Arab workers. They help me in my work from time to time."

"Arabs helping Yad Vashem? . . . I don't want them here."

Avraham looked at her, not knowing what to say. The friendly smile, or as close to it as he could manage, left his face. Naomi's eyes opened wide as she took an awkward step backwards.

"Get out of here!" she shrilled at them. "Get out of here this instant!"

Avraham kept his eyes on Naomi's as he motioned to Mustapha and Majid. They started walking slowly toward the steps. Naomi screamed again and dashed inside. She whirled around and threw herself on the door. The door swung shut with a bang that rattled the glass panes. Avraham tried the knob. The door was locked.

"Open it!" he shouted as he stood back. "Hurry!"

Mustapha and Majid both hit the door at the same time. The old-fashioned lock ripped out of the wood with a splintering crash as the door burst open and slammed against the wall. Avraham hurried through a moment later. He looked quickly about the entryway, then heard a noise above him. He looked up in time to see Naomi disappear around the corner of the stairs to the second floor. He took the steps two at a time, getting to the top as a door at the end of the hall slammed shut. The key scraped as it twisted in the lock.

Avraham rushed the door and brought both fists down on the large upper panel. The wood split with a tremendous crash. He reached inside and unlocked the door. Naomi clutched a telephone in her hand as she frantically punched the number. Avraham grabbed the line and ripped it from the wall. Naomi tried to run past him, but he reached out and grabbed her as Mustapha and Majid ran into the room. He grabbed her thin neck with his hands and started squeezing. She struggled and tried to cry out, but only a weak gasp escaped. Avraham increased the pressure, an evil smile coming to his face. Then, with a powerful wrench, he twisted, and Naomi fell limp in his hands. He dropped her lifeless body to the floor.

"Avraham, what if someone heard?" Mustapha asked.

The three hurried downstairs, where Avraham approached the gaping front door with care. He peered cautiously outside from the relative security of the dark interior. There wasn't a sound.

"I think we're okay," he said as he closed the door. "Let's get on with it."

Avraham showed Mustapha and Majid where the storeroom was and got them busy pulling out the boxes. He then left the house and walked slowly to the van. It was still quiet. He backed the truck into the space between Naomi's house and the one next door, stopping by the side steps.

"The van is outside," Avraham said as he came into the storeroom. "Start loading."

Avraham hurried to the front room. There in the corner was Naomi's writing desk. He pulled out the center drawer and rummaged hurriedly through the jumble of papers inside. Then he tried the left-hand drawer. Last he opened the right-hand drawer. There, under a stack of old letters, was the will. He checked it quickly, then folded it and put it in his inside coat pocket.

It took Mustapha and Majid almost an hour to move the boxes. Avraham ransacked the house, making it look like there'd been a robbery. There wasn't much money or jewelry, but what there was he put in a pillowcase. He pulled open all the drawers and dumped them on the floor. He then ripped open the mattress. Satisfied with the appearance, he returned downstairs, carrying the pillowcase with him. Avraham found Mustapha alone in the empty storeroom.

"Majid just took the last box out," he said. "The van is really packed."

"Good," Avraham said. "Looks like my Arab workers will have to ride up front."

Mustapha nodded.

The ride back to Jericho was uneventful but slow. It was after 5 P.M. when they arrived at the house. Avraham backed the van in beside the house and shut off the engine. Majid opened his door and jumped down. Avraham grabbed Mustapha's arm.

"Get all this inside. We've got to pull the old lady's family stuff out and work with the rest."

Mustapha nodded.

"And get the word out to those stupid kids to leave us alone," he added as he pointed to a brown face observing them from across the street.

"Right away," Mustapha said.

♦

Anne looked out over the site, everything rosy in the early-morning light. She sipped hot black coffee from a Styrofoam cup, the steam fogging her glasses momentarily.

"There's still a lot of dirt to take out," she said.

"Anxious to see what's there?" Moshe asked.

"In the worst way."

"I could bring back the dozer."

Anne glanced at him.

"Perhaps we should get some explosives," Mars added.

Moshe looked over at the American, who was trying very hard not to smile.

"Don't say that too loud. Someone from the Company might hear you. I can see the headline now: 'Mars Falls on Alhambra.'"

"The palace of the Moorish kings in Spain? That's quite a ways from here."

"I'd help."

Anne laughed. "I sure am enjoying this scholarly conversation."

"My pleasure," Moshe said.

"Mine too," Mars added.

"I suppose we *could* go down and start working on uncovering the floor," Anne said.

"What a radical idea," Mars observed. "Think we'll get the floor uncovered today?"

Moshe looked at Anne.

"Must be his first dig," he said.

"Yes," she agreed.

At the end of the day the site looked much as it had that morning.

◆

"You have something to show me?" Avraham asked.

Mustapha nodded as he picked up the box and handed it to his leader.

"This is it?"

"That fiberboard box is actually an explosive similar to the plastics we ordinarily use, except it's a better incendiary. What you're holding could blow up a car, after we stuff it with explosive paper. We'll also be inserting C-4 bombs in some of the boxes. We'll use two mechanical timers. The first one to go off will do it."

Avraham handed the box back.

"Good. What about the rest?"

"We're making the boxes now. As you know, we need a lot of them. But we'll have it done on time. We've pulled out the boxes that are to stay here, and we're stuffing the rest with explosive papers. When we get done, the contents will look fine. Then we move the stuff from the old boxes to the new. But there is one thing—the boxes are obviously new. I'm afraid to try and age them."

"Rabbi Horowitz will take care of that. I have thoughtfully provided new boxes because the old ones were disintegrating."

"Very good."

◆

Moshe drove up as Anne and Mars walked out of the hostel. He jumped out of the van and came around to the sidewalk.

"You two enjoying your evenings?" he asked.

"Oh, yes," Anne answered. "We've been poking around Jerusalem as much as we can. You could spend *years* here and not see everything."

"You're telling *me* this?" Moshe asked. "It'll be nice when we can

take it a little easier. We will change to a Monday through Friday schedule soon, once we establish the site's significance." Moshe glanced at his
watch. "Now, we can either *talk* archaeology or *do* archaeology."

"We didn't start this conversation," Anne observed.

"Such a legalist. Shall we go?"

Mars helped Anne up into the front and wired the door shut.
Moshe walked with Mars to the rear of the bus.

"A little bird told me something," he said with a grin.

"Oh? What did it tell you?"

"This very day is Anne's birthday."

"It is? How'd you know that?"

"The papers the University of Texas sent me. Plus I'm naturally
inquisitive."

"There's another name for that."

"Oh, but you are much too polite to say that."

"Hmm. Why are you telling me this?"

"You like her." It was a statement.

"How do *you* know who I like?"

"We Jews are *very* romantic," Moshe said pounding Mars on the
back. "Have you read the Song of Solomon?"

"Can't say as I have."

"You should. Anyhow, I think you can make proper use of this
intelligence."

Mars climbed into the back of the bus. He worked his way forward
and into a folding chair. Moshe opened the driver's door and got in.

"What were you two talking about?" Anne asked.

"Did I tell you about the big research project the psychology department was working on?" Moshe asked.

"No," Anne replied cautiously.

"They were trying to prove once and for all which is more curious—male or female."

"How'd it come out?" Mars asked.

"They never could finish the experiments. The women kept steal-
ing the raw data to see how it was going."

Mars laughed until Anne turned toward him.

"Moshe," he said.

"Yes, my friend?"

"We'd better cool it."

Moshe looked over at Anne.

"Yes, I see what you mean. Back to business."

◆

Michael had the crew working when Moshe, Anne, and Mars arrived.

"Anything new?" Moshe asked.

"Not much. We found a wall over to the west—and something else to be careful of." He led them over toward the eastern side of the pit. "Sewer line. Runs north and south through the site."

"From the Turkish era?"

"Probably. Means it could go anywhere."

"Is it in use now?" Anne asked.

"Can't say unless we open it. Probably is. We'll leave it alone if we can. If we can't, we'll call the Company."

"Sounds good. Let's keep clearing the dirt out."

Gradually the floor plan of the building came into view. The black and white marble floor was remarkably intact. Some of the paving blocks were smashed, but most looked quite good for having been covered for almost two thousand years. The floor was about thirty by ninety feet. Surrounding it was a stone wall with two layers.

"What do you think it is?" Anne asked.

"Herod built it," Moshe said. "I'm sure of that—the huge columns, the thick walls with beautifully cut ashlars, the use of marble. It's an official building but not a palace. There are no cisterns, drains, or anything to indicate normal human activities. We haven't seen much pottery, coins, and such—it's almost like the site was holy."

"And there is something odd about the dimensions," Michael added.

"The Temple," Moshe said. "Of course. The interior dimensions are exactly those of the Temple."

"Why?" Mars asked. "Do you suppose Herod built a model down here before he built the real one—sort of like Abd al-Malik had the Dome of the Chain built before the Dome of the Rock?"

"Perhaps. But why build it full-size? And the dimensions may be the same, but the wall ashlars aren't anywhere near the size of the Temple's."

"Could the dimensions be a coincidence?" Anne asked.

Moshe looked around the site and up toward the Temple Mount.

"No. I don't know what the connection is, but it's no coincidence."

◆

Shimon Goldberg ushered "Rabbi Avraham Horowitz" into his office and indicated a side chair as he returned to his large swivel chair and sat down. He looked at Avraham over the broad expanse of his desk.

"Now then," he said as he settled himself in the chair, "what can I do for you, Rabbi Horowitz?"

"Please call me Avraham, Mr. Goldberg," the ersatz rabbi said, sliding a business card over the director's highly polished desk.

This flustered Shimon. "Yes, yes. All this formality. And what does it get us? Please call me Shimon." He rummaged around inside his desk's center drawer until he spied a loose business card. He attempted a smile as he extended it to his guest.

"I am here on a matter of highest national interest," Avraham continued. "I have come across something . . . It boggles the mind . . . It is too much."

"No doubt. Tell me more."

"I have lived in Jerusalem for a long time now, longer than I care to admit. And it isn't often that I can get away, what with the troubles a rabbi sees."

"Yes, I understand. You can well imagine what I see here at Yad Vashem."

"I'm sure. Sometimes it gets to be too much. Some of my close friends say, 'Avraham, go to the Dead Sea. Take the baths. Lie in the sun. It will do you good.' Others say, 'Go up to Kinneret. It's beautiful this time of year. Relax. Enjoy yourself. You deserve some time off.'"

"Interesting," Shimon said, trying not to show his growing impatience. "This is leading somewhere?"

"Oh, yes. Forgive me. I must not take up your time unnecessarily. Anyhow, I took their advice, in a way, and went to Tel Aviv. But do you know what happened?"

"No," Shimon replied with ill-hid irritation.

"I'm sitting at this cafe having lunch and this elderly lady comes up. 'Are you a rabbi?' she asks. How do they know? Am I wearing a sign or something? Anyway, I admit it, and she tells me this long story. She has lived in Tel Aviv for many years. She has no relatives, so she's quite alone in this big house in a rundown neighborhood."

"Could we perhaps shorten this some?"

"I'm coming to it now. The lady's father was a photographer in Poland before the war. Almost her entire family died in Auschwitz. But when the war was over, she found out that all her father's photographs, negatives, and records had survived."

"You don't mean . . ." Shimon said, sitting up suddenly, looking as if he might come across the desk.

"She still has them. She managed to bring them to Tel Aviv."

"Have you seen them?"

Avraham opened his briefcase, extracted a bulging envelope, and handed it to Shimon. "Take a look."

Shimon tore open the envelope. He pulled out photograph after photograph, along with faded sheets of paper with names, addresses, dates, and occasions on them. "This is astounding. How much of this is there?"

"Around a hundred boxes."

"*A hundred boxes!* I must meet this woman. Can you arrange it?"

"That, I am afraid, I cannot do."

"What? You come here with this and then tell me I cannot meet her?"

"Regrettably not. I'm sure you realize what she's been through. She wants Yad Vashem to have the documents eventually. But she cannot bear being involved in the actual transfer to the Memorial. Surely you understand."

"Yes, of course. But what is the purpose of your visit then?"

"She has delivered the boxes into my safekeeping and has instructed me to see that Yad Vashem gets them. But she is to remain strictly anonymous. You are to make absolutely no inquiries concerning this."

"I see."

"Is this acceptable?"

"Certainly. I would like to meet her, but I understand. Nothing will be said concerning her identity."

"Excellent. Now, there is one other stipulation."

"What is that?"

"She does not want any work done on the documents for one year. I tried to talk her out of this, but she was adamant. She doesn't want to see any news items about this right now—it would bring back too many memories. Later, she feels, it would be more bearable."

Shimon groaned.

"I know," Avraham said. "It's unfortunate, but I'm afraid we must follow her wishes."

"What if we avoided publicity?"

"She gave me very explicit instructions—not for a year. That is the only way I can deliver the documents to you."

"We accept," Shimon said. "I regret the delay, but we accept. Now, how do we arrange for the transfer?"

"That, Shimon, is why I'm here. Please return the documents I gave you—they'll come back in the boxes—and let's arrange the delivery time."

9

THE SECRET STAIRWAY

By midafternoon the floor was completely clear except for the Turkish sewer line sitting on a wall of dirt like a miniature aqueduct.

"What next?" Michael asked.

"Look's like this is about done," Moshe replied. "We'll remove the top section of the column later. I need to get the Company to take care of the sewer line, but that can wait also. Start digging down on the rest of the site as far out as the hotel plans say."

Mars was out on the floor near the back of the building looking over the intricate geometric patterns in the white and black marble.

"Moshe," he said, kneeling down on the tiles.

"Find something?"

"Don't know. Come take a look."

Moshe and Anne hurried down the embankment and onto the floor.

"What is it?" Moshe asked.

"Look at these paving tiles. They're not exactly the same color as those on the rest of the floor."

Moshe got down close and peered through his bifocals. "You're right," he said. "It's almost the same, but not quite. How big an area?"

"About eight by eight—almost square. Do you think the guy that laid the floor ran out of marble and had to get some more?"

"If he did, he also ran out of brains. Herod was a perfectionist. He would never have allowed something like this."

"Then what is it?"

Moshe struggled to keep a straight face. "I thought you young archaeologists knew everything."

"We're working on it," Mars grumbled.

"Anne?" Moshe asked.

"Somebody dug under the floor."

"I think you're right. Sometime before 70 C.E."

"Do we open it up?" Anne asked.

"It's a shame to break up the floor, but yes. We have to see what's under there."

A few minutes later Michael marked the paving stones that would be removed and used a chisel to break the first one loose. It came up in one piece, with one corner broken by the chisel. He then placed the blade under an adjacent paving tile at the mortar line and gave the chisel a sharp blow. The marble popped loose intact. He motioned for four workers.

"Take up the rest of the tiles," he said, indicating which ones. "Be careful of the sewer line. Find a plank to put under it before you dig the dirt away."

It took over an hour to get the rest of the tiles up and chip away the mortar, exposing limestone paving stones. Michael examined the sewer line to make sure it was properly supported. The line was to one side of where they would be digging, but it was still going to be a bother.

The paving stones were about five inches thick, set without mortar. Michael watched as the first one was lifted. He reached in with his trowel and scraped around.

"Hard-packed dirt," he said with a smile. "And I do mean *hard*. Let's start digging it out."

The workers soon ran into a set of stone steps leading downward at a steep angle, perpendicular to the side of the building. The upper part of the stairway vault was a masonry arch that gave way to natural, undisturbed stone as the steps entered the Jerusalem limestone. By the end of the day, four feet of dirt had been excavated. A narrow crack appeared at the bottom of the hole where the dirt had settled beneath the ceiling of a large room.

"That's as far as we get today," Moshe said as he peered into the hole.

"What do you think is down there?" Anne asked.

"I didn't bring my X-ray eyes with me today."

"Take a guess," she insisted.

"I can tell you what most archaeologists would say. But what would the future Doctor Enderly posit?"

"The future Doctor Enderly would posit that the present Doctor Stein is evading Doctor McAdams's question."

"Would I do such a thing?"

"No more answering a question with a question," Anne said.

"But it's the national Jewish pastime," Moshe protested.

"What is it?" Anne demanded.

"You are a persistent lady," Moshe observed. "In other excavations, such stairways usually lead to a lower section of a house, a bath, or a cistern. But this isn't a house."

"So is it a bath or cistern?" Mars inquired.

"That's what most archaeologists familiar with Jerusalem would say."

"But you don't think so."

"No."

"Then what do you think it is."

"If I knew what this building was, maybe I'd have a guess. But we should know soon enough."

Moshe helped Anne up into the van and walked to the back with Mars.

"Want to borrow the machine tonight?" he asked.

Mars looked at the battle-scarred vehicle.

"Thanks, but I think I'll use a taxi."

Moshe shrugged, as if there was no accounting for taste.

◆

Anne opened her hostel door. Mars grinned self-consciously and handed her an envelope.

"What's this?" Anne asked.

"A card," Mars replied. "Happy birthday."

"Thank you," she said, pleasantly surprised and a little embarrassed at the same time. She motioned him to a chair as she closed the door. "How did you know?" she asked as she took a chair across from him.

"A little bird told me."

"A little bird named Stein?"

"Yeah. He said Jews are very romantic."

Anne felt her stomach knot up as she tried desperately to remain calm. She willed her hands to remain steady as she opened the envelope. She smiled as she saw a picture of a sunrise over the Sea of Galilee. She opened the card, looked at it for several moments, turned it on its side, then glanced back at Mars. "This is in Hebrew."

"It was all I could find."

"What does it say?"

"I can't read Hebrew."

"Then how did you pick it out?"

"I told this girl at the card shop what I wanted, and she picked it out."

"What did you tell her?"

"Is it final exam time already? My, how time flies."

"Mars! Will you be serious?"

He didn't say anything. Anne couldn't read what was in his eyes, but she knew it was deep.

Mars finally looked down, then quietly said, "I told her I wanted a card for a friend—a special friend."

"Did she read it to you?"

Mars smiled suddenly. "Yeah, she did. And it's pretty, although I can't remember exactly what it says. Moshe is right. The Jews are very romantic. It talks about beauty, and it goes into a lot of detail."

Anne flushed. "Mars, if this is your idea of a joke . . ."

"It's anything but a joke."

Anne could tell he meant it. "Mars, this is very thoughtful. Thank you."

"Would you like to go out to celebrate?"

"I would like that. What did you have in mind?"

"Moshe said the restaurant in the King David Hotel is very nice. Would you like to try it?"

"How could we go wrong?"

"Ah, Moshe said I could borrow the bus."

Anne looked at him unable to hide her stricken look.

"I declined, politely," he said with a smile.

Anne's relief was all too obvious.

"Shall we go?" Mars asked.

◆

The maitre d' seated Mars and Anne at a table for two in a corner.

"I think the guy wanted his palm greased," Mars grumbled.

"I think you're right."

"Be back in a minute," he said, starting to get up.

"Sit down. This is fine. Save your money for something important."

"You sure this is okay?"

"It's fine."

"I think that guy needs the Enderly treatment."

"I'm afraid to ask what that is."

Mars reached into a pocket and pulled out a coin. "You ask the major domo for a choice table, then pull this out and ask if anyone has change for a quarter."

Anne laughed. She could see Mars doing that.

"Is it effective?"

"Very. I've been bounced out of some pretty classy places with it. But first I make sure it's a place I really don't want to be in."

"How do you decide that?"

"If the head waiter acts like this one, that pretty much decides it. But we'll make an exception for the King David. Dave probably isn't aware he has this bozo working for him. And there's another reason."

"What's that?"

"It's your birthday."

Anne looked down at the tablecloth.

"Do you know which one?" she asked not looking up.

"No. I'm afraid the little bird didn't tell me."

"I'm thirty today. And that's quite a few years older than a certain student of mine."

"It's my weakness. I'm attracted to older women."

Anne jerked her head up. Her smile was gone. "Mars, I'm not much on playing games."

A stricken look came to Mars's face. "It's hard for me to be serious. The thought of rejection terrifies me."

"What rejection?" Anne asked in exasperation.

"By you," he replied. "I meant what I said, though not the way I said it. What I'm trying to tell you in my stupid, clumsy way is, I think I'm falling in love with you."

Anne sat there not knowing what to say.

"Please say something," Mars said when he could stand it no longer.

"I don't know if I can. I wasn't expecting this."

"Yes—I guess I understand. But I'm trying to tell you how I feel, except I don't understand it myself. I didn't come to Israel for romance. I didn't expect it—and certainly not from my teacher. But you intrigued me. And I'm impressed with you as an archaeologist. All I can say is, the feeling keeps getting stronger and stronger. And now I think I know what it is. Apparently Moshe does too. Anne?"

"Yes?"

"I have to know how you feel."

"This is quick, Mars, awfully quick."

Mars's expression tore at her.

"Please give me time, Mars. Yes, I like you very much. And if it helps, I don't have anyone back home waiting to warm my feet."

Mars's face lit up. "Does that mean I can ask you out again?"

"Yes, you can."

The waiter made his belated appearance. Mars ordered for them. The man took the menus and departed.

"Mars?"

"Yes?"

"If we're going to be special friends, would you tell me what your first name is?"

"How about a little 'let's make a deal'?"

"What sort of deal?" Anne asked cautiously.

"What does the D stand for?"

"That's not fair."

"Okay," Mars agreed with a smile.

Anne looked at him, trying not to return it. "It's my birthday," she said.

"And we're celebrating it. This has nothing to do with names."

"Please tell me," she said.

"And you'll tell me?"

"Yes," she agreed after a long pause.

"My real name is Marsh. When I was little, I couldn't say it. It always came out 'Mars.' My parents thought it was cute, so they started calling me that. It's so natural now, I use it as my real name, although I probably shouldn't. My passport says 'Marsh,' but not much else does. And if you call me that, I probably won't know to whom you're talking."

"I think that's sweet."

Mars winced. "Now it's your turn," he said.

"This is hardly fair. There's nothing deep and dark about Marsh."

"A deal's a deal. Fess up."

"Delouva," she said, her voice hardly a whisper.

"What?"

"You heard what I said."

"Ah, yes, I did. But what does it mean? I don't think I've ever met a Delouva before."

"Mars, this is not a subject for one of your jokes. As far as I know, there are only two Delouvas in the world—me and the lady my mother named me for. She was a dear friend, but I wish her name had been Judy or Gail. I'm only thankful my middle name was a little more normal."

"Boy, wait till Moshe hears this."

"Don't you *dare* tell him!" Anne ordered. "This is private between the two of us."

"Yes, ma'am. It's getting kinda warm over here. You can switch off the high-beams now. Your secret is safe with me."

Anne's scowl moderated. "I appreciate it. Very few people know my first name, and I intend to keep it that way."

"I'm glad I'm one of the select few."

The dinner was excellent and the service very good in spite of their apprehensions. But neither one of them noticed it much. Mars looked at Anne, trying to understand the feeling growing inside himself but failing utterly.

"Are you home?" Anne said, interrupting his reverie.

"What?"

"You've been staring for some time."

"Oh. Sorry."

"That's okay. Anything interesting?"

"Yes, but not something I can exactly explain. Just thinking about you."

For the first time since her youth, Anne felt totally disarmed. "That's real sweet, Mars."

"I don't know if my male ego can bear being real sweet."

"But you are."

"Hmm. To change the subject, I think Uri ben Waiter is expecting us to settle the national debt. What say I give him a broadside with my American Express and let's get out of here?"

"Sounds wonderful. May I watch?"

"Be my guest. There, the card's down. Start the timer."

The waiter was upon the tray with alacrity. It was returned moments later with the gratuity already filled in. Mars eyed it, thought of saying something, then dashed off his signature.

◆

It was cool outside. To her surprise, Anne found her hand in Mars's. She thought about removing it but was afraid of offending him. He squeezed her hand. With the slightest pause, she returned the pressure.

"Would you like to see some of the Old City under moonlight?" he asked.

"I'd love to," she said, looking up at him.

The moon seemed to hover over the ancient walls, cool and white and impossibly large. It seemed to be waiting for them as they walked, guarded by crenellated walls and towers. The Dome of the Rock gleamed gold in the distance like some spaceship ready to blast off into the night.

They entered the Jaffa Gate and turned right.

"We're at the Citadel," Mars said. "And there's David's Tower."

The square tower rose up into the night, bathed in floodlights and the moon.

"It's beautiful, Mars. I've never seen anything like the stonework in Jerusalem. It positively glows."

"That's not all that does."

"I'm the one that's Irish."

Mars laughed. "This isn't blarney."

Their hands were sweaty despite the coolness. Mars let Anne's hand slip from his. She looked around at him. He held out both his hands. She took them, and he pulled her slowly to him, putting his arms gently around her as if in slow motion. Their bodies touched, and he pulled her close. He closed his eyes and kissed her, a brief kiss that made the night suddenly warm.

"Anne?"

"Yes?"

"I love you."

"Mars, this is awfully . . ."

"Sudden?"

"Yes. Don't you think . . ."

He pulled her close again and kissed her. After a brief moment Anne responded, and they clung to each other not daring to breathe. They both gasped as they separated.

"Mars," she said in a small voice.

"I love you," Mars repeated, his voice husky with emotion.

She was silent.

"Anne?"

"Yes?"

"Please tell me how you feel."

"Mars, I said this was sudden. It *is* sudden."

"Well, yes," he said, "I guess it is. But . . ."

"But what?"

"I can't change how I feel," he said, so serious Anne couldn't help smiling.

"What's funny?" he demanded.

"You are."

"I don't see why."

"It's the way you are. It's one of the wonderful things about you."

"Hmm," he said, looking at his feet. "That mean I can call on you again?"

"I'd be awfully blue if you didn't."

"Really?" he said looking up suddenly.

"Yes, really."

He drew her close, and she did not hesitate.

◆

The following day Moshe left the site in the early morning and did not return until the afternoon. Anne and Mars watched him as he trudged across the black and white paving tiles.

"That must have been *some* meeting," Mars commented.

Moshe glanced at his watch.

"Probably thought I had abandoned you," he replied. "I avoid committees like the plague, but some I can't get out of. Ordinary committees are bad enough, but committees of academicians have to be previews of hell. But at least I knew the site was in good hands. Find anything?"

"Lots of dirt," Anne said. "A little after 2 we found a few coins—Roman, first-century. But nothing else. Looks like the room is quite large, but we've only reached one wall yet and it only barely."

The muffled sound of digging stopped. "A mosaic! There's a mosaic on the wall!" Michael Shapiro shouted up from below.

Moshe dashed down the steps, followed closely by Anne and Mars. He stooped low to get under the stone vaulting and duck-walked to the wall. He waited as his eyes grew accustomed to the shade, absently running his rough hands over the ancient art.

"Looks to be about fifteen feet wide with a geometric border. Small tiles in contrasting tans and browns. Typical for the period, but exceptionally well done. Mars, your sharp eyes may have discovered the greatest find in Jerusalem. If you hadn't noticed those discolored paving tiles we'd never have found this room."

Mars smiled self-consciously. "You really think so?"

"I do. This room hasn't been touched since it was buried. So whatever's down here hasn't been disturbed. Let's get out of the way so these men can get back to work."

"I presume you want us to dig this out first," Michael said with a straight face.

"No, you old goat. I want you to leave it for last so we can savor it."

"Archaeologists . . ."

Moshe led the way out of the dirt-filled room.

"He says that like he's *not* one," Moshe chuckled as he walked up the steps. "He may not have the degree, but he's got the smarts. Well, we won't find out any more today. When the dirt gets lower, we'll be able to get some more people down there. But it'll still take a few days to get it all out."

10

DECEPTION
UPON DECEPTION

A ny action on our Arab friend?" David Kruger asked.

"Not yet," Ya'acov Isaacson answered. "I've tried everything I can think of, including keeping him awake around the clock. But he's a tough nut. There's nothing else I can do." Ya'acov wasn't sure he entirely agreed with the regulations for dealing with prisoners, but he felt more secure knowing he didn't have to decide.

"This is serious," David said after a short pause. "The Defense Minister thinks this whole incident may lead to an invasion. The Arab saber rattling is getting pretty loud."

"I still don't see what more we can do."

"The regulations have been suspended on this prisoner."

"What?"

"You heard what I said perfectly well. Look at this . . ." David opened the folder in front of him, picked up a letter, and pushed it over to Ya'acov. Ya'acov picked it up and scanned it, whistling when he saw the signature.

David looked as if he tasted something bitter. "You recognize the Defense Minister's name?"

"Yes, of course. This is about as nice a can of worms as I've ever seen."

"I'm not asking for your opinion," David said as evenly as he could.

Ya'acov paused before answering. Although he didn't mean to be, he knew he was a royal pain to his boss. "No, sir, I know you weren't. But there is a problem, and it affects us both."

"I will probably regret asking, but what is the problem?"

Ya'acov took a deep breath as he contemplated how far into the den he wanted to go—or had to. "Sir, let's leave morality out of it for the moment. This letter is of questionable legality."

"It comes down the direct chain of command from the top."

"Actions taken under it could end up before a military tribunal or even the Supreme Court. The Court could find against any soldier taking illegal actions, from the top right down to the bottom. And 'following orders' won't save anyone—not if the orders are illegal."

"Are you telling me you will not obey a direct order?"

"Sir, may I make a suggestion?"

David looked around his office as he struggled with his anger. It was several moments before he could face Ya'acov. "I get plenty whether I ask for them or not."

"Sir, I want what you want. This Arab is the only link we have with the terrorists. I want information out of him, and I'm doing everything I can think of to get it—legally. Please don't back me into a corner."

Ya'acov felt sorry for his boss. He knew the colonel's career was circumscribed by the Defense Minister on one side and, potentially, by the Supreme Court on the other. If Ya'acov decided to bolt, it could be disastrous for them both.

David's earlier grimace eased a little. "Keep me posted," he said as he closed the folder.

"Yes, sir."

Ya'acov rose quickly, thankful the interview was over. He hurried out and closed the door carefully as if he were afraid of setting something off.

"Ya'acov." A familiar voice sounded behind him.

He turned to see Ari Jacovy coming down the hall.

"Been in to see the old man?" Ari asked.

"Why don't you step in and ask him?"

"That bad? What was it about?"

"My friend, we both work in Intelligence."

"And you can't tell me. Is it my imagination, or do I smell some burned tail feathers?"

"I might be able to find a special job for you, Lieutenant. As a matter of fact . . ."

"No, please. I'm quite busy right now. That's one of the reasons I was looking for you. I've got a weird case I'd like to talk with you about."

"I'm not sure I want to know, but what is it?"

"Murder case in Tel Aviv."

"What? We're not the police department."

"I know. The Tel Aviv police referred it to us." Ari held up his hand when he saw Ya'acov was going to object. "I know what you're thinking. There was probably no good reason for them to do it, and we'll probably give it right back to them, but I've got to take a look. This guy—Dan Braun—raised a stink with the police and insisted they contact us. Says his cousin, Naomi Braun, was murdered by terrorists."

"I suppose he has proof."

"Haven't talked to him yet. Care to come along?"

Ya'acov shrugged and followed his friend down the hall to one of the interrogation rooms. Dan Braun was already there and jumped to his feet as the officers came in.

"It's about time," Dan said. "First I had to argue with the police, then the IDF. Why does it take so long to get anything done?"

"Please be seated, Mr. Braun," Ari said. "I am Lieutenant Ari Jacovy, and this is Captain Ya'acov Isaacson. Before we begin, do you object to this meeting being taped?"

Dan hesitated before answering. "No, I guess not."

"Good." Ari pressed the Record and Play buttons and set the portable recorder on the table between them. "I am Lieutenant Ari Jacovy, and with me is Captain Ya'acov Isaacson. Please state your name."

"Dan. Dan Braun."

"Mr. Braun, do we have your permission to tape this interview?"

"Yes."

"Thank you, Mr. Braun. We're here to discuss this case with you at the request of the Tel Aviv police. I've read their report, and it appears to be an ordinary homicide. Unless you can convince me otherwise, this case goes back to the police."

"But terrorists did it!"

"What proof do you have?"

"All the pictures are gone."

"I have read the police report. 'Over a hundred boxes of old photographs, written records, family documents, some jewelry, an unknown amount of money.' Where do the terrorists come in?"

"Okay—the police said it was burglary. Fine. Burglars break in and steal a hundred boxes of pictures. That really makes sense!"

"You may have a point, but stranger things have happened. Maybe it was crazies or druggies."

"It was terrorists!"

"So you say. But where is the proof?"

"You don't believe me?"

"It's not a matter of believing or not believing, Mr. Braun. It's a matter of whether or not I think your conclusion is correct. At this time I don't think it is. Again, do you have any evidence?"

"No."

"Did you see your cousin on a regular basis?"

Dan hesitated before answering. "Not very. Naomi didn't like me very much."

"When did you see her last?"

"A little over a week ago. I was there when this rabbi came by with this lawyer. They were going to do her will, she said. I tried to help her, but she got mad and threw me out."

"These men had names?"

"Yes. The rabbi's name was Avraham Horowitz, and the lawyer's was David Rubinstein. And that's another unusual thing. I had met this Horowitz guy a month earlier in Jerusalem. Don't you think that's strange?"

"I don't know enough to say one way or the other."

"Why was she doing a will when she didn't tell me about it? I'm her next of kin."

"You said she didn't like you," Ari reminded Dan.

"Well, yes. But I'm still her next of kin. And it seems odd that this happened just before she was murdered."

"You have seen the will by now?" Ari asked.

"No. We haven't found it yet. I called Rubinstein, and he said Naomi kept it with her."

"Do you know what was in it?"

"The lawyer won't tell me. But she told me she was leaving everything to Yad Vashem. Why would she do that?"

"Why not? Many Israelis leave their estates to Zionist organizations, many of them to Yad Vashem."

"But I'm her next of kin. Why didn't she leave everything to me?" Dan scowled at the officers.

Ari glanced at Ya'acov, who shook his head.

Ari turned back to Dan. "Thank you for coming in, Mr. Braun. You did the right thing in cooperating with the police and in having them refer the case to us. We're trained to evaluate such things. At the present time I see no evidence of a terrorist tie-in. However, the Tel Aviv police will contact us automatically if such a connection shows up later. Now, if there's anything further you require, the sergeant at the front desk will be able to help you. Good day, sir."

Dan left the room trailing a sullen cloud behind him. Ari clicked off the tape recorder. "There goes a happy man. Terrorists did in his cousin and stole her pictures. Why not extraterrestrials?"

Ya'acov laughed. "That would have been better. Then we could have handed it off to the Israel Air Force."

◆

A whole day had not changed the room much. Michael was using two more men, and they were all concentrating on the mosaic. But tons of dirt filled the room, packed as only two millennia of rest could do. The three archaeologists were gathered around the steps like vultures. Moshe cocked his head to one side as he listened to the digging below.

"You're not holding your mouth right," Mars observed.

"What?" Moshe asked. The quizzical expression was quickly replaced by a suitable glare. "You had best be careful, young man. Your professor and I have not discussed your grade as yet."

Moshe glanced at Anne, who had to look away quickly, but not before Moshe caught the amusement on her face.

"I am surrounded by Philistines," Moshe observed.

Anne was about to reply when a muffled cry came from the excavation. She watched in awe as Moshe rushed down the stairs faster than she thought possible. She and Mars followed him.

"Look at it," Michael shouted.

"I'm trying to," Moshe said as his eyes began to adjust to the dim light.

The top of the mosaic was clearly sky and clouds. But in the center, nearly halfway down, was the top of a massive building somber against a summer sky.

"The Temple," Moshe said. "The Second Temple. We're looking at something that hasn't been seen for nearly two thousand years—since 70 C.E. For the first time we know exactly what it looked like."

"Looks like the Holyland Hotel model isn't far off," Anne said.

"Considering the historical record, they didn't do badly at all," Moshe agreed.

"I think we have company," Michael said, pointing up the stairs.

"Daniel," Moshe said. "What a surprise. Come on down."

Dan Adov picked his way carefully over the debris-strewn steps, his eyes never leaving the mosaic. "That's the most beautiful thing I've ever seen," he said. "I thought what I saw up above was magnificent, but this is beyond comparison. What have you found?"

"Only the greatest art treasure of the ancient world. A mosaic executed some time before 70 C.E., probably commissioned by Herod the Great. How fortunate you happened by."

"I didn't happen by. You left a message for me at the paper."

"No need to go into that. You're glad you came, aren't you?"

"Yes, of course. And just in time for my deadline. I wonder if that's a coincidence too?"

"I'm sure it is," Moshe said.

"There wouldn't happen to be some background information lying around, would there? Perhaps in a jar or hiding under a column?"

"You mean something like this?" Moshe asked, pulling several typewritten pages out of his pocket. He unfolded the pages, smoothed them out, and handed them to Dan.

"How about some pictures?"

"It's sad," Moshe said. "Reporters get so lazy when they get old."

"On the contrary. I learned years ago that you like me to write these stories using all the facts, which you conveniently provide."

"So as to keep them straight."

"I haven't had too many complaints."

"You do good work, I have to admit. But as to the pictures, if you will take a look in your mailbox at the *Post*, you will find a good selection of black-and-whites on the work upstairs. This we haven't had a chance to photograph yet."

"And you won't today," Michael interrupted. "It's quitting time."

"Think we'll get to the bottom tomorrow?" Moshe asked.

"There's a lot more dirt to come out, but, yes, I think so. We'll give it our best shot."

"Couldn't ask for more." Moshe turned to Anne, Mars, and Dan. "Let's get out of the way so Michael can pack up."

♦

Abdul Suleiman fought his way toward consciousness. It had been the first night they had let him sleep without rousing him every few minutes. He heard a key in the lock, the cell door flew open with a crash, and a burly hand reached in and snapped on the light. Abdul winced as the brilliant light stabbed at his retinas. He forced his eyes open a little and squinted at the door. The Israeli guard glared in at him. "Okay, come out of there."

Abdul looked at the man.

"If I have to come in there, I guarantee you'll regret it."

Abdul sat up and swung his feet slowly to the floor. He was tempted to take the Israeli up on it, but knew he couldn't very well fight the whole garrison.

"A wise choice," the guard said. "Have we got a deal for you! Since you've been so cooperative, we're going to move you to a deluxe prison. Now let's see some hands."

Abdul stuck them out. The soldier snapped the handcuffs on in one smooth motion and pointed down the deserted corridor. "Let's move it. Can't keep the limo waiting."

The guard quick-marched Abdul to the loading dock in the back of the building. One of the dock doors was open. Pulled up to it, framed by the early-morning darkness, was an IDF van, its engine running. The driver was on the dock talking to another soldier. They both looked around as the guard brought Abdul up.

"Here he is," the guard said.

"Get in," the driver ordered, pointing to one of the benches inside the back of the van.

Abdul glared at the driver as he ducked his head and went where he was told. He looked at the bench, then back at his captors.

"Sit down!" the guard commanded as he extended a clipboard to the driver.

The driver glanced at it, signed his name in the indicated blank, and handed it back to the guard.

"All yours," the guard said.

"Thanks a lot. I'll try and do something nice for you sometime." He turned to the soldier with him. "Close it up. Let's get rolling."

The other soldier pulled down the van's steel roll door and secured it with a padlock.

Abdul got up and crept to the back of the van. It was completely dark except for a thin line of light where the door met the van's bed. He heard two thumps as the soldiers jumped to the pavement. A few moments later he heard the van doors open, then clump shut. The emergency brake thumped off, and the van lurched on its way, almost causing Abdul to lose his balance. He stumbled his way forward and sat down on the bench. He put his ear against the steel wall behind the cab and listened. Nothing.

Abdul leaned back, his head resting uncomfortably on the side wall behind him. Where were the Israelis taking him—and why? He had been expecting a transfer when they figured out they weren't going to get anything from him, but not this soon. The possibility of a secret prison where prisoners would be beyond the reach of Israeli law came to mind. That was frightening. If the Israelis were planning something nasty, it would certainly be done in some remote location. He tried not to let himself dwell on that.

He tried to figure out what direction they were going but had to give up. With no references, it was impossible. How long the trip took was far more important. Gradually the adrenaline began to wear off, and weariness began to seep back in. He felt his eyes drifting shut. He shook his head and stood up. He walked back and forth in the dark until he could feel the drowsiness leaving.

He almost fell as the truck slowed, then made a tight right turn. The driver downshifted, and the engine started laboring as they started up a hill. A familiar whine came clearly through the steel sides of the van. Abdul cocked his head as the sound grew louder. It was going to be close. The driver slammed on his brakes, throwing Abdul off his feet and into the forward wall. His head exploded with light as it hit a glancing blow on an unseen sharp corner. He fell to the floor in a crumbled heap and clamped his eyes closed to try and shut out the excruciating pain.

When the mortar round hit, the concussion threw Abdul into the air and down flat on his back. Something else was happening, but he wasn't sure what because of the ringing in his ears. Something was violently rocking the van. After a few moments he could distinguish the staccato rattle of automatic weapons and a sound much worse than hail as slugs tore into the truck. Abdul tried to merge with the floor as he imagined the bullets tearing through the air above him.

Then everything was silent. The quietness was almost as unnerving as the racket had been. As the ringing in his ears began to subside, Abdul started to hear other things—the *tink-tink-tink* of the engine as it cooled and the spatter of the coolant as it drained from the bullet-riddled radiator. But all else was silent.

Abdul staggered to his feet, bumping his throbbing head against the top of the van. He stumbled to the heavy roll door and knelt down. He forced his fingers under the bottom and pulled up with all his strength. He pulled until it felt like his muscles would part, but the door only clanked against the padlocked latch. He gave up and sat back.

At first he thought his hearing was playing tricks on him. But then he heard it again—voices outside, barely audible. Then rapid footsteps as someone ran toward the van. Whoever it was opened one of the front doors. Something heavy hit the ground. An assault rifle fired three times in quick succession. The truck swayed again. The rifle fired two more times.

When the man ran to the back of the van, Abdul crawled into a front corner, as far from the back door as he could get. The man outside rattled the padlock and a few moments later emptied his clip in a horrible din, then struck the padlock with his rifle. Somehow it had held.

"Bring me a grenade!" the man shouted in Arabic.

"Not with me in here!" Abdul shouted.

The man outside paused before asking, "Who's in there?"

"No friend of the Jews," Abdul replied. "Who are you?"

"I will wait until I see who I'm talking to."

"Don't use a grenade! You'll kill me!"

"You don't . . ." the man began.

Another man near the front of the van said something Abdul couldn't hear, and one of the men ran off. The other one came around to the back door.

"Bring it here," the man said.

The roll door began creaking and banging against the floor as the man pushed on it.

"What are you doing?" Abdul demanded.

The man made no reply as he continued working. There was a rustling noise, followed by silence.

"Cover your ears!" the man shouted.

"What are you going to do?" Abdul demanded.

"Shut up and do what I say! You have ten seconds."

Abdul heard two men run away from the truck. He covered his ears and waited. The ten seconds seemed like an hour. When the explosion came, it was almost a surprise. The sound was deafening even through his hands. The truck lurched as if it had been rear-ended. The door rattled and shrieked in protest, then rolled up a few feet before it jammed. Black shapes were silhouetted against the moonlight.

"Come out of there," one of them said.

Abdul crawled forward and under the door. He got shakily to his feet and felt where the lock had been.

"Plastic?" he asked.

"Yeah. Now hold still."

One of the men checked him quickly for weapons.

"He hasn't got anything. He's cuffed though."

"What do you expect?" another man asked. "He's got prison clothes on, and they had him locked in the back." The man pointed with his rifle. "Come on, you. We've already been here too long. Do exactly what I say or you'll get what we gave the Israelis."

Abdul hesitated until he heard a rifle safety click off.

"Lead the way," he said.

"Turn around. There's a man directly in front of you. Keep up with him. I'll be right behind you. If you give me the slightest trouble, I'll drop you. Understand?"

"Yes."

"Good. Move it."

Abdul glanced to the side as they started off. Although past full, the moon was high in the sky and provided ample light, if not much color. The van was riddled by heavy-caliber slugs. The left front was on the edge of the mortar crater—the driver had stopped in time, for all the good it did him. He was sprawled on the ground where the black pool of his blood grew wider and wider. The other guard was slumped in the front seat, his head tilted at a crazy angle, eyes gazing vacantly at the stars. Abdul tripped on a stone.

"I'm not going to warn you again," said the man behind him.

They rushed down a steep ravine, then started up the opposite side. Ordinarily Abdul would have had no trouble keeping up, but he was out of condition from his captivity. He puffed with exertion as he followed the man in front. Finally they reached the top and walked out on a narrow road on the top of the ridge. Where they were, Abdul had no idea except it had to be somewhere in the Judean Hills.

In a few moments an ancient bus groaned around the bend and pulled up to the group. The door popped open, and the men started climbing in.

"Okay," the man behind Abdul said, "get in and go all the way to the back. When you get there, lie down on your face and don't make a move. I'll be watching you the entire trip."

Abdul did as the man said. He could wait. At least he was no longer in the hands of the Jews.

◆

The trip took around an hour. Finally the bus lurched to a stop.

"You can get up now," Abdul's guard said. "When you get off the bus, turn left, walk straight ahead, and enter the first door you come to."

Abdul walked forward and down the steps. The wall of a building was a few feet away. He turned left and immediately saw a black doorway in front of him. He turned in, his guard following. As soon as the last man was in, someone closed the door.

One of the men flipped on a switch, bathing the room in a dim light that obscured more than it revealed. Abdul saw the Palestinian flag immediately.

"Are you PLO?" he asked.

"You will *not* ask the questions," his guard reminded him. "We don't know who you are. And until we do, we have nothing to say. Now, who are *you*?"

Abdul looked at the man, apparently the leader. He scanned the other faces, taking time to gather his thoughts. One of the things Avraham had told him again and again was, "No one is to know who is in the Palestinian Revolutionary Force. No exceptions. Ever."

"I cannot tell you," he said, facing the leader.

"That will not do," the man said.

"I do not know who *you* are. Why should I tell you about me?"

"Because I'll kill you if you don't." The man brought up his AK-47 for emphasis. "Right here and right now."

"But I'm Palestinian!"

"Says who? We set up an ambush for the IDF, and this stupid truck drives into it. We kill the soldiers and find you in the back. We have no idea who you are or what the Jews were doing with you."

"They don't carry their friends around locked in the backs of trucks! They were taking me to a new prison."

"So he finally tells us something," the leader said with a laugh. He looked around as his men joined in. "And what prison were they taking you to?"

"I don't know. They didn't tell me."

"What sorts of things *did* they tell you?"

Abdul glared at the man. How could someone be so stupid?

"You are Palestinian, you say?" the leader asked. "You are PLO?"

"No."

"So you are Palestinian, but you are not PLO. The Jews put you in prison. What did you do? Squat down where you weren't supposed to?"

"You idiot!" Abdul stormed. "You don't have the brains of a dung beetle."

The leader swung his AK-47 up and thumbed the safety off in one fluid motion. Abdul looked right down the black bore. The silence was abrupt and stifling. Not a man moved. Abdul shifted his gaze to the man's trigger finger. He was sure it was slowly squeezing. Then slowly the gun went down. But the safety stayed off.

"Next time your brains will be on the wall. You will tell us who you are. Now! I am done. I don't care if you answer or not. We have important things to do—and you're in the way. If you are Palestinian—really Palestinian, and not a collaborator, you'd better convince me right now. If you don't, you're dead. Is that clear enough for you?"

Abdul knew the man meant it. There was no one he could appeal to. He did Avraham no good in captivity or dead. And Abdul did not want to die, not when there was no purpose for it. And certainly not at the hands of a fellow Arab.

"I am a member of the Palestinian Revolutionary Force," he said slowly.

"That's easy enough to say. Prove it."

"You don't know what you're asking! My leader . . ."

"I know the importance of security," the chief interrupted smoothly. "I have the same problem—with you. I have no desire to kill a brother, but how can I be sure you won't inform on us? I am not entirely ignorant of other groups. Give me something I can trust."

"My leader's name is Avraham Abbas."

"More."

"But you don't know Avraham!"

"You young fool! You don't think *I'm* going to tell him any of this, do you? Can I turn you loose or not?"

"We did the Dome of the Rock attack."

"What? The Jews are telling the truth about that?"

"Yes. That's where they captured me."

"Why in the name of Allah would you do such a thing?"

"I don't know. Avraham did not tell me."

"You are not high in the organization then."

"Not high?" Abdul snorted in derision. "I am second in command!" Abdul hung his head, then looked back up. "I know how that sounds," he continued. "But you don't know Avraham. Some things he confides in no one. I did not like having things that way, but he is the leader. He is hard to work for, but I have seen him do some amazing things. Things I would not have thought possible."

"I would ask you what, but I don't have time. I think you are telling the truth, but I have to be sure. Where do I find this Avraham Abbas?"

"In East Jerusalem, number 7 Sha'ar haArayot."

"I am convinced," the leader said slowly. "Now, who am I speaking to?"

Abdul remained silent.

"Come, come. One Arab to another. I am Naif Tarif. I must know what brother I am talking to."

"Abdul Suleiman."

"A good name."

"Yes. Now get these cuffs off me. I must get back to Avraham as soon as possible. He needs me."

"I'm sure he does, but I am afraid he will have to do without you."

"What? I told you what you wanted to know. You said you were convinced."

"I am," Naif said as he slowly raised his rifle.

"Then what are you doing?" Abdul screamed.

"You can come in now," Naif said, raising his voice.

The door opened, and two IDF soldiers came in followed by Captain Ya'acov Isaacson.

"Got the tape?" Ya'acov asked.

The man who said he was Naif held out his hand. One of his men placed a small cassette recorder in it. "Naif" handed it to Ya'acov.

"That was nicely done."

"Naif" nodded.

Abdul looked at Ya'acov and then at the soldiers with him. One of the soldiers had ragged holes in his shirt and appeared drenched with blood, although he appeared in no pain. Then he looked closer. It was the driver of the truck.

"You're dead!" he said before he could stop himself.

"Sometimes I wonder," Ya'acov said, giving the man a wink.

"But I saw it. That truck was ripped to shreds."

"What you saw was the work of the best Israeli special effects man in the movie business. My men were pretty good actors, wouldn't you say?"

Abdul started forward in a blind rage.

"Naif" brought his rifle up and let Abdul run into it. Abdul backed up, blinking away tears as he clutched his chest.

"This is a real AK-47, and it doesn't have plastic bullets in it."

Abdul spat in the man's face.

"He's my prisoner," Ya'acov said, seeing "Naif's" finger move to the trigger.

"Naif" glanced at Ya'acov. He wiped his face and stood aside. Abdul walked past and stopped next to the captain. Ya'acov looked at him. Never had he seen such hate in a man's eyes.

11

THE HIDDEN
ROOM

Moshe waved as a group of his colleagues from the Hebrew University skirted the edge of the barricade and got back in their Land Rover after their early-morning visit to the site.

"News gets around fast," Mars commented.

"Yes," agreed Moshe. "At least among the archaeologists."

"Now that you mention it," Anne said, "no one but archaeologists has been here. That story Dan did in the *Jerusalem Post* was great. But it's the only media interest there's been. And this has to be one of the finest archaeological finds in a very long time."

"I must hire you to be my press agent," Moshe said. "You are learning an important lesson about public opinion. About all you can say for sure about public opinion is that it's public. Somehow this isn't up there with the vital issues of our day, like flying saucers or Elvis sightings or some woman giving birth to a tabloid editor."

"Inquiring minds want to know?" Mars suggested.

"That's what I've heard, but I haven't seen any evidence of it. But don't let that bother you. We may get some polite interest, but it won't be in depth and it won't last long. What we're doing, we're doing for science. *We* know it's important, and that's enough."

"I guess I agree," Mars said after thinking about it.

"Bless you," Moshe said with a smile. He sat down and tried to make himself comfortable. Workers staggered up the stairs with baskets of dirt as the digging slowly progressed.

♦

The three archaeologists wolfed down sandwiches at lunch, not daring to leave for fear of what they might miss. It was midafternoon before Moshe heard what he had been waiting for.

"We're at floor level," Michael shouted. "The mosaic's entirely exposed."

Moshe led the other two down the stairs and looked for the first time at the complete mosaic. He stood gazing at it for several minutes. "That's the most beautiful thing I've ever seen," he said at last. "Look at that detail. If we could back off far enough, it would look just like a photograph. The Temple, the walls, the Antonia fortress—everything! Looks like you could walk right up the hill and into one of the gates."

"How does this fit in with what we've already found?" Mars asked.

"I think the mosaic definitely links this building to the Temple. My guess is that the building above is the Temple Treasury."

"But the Temple itself had a treasury, didn't it?" Anne asked.

"Yes, according to the Bible it did. Maybe the one in the Temple wasn't big enough to hold the bulk of the treasure."

"But this room was sealed before the building was destroyed."

"Yes, that's a problem. Well, we're in the way again. Back upstairs."

It was late afternoon by the time the men had cleaned out the rest of the dirt.

"That's all that's down here?" Mars asked, nodding toward the mosaic.

"Isn't it *enough*?" Moshe demanded.

"That's not what I meant. This is the most fabulous thing *I've* ever seen, ancient or modern. But that's all that's down here. Something's missing."

"What?"

"I don't know," Mars said, very much aware of his lack of experience.

Moshe smiled. "It's a good observation, Mars. This room is strange, very strange. But so is the building above. The whole site is unique." Moshe's eyes narrowed as he contemplated the American. "Assuming the Temple Treasury is what's above us, what would be the function of this room?"

"I think the building above was administrative and the vault was down here."

"But there's nothing here, Mars. Natural, untouched rock is all around us. There's nothing more to excavate—no more stairs, no door-ways. This is it."

"Maybe the door's behind the mosaic. It's been bricked up, and they covered it with the mosaic to keep anyone from finding it."

"My friend, you watch too many movies. You can't move treasure in and out of your vault if you've sealed the only door in."

"I can't argue that," Mars said after a moment's thought. "But I still say there's something behind that mosaic. There's more down here than an empty room. Otherwise, this is an art gallery under the Temple Treasury."

"Doesn't seem very likely, does it?" Moshe admitted.

"What if we look behind it?"

Moshe turned on Mars in utter disbelief. "Touch that mosaic? The University would stick me in the Hadassah psychiatric ward. This is the greatest art treasure of the first century."

"Could we tunnel around from the side or underneath?"

Moshe looked at the floor and scraped his foot along the rock. "No. I'm intrigued with your theory, but without hard evidence, tunneling through the rock would take too long. And there would be too much danger to the mosaic. I'm sorry."

"Moshe, what if something *is* back there?" Anne asked.

"This room will remain exactly as it is. Perhaps we can investigate later."

Anne was not ready to give up. "And what if someone else finds it? And what if what's back there puts what we've found in the shade?"

"What a nightmare," Moshe said with a wince. "But we still can't do it. The Company will not allow it. And without proof, I can't put off their work any longer. Unless we find something else, this site is finished."

"Moshe?" Mars said.

"Yes."

"Please listen. What if we dig a little pit in the floor in the center of the mosaic and drill up under it to see if there's something hollow

behind there? That ought to be quick, and it would give us the proof
we need."

"Or the lack of it."

"Yes."

"And what if the door's offset to either side and we miss it?"

"That's possible. I just thought the mosaic would be centered on the
door."

Moshe glanced around the room. "I think your reasoning is sound.
Looking at the room, I'd place a door in the center too."

"Then we'll do it?"

Moshe sighed. "Against my better judgment, yes. Michael, set up
the portable generator and get the heavy-duty drill down here and the
masonry saw. Looks like we're going to be here for a while."

A few minutes later the generator started up, and a worker started
snaking the heavy-duty cables down the stairs. Michael rigged the
work lights, then set up the rock drill and the masonry saw. The lights
clicked on, dispelling the growing shadows of evening.

The three archaeologists retreated as the worker donned his respirator and goggles and started cutting with the masonry saw. He made
two deep cuts perpendicular to the wall about two feet apart. He then
sectioned the inside rock with cuts parallel to the wall. Finished, he cut
off the saw and removed the respirator and goggles, his flesh making a
sharp contrast with the white stone dust.

He made quick work of breaking out the segments with a hammer
and chisel. When the rock was cleared away, he worked on the area
closest to the wall to dig away enough rock to accommodate the drill.

"That looks like enough," Michael said, lying down on the floor to
check the perspective. "Put the bit under the mosaic's border and get a
good up angle. Start slow," he instructed one of his helpers.

The bit cut quickly into the soft stone. In minutes it was in up to the
chuck. The worker stopped and backed the bit out.

"The end of the bit's above floor level where the door should be,"
Moshe said. "And there's no change in the color of the dust. Looks like
solid rock."

"They probably walled off the door with rock from down here,"
Mars replied. "Let's keep going. It's got to be hollow."

Moshe nodded to the worker. The man ran the bit back into the hole, attached an extension, and continued drilling. The progress slowed as more and more of the bit disappeared into the hole. The worker stopped when the chuck started grinding against the rock.

"I've got one more extension," he said.

"Well, we've gone this far," Moshe said. "Put it on. But if this doesn't hit something, we quit."

Mars watched as the last section slowly entered the hole. After what seemed hours, less than an inch of the extension remained. Still the drill ground away.

"It's not there," Moshe said.

"The wall could be thick. Or the door could be off to the side."

"'Maybe' won't stop the Company from shooing us off this site tomorrow. We've done all we can do."

Just then a sharp *snap* sounded outside. The lights went off, and the drill ground to a stop. Moshe flicked on a flashlight.

"The circuit breaker on the generator tripped," Michael said. "Want me to go reset it?"

"I don't see why. We're all the way in and still drilling through rock."

"There's an inch to go," Mars said.

"If we haven't hit something by now, we're not going to in another inch."

"What have we got to lose? We've put in all this time. Why not go as far as we can?"

"Reset it," Moshe grumbled.

A minute later the lights flicked back on, bathing the hole with what seemed a blinding glare after the darkness. The worker grasped the drill and squeezed the trigger. The extension shaft continued rotating as it slowly traveled the last inch. The chuck was grinding against the rock when the drill suddenly picked up speed.

"Did you hit something?" Moshe asked.

"I don't know," the man said. "Let me back it out and see."

The man loosened the chuck and removed the drill. He then pushed the extension back up the hole. It went all the way in.

"It's hollow in there!" he shouted.

"Well, well, well, Mr. Enderly," Moshe said with a smile. "It seems we are very much indebted to your perseverance. Assuming we haven't hit some rock cavern, may it never be, we seem to have hit your hidden doorway."

"We can stall the Company?" Mars asked.

"We can stall the Company. They won't like it, but they'll have to wait. I think this is quite enough for one night. Let's pack it up and get some dinner."

12

ASSAULT ON
YAD VASHEM

Mustapha Kabran watched as Avraham put on his black coat and adjusted it to his liking. No matter how handy the disguise was, it still bothered him when his leader masqueraded as a Jew. Avraham glanced up.

"Something the matter?" he asked.

"Nothing. I was thinking about what we have to do."

"Good. I hope you remembered everything. What about the timers?"

"They're set for 2:30 P.M. But once we leave here, there's no way I can adjust them without giving everything away."

"This will come off on time!" Avraham glared at Mustapha, again wishing he had Abdul back.

"You and Majid have your identity cards?"

"Yes. I have checked off everything, as you instructed."

Avraham glanced at his watch. "Time to go. Call Majid."

Mustapha shouted for the man. "You want us in the back? Not much room the way we had to load the boxes."

"No. Too dangerous in case we're stopped. I've hired two Arabs to do this work for me—that is the explanation for your presence. It will look perfectly natural. I want Majid in the middle and you next to the door."

The ride into Jerusalem was uneventful, even though Avraham

looked for trouble around every bend as Road 1 made its steep ascent into the eternal city. The beauty of the rugged Judean Hills was lost on Avraham as he kept watching for IDF patrols.

Avraham slowed as he made the sharp turn to head north on Derekh Yeriho, with the Old City on the left and the Mount of Olives on the right. At the northeast corner of the Old City he turned left onto Sultan Suleiman.

Avraham glanced at his watch. It was almost 10:45. "Looks like we'll be right on time."

"Should give us plenty of time to unload and get out," Mustapha agreed.

"Of course there's plenty of time! That's the way I planned it."

"Yes. Forgive me. It's my nature to worry."

"I've noticed."

Mustapha looked quickly out the window, taking no chance that Avraham might see his expression.

Avraham followed a sinuous series of streets, trending generally toward the southwest corner of Jerusalem past the southern corner of the Hebrew University's West Jerusalem campus, then back to the northwest up Shemu'el Beyth until it ran into Sederot Herzl. There he turned left and abruptly ran into a line of cars that were barely moving. Several hundred feet ahead the street to Yad Vashem was barricaded by the IDF. That the line of cars was moving at all was because most of the cars were continuing straight, passing those that were trying to turn into the Memorial. Of the latter, most were being turned away.

"What's going on?" Mustapha asked, leaning forward to look over at Avraham.

"How should I know?" Avraham snapped.

"Shouldn't we turn around? We can disarm the bombs back at Jericho."

"There is no reason to quit. We have every right to be here."

Mustapha shifted uncomfortably in his seat. He watched in horror as the line of cars in front dwindled. Finally there was only one, and it was turned away by the young Israeli soldier. Avraham slipped the clutch smoothly and drove up to the barricade. He smiled at the soldier and handed him his identity card without being asked. The young man studied it carefully and handed it back.

"I'm sorry, Rabbi," he said. "The Memorial is closed until late this afternoon."

"But I have an appointment at 11 o'clock with Shimon Goldberg."

"The director?" the soldier asked in surprise.

"He doesn't sweep the floors."

"Please wait here."

Avraham watched the man walk over to a group of officers and tried to look at ease as two soldiers watched the truck, their hands resting lightly on their assault rifles.

"I wouldn't think of moving," Avraham muttered through his teeth.

One of the officers looked over at the truck. Avraham put on his best smile. The officer glanced at the lengthening line of cars behind the truck, then started over.

The lieutenant's smile was strained as he looked up at Avraham. A horn sounded, followed immediately by several more.

"You have come at a bad time, Rabbi," the man said with an obvious lack of respect.

"The time was agreed upon by Shimon and myself. And I believe the appointments of the director are his business."

"But I have my orders. I have a list of people who are allowed in, and your name is not on it. And I haven't even checked the men with you."

"A mistake's been made. If you will check with the director, he will verify our appointment."

"That's not possible."

The officer caught a movement out of the corner of his eye, and much to his horror saw General Ezer Levy approaching with something more than the time of day on his mind.

"Lieutenant!" he thundered.

"Yes, sir?"

"What's the meaning of this holdup? My staff car hasn't moved in five minutes."

"Sir, this rabbi wants in, and he isn't on the list. Says he has an appointment with the director, but I can't verify it right now. And there's no way past until I can get this truck out of here."

"Shimon's not going to like this," Avraham said.

"What?" The general turned his glare on Avraham.

Avraham tried to smooth over the tense situation. "The director was going to show the Prime Minister the Holocaust documents we're bringing him. If you don't let us through, he has nothing to show the Prime Minister."

"May I see your identification?" Ezer asked.

Avraham handed it over.

"Rabbi Avraham Horowitz. Do you have something to confirm your appointment?"

Avraham reached into a pocket and drew out the business card Shimon had given him at their last meeting.

"That's all?"

"What else *should* there be? It's on his appointment calendar."

Ezer looked at the lieutenant in exasperation as he handed the ID and business card back to Avraham.

"Let them through," he said.

"But I haven't checked the others' identity cards."

"Let them through! Do you want it in writing?"

"No, sir."

The lieutenant waved to two of his men. They moved the barricade and allowed the truck to drive through. General Levy turned around and stormed back to his staff car. Avraham smiled at the lieutenant as he drove past the guards and up the winding road to the Memorial.

"It's a good thing I know the right people," Avraham said with a rare laugh.

Mustapha looked over at Avraham. "You got us in, all right. But what in the world is going on? I've never seen so much IDF brass in my life."

"Who cares. All we have to do is unload the boxes and get out of here. Maybe the IDF officers will be inside when the bombs go off. That would be a nice bonus."

Avraham found the loading dock Shimon had told him about and backed the truck in. "Wait here," he said as he jumped out.

He walked to the large double doors and pressed the button below the admittance sign. A buzzer went off inside, sounding remote and ineffective. After nearly a minute Avraham heard muted footsteps. A bolt clicked, and one of the doors swung open. The man framed in the doorway squinted into the bright sunlight.

"What do you want?" he asked in a way that implied he had been taken away from something he considered important.

"I am Rabbi Avraham Horowitz. The director is expecting me."

"I'm sorry, he's not here."

"What do you mean? I made this appointment with him a few days ago."

"All I know is, he's not here. As you perhaps have noticed, there's quite a lot going on right now."

Avraham paused. "What exactly is going on?" he asked.

"You don't know?"

"If I did, I wouldn't be asking, would I?"

"No reason why you should, I guess. The Prime Minister is holding a press conference here at 2 o'clock to discuss the Dome of the Rock incident. A lot of the minority parties are here early to try and figure out what he's going to talk about so they can oppose it. And of course there's the security."

"And you have no idea where the director is? It really is urgent that I see him."

"No, I'm sorry, but I really don't know. I'm sure it has something to do with the press conference, but he left here about an hour ago and didn't tell anyone where he was going. I know—*I've* been trying to find him. Would you like to wait in his office?"

Avraham thought this over. "No. I'll wait in my truck. It's such a nice day."

"Yes, it is," the man agreed. "Not to worry. As soon as I see him, I'll tell him where to find you."

Avraham thanked the man and watched as the door swung shut and the bolt thumped home.

"What is going on?" Mustapha asked as Avraham climbed back into the cab.

"The director's not here."

"Oh great! We're going to sit here until the bombs go off?"

Mustapha knew he had gone too far. He looked at Avraham out of the corner of his eye. The man was glaring at him with unspeakable hate. What made it worse was the silence that accompanied it.

After a long time Avraham turned to look out through the windshield. He tried not to think about what would happen if someone got curious about why they were there. Avraham glanced down at his hands. They were unconsciously gripping the steering wheel and were white as death.

◆

David Kruger thought about knocking but decided not to. He swung the door open and walked into Ya'acov Isaacson's office.

"Ah, you're both here," he said, spying Ari Jacovy seated across from Ya'acov. "Saves me the trouble of finding Ari."

Both officers stood, looking rather like trapped animals.

"Good afternoon, sir," Ya'acov said, which was echoed by Ari a fraction of a second later.

"Good afternoon, gentlemen. I suppose you're wondering why I'm here."

"Yes, sir, now that you mention it."

"And you suspect that whatever it is, it probably isn't pleasant."

"I would never say such a thing," Ya'acov answered.

"I was talking about thinking, not saying. Anyway, I won't keep you wondering any longer. You gentlemen are going to be my guests today. We're going to the Prime Minister's press conference."

"To hear him talk about some recent happenings," Ya'acov said.

"How astute you are." David paused as he pondered what he wanted to say. "Ya'acov, that was fine work you did in finding out who our guest terrorist is. And as you've probably guessed by now, the information was quite well received by Prime Minister Beker. Incidentally, he instructed General Levy to tell you that Israel is very grateful. The general is otherwise occupied, so I'm saying it. Anyhow, I want you both with me at the conference. The press is going to have a field day, and I want sound observations on who's there, their reactions, and so on. Any questions?"

"No, sir," Ya'acov answered for both of them.

"Okay, let's go. We'll take my car."

◆

Avraham glanced at his watch, silently cursing himself for the weakness that action showed. It was nearly 1 P.M. and still no sign of Shimon. He thought again about driving back to Jericho. Assuming they had no trouble getting out, they had plenty of time to get back, disarm the bombs, and make another appointment with the director. But that meant admitting failure. And there were so many important Jews around . . . If the bombs went off while they were at the Memorial, that would have an impact far greater than he had planned.

"Trouble," Mustapha announced while trying to look impassive.

Avraham glanced to the left. An Israeli lieutenant was striding toward them with an air of self-importance. Avraham smiled down at him through the open window.

"Shalom," he said, to get the first word in.

"Shalom," the soldier replied in irritation. "May I see your identity cards?"

Avraham handed his down with the director's business card on top of it.

"What's this?" the officer demanded.

"It's a business card. Have you never seen one before?"

"Of course I have. I only asked for your identity cards, nothing more."

"I thought you might be interested in knowing who I am meeting here. It's only the director of the Memorial."

The Israeli paused before continuing. "Who you are meeting is of no concern to me."

"I will inform Shimon of that when he gets here."

The officer shoved the business card back through the window. Avraham took it and slowly returned it to his coat pocket.

"Rabbi Horowitz, your card appears in order." He handed the card back. "Now, let me see the cards for the men with you."

"Is this really necessary? We passed through security to get up here. And as I mentioned, I do have an appointment with Shimon Goldberg."

"I'm sorry, Rabbi. I regret the inconvenience, but I have my job to do. I must see all your cards."

Avraham sighed and turned to his men. "This gentleman needs to see your cards."

Majid and Mustapha pulled their cards out and gave them to Avraham. Avraham extended them to the officer.

The lieutenant looked at them in horror. He quickly scanned the first card and then the second. He stepped to the window and looked closely at Avraham's companions, comparing their faces with the ID photos. "You've brought Palestinians up here?"

"What is the big deal? Yes, they're Arabs. I hired them to move the documents I am giving to the Memorial. You can't get Israelis to do that kind of work, or if you can, they want too much. And then they don't really work."

"I can't have them up here right now."

"*You* can't have them up here right now?" Avraham grumbled. "I'm not moving these boxes by myself. Suppose you tell the director he can't have these precious documents that God has provided for Israel."

"I'm sorry, Rabbi," the officer said. He pulled his hand radio out of its holder and turned the volume up.

A movement behind the lieutenant caught Avraham's eye.

"Avraham," Shimon said as he rushed up out of breath, "I'm sorry for not being here. I was called to the Prime Minister's office to discuss the arrangements for his press conference with him. I had to drop everything. Didn't even have time to let my staff know where I'd be."

"These things happen," Avraham said with a smile. "The running of a great nation has its price, of course. Now perhaps you would be so kind as to tell this lieutenant that we have a right to be here."

"What?"

The lieutenant looked like he wanted to be elsewhere. "I'm sorry, Mr. Goldberg. I'm afraid we have a security problem here."

"Yes, yes. Security, always security. *I'll* vouch for the man."

"It's not quite that simple." The officer nodded to the two Arabs. "He has two Palestinians with him. They *absolutely* cannot remain."

He held up his hand as he saw the director was about to protest. "No exceptions, sir, and that's straight from my commander. Either Rabbi Horowitz leaves this instant or I'll have to radio for help."

"We'll go," Avraham said hurriedly.

"Wait!" Shimon shouted. "Lieutenant, I don't think you understand the importance of what Rabbi Horowitz has brought us. These are documents from pre-war Poland."

"It doesn't matter."

"If you will hold your tongue for only a moment—it so happens that I told Prime Minister Beker about these documents. His relatives were from Poland, and he wants to see what we have after the conference."

Avraham's mind was racing. "But you can't do that. The donor requires they remain sealed for a year."

Shimon composed his thoughts before replying. "I have kept our agreement. I could not help telling the Prime Minister, and the agreement doesn't cover that. And letting the PM look at a few photos isn't telling the world. The press will never know, and we will keep the boxes sealed for a year, as I promised. Under the circumstances, I was sure you would understand."

"Well . . ." Avraham said as if unsure.

"Not a word will leak out, I give you my word."

"Sir, there's still the security problem," the lieutenant interjected.

"Hang the security! What do I tell the Prime Minister? 'Oh, we couldn't get the photos because of security.' And what will he say to that?"

"But I have my orders! I don't have any choice."

"Listen," Shimon said, trying to keep himself under control, "I have a proposition for you. The press conference isn't until 2. We can bring the boxes into the Memorial and let these men be gone long before then. Wouldn't that satisfy Security and the Prime Minister as well?"

The lieutenant looked down as he thought this over. "I'll have to stay with you while you do it."

"There now," Shimon crowed. "There is reason in you after all. Solomon would be proud." He turned to Avraham. "If you would be so kind?"

"Lieutenant . . ." Avraham said. The young man looked at him. "If you could return the identity cards to my men."

The soldier handed them to Avraham. Majid and Mustapha quickly pocketed them.

The officer required Avraham and his men to remain together at all times, and they never left his sight. It was almost 1:30 by the time the last box was in the storeroom and the door locked under the watchful eye of "Rabbi Horowitz." The walk back outside was a relief for all concerned.

"Thank you so much," Shimon said, almost wringing his hands in delight. "You have no idea what this means to Israel."

"The time . . ." the lieutenant reminded him.

"Yes, yes. Well, thank you."

"You are most welcome." Avraham smiled down at him as he started the engine. "For Israel."

"For Israel," Shimon agreed.

Avraham let off the brake, engaged the clutch, and drove out of the parking area.

"Thank goodness that's over," the officer said.

Shimon looked at him in disgust.

◆

"This looks like as good a spot as any," David Kruger said as he wheeled his personal car into an empty slot. The three officers got out and looked over at the Memorial.

"Where's it going to be?" Ya'acov asked.

"Inside," David replied. "The Prime Minister wanted Holocaust exhibits for a backdrop."

"Nice touch," Ya'acov replied.

David glanced at him and almost smiled. "Never enter politics, my young friend," he said. "Let's go inside and look it over."

The guard at the door saluted as the officers approached. The interior seemed dark in contrast to the sparkling clear day outside.

"Isn't that the director?" Ya'acov asked, pointing to a man watching the technicians run their endless snarls of cable.

"Yes," he replied. "Just the man we need to see."

"Mr. Goldberg," David said as they approached. "I don't know if you remember me or not—David Kruger, Military Intelligence."

Shimon looked blank for a moment. "Why, yes," he said. "How are you, Colonel?"

"Very well, thank you. These two officers work for me—Captain Ya'acov Isaacson and Lieutenant Ari Jacovy."

"Pleased to meet you both."

"We won't interfere. We're here to observe. You know, Intelligence stuff."

"Yes. If you need any assistance from me, please let me know. Glad to cooperate in any way I can."

David thanked him and led his officers to a graphic life-sized print of a scene from Dachau. They watched as the television crews tested the lights. Suddenly it seemed as bright as outdoors.

"It's 1:30," Ya'acov observed. "Where is everyone?"

"The Prime Minister will be here in about fifteen minutes. The gallery will be almost entirely media types, as carefully selected as the government could get away with. The rest will be dignitaries—a few important foreigners who happened to be in Jerusalem, a fair number of government big-shots. They're all enjoying the PM's hospitality in a fancy buffet outside."

"Prejudicing the witnesses?" Ya'acov inquired.

David cocked an eyebrow at him. "*You* might say that. I wouldn't."

"Yes, sir."

Loud thumps sounded behind them as the large double doors opened and the press and dignitaries started in, vaguely gravitating toward the lights. The former started jockeying for position around the equipment, while the latter headed for their reserved seating behind a crimson rope. Ya'acov started his pocket recorder and checked to make sure the tiny microphone was where it would pick up clearly.

David turned to see Shimon Goldberg returning. "Aren't you sitting over with the dignitaries?" Kruger asked.

"I have my assigned seat over there, of course, but I have to be ready to slip out as soon as the conference is over."

David almost smiled when he realized a question was expected of him. "Tight schedule today?" he obliged the man.

"Tell me about it. First the Prime Minister decides he has to have the conference here. Naturally he had to see me to make the arrangements. Then I happened to tell him about the boxes of Warsaw documents we are getting today. So he wants to see them, but it has to be right after the conference because *he's* on a tight schedule. I couldn't let the Prime Minister down."

"I would think not."

His duty done, David went back to observing the final preparations for the conference. A hush fell over the room as the television cameras focused on the podium. A man in the corner held up a mike. "Ladies and gentlemen, the Prime Minister of Israel."

Everyone stood as a rather short, stocky man entered the room dressed in an expensive suit that hung on him as well as could be expected. He squinted as the full force of the television lights hit him. He took his position at the podium and glanced briefly at the arsenal of microphones pointing up at him as if in ambush.

"Good afternoon," he said, with a moderate accent that identified him as an Ashkenazi Jew. "Before we begin the questions, I would like to make a brief statement.

"As you will recall, we have identified the Palestinian Revolutionary Force as the terrorists behind the Dome of the Rock attack. Even so, there has been skepticism among some of the press about the accuracy of our report. Today, I am happy to say, we have positively identified the man we captured in that raid, and he was indeed with the PRF. The man's name is Abdul Suleiman.

"At present, our knowledge of the PRF is limited. But we do know that their goals are roughly the same as the more radical wings of the PLO, and their methods are definitely the same—terrorism with absolutely no regard for the innocent victims.

"In addition to learning our prisoner's name, the man identified the group's former Jerusalem headquarters. I say former, because we had already raided it. And we have also discovered who heads the PRF. His name is Avraham Abbas. With these discoveries, I pledge to you that we will root out this terrorist organization and bring its personnel to justice.

"I will now entertain questions from the press."

The room was transformed into bedlam in an instant. Beker looked bewildered for a moment, until a reporter for the USA's NBC news got the nod and a live microphone.

"Mr. Prime Minister, why would Arabs attack the Dome of the Rock?"

"That we don't know. It is a puzzle, I must admit. But we have the proof. This terrorist's statements have checked out completely. As I said, he identified their former headquarters."

A reporter near the front was frantically waving his notepad. "Mr. Prime Minister, isn't it true that the ultra-Orthodox Jews are ready to build the new Temple if a way can be found to tear down the Dome of the Rock?"

All the color drained out of Beker's face. "The official position of the State of Israel on religions in general and the Temple Mount specifically is crystal-clear. But for those with short memories, I will repeat it. Israel respects all world religions. People of all faiths are welcome in Israel and especially in Jerusalem.

"The entire Temple Mount, although totally within the sovereign State of Israel, is administered by the Muslims. They say who can visit the Mount and what behavior and dress is required. The only time Israel becomes more involved is to provide assistance in case there are incidents such as the terrorist attack that is the subject of this conference. May I point out that the PRF are not, to my knowledge, ultra-Orthodox Jews."

Laughter swept through the room. But the man was not quite through. "Isn't it true, Mr. Prime Minister, that the IDF was planning to blow up the Dome of the Rock after the Six Day War and in fact had placed charges around it before they were stopped?"

The room became very quiet.

"Does your mother know you're out?" Beker replied.

Ya'acov shut his eyes and passed a hand over his face as the crowd howled their glee. The Prime Minister took a firm grip on the podium, causing the microphones to thump.

"The Dome of the Rock is still there. Speaking for the State of Israel, I will do everything in my power to make sure that no harm comes to it or to any other sacred shrine in our nation. We did not have anything to do with the heinous assault on the Dome. We have very clearly shown the world, in an open press conference, who did. The answer is there for anyone with an open mind."

Ya'acov glanced at his watch. It was only 2:05. He did not envy the Prime Minister his job. The floor moderator wrestled the mike away from the reporter and handed it to the first person who looked like he wanted it.

"Mr. Prime Minister, how did the government discover the terrorist's identity? The first reports said the man refused to talk. What happened?"

Shlomo smiled his gratitude to the man. "Quite simply, we tricked him. We told him we were transporting him to a new prison. Out in the country we staged an attack that convinced him he was in the hands of an Arab terrorist group. We tricked him into revealing this information as the price of letting him go."

"Just like that?" the reporter asked.

"If the truck you were riding in was hit by a mortar, then machine-gunned, and you saw the driver and guard murdered before your own eyes, what would you think?"

"This actually happened?"

"It *appeared* to happen. It was a very carefully staged stunt."

Ya'acov sighed. The Prime Minister obviously did not know that what you didn't say was as important as what you did say. Ya'acov listened as the questions kept coming, marveling at all the different ways reporters kept asking the same questions because they hadn't heard the answers they wanted. After a particularly stinging question, Beker again paused before answering. Ya'acov braced himself for the lash, but it did not come.

"Look around you," the Prime Minister said very softly. "You are standing in the memorial of memorials—a monument to man's inhumanity to man. What some of you are accusing Israel of is basically intolerance to the Muslim faith. We, the descendants of Hitler's Holocaust, deny this with every fiber of our being. Six million martyred Jews are my witnesses.

"What is housed here is the greatest archive of the Holocaust that will ever be, and it is still growing. Only today we received over a hundred boxes of photos and documents of Polish Jews, perhaps some of my relatives, who were brutally murdered by Hitler and his Nazis. I ask you, how could the Jewish people be intolerant of others?"

The room became very quiet again.

Ya'acov looked around. Shimon was watching the Prime Minister with rapt attention. "Where did those boxes come from?" Ya'acov whispered.

Shimon blinked in irritation. "I'll tell you later."

"Tell me now. It may be important."

"I'm not supposed to tell, but Rabbi Avraham Horowitz arranged for us to get them. He brought them himself this afternoon."

"Did he say where he got them?" Ya'acov asked.

David Kruger looked around in irritation. "Hold it down. We're getting some nasty looks from the media techies."

"Sir, this could be very important. Where did he get them?"

"From a lady who lives in Tel Aviv."

"Oh, no!"

"What's the matter?" David asked in irritation.

"Show me the boxes!" Ya'acov demanded, ignoring his commander's question.

"I can't."

"Show them to me right now!"

"Ya'acov, what's gotten into you?"

Ya'acov tried to quell the awful feeling in the pit of his stomach. If he was wrong, it would go very badly for him. But if he was right . . .

"Colonel, I think we may have a bomb here."

"What?"

"Sir, I strongly suggest we look!"

David knew his man. "Mr. Goldberg, take us to those boxes."

"But . . ."

"You may consider this a command from Military Intelligence. Take us there at once."

Shimon shrugged and led the officers away from the gallery and down a long corridor. Along both sides were anonymous doors and at the end a door with an exit sign above it. Shimon stopped before a steel door and pulled out a ring of keys. He selected one, opened the door, and flicked on the light. "They're stacked against the far wall."

Ya'acov rushed to the stack and pulled one off the top, lowered it carefully to the ground, and slowly lifted the flap, hoping it wasn't booby-trapped. "Ari, start checking the others."

Ya'acov pulled out photos, obviously genuine, and poked around in the box. He had almost decided to check another box when he pulled out a folder. He flexed the cardboard and sniffed it. Then he licked the surface. "Don't anyone strike a match," he said.

"What did you find?" David asked.

"Explosive paper. The documents appear genuine, but these boxes are crammed with explosive paper—the file folders and the box as well, I suspect."

"That's not all!" Ari exclaimed. "There's enough C-4 plastic in this one to blow the roof clear to Jordan. And it has a timer."

"Can you see what it's set for?"

"No. It's sealed in a box, and there are a bunch of tiny wires under the lid. No way I'm going to look inside."

"Evacuate the building!" Ya'acov ordered.

"You can't do that!" Shimon exclaimed. "The press conference is still going on."

"It's either that or adjourn to Abraham's bosom!"

"Wait, both of you!" David commanded. "The director has a point. There'd be a panic, and we may not have enough time to get everyone out anyway." He turned to Shimon. "You got any men we can get real quick?"

"Yes, but . . ."

"No buts! Go get them right now. And give me the keys to that exit at the end of the hall."

Shimon handed over his ring of keys, pointing out the one to the door, and hurried out. David pointed to the boxes. "Grab some of those boxes. I'll open the door. We have to get these boxes out of here. When the others arrive, I'll tell them how to handle the boxes and where to take them."

David led his two officers to the door and let them out, propping the door open with a large rock. He had just reentered the storeroom when Shimon puffed up, mopping his florid face as he tried to catch his breath. "What do you want us to do?" he asked, waving a hand at the six men he had brought with him.

"Start taking those boxes outside—my men will show you where. Bombs are inside, so take it nice and easy. Set them down carefully."

The men hesitated as if David were speaking in an unknown tongue. "*I mean right now!* Get your butts in gear or we're going to have this place come down around our ears!"

He spoke with a volume and authority usually reserved for drill sergeants. Each man grabbed whichever box was closest and hurried out. David grabbed a box and glanced at Shimon, deciding he had better not include the director. "You keep an eye on things in here. We don't want anyone coming in this storeroom until we get done."

Shimon nodded, grateful to be excused from further exertions. Ya'acov hurried in, sweat already soaking through his uniform shirt.

"Where are you putting them?" David asked.

Ya'acov grunted as he hefted another box. "The ground slopes off rapidly about a hundred feet from the door. We're taking them down the hill a short distance. Just out of line of sight."

David nodded as he grabbed a second box for himself. As long as the Memorial building was not in line of sight of the bombs, there was much less chance of severe damage.

"Lead the way," he said, trying not to think of what would happen if the bombs went off right then.

At first it seemed as if the room would never be cleared in time. But with nine men putting everything they had into it, the stack dwindled quickly. Fifteen minutes after they had begun, the last box went outside. David stood by the door anxiously as the last three men hurried back in. He pulled the door shut and locked it.

"Ya'acov, go out the front and round up an IDF detail. Post two groups at opposite ends of the building to keep people from wandering back there. And radio out for a bomb disposal team. And . . ."

His last words were obliterated by a deafening explosion. Rocks and gravel pelted the door like hail. It was over in seconds, but it seemed like minutes, a final rattle of pebbles indicating the all-clear. The lights flickered twice, then went off, accompanied by an electrical explosion. The ventilation fans, unnoticed a moment before, whined to a stop. Everything was quiet.

"What's going on?" Shimon demanded.

"Some people never get the word," Ya'acov whispered to Ari. Although a whisper, it was clearly audible in the silence. Ya'acov's ears burned as he realized everyone had heard him.

"It was the plastic explosive," David finally answered the director. "It apparently knocked out your transformer."

"Then the press conference . . ."

"Is over," David finished for him. "Unless the crews brought emergency generators, which I doubt."

"I need to get back in there."

"We all do."

As if in answer to their need, a flickering light appeared at the end of the corridor. The beam swung and bounced, throwing grotesque shadows on the walls and ceiling. The beam fell on David and remained on him.

"Colonel, I'm Captain Asher Makovsky," the man behind the light said. "Sir, things are pretty tense at the conference. Do you know what happened?"

"Yes, Captain. I'm Colonel David Kruger, Military Intelligence. Captain Ya'acov Isaacson and Lieutenant Ari Jacovy are with me. And, of course, Mr. Shimon Goldberg, the director."

"Thank God. General Levy sent us out to search for Mr. Goldberg and to find out what happened."

"The director is here. And a terrorist bomb is what happened."

"What?"

"Later, Captain," David interrupted. "Take us to the general."

"Yes, sir."

The light turned, and the wavering beam began to trace its way back into the gallery. The three officers and the director followed the captain as he led them to the front, where General Levy was talking with the Prime Minister. The reporters were as close as they could get, their tape recorders still running. The general turned as the group approached. He squinted, trying to see through the glare of the flashlight.

David spoke first. "Colonel Kruger, General."

"David, what's going on here?"

"Terrorists managed to get multiple bombs into the Memorial, General. We discovered them in time and hauled them outside. That was the explosion you heard, which also took out the power."

"Bombs *inside* the Memorial?" Prime Minister Beker demanded. "How?"

"Mr. Prime Minister, I . . ." Shimon began.

"Excuse me, Mr. Prime Minister, Director Goldberg," David interrupted smoothly. "Gentlemen, this is a very sensitive subject. May I suggest we retire to discuss this in privacy?"

Beker looked at David, his eyes looking hunted. Finally he nodded. "Yes, Colonel. I think that would be wise." He thought for a moment. "I suggest we travel to my office—at once."

The Prime Minister turned back to the reporters. They had not, as he could have wished, disappeared.

"Ladies and gentlemen, you have, of course, heard what happened. Even as we have been discussing Israel's innocence in the Dome of the Rock incident, this very Memorial has come under a terrorist bomb attack. We will have further releases for the media when we have more information." He could clearly see the frantic hands waving for attention. "This conference is closed." He followed an aide out of the room.

"See you at the Prime Minister's office," General Levy said.

"Yes, sir. At once," David answered for them.

13

THE PRIME MINISTER'S DEMANDS

Shlomo Beker's press secretary tried to look disinterested as the Military Intelligence officers filed into the Prime Minister's office, followed by Beker himself. The Prime Minister's glance was completely clear: *no interruptions.*

Shlomo closed the door and walked quickly to his chair. "Seats, gentlemen," he snapped as he sat down and turned toward General Levy. "Ezer, *what is going on?* First we almost get the Dome of the Rock blown up. I ask for answers, and I get, 'Maybe it's this and maybe it's that.' I have to pester you and finally you tell me it's the Palestinian Revolutionary Force. So I hold a press conference, and we almost get blown up—in Yad Vashem of all places! Is it too much to ask: *what is going on here?*"

General Ezer Levy glanced at David, then back at Shlomo. "I share your concern, Prime Minister. I . . ."

"You don't share the heat!" Shlomo thundered, slamming his fist on the desk. "It's one thing for you to sit in your comfortable office telling me, 'I don't know; I don't know!' It's quite another to face Israel's enemies. They're not as understanding as I am. So do I get some answers or do I look elsewhere?"

"Prime Minister," David interjected quickly, "we have the best brains working on this. Captain Isaacson in particular has some views that I think will interest you—new since your last briefing with General Levy."

"Captain?" Beker said, turning toward the young officer.

Ya'acov wished for some Maalox as his mouth went dry and his stomach started burning. "Prime Minister," he began as his mind raced for a reasoned argument, "as Colonel Kruger says, we have made an interesting discovery—we made it at your press conference as a matter of fact."

"The press conference?" Ezer asked.

"Yes, General. The group that planted the bombs in Yad Vashem is the same one that tried to blow up the Dome of the Rock. The bombs were identical to the ones found at the Dome and the PRF headquarters. The Palestinian Revolutionary Force did both jobs."

Beker looked at the officers as he thought over the unexpected response to his demand. "Then I must arrange a press release immediately. The world must accept the truth! This is just what we need."

Ya'acov knew he was in danger. "Excuse me, Prime Minister, but there is a problem."

Beker looked at the young officer, then at Colonel Kruger and General Levy. David's lips were compressed in irritation, while Ezer looked as if he wished he were elsewhere.

"Go on," Beker said, his forehead creased in an ominous scowl.

"Sir, the world is not going to buy your statement that the PRF staged the Dome attack, in spite of the evidence you gave at the press conference."

The Prime Minister made a steeple with his hands as he held the young man's eyes with a gaze that did not waver.

"I gave them the proof," he said slowly and deliberately. "And I can back it up."

"You are expert in gauging public reaction, Prime Minister. You saw the way the questions were going. The reporters won't look for proof. They'll report their biases."

Ya'acov was well aware of Prime Minister Beker's penchant for blowing up and the usual aftermath. He hoped he was not crossing the line.

"So, they do not believe me?" the PM asked.

"A few do, sir. But most do not. And this is complicated by one other point."

"And what would that be?"

"Telling what we did to Suleiman will damage our credibility, I'm afraid. We doctored reality to trick Suleiman into confessing. The press will ask if we've done the same thing concerning the Dome attack." Ya'acov checked himself before he could add that in his opinion it was a fair question. He suspected they were moments away from a fatal explosion.

"You are a bold young man," Beker said at last. "And brave. Foolhardy? Perhaps. Who can say. So, what do we do about Yad Vashem, hmm?"

"That is your decision, Prime Minister."

"Surely you have an opinion."

"Prime Minister, perhaps we should prepare a special report for you," David said as Ya'acov was opening his mouth to reply.

"No, David. I would like to hear what Captain Isaacson has to say."

"Sir, I'd recommend attributing the attack to the PRF, citing the bombs and timers we found at their headquarters. However, I would not tie it to the Dome attack for the reasons I stated. It would only fan the flames without changing any minds."

"What about proof?"

"C-4 residue is quite distinctive. Also, we're bound to find enough of the timers to positively identify them."

"So the world will accept this much at least?"

"Probably. An Arab terrorist group attacking Yad Vashem makes sense, especially after the Dome attack. The only problem is that most people have never heard of the Palestinian Revolutionary Force. How does the average citizen understand something he hasn't seen on CNN?"

"This is not very encouraging, Captain."

"No, sir, it's not."

Beker pursed his lips as he thought about what Ya'acov had told him. Then he turned toward David. "You have a sharp young man working for you, David. Perhaps two?" He turned quickly to Ari. "Lieutenant . . ."

"Jacovy." David provided the name.

"Lieutenant Jacovy, what are the PRF up to?"

Ari looked dazed for a moment. The Prime Minister looked at him expectantly. "Prime Minister, the PRF is composed of hearts and minds having the object of attaining political power. It is possible that the leader—this Avraham Abbas—is crazy, but I think not, even though the Dome attack is strange. Abbas is leading a small group and probably wants to be a leader among the Palestinians. This he can't do directly because some bigger frogs have gotten to the pond before him. So a time of political turmoil is his only chance. Get the Arabs mad at the Jews and the Jews mad at the Arabs. When the fighting starts, he might have a chance to make a name for himself."

"You have a vivid imagination, Lieutenant."

"Military Intelligence has paid off for Israel many times, Prime Minister."

"Yes, I have to admit it has. So, General, what do you propose to do about this? I want this Abbas caught and his group smashed."

Ezer shifted uncomfortably as the focus shifted to him. "The group may be somewhere in East Jerusalem, but most likely they have fled to an Arab town. We'll intensify our searches and check with our paid informants. I assure you, we will leave no stone unturned."

"See that you don't. Now if you gentlemen will excuse me . . ."

The four officers were out of their chairs before the Prime Minister finished speaking.

◆

Ari Jacovy glanced at his watch, wondering if Ya'acov was still in the building. He opened Ya'acov's door and stuck his head in. "You're in," he said, coming in and closing the door behind himself.

"And so are you," Ya'acov remarked. "Perhaps I can invite you to sit before you do so."

"We've got a breakthrough of sorts," Ari continued, ignoring the jibe.

"Which is?"

"We've found out where the PRF got the truck they used at the Memorial. It seems a Rabbi Avraham Horowitz rented it from Eldan in Tel Aviv. The truck's overdue, and they've reported it stolen. They're quite distressed that a nice rabbi should do such a thing. Anyway, we've sent out the full description to all police and IDF units—and to our informants."

Ya'acov rocked back in his chair and looked up at the ceiling. "Certain individuals, who will remain nameless, will get quite excited about this," he said.

"Think we'll find the truck?"

"Probably not, unless we're dealing with complete idiots, which I doubt. Does the colonel know about this?"

"You are the first. I took the report myself."

"Do you want to tell him?" Ya'acov asked with a grin.

"You're senior."

"Big deal. Give me the report."

Ari handed over several typewritten pages. "Ah, the responsibilities of rank," he said as he got up hurriedly.

"Make yourself available in case we need some clarification," Ya'acov said as his office door closed.

◆

"Have you taken care of the truck?" Avraham asked as Mustapha came in from outside.

"We're working on it right now. The plates are already swapped. Majid is working the body over. We'll paint it as soon as he's done beating it up."

"Very well," Avraham said.

"Is there anything else you want me to do?"

Avraham looked out the window where Majid was still pounding on the truck. Already it looked quite different. "No. Not at this time."

14

DEATH AT THE WAILING WALL

Allen Siegel was again praying at the Wailing Wall. As he meditated and prayed, he reflected on all that he knew of the Wall. Called the Western Wall by Jews and the Wailing Wall by others, this most famous of all walls is part of the western perimeter of Haram esh-Sharif, otherwise known as the Temple Mount. It is a tribute to Herod the Great's being a master builder that anything of the second Temple still exists.

What has been preserved is not actually a part of the Temple itself, Allen remembered, but rather a portion of the retaining wall. Herod used the resulting platform to refurbish and embellish the Temple, which had been standing when this great but warped man became king under the Roman overlords.

Allen knew that the bottom sections of this massive wall are definitely from that period—huge ashlars incised in typical Herodian fashion. The middle and upper courses are probably of later construction and repair. The overall impression is one of immense age.

The wall is revered by the Jews as their only link with the second Temple. It is a focus of prayer, and Allen again noticed the countless slips of paper jammed into the crevices between stones to insure that the prayers remain close to where God's house once stood.

But the wall had also suffered the ravages of time, as well as that of repeated conquerors. The imposing stone face is now pockmarked by slowly crumbling rock and by bushes growing from the cracks.

Allen Siegel did not come from an Orthodox Jewish family. The Siegel family had lived in Los Angeles for years, comfortably ensconced in a Reformed synagogue in the San Fernando Valley. But introduced to Orthodoxy, Allen had decided it was the way. And one of the consequences of that decision was *aliya* to Israel, settling in Jerusalem.

Thus it was quite natural for him once again to be praying at the Western Wall, standing only inches from an immense ashlar. More than halfway up the stone face was a smaller block, though still almost as tall as he was. Time had not been kind to it. Years ago it had developed a longitudinal crack near the bottom, and repeated weathering from water and freezing temperatures had done the rest. The fracture would soon be complete, requiring only the slightest disturbance to break it loose.

Allen sighed as the early afternoon sun warmed his shoulders. The sun was also heating the wall above him, and the rock expanded, causing an imperceptible movement. With a sharp crack followed by an ominous grinding noise, the huge section of rock broke away and began to fall.

Allen looked up in puzzlement but never comprehended the shape that was hurtling toward him as over a thousand pounds of rock hit him at well over a hundred miles an hour. In an instant it was over. Allen Siegel was dead, mostly obscured by the block of limestone lying on him. Dark red rivulets starting fanning out from the crumpled mass.

The crowd surrounding the victim stood transfixed for several heartbeats. Then one of the men looked up at the top of the Western Wall. "Filthy Arabs!" he shouted as he pointed upward.

"Death to all Palestinians!" another shouted a moment later.

The crowd erupted with shouts and screams as the people began to mill.

"Remember Yad Vashem!" carried clearly above the clamor. Then the catalyst: "To the Moslem Quarter!"

As a body the mob poured out of the square and headed north beside the Temple Mount, growing as it went. They crossed the Via Dolorosa and bore to the right.

The lucky Arab merchants saw them coming and quickly shuttered and barred their shops. But the violent wave was too quick and unexpected for most. Tables of merchandise were turned over, shop fronts smashed.

A shoeshine man on El-Hamra saw the wall of people round the corner, sweeping directly toward him. He hastily threw the tins, brushes, and cloths of his trade into the battered box that was his sole business asset. He started to get up but had misgauged the crowd's speed and violence. A hand reached out and ripped an awning pole loose from the side of a building. The old Arab looked up in horror as he saw the slim pole come scything down. He died as instantly as Siegel had when the bludgeon crushed his forehead. He collapsed in an untidy heap, his dirty robes providing a rumpled shroud. His lifeblood spilled onto the pavement as the mob swept on.

In the next block the proprietor of a carved wood products shop was trying desperately to pull down the steel shutter in front of his shop. But it jammed, and no matter how he pulled on it, it would not come free. He gave up when the crowd was only a few feet from his door. He dashed up the back stairs to the family apartment above the shop. He rushed through the door as his wife and children gathered around him demanding to know what was going on.

Downstairs several men turned over tables and swept wood carvings off the shelves, while those outside became even more angry because they could not get into the tiny shop. One of the men started a box of wood fans burning with his lighter, then scattered the fiery contents on the wooden destruction.

In moments the shop was ablaze. The flames jumped quickly to wooden counters and finally to the overhead beams. Those inside the shop beat a hasty retreat and watched as the fire spread, while the bulk of the mob continued deeper into the Quarter.

The Arab family had nowhere to go. They huddled in the back of the one-room apartment, cut off from the windows that faced the street as the flooring collapsed and the blast-furnace flames roared up the walls to the roof. Moments later the rest of the second floor fell in, followed quickly by the heavy, domed roof. The next-door shop burst into flames as the common wooden framing burned through.

Sirens screamed outside. The mob continued down the street for a while, then began to disperse as the wail drew nearer.

When order was restored, over a hundred people, mostly Arabs, were dead. Added to this was an entire block of businesses and homes in blackened ruin.

♦

Moshe looked up as Michael Shapiro came down the stone steps with the toolbox.

"What took you so long?" he asked.

"Some kind of disturbance down by the Wall. Couldn't see what it was, but this huge crowd stormed out of there heading north."

Moshe looked at the two Americans. "Anything we need to be concerned about?"

"Don't think so. Probably some women pestering the Hasidim. They're pretty touchy about that."

"The men or the women?" Moshe couldn't help asking.

Michael glanced at Anne before answering. "I think I'll pass on that."

"He's not as brave as he once was," Moshe said to Mars.

"When you men are through, perhaps we could continue our work," Anne observed.

"Perhaps those are words of wisdom," Mars said.

"Mars . . ." Anne said, giving him her full attention.

"Yes, dear?" The last part slipped out, and as much as he wished to take it back, it was gone.

"Dear?" Moshe inquired, his bushy eyebrows arching upward. "Did I hear correctly?"

"Moshe, I was only . . ." Mars started.

"Michael," Moshe interrupted, "this sounds serious. I can't recall a dig going this way before."

"Moshe, we really do have work here," Anne said in a deceptively sweet way.

"Indeed we do," he agreed. "Now, if the rest of you are done with this idle chitchat, perhaps someone would be so kind as to fetch the wooden drum. Ben should have the first one put together by now."

"I'll go get it," Anne volunteered.

"No, no," Mars said. "I'll go for it."

Anne started to argue but stopped when she saw the look in his eyes. She smiled at him. "Okay."

He was halfway up the stairs when Moshe called after him. "Mars, my boy . . ."

"Yes?"

"You have good taste." Moshe looked to the side, taking in Anne's complex expression.

"Now, Dr. McAdams, if you will kindly assist me."

Mars bolted up the steps.

Moshe examined the loose-weave cloth that was glued to the face of the mosaic. "I feel like a surgeon when I do this. Hammer."

Anne handed him a leather mallet and a chisel. She held the edge of the cloth away from the wall as Moshe put the chisel against the mortar joint of a tile near the top of the mosaic. With a sharp rap, the ceramic chip popped cleanly away, remaining securely fastened to the cloth strip.

"Good. Mortar bond to the limestone is very poor. This should go quickly. Let's go at it from both ends. As soon as Mars gets back, why don't both of you work on the other end while Michael and I do this one."

Mars had no trouble finding the wooden drum. Ben had finished it and was working on another one. It was about five feet in diameter and looked like a large, wooden wheel. The drums were to hold the strips of the mosaic until it could be reassembled at a permanent exhibit.

Mars lifted the drum upright, surprised at how light it was. It wobbled as it crunched its way over the black and white tiles. Mars stopped it short of the stairs and stepped to where he could look down into the shadows.

"Anne?" he yelled.

"Yes, Mars?"

"Could you help me with this?"

"Be right up."

An ominous crunch sounded behind Mars. He whirled around to see the drum lurching toward him. He took a step toward it and caught his foot on an uneven paving tile, falling headlong in the path of the errant wheel. Reaching out, he shoved the side with a sweeping motion that swung the drum around parallel to the stairway but failed to stop it. He watched in horror as it rammed the board supporting the Turkish sewer line, breaking it neatly, directly over the stairs. A dark stream poured out, making a wet spattering noise below, followed immediately by a healthy scream.

"Anne!" Mars shouted.

Moments later Anne emerged from the stairs, her hair wet and hanging over her face in strands. Filth covered her face and ran down her blouse and trousers.

"Oh, Anne, I'm so sorry."

Anne looked at him through her disheveled hair.

Ben rushed over. He stared at Anne, then glanced at Mars. He muttered something in embarrassment and returned to the drum he had been working on.

Moshe came slowly up the stairs, treading carefully around the mess. He couldn't see Anne's face, but Mars's was white with shock.

"Michael . . ." Moshe said, barely loud enough to be heard.

"Yes?" Michael answered, not wanting to come up the stairs.

"Go find a phone and call Samuel Kretzmer. Tell him we need this sewer line relocated."

"It was my fault," Mars said. "I let the blasted drum get away from me."

"Nonsense," Moshe rumbled. "I should have had the line removed as soon as we found it. Then this wouldn't have happened."

"But . . ."

"If you two could argue about this some other time . . ." Anne snapped.

"Yes," Moshe agreed quickly. "Yes, of course. Mars, take Anne back to the hostel." He thrust the keys to the bus into his hands before Mars could protest.

"Go, go," Moshe insisted.

Moshe escorted them to the bus and helped Anne up into the seat, wiring the door shut. Mars climbed up behind the wheel. The engine caught after a few cranks and settled down into an uneven idle.

"I must get it tuned," Moshe muttered as Mars drove away. He turned back to Michael. "So go phone Kretzmer!" he said with uncharacteristic irritation. Michael bolted off to find a pay phone.

◆

It was midafternoon when Mars and Anne returned. Mars shut off the engine, then looked over at Anne, her hair still wet from her shower. The trip back had been in complete silence.

"Well, we're back," Mars announced, trying to cover his embarrassment.

"Yes," Anne said simply, staring straight ahead.

"Anne?"

She turned toward him.

"Are you still mad at me?"

Anne frowned as she tried to sort out her feelings. "I wasn't mad in the first place," she said finally. "I was shocked—who wouldn't be? I was embarrassed and . . ."

"And what?"

"And I didn't want you seeing me like that."

"Oh," he said, looking down. "Then you forgive me?"

"There's nothing to forgive," Anne replied, nearing exasperation. "You didn't mean to do it. It was an accident."

"I'll say."

Anne looked at him. He was impossibly serious. Her self-consciousness disappeared, and suddenly it was funny. She smiled and turned away quickly. Mars caught the movement out of the corner of his eye. "Are you all right?" he asked.

"I am now," she said, stifling a laugh.

"What's funny?" he asked.

"You are, as usual."

He looked at her in bewilderment as he tried to understand what was going on. "Hmm," he said. "I guess we'd better get out."

She turned back to him. "Mars?"

"Yes?"

"You called me 'dear' just before all this happened."

"Ah, yes, I guess I did."

"You *guess* you did?"

He cleared his throat nervously. "Yes, I *did*, actually and factually."

She felt a warmness steal over her. "Do you remember my birthday?"

Mars smiled. "How could I forget it?"

"You said something to me."

He raised his eyebrow as he looked over at her.

"I feel the same way about you," she admitted.

"Do you mean . . . ?"

"Yes, I do," she said.

He sat there looking at her. Then he started to smile. He leaned over and brushed his lips against hers gently, then firmly. When they parted, his pulse hammered even though the kiss had been brief.

"I see you still feel the same," she observed.

His smile broadened. "Yes, ma'am."

"And your humor has returned."

"Uh huh."

"You'd better get out and let me down. Moshe will wonder where we are."

Mars smiled as he opened the door and got out.

◆

Moshe looked up the stairs as he heard the Americans start down. As soon as he saw Anne's expression, he started to smile but quickly became serious as he looked back at Michael. "I really must do something about that car door," he said as Anne reached the bottom. "It's getting harder and harder to unwire. It's been a good half-hour since they drove up."

"It has not been a half-hour," Anne observed.

Moshe examined his mallet carefully. "How long *has* it been?"

"Oh, I get it," Mars said. "Dad is grilling us because I got home late with his car." He threw the keys to Moshe, who caught them and thrust them into a pocket.

"This younger generation worries me," he muttered as he looked over at Michael.

◆

Moshe and Michael carefully lifted the strip of cloth away, each mosaic tile securely glued to the back. They carried it over to the wooden drum and laid it over the curved surface.

An uneven crust of yellowed mortar remained where the tiles had been. Moshe took a wide chisel and chipped away the crumbling material near the center. A sharp line came into view where the rock was a slightly different color.

"Well, Mars," Moshe said, standing back, "there's your door."

♦

Long, dark shadows joined in a macabre dance on the Damascus streets as the sun inched toward the horizon. President Hashem Darousha smiled as he looked down on the crowd. Atallah Jubran smiled too, grateful that Darousha was pleased. The shouted slogans could be clearly heard through the closed windows as thousands of signs moved up and down in unison. Most of the placards were filled with flowing Arabic script denouncing the Dome of the Rock attack and calling for the death of all Jews. Some signs had graphic pictures of the Israeli Prime Minister or the United States President in various stages of predictable physical distress.

The media camera crews were present, of course, each allowed to tape the event without hindrance, even though the crowd appeared to be in the last stages of hysterical frenzy.

"You have done well," Hashem said with a sidewise glance at his special assistant.

"You are most gracious," Atallah replied, touching his forehead in salaam.

Hashem paused, then came to a decision. "We must find this Avraham Abbas. He could be useful to us."

Atallah frowned at the change in subject. "Are we sure he exists? Was the Jew telling the truth?"

"He exists, and our Intelligence thinks they know where to find him. They haven't approached him, on my orders. That's what I want *you* to do."

Atallah nodded.

♦

The IDF guard shook his head as he read the release order. It was only 8:30 in the morning and already he was having fun. The document was entirely correct. It specified that Abdul Suleiman was to be released; it listed his cell number and had all the correct signatures. Prisoners were released every day, but usually not notorious terrorists, unless some political angle was involved. The guard thought about asking his superior about it, but only briefly. The minor brass, he knew, did not take the questioning of their orders kindly.

He shrugged as he unlocked the door and pulled it open. Abdul rolled over on his cot and scowled at his captor. The man's look angered the guard, tempting him to have a little trouble escorting the prisoner.

"Come out of there!" the guard growled.

Abdul took his time getting to his feet. The IDF soldier backed away, keeping his rifle ready. The Palestinian marched ahead of the guard and was surprised when they did not make the turn toward the interrogation rooms. Instead they followed a different path and ended up at the release station. Abdul changed quickly into the clothes he had worn on the day he was captured. He then signed the forms where the desk clerk indicated. That done, the guard opened the door and let him walk out.

Abdul walked out on the busy Jerusalem street. Was this another trick? he wondered. He couldn't believe the Jews would let him go, but he certainly wasn't going to ask questions. He hurried away, looking over his shoulder frequently. There was no indication that anyone was following him.

Inside the prison was another man. That man had just finished serving a six-week sentence for throwing rocks at border guards. His name too was Abdul Suleiman.

The rock-throwing Suleiman probably would have been pleased with what the mistaken identity had accomplished, had he ever found out. Accusations and counter-accusations traveled up and down the Intelligence structure and up to the highest offices in the government.

Ya'acov knew a "lose-lose" situation when he saw one. He reported the mistake to his boss and stood by to weather the reverberations that went on for the rest of the day.

15

HERODIAN
TREASURES

It had come as no surprise to Abdul when he discovered that the PRF headquarters had been compromised. He had spent the night with friends in East Jerusalem and had resumed his journey when the mid-morning bustle of the Old City made it safe.

Abdul crouched behind a boulder as an ancient Chevrolet truck slowed to make the sharp curve on the Jericho road. He leapt out as the truck went by and sprinted for the tailgate, his robes flapping madly. He jumped up and caught a wooden slat on the rear gate and pulled himself up and over, falling in a heap on the littered truck bed. The sweet smell of oranges told him what the cargo had been: Arab citrus for Jewish tables.

He stood up and held onto a side rail as he looked back at the city walls of East Jerusalem receding into the distance. He wondered if Avraham would be in the safe-house in Jericho or if that had been discovered as well. It would not take long to find out as it is only a little over twenty miles to Jericho over a tortuous road that starts at an elevation of 2,500 feet above sea level, then drops to 700 feet below sea level.

Abdul lurched his way forward until he could look over the roof of the cab. The view was spectacular as the road made its sinuous way down the Judean Hills toward the Jordan Valley. But the ride was uncomfortable as the driver tried to make the best speed he could.

A flash of light in the distance caught Abdul's eye. He blinked away
the tears caused by the wind, squinting to look toward the sun. A small
vehicle had topped a hill over a mile away followed by what looked like
a truck. Abdul watched as the two started down the incline. In a few
moments he was sure. It was an IDF patrol.

An icy pang sank into his stomach. He thought about jumping out.
Up ahead was a secondary road to the north, leading to Highway 3,
which offered an alternate route to Jericho and Ramallah, both Arab
towns. The distance dwindled to a half-mile as the patrol approached
the intersection. Just when he thought he could relax, the jeep pulled off
the road, followed immediately by the truck.

Abdul cursed as he saw the soldiers jump out and start setting up
the roadblock. The only bright spot was that they were setting it up
about a hundred yards on the other side of the intersection.

Abdul restrained an immediate reaction and decided to wait until
he was abreast of the intersection. Regardless of when he jumped, the
patrol was sure to see him. A few moments later he regretted his decision. The Arab driver roared down the steep hill, making it impossible
to jump without grave danger.

Abdul ran up to the cab, almost falling as the truck rumbled over a
chuckhole. He clenched his fist and brought it down on the cab roof
hard enough to dent it. He crashed against the front railing as the startled driver jammed on the brakes. Blue smoke boiled up in a pungent
stink as the driver tried to maintain control of the fish-tailing truck.
Abdul struggled toward the rear gate as the truck went broadside.

He jumped, rolling as he hit the rock-strewn ditch. Rocks dug
painfully into his back and tore at his hands. He jumped to his feet and
looked past the still-sliding truck. The Israelis had seen everything.
With a shout, two soldiers were running toward him, rifles at the ready.

Abdul glanced left. He started running north up the road, hugging
the left-hand side. He clearly heard one of the soldiers order him to halt.
He glanced over his shoulder. The patrol was more than a hundred
yards away. A shot sounded behind him, followed by another.

To both right and left were steep hills. Abdul chose the right side
and started scrambling upward, trying to ignore the sharp pain in his
side as he tried to catch his breath. He paused briefly and looked down.
The patrol was nearing the bottom of the hill. He ducked instinctively

as one of the soldiers brought up his gun. Fine grit peppered him as the bullet struck at his feet. These were not warning shots.

He ducked under the canopy of a large bush and lunged upward. He struggled to the top of the hill on the verge of total collapse. He looked back. The nearest soldier was barely a hundred feet away— much too close. Up came his rifle. Abdul whirled around and jumped down between two bushes as he started down the far side of the hill. A shot rang out as he flew between the bushes and started skidding. The brush tore at his robe, and the dirt in his sandals ground painfully into his feet. Abdul risked a glance. The soldiers were having as much trouble as he was as they flew down the steep slope.

Abdul rounded a small tree and for the first time understood what he had glimpsed moments before. The even line ahead was a ridge, and it was less than fifty feet away. He slid to a grinding stop as the slope leveled out to a narrow, rock rim. He stepped forward and looked over. It was a sheer drop of over a hundred feet into a narrow canyon. The rim continued for hundreds of yards in both directions. He looked back at the soldiers. They were about fifty feet away now.

Abdul turned back to the dropoff. He looked up into the sky for a moment, then jumped out over the chasm. The moment his feet left the cliff, time seemed almost to stop. Every detail was crystal-clear as he did a slow forward roll. He was head-down now—looking back at the cliff, seeing the rock striations where the elements had worn it. Here and there grass and small bushes clung to their precarious holds as they struggled for survival. The scene tilted, and he was looking back up at the cliff top as the two soldiers came into view, looking down at him as he fell. Now he was on his back looking straight up. He looked to the side, noting almost indifferently that he was near the bottom. The strange dilation of time ended with a blurred rush. Then everything went black.

◆

The two Israeli soldiers watched as Abdul disappeared between two trees. A split-second later the crashing noise reached them, going on for a surprisingly long time. They couldn't see the man because his resting place was hidden beneath the crowns of the two trees. They didn't even think of trying to find a way down. The man was surely dead. They turned to make their way back the way they had come.

◆

The sound was familiar. Abdul struggled to recognize it despite the agony that almost overwhelmed him. He opened an eye and was instantly sorry as pain stabbed deep into his brain. Everything hurt. But at least he knew what the sound was. A small brook trickled down the narrow canyon a few feet away, a strange brook that spun around him in sickening whorls. He shut the eye.

How he could be alive, Abdul had no idea. But the way he felt, he was sure it was a temporary condition. Surely he was bleeding to death from internal injuries. He lay still waiting for the final blackness to come. But it didn't, and things certainly were not becoming dim. What they were becoming was painful.

He was lying on his side. He rolled over on his back, crying out in agony. Slowly he opened his eyes. It took a few moments to become oriented. He was in a little pocket with a rise on either side. Two trees were at the top of each rise, and he was at the base of a tree between them, its crown hidden by the ones above. He followed the line of smashed branches upward. He had hit the top of the tree dead-center.

He carefully moved his arms and legs. There wasn't a part of his body that did not ache, but there were no broken bones. After a long time, he rolled over and staggered to his feet. When the bright flashes of pain tapered off, he started following the brook to the north.

◆

Atallah Jubran glanced at the luminous dial on his watch as he swallowed, trying to quell the airsickness that had plagued him the whole trip. It was after 1 o'clock in the morning, and it was dark. The Russian-made Hind helicopter turned a little to the right and started descending. They were over Jordan with the assurance that there was no official notice of their presence. They left the mountains and angled toward the Jordan rift.

The huge aircraft slowed and came to a hover near the ground, supposedly off the Israeli radar. The pilot checked his low-light goggles and turned the helicopter back to the north and flew for a few minutes, skimming the rugged Jordan Valley. He then banked west and crossed the Jordan, picking his way carefully among the tumbled terrain.

Ahead a light winked once. The pilot adjusted his heading and pulled back on the stick, flaring the cumbersome helicopter into a hover. He slowly settled the aircraft onto the ground.

The door swung open, and a crewman motioned for Atallah to hurry. Atallah jumped down, almost falling when the stinging blast intensified as the pilot lifted off. The Hind started a ponderous turn back toward Jordan and safety.

Atallah looked around. The light winked again. He started walking toward it. A large shape loomed suddenly, slightly darker than its surroundings. A door opened, turning on squeaking hinges, but no interior light came on.

"Get in," someone outside the vehicle said.

"Who's there?" Atallah asked, trying to see the man. For the briefest moment he feared it was a trap.

"You're late!" snapped the man, stepping from behind a large boulder. "Get in!"

Atallah almost fell on his face as he missed the door sill. He felt with his foot and found a step. He climbed up into what turned out to be a truck.

"Move over," commanded the sentry as he got up beside Atallah and slammed the door. The driver started the engine and drove off without using his lights. A few miles later they turned south onto a highway. The driver turned on the lights as they sped into the night.

◆

The door closed with a solid thud. Atallah blinked as someone flipped on the lights.

"So you are from President Darousha?" Avraham asked.

"I am. And you must be Avraham Abbas."

Avraham nodded. "Please come in and sit down." He motioned toward a table in the next room. Atallah picked a chair and sat down.

Avraham joined him on the opposite side. He glanced at the open door. Mustapha Kabran quietly closed it.

"And what does President Darousha wish of Avraham Abbas?"

Atallah smiled at the man's vanity.

"This is amusing?" Avraham asked, a hard edge to his voice.

"Refreshing, shall we say. You are a very direct man."

"I know where I am going."

"I have no doubt," Atallah said, remembering his diplomacy. "And that is precisely why I am here. President Hashem Darousha has taken notice of you. He is very impressed with what he has heard. He is, of course, sympathetic to the Palestinian cause."

"I am glad to hear that," Avraham said.

"Which brings me to the point of my visit," Atallah said after a slight pause. "President Darousha would like you to visit him in Damascus. He wishes to hear more fully your views on the Palestinian situation."

"I am most honored."

"Then you will come?"

"Most assuredly."

"Very good," Atallah said with a sigh. He pulled out a sealed envelope and handed it to Avraham. "Here is everything you will need for your journey. In addition to instructions, you will find money for your expenses. Now, as I must be out of here before sunrise, I must be going."

Avraham nodded. "Mustapha will see that you get to your rendezvous."

◆

Ben lifted the saw clear and waited as the masonry blade spun to a stop. He set the tool down on the blade guard and removed his respirator and goggles. The dark circles around his eyes and nose were in sharp contrast with the light-colored rock dust on the rest of his face.

"It's almost free all the way around," he said.

He took a large hammer and struck the stone a sharp blow. It broke loose and moved inward a fraction of an inch. Using the chisel, he worked the block back out. Mars grasped one end while Ben took the other. Together they lowered it to the ground.

Mars straightened up and looked into the hole. He sniffed around the opening. "Dry and musty," he announced.

"Just the way we want it," Moshe said. He handed Mars a large flashlight.

Mars brought the light up and switched it on. The brilliant beam cut through the darkness, touching object after object without revealing much. The circle of light stopped on a jumble of boxes about twenty feet from the door.

"What do you see?" Anne asked, standing on her tiptoes trying to see past him.

"Oh, sorry," Mars said, stepping back. "Looks like boxes." He handed her the light. She stood on the block of stone and swept the beam from side to side. Column after column marched down the length of the room until the flashlight beam reached the back wall. The interior was immense, larger than the floor plan at ground level.

Anne turned back to Moshe. "Want to see?"

He shook his head. "Let's get the door open. Then we can all get a good look."

◆

Ben dragged the last block away and stood up. The work lights shed a little illumination near the doorway, but the bulk of the room was in Stygian blackness. Michael looked expectantly at Moshe.

"I think our American friends should go first," Moshe said, handing the flashlight to Anne. "Mars's observation and persistence enabled us to find this." He looked at Anne. "And of course the student's professor must share in the credit as well."

"You are very thoughtful," Anne said, waggling the flashlight at him.

"I have been accused of that from time to time. Press on, press on."

Anne clicked on the light and stepped over the threshold with Mars close behind. She stopped about fifty feet inside and slowly panned the light around. The ceiling, about eight feet high, was smooth, with no chisel marks to indicate it had been carved from previously undisturbed rock. In fact, the entire room was smoothly finished. This was no cave. Two immense stone columns were on either side of her, left in place when the room was excavated. A jumble of large boxes was straight ahead, with more orderly rows beyond and two more sets of columns further in.

Anne swept the light to the right and followed the wall to the corner closest to the door, revealing a large table. The beam continued past into the opposite corner. There it stopped on something that glinted brightly.

"Look at that menorah," she gasped.

"It's huge," Mars agreed. "Looks like it's made of gold."

Anne let the flashlight beam drop to their feet. Dark footprints led backwards to the door.

"Think of it! No one's been in here for almost two thousand years," Anne said.

"Yeah. But the dust surprises me. I would have thought there'd be more in that length of time."

"This is typical of ancient sites that have been sealed up."

"I yield to experience."

Anne glanced at him. She couldn't see his face but decided he was being serious. "Not personal experience, Mars. Only what I've read."

"Yes, Doctor McAdams," Mars said with a chuckle.

"I've still got the flashlight."

"Yes, ma'am. Shall we continue?"

They worked their way around the jumble of boxes and back toward the center of the room. Beyond the mess was row upon row of boxes, each precisely aligned, although the individual boxes varied greatly in size. A narrow aisle neatly divided the room.

"There must be *hundreds* of these," Mars said in an urgent whisper. "This is fabulous. Nothing I've ever read about touches this, unless it'd be Tutankhamen."

"This beats Tutankhamen, even counting the gold and jewelry."

They stayed within the aisle and walked its length until they reached the far wall, some one hundred and fifty feet into the room. There, one behind the other, were two stone boxes each fully ninety feet long, exquisitely carved with cherubim.

"Is that in one piece?" Mars asked.

Anne played the powerful beam over the side of the nearest box.

"Don't think so. Looks like it's jointed. Each section appears to be about ten feet long."

Mars reached down to feel the box.

"Better not do that," Anne advised.

"Think it's cursed?" Mars asked.

"No—nothing as wonderful as that. Moshe will want to photograph everything first."

"Right. And I *know* that, too."

"It's easy to forget. I guess we'd better get back before he wonders what happened to us."

"Eaten by giant snakes left to guard the place."

"You watch too many movies," Anne observed with an expression Mars could not see but could well imagine.

"Oh no, I'd never watch any trash like that."

Anne turned without comment and retraced her steps. The work lights seemed blinding as they framed the doorway. But the light that poured in was soon swallowed up in the immenseness of the room. Anne panned the flashlight over the menorah one last time, then back over on the table on the opposite side.

"What do you suppose they used that for?" she asked.

"Looks like a work bench. Maybe if we knew what this room was used for, we could figure it out."

Anne stepped through the doorway and switched the flashlight off.

"Well?" Moshe prompted.

"I don't know where to start," Anne began. "The room is about a hundred and fifty feet long, a hundred wide, with about an eight-foot ceiling. Six natural rock columns are arranged in symmetrical pairs. There's a large menorah—about six feet tall and seven wide—against the left-hand wall. Looks like it's gold or gold leaf. There's a large table against the right, and hundreds and hundreds of boxes. And something really strange against the far wall."

"Oh?" Moshe asked.

"Two stone boxes about ninety feet long, four deep, and four high. Looks like they're built in ten-foot sections. They're exquisitely carved in relief, the main art motif being cherubim."

"Ninety feet long . . ." Moshe repeated as he looked absentmindedly through the doorway.

"At least," Anne confirmed.

Moshe continued to look into the vast chamber as his mind journeyed back through the millennia. After several moments he looked back at Anne with an uncharacteristic seriousness. "This may well go down as the greatest archaeological find of all time. Nothing else can touch it."

"Do you know what it is?"

"First things first. Guessing's one thing, proof's another. Michael, my friend, let's set up some work lights inside the door—enough so we can see what we're doing. I'm going to get the Israel Museum to photograph every square inch before we touch anything. Then we measure and map it."

He turned back to Anne and Mars. "*Then* we open our presents."

16

THE TEMPLE GENIZA

Photographic strobes went off every few seconds, punctuated by strident instructions from Michael.

"He's truly in his element," Moshe commented to Mars and Anne. "The Museum photogs know what they're doing, but Michael is going to make sure. And heaven help anyone who makes a mistake."

"How long have you worked with him?" Anne asked out of curiosity.

"I don't really know. He's been on every dig I've had, except for undergrad days. He's the best there is. And he's a friend."

"I think that's sweet, Moshe," Anne said.

"Don't let *him* hear you say that," Moshe responded. "I'd never hear the end of it."

"My lips are sealed."

"Somehow I'd feel more secure if you weren't of the feminine persuasion."

"Take care, Moshe," Mars advised.

"Yes, children, it's back to work. And such wonderful work it is."

The archaeologists stepped aside to make way for a photographer who was working on a wide-angle shot of the jumbled boxes near the door. Moshe gravitated toward the gold menorah since it had already been photographed. He admired the heavy branches that shot straight out of the central trunk before turning upward, ending in graceful oil sockets—the menorah's lamps. Moshe traced the lower branch to the right and upward toward the lamp socket. There a small piece of gold had broken away. He probed the rough surface with a fingernail.

"Now we know what this place is," he said.

"What did you find?" Mars asked.

"The menorah is defective," he said, pointing to the lamp. "An undetected crack probably. Unnoticed at first, until the piece broke away."

"What's the big deal?" Mars asked. "You can hardly see it."

"It's less than perfect. And that makes it unfit for service in the Temple."

"*This* was in the Temple?" Anne asked.

"I think so. This room, if I am correct, is the Temple *geniza*."

Moshe watched Anne as she thought this over. "You mean, like the Cairo *geniza*?"

"Very good. The Cairo *geniza* was for a synagogue. This one was for the Temple."

"But there's no historical record of a Temple *geniza*."

"Correct. No reason why there should be. The function of a *geniza* is to store religious items that are no longer suitable for worship. The *geniza* is the forgotten place. The place of worship is what's important. It stands to reason the Temple had a *geniza*. It had to. If a lowly synagogue must be careful about religious articles, how much more the Temple?"

"So what's in the boxes?" Mars asked after a few moments of silence.

"That indeed is the question," Moshe agreed. "Whatever's there, you can bet it'll stir up all our fellow rock-scrapers."

Moshe turned as he heard someone come in the door. "Ah, Dan," he said. "I see you still check your mailbox from time to time."

"What in the world *is* this?" Dan demanded, trying to see everything at once.

"My friend, have I ever told you I've made the most fantastic find in history?"

"Many times."

"Well, this time I have. Or rather, *we* have. We are standing here courtesy of the observation and persistence of Mr. Mars Enderly and Dr. D. Anne McAdams."

"I've got to get a photographer," Dan said, starting to leave.

"Don't go. The Museum will provide whatever you want. Get out your pad or whatever you reporters use nowadays, and I'll give you your story."

Dan turned his pocket recorder on and pulled out a small notepad. He clicked his ballpoint pen. He didn't miss a word as Moshe told him what they had found.

◆

Abdul Suleiman tried to get comfortable as he sat wearily in the chair offered by his Arab host. But there wasn't a part of his body that did not ache. After walking up the canyon, he had found a path over the hills where the cliff ended. A passing Arab truck driver had been only too happy to give him a ride. And since the driver was going to Ramallah, that was where Abdul had decided he wanted to go also.

He now fought with his conscience and his dread of contacting Avraham. It was late. He was exhausted and hurt all over. Waiting until the morning was very attractive, but he dared not wait.

He struggled out of his chair, trying to ignore the pain. He punched in the number on the wall phone and waited while it rang. Someone picked up on the other end but said nothing.

"The fruit has been delivered," Abdul said, hoping whoever was on the other end knew the code.

"Very good. Let me check and see if there are any more deliveries."

There was a klunk as the receiver was put down. Abdul sighed with relief. It was Mustapha Kabran.

"No, no more deliveries for today," Avraham said, coming to the phone. "What's your first stop tomorrow?"

Abdul frowned. This wasn't part of the code. What did Avraham want? Abdul decided it had to be his present location. "I have a delivery to make in Ramallah." He held his hand over the mouthpiece while he asked his host a question. Then he gave Avraham the street address. "I presume you still want me to make the delivery," Abdul added.

"Yes. It is required." Avraham hung up.

Abdul replaced the receiver and sat back down.

◆

Several hours later a knock came on the door. Abdul's host answered and let the man in.

"Abdul," Mustapha said in relief. "I didn't know if I'd ever see you again."

"You almost didn't, but that can wait. Are you alone?"

"Just me. Avraham is quite anxious to see you."

"Yes, I imagine he is. Are you ready to start back?"

Mustapha nodded.

Abdul thanked his host, and the two men left for Jericho.

◆

It was 3 in the morning when Mustapha parked the truck. Abdul had slept most of the way from Ramallah, but he was still exhausted. Mustapha hurried around and started to help Abdul down. The other waved him away angrily as he got out and started walking stiff-legged toward the front door. Mustapha rushed past and knocked. The door swung open immediately. Abdul shuffled inside.

He had hoped to see Avraham in the morning, but this was not to be. The PRF chief was seated at a table in the room to the left that served as his command post. "Come in," Avraham said without getting up.

Abdul joined him at the table. Mustapha closed the door without being told, glad he wasn't invited to stay.

"So, my talkative friend, how did the Jews get you to talk? Did they peel your fingernails back or jab you with needles?" Avraham looked down below the tabletop. "Or was it worse than that?"

Abdul dared not look away. He knew he was very close to being a dead man. "They tricked me."

"They *tricked* you?" Avraham thundered.

"Yes. But I was following the intent of your instructions, if not the letter."

"This had better be good."

"If you had been there, you would understand and agree."

"You take too much on yourself! No one speaks for me!"

"Please let me explain. I thought the Jews were moving me to another prison. They faked an attack on the truck. I thought they were PLO."

"Go on," Avraham said.

"The terrorist leader—or whoever he was—said he was going to kill me rather than let me compromise them. The price for my freedom was convincing him I was not a collaborator. He wanted to know who I was and who I was with."

"So you told him."

"It was that or die! I was absolutely convinced of that. To what purpose if they were fellow Palestinians? We ought to fight *Jews*, not each other."

"You still disobeyed orders."

"The Jews haven't caught us."

"No thanks to you!"

"Have operations been going smoothly?" Abdul asked, hoping his timing was good.

Avraham glared at him for almost a minute, then looked away.

"I renew my vow to you," Abdul said. "If you will accept me back, I will do whatever you ask. My loyalty has always been to you and the PRF."

"Yes, I know that. But those Jews have made fools of us."

"What shall we do about it?"

Avraham sighed. He then told Abdul of his coming trip to Damascus. And he detailed what he wanted done in Jericho in his absence.

◆

Moshe and Michael met Anne and Mars at the police barricade.

"I forgot to warn you about this yesterday," Moshe said as he conducted them through. "With a find of this magnitude there could be difficulties. The press will hound us for a while. And certain groups don't like archaeologists poking around."

"He means the Orthodox," Michael interpreted.

"Now, live and let live," Moshe said. "They are very sincere, and I do not wish to disturb them."

"Did you see the piece Dan did in the *Jerusalem Post*?" Mars asked.

"Yes, I did. It was very nice, even for Dan. Big story complete with color photographs even. I must thank him when I see him."

"Now, people," Michael interjected, "we're not done with the photography or the mapping."

◆

It was midmorning when Michael came to find Moshe.

"Trouble topside," he said as he entered the *geniza*.

"What flavor?" Moshe asked.

"The fourth estate—bunch of TV crews—CNN, Israeli television, some others. They tried to grab me, but I convinced them the real archaeologists were down here. I gather it's either you come up there or they're coming down after you."

"We can't have that," Moshe said emphatically. "Anne, go see what they want."

"Moshe, this isn't my dig."

"You'll do fine. You can handle them much better than I can."

"What do you mean? I've never dealt with the press before."

"It's high time you started."

"But . . ."

"Go, go. Mars will accompany you."

"That's nice, but . . ."

"Unless it would be too distracting."

"Moshe!"

"You're welcome. Now go. We'll carry on down here."

Anne walked out with Mars in tow.

"You have no conscience," Michael observed.

"It's good for them. Now, don't you have something to do over there?"

◆

By the time Anne and Mars reached the barricades, there were five reporters trying to get through along with their associated cameramen.

"You ever heard of 'freedom of the press'?" shouted the CNN

reporter as he tried to push past a policeman. Then he saw Mars. "Hey, tell these bozos to let us through."

"This is a closed site," the policeman repeated, his tone indicating this was not the first time he had said it. "No one comes through unless Dr. Stein says so."

"You one of the archaeologists?" the CNN reporter asked Mars.

"I'm a graduate student in archaeology," Mars replied.

"Student, huh? How about getting one of the archaeologists so I can do an interview?"

"There's an archaeologist right here," Mars replied. "This is Dr. Anne McAdams, professor of archaeology from the University of Texas at Austin." He winked at Anne.

"You're an archaeologist?"

"Try me," Anne said evenly.

"Oh. Ah, what have you found here?"

"Did you read the *Jerusalem Post* story?"

"Why, yes, of course."

"Then you know what we've found."

The NBC reporter laughed. The CNN reporter shot him a nasty look.

"Well," the man continued, a little contritely, "could we set up for an interview—say over there with that tiled floor as a backdrop?"

"Make that interviews," the NBC reporter added. "You're not the only crew here."

"Not without Dr. Stein's approval," the policeman said.

"I am Dr. Stein's assistant. I see no harm in conducting the interviews on the floor."

The policeman hesitated, then opened the barricade to let the crews through. The reporter from CNN led the way out onto the marble floor, selecting a view that had the stairway as a backdrop.

"The hidden room down there?" he asked.

"Yes," Anne replied.

"Why can't we go down there?"

"Because I say you can't."

"But . . ."

"You can do it here or not at all."

The reporter started to argue, but something in Anne's expression convinced him not to. "Okay. Dr. McAdams, if you will stand over here, my cameraman can get us with the floor and the stairway in the back-ground."

"There are other crews here, bud," the NBC reporter pointed out. "Where does it say CNN gets first shot?"

"Hey, man, CNN *means* news. Besides, I got us in here."

"You did no such thing," Anne said in growing irritation. "And you can find yourself outside as quickly as you got in."

The CNN reporter started to object, but Anne held up her hand. "One more word and you'll be doing your taping from outside the bar-rier. Now here's the way it's going to be. You are guests of the Hebrew University and will conduct yourselves as such or be expelled."

Anne quickly counted the crews. There were five of them, she noted grimly. "Okay, this is the order we'll do the interviews." She pointed to each of the reporters in turn. She pointed to the CNN reporter last. The man kept his irritation to himself.

The NBC reporter was first. He rigged Anne with a wireless mike and set up a two-person, side-by-side interview. He nodded to the cam-eraman.

"Rolling," the cameraman replied.

Anne felt her stomach tighten and her mouth go dry.

"This is Peter Cooper standing at an archaeological dig in Jerusalem, a few blocks from the Wailing Wall. With me is Dr. Anne McAdams, assistant to Dr. Moshe Stein. Dr. McAdams, what have you found here?"

"We are standing on the site of a building that we believe is linked to the second Temple, the one Herod the Great ordered rebuilt on a grand scale. This building has the same perimeter dimensions as the Temple and exhibits Herod's architectural extravagance and attention to detail. But the most spectacular find is down those stairs. We have found a hidden room measuring about a hundred and fifty feet by a hundred. Inside are hundreds of sealed boxes and one large menorah. Dr. Stein has identified the room as the Temple *geniza*."

"What is a *geniza*?"

"It's a storeroom for religious articles no longer fit for worship ser-vices. The most famous *geniza*, prior to this discovery, was found in Cairo."

"What sorts of things have you found?"

"Just what I told you. The only identifiable article so far is the menorah. Nothing can be touched until everything is photographed and mapped."

"Do you think you'll find the lost Ark?"

"What?" Anne asked incredulously.

"The Ark of the Covenant. Do you think you'll find that?"

Anne paused as she suppressed what she wanted to say. "No, we do not expect to find the Ark of the Covenant. The Ark disappeared sometime after it was installed in Solomon's Temple, probably when the Babylonians sacked Jerusalem in 586 B.C.E. The only place you'll find it nowadays is on movie screens."

Peter's smile wilted a little as he continued to look into the camera. "This is Peter Cooper for NBC News, Jerusalem."

The cameraman took his camera down while the reporter retrieved Anne's mike.

Anne breathed a sigh of relief, until she remembered there were four more interviews. "I don't see why a certain graduate student couldn't do this," she said with a smile.

"I'm not a Doctor of Archaeology. Besides, you're doing fine."

The Israeli reporter was next.

◆

"That's the last of it," Moshe said as he tucked away the last drawing into the portfolio. "A nice day's work. Photographs done and maps done. Tomorrow the fun begins."

"Could we look in just one box?" Mars asked half-seriously.

"I'm shocked, young man. I'd speak to your professor, but I'm afraid she's not quite objective concerning you."

"Moshe, it's getting late," Anne observed.

"So it is. Let's be off."

They were halfway up the stairs when they heard it. They stepped out on the paving tiles under the last vestiges of a glorious sunset. Most of the sky was midnight blue going to violet in the west with a touch of red on the horizon in the direction of Tel Aviv.

Shadowy figures milled outside the barricades. Angry voices

drifted toward the archaeologists. As they got closer, they saw that the
policemen had been augmented by Israeli border guards.

"What's going on?" Anne asked.

"There's no telling," Moshe answered.

They stopped short of the barricades. In the fading light, they saw
an unusual gathering. Ultra-Orthodox Jews and Arabs protesting
together but taking care to remain separate.

"This has got to be a first," Moshe said as he tried to hear what was
being shouted. After about a minute he put a hand over his eyes
momentarily in amazement. "This is wonderful. The Hasidim think we
are desecrating Temple articles and possibly ancient Jewish graves. The
Arabs think all the publicity about the find is a pretext to tear down the
Dome of the Rock. I think we need Solomon here."

Moshe stepped up to the wooden saw-horses and shouted for the
crowd's attention. He gave a short speech in Hebrew, followed immediately by one in Arabic. When it was over, the two factions looked suspiciously at each other and began to drift off.

"What did you say?" Mars asked.

"I told the Hasidim that the Chief Rabbi of Jerusalem would par-
ticipate in investigating the finds. I told the Arabs that anything the
Jews were mad at couldn't jeopardize the Dome of the Rock."

"Who needs Solomon?" Mars replied.

Moshe led them through the barricades to his bus.

◆

"They don't give up easily," Mars remarked the next day as they
descended the stairs to the *geniza*.

"Sooner than you might think," Moshe replied. "The reporters and
religious zealots of one stripe or another only have a limited attention
span. Give it a few days."

"I'd as soon they quit now."

"Patience. Anyway, they can't bother us down here. Now, what do
we open first?"

"That's a good question," Anne agreed. "This feels like my first
Christmas."

"Hanukkah," Moshe corrected, then turned to Mars. "We'll let Mars decide. He made it possible. What shall it be?"

Mars shaded his eyes against the glare of the work lights. "I'd really like to see what's in those stone boxes at the back, but that's probably not practical. Let's open one of the boxes in the jumble."

He walked to the nearest box and got down on his hands and knees to examine it.

"Let's open this one," he said at last.

"Michael," Moshe said, "don't stand there. Give him a tool."

Michael handed him a thin pry bar. Mars put it in a crack where one of the top boards was fastened to the side. He gave it an experimental twist and the board came loose, revealing two thin, copper nails. He stopped before continuing.

"What the matter, Mars?" Anne asked.

"I was thinking—the last man who touched this box died about two thousand years ago." He shrugged and pried the rest of the board off, carefully laying it aside. Mars peered inside with three heads looking over his shoulder.

"Looks like a scroll," he said.

"Let's take it over to the table," Moshe said, unable to hide his excitement.

Mars lifted the scroll carefully from the box and carried it to the table.

"This is extraordinary," Moshe said as he rolled the scroll back enough to see one frame of Hebrew. "The condition is excellent. Apparently being in the box and inside this sealed room saved it from the Jerusalem humidity."

"What is it?" Anne asked, looking at the neat Hebrew lettering.

Moshe pulled out his reading glasses and perched them precariously on his nose. He moved the scroll slightly to get better light and squinted at the text.

"It's an inventory, as nearly as I can make out. I think it's a list of what's stored down here."

"What's the last entry?" Mars asked.

Moshe read the Hebrew date and made the necessary mental calculations.

"A scroll of the prophet Isaiah, stored in the year 33 C.E.," he said.

17

THE TEMPLE VEIL

T his will blow the socks off biblical archaeologists," Moshe said with a self-satisfied grin.

"What will?" Anne asked.

"This box has Torah scrolls that were stored in about 10 B.C.E. The scrolls are complete, and, not only that—we have more than one set down here."

"How can you tell?" Mars asked.

"This inventory lists *everything*," Moshe answered, waving a photograph of one page. "And except for the jumbled boxes near the front, the boxes are stored in order."

"So the stone boxes are at the head of the list," Mars concluded. "What's in them?"

"Bad assumption. Not only are the boxes not at the head, they're not on the list at all. I've checked. Twice. I did discover something else, though."

"What's that?" Mars asked.

"The jumbled boxes were originally where the stone boxes are now. They were apparently moved out of the way so the stone boxes could be put there."

"Why?" Anne asked.

"I was off that day."

"And here he had me convinced he knew everything," Mars said.

"I would talk to your professor about disciplining you, but I'm afraid she's compromised."

"There's plenty of room near the front to store the stone boxes," Anne said, ignoring Moshe. "Sure seems like a lot of extra trouble."

"A lot of trouble, and done in a hurry," Moshe agreed, pointing at the disarray.

Michael entered the room trailed by two workmen lugging heavy wooden beams.

"We won't have to wonder much longer," Moshe said.

Michael set down a box containing two chain hoists as the men started erecting a beam above one end of the outer stone box.

Michael placed four prefabricated clips on the first section of the stone lid. He then attached the chain hoists to the beam. He hooked wire bridles to the clips and slipped them over the chain hoists' hooks.

"I don't know when I've seen such efficiency," Moshe commented.

"The last time we did a dig," Michael replied.

"And modest too. Such a man."

"The seals," Michael reminded.

"Yes, the seals. Come, children, we've work to do before we can peek inside."

Moshe handed Mars and Anne hammers and chisels and showed them where to chip away the resin sealing the lid sections.

◆

It was harder work than they had counted on. Mars stretched out on his back, waiting until the fatigue left his right wrist. "I bet I know what we're going to find in there," he said.

"I know I'll regret asking, but what?" Moshe asked.

"A very tall mummy."

"And I was not disappointed. But since you suggested it, it could be Nebuchadnezzar's golden image."

"What's that?" Mars asked cautiously.

"Each of these boxes is very close to the dimension of the king's image. According to Daniel, the golden image was ninety feet tall and nine feet wide. Most biblical commentators suggest that the image was of Nebuchadnezzar, but this seems unlikely."

"Why?" Mars asked.

"A six-foot human built to the same scale would have shoulders seven inches wide. The original thin man perhaps."

Mars groaned and tried to make himself comfortable lying on the resin chips as he continued hammering away at the seam under the stone lid.

♦

Moshe finished his examination of the lid's joints. He straightened up and nodded to Michael. "Should come free now," he said. "Gently. It may be stuck."

"I'm new at this," Michael grumbled. "You better watch me carefully."

"There's no end to it," Moshe groaned. "Get on with it, will you?"

"Mars, if you will take the other one," Michael said, ignoring Moshe. "Get your hoist taut. Then pull slowly until the lid comes free."

Mars pulled the chain on his hoist until the slack in the bridle was gone. The beam began to groan ominously as it started bearing the load. Mars eyed Michael and saw he was continuing to apply force. A sharp crack sounded as the lid came free suddenly, jumping about a half inch above the box.

"Nothing to it," Michael said as he let out his breath. "Now raise it up about a foot. Then we'll adjust the bridle so we can angle the lid to get it down."

Mars followed Michael's example as he grabbed the rear edge of the lid and pulled it up, slipping the bridle through the chain hoist hook. Soon the forward edge of the lid was angled down, almost touching the box. The two men got behind the lid and pushed it forward, letting the chain hoists down as they went. The lid slid down the front edge of the box until it hit the dollies positioned on the floor. As soon as the lid was clear of the box, Michael and Mars lowered it quickly onto the dollies.

"One down and nine more sections to go," Michael said with relief.

The four converged on the box. Moshe clicked on his large flashlight and swept the beam over a striped object—broad bands of scarlet, purple, and blue. A neat series of golden emblems marched enigmatically across the object.

"What is it?" Anne asked.

Moshe reached down and touched it. It was cloth, the heaviest Moshe had ever seen, and surprisingly soft for its age.

"It looks like a curtain of some kind," he said. He turned his head to get a new perspective on the golden objects.

"Cherubim," he said softly.

"Do you know what it is?" Anne asked.

Moshe clicked off the flashlight. For a while it appeared he had not heard. Then he glanced at Michael before looking at Anne.

"It's the veil from Herod's Temple," he said in a strangely quiet way.

"What?" Mars asked.

"It can't be anything else. We've already identified this room as the Temple *geniza*. The Temple veil was ninety feet high. It was very thick, constructed of scarlet, purple, and blue panels. And it was embroidered with cherubim. What we're looking at is the curtain that separated the Holy of Holies from the Holy Place. This box contains one of the veils and the other box the other one."

"Like stage curtains?" Mars asked.

"No. They were hung one behind the other. One was firmly attached to the north wall of the Holy Place and was open about a foot on the south side. The one behind it was attached on the south wall and open on the north. There was a one-and-a-half foot corridor between them for the priests to use. On the west side, behind the veil's halves, was the Holy of Holies."

Moshe touched one of the cherubim. "I don't know about you, but I feel awfully strange. The tradition of the veil goes back to the Tabernacle Moses built in the wilderness. And this is the last one that ever was, or next to last, assuming the last one was destroyed by Titus in 70 C.E."

"Michael," Moshe said, standing up straight, "we've got work to do—a lot of work. We'll need some help in chipping these lids free. Do whatever you think necessary, but we've got to move these veils to the Israel Museum as soon as possible, so we can get on with cataloging the rest of the finds. The boxes can stay where they are for now. I'll make the arrangements with Yitzhak Yadin at the Museum. I can't wait to see his face when he hears what we've found."

"Do you want me to arrange for transportation?" Michael asked.

"No. I'll get Yitzhak to do that. Let's concentrate on getting the boxes opened."

Michael turned and left.

"This is an archaeologist's dream come true," Moshe said. "First we find the building above us, then that fabulous mosaic, then this room. This isn't some totally destroyed site with a few badly weathered artifacts, a few things somehow overlooked by grave-robbers. We're standing in a *warehouse* perfectly preserved for two thousand years, with who knows how many treasures. *And* the Temple veil. There isn't anything else that will touch this. My friends, our place in the history books is assured."

"Makes me wish I already had my Ph.D.," Mars said with a wry grin.

"Degrees, degrees," Moshe grumbled. "You're an archaeologist, too, and you'll get your credit. I'll see to that. We can't forget the discoverer, can we?"

Mars smiled.

"Now if you and Anne will continue cataloging the boxes, I need to make a little trip over to the Israel Museum."

◆

It was near the end of the day before the truck from the Museum arrived. Dr. Yitzhak Yadin peered through the doorway into the *geniza*, his lively brown eyes flashing when he recognized Moshe. He strode across the floor with surprising vigor for a short, stout man. His round face was framed by gray hair and a full beard, both perfectly groomed.

"Moshe," he said, "what have you found here?"

"Yitzhak, I'd like you to meet my colleagues. This is Dr. Anne McAdams and Mars Enderly."

Yitzhak asked a quick question in Hebrew. Moshe looked momentarily embarrassed. "Yes, they are goyim. Not much chance 'McAdams' or 'Enderly' could be Jewish, I would think. But they are fine archaeologists. Mars is responsible for our finding the mosaic and the *geniza*." Moshe paused before continuing. "And they're my very good friends."

"That's good," Yitzhak said without feeling. He did not extend his hand. "I see you have the boxes open," he continued. "Shall I have my men come and get the veil?"

Moshe nodded and waved an arm at the boxes against the far wall. Yitzhak gave a barely perceptible nod toward the doorway, and twenty men filed into the *geniza*. Yitzhak strode to the nearest box to see the veil before it was removed. He leaned over and felt the heavy fabric. Satisfied, he turned to his men.

"Gently now. Spread out. Get this first one up to the truck, then come back for the other. And be careful. Anyone damaging this is going to be looking for another job."

The men did exactly what Yitzhak said without a murmur. They struggled to get their arms around the veil, straining to lift the surprisingly heavy object. Finally they hoisted it free and carried it out of the room like some immense snake. Moshe felt a strange sense of loss as he watched it go out the door.

"You will take care of it?" he asked absentmindedly.

"Of course," Yitzhak replied testily. "I didn't get to be Director of Antiquities by being careless."

"No, of course not," Moshe replied. "It's just that it's our baby."

Yitzhak gave a short, mirthless laugh. "I'll take good care of your baby." He left without another word.

◆

The male receptionist picked up the phone on the first ring. He listened for a few moments, then calmly replaced the receiver.

"You may go in now," he said.

Avraham heaved a sigh of relief but wished for a chance to go to the bathroom. First had come the pre-dawn trip at low altitude in the Hind helicopter. Then sitting for hours in the anteroom drinking endless cups of coffee. Avraham's stomach was less than steady.

Atallah Jubran stood expectantly at the door. Avraham rose to his feet and made his way unsteadily to the door. Atallah opened it for him and followed him inside.

President Hashem Darousha looked up from his immense walnut desk, fresh and alert despite the early hour. "Avraham Abbas," he said as if they were old friends. He came around the desk and embraced his guest. His smile radiated as he returned behind his desk.

"Please sit down," he continued, indicating an overstuffed chair in front of the desk. He gave the briefest nod to Atallah, who touched his forehead in salaam and left, closing the door softly.

"So how was the trip?" Hashem asked with just the right amount of concern.

"It was interesting, Excellency," Avraham replied carefully. "You were most gracious to send for me."

"The cause," Hashem said. "The land to the south is ruled by usurpers. This must end."

"I am committed to this," Avraham said.

"I am aware of this," Hashem agreed, "and not from the petty revelations of the Jewish puppet. President Darousha's sources of information are quite pervasive. And so, how can I help my brother Abbas?"

Avraham's mind raced. He had not expected this offer, at least not this soon. "Many things, Excellency. But most urgent is explosives and assault rifles. Oh, and handheld ground-to-air missiles if they are available."

"What, no tanks?" Hashem asked with an easy laugh.

Avraham colored in embarrassment. "Please accept my apologies," he said.

"None necessary, my friend. All this can be arranged." He paused for a moment. "And the missiles. You are an audacious man. If you say you need them, I'm sure you have a good use for them. It so happens I have some Russian-made SA-16 missiles I can let you have."

"You are too kind," Avraham said with a nod.

"Not at all. Your enemy is our enemy. You will keep me informed?" It was not exactly a question.

"Of course, Excellency."

"Very good. Now, I'm sure you are anxious to get back, but daylight is not the best time for travel. Atallah will see to your needs until evening. Again, thank you for coming."

The door opened on cue. Atallah looked in and motioned to Avraham. The PRF leader rose, grateful that he could now seek a restroom.

18

THE UNEXPLAINED
TEAR

D r. Jon Arnon looked out over the nearly deserted storeroom. As head curator under Yitzhak Yadin, he had ceased to be surprised at what his boss could accomplish. Only this morning the storeroom had been crammed with all the things the Museum didn't currently need but was disinclined to throw away. Now it contained one thing—the veil from Herod's Temple, consisting of two curtains. Both were up against the only wall long enough to take them without folding.

Yitzhak had been there while the veil was brought in. Then had come the detailed instructions covering the investigation. Jon had listened dutifully even though he knew exactly what to do. He liked his job and wished to keep it. Now he was alone with his crew.

He watched as ten men slowly and carefully started unfolding the first curtain. This proceeded smoothly until about fifteen feet had been exposed. There a jagged tear separated the heavy fabric into two pieces. When the men completed their task, thirty feet of four-inch-thick cloth lay on the floor. They straightened the pieces while the photographer prepared his cameras.

Jon knelt and examined the tear. Both halves of the veil were in remarkably good condition. It was definitely not in a state of decay, and yet there was this tear. He felt the edges and looked at the fiber ends. The veil had been torn, not cut; of that he was certain. He moved to the side as a draftsman shuffled past with a tape measure.

"Where do you want us to remove the samples?" a man in a white coat asked.

"Take two from this half and two from the other one. Pick a point at the top near one of the ring holes and one along the bottom hem. Take enough for a good test."

The man nodded and started removing material from the top near the tear.

◆

"What have we found today?" Moshe asked as he entered the *geniza*.

"We've hardly made a dent," Mars answered. "So far, it's what the inventory said we'd find. Lots of oil lamps, a chair, two tables, some pitchers, a money chest—nothing in it—and a marble tray. A regular treasure trove. Some of the defects we've been able to find, some we haven't. All I can say is, the Temple priests must have been *very* particular."

"They were," Moshe said with authority.

"Anything on the veil?" Anne asked.

"Just got back from visiting Yitzhak. They've barely begun. May be a while before we learn anything."

"If ever," Mars added.

"Yitzhak is a little, what should I say, austere. But he is a good scientist. He has his work to do, and we have ours. And ours seems to be stopped at the moment."

Mars eyed Anne. "Well, Dr. McAdams, I guess we better get back to it."

Moshe grinned. "You children play nice now. I've got to go see Michael about transporting the mosaic."

◆

The cockpit instruments glowed in the darkness of pre-dawn. The pilot grinned like a little kid. He loved flying, and the less restrictions the better. He pushed the Phantom 2000's throttles to 100 percent, released the brakes, then shoved the throttles into full afterburner. The newly repaired fighter surged down the runway as if eager to prove it was ready to serve again. The backseat weapon systems officer thrilled to the raw power of the heavy fighter. Weapon systems officers go by many shorter names, the most common being wizzo, a variation of WSO. Right now the wizzo was only a passenger, since he and the pilot would not test the weapons and electronics suites until they were airborne.

The young Israel Air Force lieutenant hauled back on the stick, and the Phantom leapt into the air. The pilot pulled back into a near-vertical climb, leaving the engines in afterburner. At eight thousand feet the plane went through vertical and onto its back as the pilot executed a half snap-roll and a sharp left turn to bring them onto their departure heading. He reluctantly brought the throttles out of afterburner. In a few minutes they would be over the Jordan River north of Jericho.

A month earlier the Phantom had suffered minor damage when the nose wheel had collapsed on landing. The plane was repaired now, which required a test flight. The pilot and his wizzo loved test hops. You were by yourself and could do almost anything you wanted, as long as you tested the bird. Since this was a test flight, they had no missiles, though the twenty-millimeter gatling gun was loaded with 640 rounds of ammunition.

◆

Abdul Suleiman shielded his eyes from the first rays of the sun as he looked out the broken side window of the beat-up Chevrolet truck. He scanned the eastern horizon impatiently. He and Majid were about ten miles north of Jericho on a secondary road near the Jordan River. The pilot was a half-hour late, and Abdul had almost decided he was not coming.

He turned his head slightly as he heard a low turbine whine. What began as a speck quickly resolved itself into a silhouette as the Mooney MU-2 came right out of the sun, flying a little higher than Abdul would have wished. *Probably afraid of running into a hill*, he thought in derision.

The small turboprop banked quickly to the north and slowed as the pilot dropped the gear and flaps. He descended precipitously to a hundred feet and began a very low, high-speed downwind leg as he swept over the rolling hills. A few moments later he racked the plane over in a tight left turn, centering on the road in a diving approach. Abruptly he pulled the power back and set the plane down. The low whine increased to a roar as the pilot selected reverse pitch and shoved the throttles forward while standing on the brakes as hard as he dared.

Abdul began to wish he had parked the truck off the road as he saw the plane begin to loom in size. The speed bled off quickly as the pilot got the plane under control. He killed the left engine and swung the plane abruptly to the right, leaving the right engine running. The copilot had the passenger door open the moment the Mooney lurched to a stop. He motioned for Abdul and Majid to board.

Abdul bounded up the ladder and ducked to enter the fuselage. He glanced forward and saw the pilot looking back through the cockpit door, obviously not intending to help. Abdul turned back to the copilot. This man was ready to do whatever it took to cut down their stay in Israeli-occupied territory. He already had the first box of plastic explosive and was heading for the door. Abdul and Majid grabbed one each and dashed after the man.

The copilot didn't say a word as they unloaded the explosives and the crates of AK-47s. The last things on the plane were six well-built wooden crates. Abdul cornered the Syrian after the last of the crates was on the truck.

"What's in those last boxes?" he asked

"SA-16 missiles," the man replied, obviously in a hurry to go.

"Are they assembled and ready to go?"

The copilot glanced up at the pilot, who was motioning frantically for the man to get back on board. He turned back as he heard the left engine start turning.

"Yes. Do you know how to use them?"

"Yes."

"Good. I have to go. Good luck."

The man dashed up the stairs and quickly operated the door controls. The stairs folded up and disappeared. The door closed and latched.

Abdul and Majid pulled the tarp over their cargo and tied it down. Abdul turned his back as the MU-2 turned to the north, pelting him and Majid with sand and gravel. The turbines roared as the pilot applied full power. The plane lurched and hopped as it gathered speed down the uneven road. Finally it lifted off and began a gradual turn to the east.

◆

"They sure fixed it good!" the wizzo grumbled into the intercom. "The radios just went dead."

The pilot heard this, but at the moment it was a minor irritation intruding on something more important. He rolled the Phantom 2000 onto its side so he could be sure. "Got a transport taking off down there. And a truck. The river is only a few miles away. That's a terrorist supply run for sure."

The wizzo looked where the pilot was pointing. "Looks like it. And us with no radios. What do we do?"

"Splash the bird, then service the truck."

"With no warning?"

"With the transport cranking for Jordan? I'm not about to let him get away."

"You're the boss."

"Right you are," the pilot said. "Let's hope the gun still works." He flicked the arming switches, lifted the switch guard, and threw the Master Arm toggle. "It's showtime," he added as he pushed the heavy fighter over into a steep dive.

◆

Abdul motioned for Majid to get in the truck, then froze in his tracks. A dark, sinister shape was hurtling toward them, trailing two black exhaust plumes. The Phantom flashed past less than fifty feet off the ground. Abdul clearly saw the helmeted pilot and his backseater look them over as they swept past. The fighter racked around in a tight turn and lined up on the departing MU-2. A few moments later the Israeli pilot fired the twenty-millimeter gatling for less than a second. The Mooney's tail disintegrated as the hail of cannon shells tore it to pieces. The turboprop abruptly nosed over and dove into the ground. The fireball rose high in the sky, followed several seconds later by the sound of the crash.

Abdul felt his blood run cold as he jumped up into the cab. He watched as the Phantom pulled into a near vertical bank to the left. He started the engine and jammed the gearshift into first, letting out the clutch so quickly the engine stalled. The jet was almost all the way around now. Abdul got the truck going and turned it around on the narrow road, crumpling the right fender against the rock embankment. The tire whined in protest as it ground against the metal. Abdul pushed the accelerator to the floor as he glanced into his right-hand mirror. The Phantom was in a shallow dive aimed right at the truck. Abdul shoved the gearshift into second, willing the truck to go faster. The grade steepened as the truck neared the top of the hill. The Phantom loomed larger and larger. Why didn't he shoot, Abdul wondered, knowing that one burst of the gatling gun would blow the truck into tiny pieces, and themselves with it. They crested the hill with a feeling of weightlessness, landing with a crash as the springs bottomed out. Abdul jammed on the brakes, trying to keep the truck straight as they slid to a stop. The Phantom thundered past mere feet above the crest, the pilot unable to bring his gun to bear.

Abdul set the emergency brake, threw open the door, and jumped out.

"Get over here!" he ordered Majid as he headed for the back of the truck. "Turn the truck around, and when I tell you, head back over the crest!"

Abdul untied one corner of the tarp, grabbed two crates and a wrecking bar, and sprinted for the ditch. He ripped frantically at the crates as Majid started turning the truck. The Phantom pilot was making a leisurely turn to the left. The truck was a sitting duck.

Abdul pulled an SA-16 launch-tube and missile from one crate and its handgrip from the other. Although he had never fired one, he had attended a clandestine training camp in Libya several years before that had covered SA-16s. He connected the missile tube to the handle and flipped the seeker on. He then swung the SA-16 up toward the turning Phantom. The seeker chirped as it picked up the heat from the jet's twin turbines. *Good*, Abdul thought. *Now come back around.* He ducked behind a large boulder, holding the missile at the ready.

Majid glanced nervously at Abdul through the truck's side window. The timing had to be exactly right. Too soon and the Jews would break off and get them on the next pass. Too late and half the mountain would get blown away on this pass.

The Phantom was all the way around now and coming back. It was noticeably slower, as the pilot settled into a confident, low glide. Abdul waited as long as he dared.

"Go!" he shouted at the top of his lungs.

Majid let out the clutch too quickly and almost stalled the truck. The engine backfired as the truck lurched off. Majid stood on the accelerator and wished for the ridge. He wound the engine higher than was wise, then shifted into second. He looked frantically out the side mirrors but could not see the jet. Slowly the ridge crept toward him.

The pilot cursed as he saw the truck heading for the ridge. He was lower and slower than he wanted to be. Although the outcome was not in doubt, he could not be sure of a kill on this pass. The next one would be a dive from the side. He pushed the throttles forward just short of the burners and waited for the engines to spool up. He lined up on the truck and jazzed the trigger. A wall of cannon projectiles sprayed out of the gatling gun. Fountains of dirt kicked up on the road well behind the fleeing truck. He wasn't in range and wouldn't be on this pass. He cursed again as he pulled back hard on the stick and shoved the throttles into full afterburner.

Abdul smiled as Majid disappeared over the crest. He watched as the big fighter pulled up abruptly into a near vertical climb, tongues of flame shooting out of both tailpipes. He swung the SA-16's launch-tube up and pointed it at the ascending Phantom. Immediately the seeker chirped. This was too easy.

Abdul squeezed the trigger. The launch-tube bucked as the missile leapt upwards trailing a white smoke trail. He watched with glee as the missile's yellow exhaust merged with the Phantom. The rocket disappeared up the right-hand tailpipe and exploded. Both engines were destroyed instantly, along with all hydraulic systems.

"Missile hit," the pilot announced to his wizzo, who was more aware of the damage than his partner was. He watched glumly as their airspeed bled off. He stabbed the left rudder pedal as hard as he could, but nothing happened. "Punch out! Now!"

The officers closed their visors and made sure their legs and arms were pulled in. The wizzo pulled his emergency jettison handle. The rear canopy separated cleanly from the aircraft. He pulled the ejection handle between his legs and felt the kick of the ejection. The seat raced up the rails and the rocket fired, shooting the seat and the backseater out over the desolate landscape. The seat separated and the parachute deployed, just like the manual said they would.

Now that his partner was out, the pilot went through the same sequence, his heart racing as his seat shot out of the fatally wounded plane. He almost blacked out from the 12-G acceleration. The seat separated, the auxiliary parachute deployed, and the main parachute snapped open with a sharp crack. The pilot cried out in pain and looked down. The left knee of his flight suit was a red mess. He had apparently hit something on ejection, although he hadn't felt anything at the time. He cursed as he looked down. He saw one of the terrorists sprint for the truck, tie the tarp down, dash for the driver's-side door, wrench it open, and jump in. Moments later the truck was turning around and heading south down the road. The pilot reached for his emergency radio.

◆

Majid had nothing to say to Abdul, but then he rarely did. He sat there looking straight ahead as Abdul pushed the truck as hard as he dared on the narrow, rutted road.

Abdul looked back. Both aviators were below the ridge line now. Abdul wrenched the wheel to the right and turned onto a road bearing almost due west. The Israelis, he hoped, would assume he would continue south. A little more than a mile later he stopped at Highway 90. After a brief hesitation, he turned right and started north at a leisurely rate, resisting the urge to speed up. A few minutes later a flight of four Phantoms flew over at low altitude heading east. He breathed a little easier as they flew past. It was going to be a long trip, but Abdul was confident they would make it.

◆

"His majesty awaits without," Michael said with not a trace of a smile.

"I presume you mean Dr. Yitzhak Yadin," Moshe said, playing the game.

"The same."

"I'm glad to see you are paying him the respect he deserves."

"Indeed."

"Perhaps someday I'll get the respect I deserve."

"Oh, you already do."

"Thanks," Moshe grumbled.

Yitzhak was pacing impatiently when Moshe emerged from the stairs leading to the *geniza*. He approached the archaeologist as soon as he saw him. "Where have you been?"

"Down in the *geniza*."

"I asked what's-his-name and he said he didn't know. Then he disappeared."

"Michael Shapiro is his name. I *am* sometimes hard to find, but enough pleasantries. To what do I owe the honor of this visit?"

"Your signature on some work requests. I have to charge this work to the University."

"Oh, yes," Moshe said with a sigh. "First things first."

"Listen, we've been through this before. Unless the paperwork's correct, the University kicks it back."

"And we always get you paid, don't we?"

"Eventually," Yitzhak agreed grudgingly.

"Let me see the clipboard, and I'll get you all fixed up."

Yitzhak handed him the board and a pen.

"Thanks," Moshe said as he dashed off the first signature. "Now, my friend, what have you discovered in that fabulous lab of yours?"

"We ran a date on the veil. Came out 350 B.C.E., plus or minus a hundred."

"Not possible. Can't be earlier than 19 B.C.E."

"I ran it four times."

"Your results are wrong four times. But never mind that. Anything else?"

"Yes. I don't know what to make of it, but both halves of the veil are torn in two."

"In two? Completely?"

"Completely. The material's in good shape except for that."

"Any idea how it was torn?"

"Not a clue."

"You said torn. Could it have been cut?"

"I said 'torn.' We have examined the edges carefully. There are no tool marks, and the fiber ends are rough, not smooth. The weave displacement indicates a tear starting at the top and progressing downward."

"Torn in two," Moshe muttered.

Yitzhak pointed to the clipboard. "If you will sign that last paper, I really must get back to my lab."

Moshe signed and gave the clipboard back to Yitzhak.

♦

Mars and Anne looked expectantly at Moshe while Michael feigned disinterest.

"Let's go outside so we don't disturb Michael," Moshe said, motioning to the Americans.

"You won't bother me," Michael said a little too quickly.

"Are you sure?"

"I'm sure."

"Radiometric dating puts the veil at about 350 B.C.E."

"What?" Mars exclaimed.

Moshe laughed. "I have already given Yitzhak our official position on that." He grew thoughtful. "But what's really interesting is the fact that both sections are torn in two. Not cut—torn."

"Torn?" Anne asked.

"In two, as in ninety feet worth—from the top to the bottom. But other than that, the veil's in excellent shape for something that's two thousand years old."

"How do you suppose it happened?" Mars asked.

Moshe arched his eyebrows as he thought that over. Finally he said, "The Christian Bible says that when Jesus died on the cross, the Temple veil was torn in two from top to bottom."

"You don't take that claptrap seriously!" Mars said. It was a statement rather than a question. "The Bible's full of fairy tales and errors."

Moshe shook his head. "We scientists have to be careful what we state as fact. It so happens that the Bible is the most accurate ancient book there is. I can't tell you how many archaeological finds we've made because we looked for things where the Bible said they were."

"Do you really believe the miracles and supernatural stuff?" Mars challenged.

"No," Moshe said after a brief pause. "No, I don't. But it sure causes me to wonder—what did cause the tear?"

Anne looked at Moshe, struggling with what she wanted to say. "Moshe, I remember hearing about this when I was a little girl. But why would you be interested in what's in the New Testament?"

An embarrassed smile came to his face. "I guess it's because of my interest in what you call the Old Testament. For history. Except for one writer, the New Testament was written by Jews, and it's obvious that Christians read the two halves as one."

Anne could tell that Moshe's feelings ran deep, and she sensed hers being dragged along, almost against her will. A glance at Mars's angry scowl told her what he thought about all this. So the Bible said the veil had been torn—from top to bottom, and that's the way they found it with no explanation of how it had been done. And the Bible said the most fantastic things about Jesus, things that couldn't possibly be true, could they? She hid the thoughts in her heart. An icy chill ran down her spine. She again sensed an unseen threat and didn't know what to do about it.

◆

The dust boiled heavenward as the tank transporters carried the Russian-made T-72 tanks down the Beirut highway, much to the irritation of the Syrian drivers who were kept lining the ditch. On they rumbled toward Damascus until turning southward on the road leading to Qatanah. At the same time the lead transports were turning off, two more armored convoys were heading for the same rendezvous, one traveling southwest from Damascus and the other northward toward the capital from southern Syria.

The northbound convoy turned west at Kissoue. A few miles further on, it halted to let the Damascus column make its turn toward Qatanah. The order fell into apparent disarray as the transporters, armored personnel carriers, and artillery pieces began arriving on the south side of the town, trying to find their assigned stations.

♦

Ya'acov wondered if he had made a mistake as the old Piper Comanche
250 bumped one last time on the grass strip before becoming airborne.
He checked the tightness of his seat belt as he scanned the instruments
in front of him. He made a conscious effort to stay clear of the control
wheel and rudder pedals as he glanced out the side window. He had
seen Jerusalem from the air before, but its beauty never failed to catch
his heart. He continued to look at the Old City until the pilot turned to
the north.

"You ever get tired of it?" Ya'acov asked the Israel Air Force lieutenant.

"No, sir. There isn't anything better than flying up to Hermon. You
know how to pick your duty assignments."

"It wasn't planned for that."

"Whatever you say, sir. And for a bonus, we get to see the sunset as
well."

Ya'acov glanced to the west. The sun was on the horizon, causing
brilliant reflections off the almost black Mediterranean. The rugged hills
were backlit with peaks in clear relief against the dark valleys. The sun,
huge and red, touched the horizon and visibly began to merge with it.
In a minute it was gone, leaving the western horizon in a luminous red-
orange glow shifting to dark blue in the east.

"How long will it take to get there?" Ya'acov asked.

"About a half-hour or so. Should be some light when we get there.
I'll come in from the west so you can see Mount Hermon. It's also a tad
safer from that direction."

"By all means," Ya'acov replied with a wry smile.

The Lycoming engine droned away happily as the Comanche flew
through smooth air at eleven thousand feet. Ya'acov kept his head on a
swivel as the land of Israel rolled underneath. Ten minutes later the Sea
of Galilee was well in view and beyond it the rugged splendor of Mount
Hermon.

"Want to take it for a while, Captain?" the pilot asked, taking his
hands away from the wheel and his feet off the rudder pedals.

"I don't know how to fly," Ya'acov said in alarm.

"No problem. Just try to keep us right-side-up. Pull back on the wheel to go up, forward to go down. Turning is obvious—you can use the wheel without the pedals if you want. Slow, gentle movements is all it takes."

Ya'acov looked at the man to see if he was serious.

"You've got it," the pilot said. "You can see Hermon from here. Aim our nose a hair to the left where the base of the mountain is."

"What if . . ."

"I'm not going anywhere."

Ya'acov grasped the wheel as if it might start twisting violently. The control was absolutely steady. He carefully put his feet on the rudder pedals. Ya'acov looked out over the engine cowling. They were heading straight for Mount Hermon, although it was still over forty miles away. He turned the wheel slightly to the left. The nose obediently swung to the left, a little quicker than he intended. Ya'acov centered the wheel quickly, and the turn stopped. Their track was now too far to the left. Ya'acov turned the wheel slightly to the right. He smiled as the nose came slowly right. He centered the wheel when their track was on the western base of Mount Hermon.

"See, nothing to it," the pilot observed. "Now, see that gauge there? That's the altimeter. We're supposed to be at eleven thousand feet. We're at ten nine right now and going down a couple of feet a minute. We need to get back to eleven."

Ya'acov pulled back gently on the wheel and watched the altimeter dial as it spun its lazy way back to eleven thousand feet. Finally he pushed the wheel forward as the long pointer hit zero. Unseen by Ya'acov, the pilot adjusted the stabalator trim slightly.

"You ought to consider transferring to IAF," he said with a smile.

"I think I'll stick with what I know," Ya'acov replied. "Although I could get to like this."

"Spoken like a true aviator. You're doing fine. Keep us heading where we are now and glance at the altimeter from time to time."

◆

All too soon it was over. The pilot pulled back on the throttle, set the mixture at full rich, and pulled on the carburetor heat. The airspeed indicator crept toward the caution line as speed built up in the fast descent. They skirted the southern slopes and started turning gently toward the east.

"Getting kinda dark," the pilot observed as he looked for something on the ground.

"Are you going to radio them?" Ya'acov asked.

"Don't have to, sir. They're expecting us. This is something of a hot mission, as the captain informed me."

Runway lights flicked on below as if in answer to their conversation.

"Right on the money," the pilot said.

He lowered the landing gear and seconds later full flaps. Without warning he cranked the aircraft into a near vertical turn and rolled out onto a short, low final. He applied power as the Comanche settled on the approach speed. The moment the first set of lights swept past, the pilot chopped the throttle and pulled back slightly on the wheel. The main wheels touched down, bounced once, and remained planted. The aircraft jounced along the rutted runway as the pilot pulled on the brake handle, keeping the wheel full back to protect the nose wheel. The speed bled off quickly until they were taxiing toward a light pickup truck. The pilot brought the plane to a stop, set the parking brake, and shut the engine down.

"I'll see you later, Captain. I'll be here when you're ready to go back."

Ya'acov nodded as he opened the door and walked gingerly over the wing until he could jump heavily to the ground.

His driver saluted as he stood by the passenger-side door.

"Good evening, Sergeant," Ya'acov said as he saw the man's stripes in the fading light.

"Good evening, sir. I'm Sergeant Avi Barak. We've already got the bird up and headed in the direction your message specified. Sergeant Tennenbaum is in the trailer guiding it."

Ya'acov nodded and got into the truck. Avi closed the door and ran around to the driver's side. He jumped in, seeming to close the door and hit the starter in the same instant. They lurched off, bumping along a rough dirt path Ya'acov could barely see. In a few minutes a lump appeared by the side of the road—an antenna-festooned trailer.

Avi jammed on the brakes, bringing the truck to an abrupt stop. He jumped out, ran around the front, and opened Ya'acov's door. The guard at the trailer opened the door for them. Ya'acov walked up the steps and into the trailer, Avi closing the door behind them.

Although once considered a wacky invention, the Unmanned Air Vehicle, or UAV, had emerged as a useful intelligence and tactical tool. Starting out life as the Israel Aircraft Industries Remotely Piloted Vehicles, these radio-controlled aircraft with their cameras and infrared sensors had proven themselves against Syrian missile sites in the Beka'a Valley and later in the Gulf War against Iraq, where they were used by the U.S. forces. Stealth, considered an American invention, started with the UAV.

Ya'acov quickly scanned the racks of electronics crammed into the trailer.

"Sergeant Yehuda Tennenbaum is your pilot for this mission," Avi said, pointing to a soldier slouched back in his chair watching a console video display.

Yehuda stood quickly and saluted.

"What about the drone?" Ya'acov asked in alarm.

"Actually it's called an Unmanned Air Vehicle or UAV. And it knows more about where it's going than I do."

"That's a slight exaggeration, sir," Avi added as he replaced the man sitting next to Yehuda. "He has a map in front of him, but the UAV's autopilot is programmed to take it to the coordinates you sent us. And if we lose the data link, the UAV's computer will automatically return it here."

"What does your console do?" Ya'acov asked.

"This is the Payload Manager's station. I control the video camera and the Forward Looking Infrared or FLIR. I also monitor some of the telemetry and recording. Yehuda gets us there, and I snoop around."

Avi looked around at Ya'acov. "May I ask you a question, Captain?"

"Sure," Ya'acov answered as he brought a swivel chair over and sat down between Yehuda and Avi.

"I thought sure when we got the message about you that you were a Visual Intelligence officer. They're assigned to the Forward Command Posts, but they quite often come back here to see what we're doing, unless we're in combat operations."

"So what's an Intelligence officer doing here who doesn't know what you're doing?"

"I don't believe I would put it that way, sir."

"It's a fair question. I am familiar with the intelligence your units provide. And I know basically how you do it, but obviously not in detail. But there's one specific thing I want to know, and you guys are the only ones who can help me."

"You want to know what's on President Darousha's mind?"

"How'd you guess?" Ya'acov asked.

"Sir, we were the ones who programmed the bird."

"Very good. So where is the little beast?"

Avi glanced at the video display and then down at the map. "We're a few miles from Qatanah. Let's slew the camera around and take a look."

The video display swirled, then steadied on a crossroad slightly to the right of the UAV's course. The image grew rapidly as Avi zoomed the camera lens.

"That's a good image," Ya'acov remarked.

"The charge-coupled device does a nice job in low light. And here's our FLIR image."

The screen changed to a surrealistic painting of hot objects glowing against the dark, cooler background. Avi did a slow pan from west to east.

"Is that what you expected, Captain?" Avi asked.

"More than. Looks like about a hundred tanks down there now and a lot more coming from the north and east. And a bunch of armored personnel carriers are also rolling into position, along with some artillery pieces."

"So Darousha is planning something nasty for us," Avi said.

"It's not quite that easy. He's announced an armored exercise, so he's got an excuse for moving his tanks around."

"We would have found this anyway, without your mission. We fly over southern Syria on a regular basis, almost as regular as southern Lebanon."

"Yes, and he knows that. And it *could* be an exercise."

"Do you believe it is?" Avi asked.

"Not on your life. But there are some that will need convincing."

"Seems clear enough to me," Avi commented as he glanced at the map coordinates on the screen. "Big Bird is on station now. What do you want to do?"

"Let's see how much armor is down there."

Avi started counting rapidly as he swiftly panned the FLIR up the approach roads and finally across the camp area near Qatanah.

"I count around four hundred tanks, all T-72s it looks like," he said after a few minutes. "Add to that about two hundred and fifty BMP armored personnel carriers and a little over a hundred artillery. But I'm probably off a little with them moving around like that. We'll do it again after they get settled down."

"That's close enough," Ya'acov said, standing up. "Looks like a reinforced tank division—about what the Syrians said in their press release. Continue the mission as directed. When can I expect the tapes?"

"Oh, say three hours at the most. The courier will take them to Jerusalem. Sure you don't want to stay for the whole show?"

"Love to, but I've got a tight schedule. Thank you for your kind assistance."

◆

Ya'acov squinted against the glare of the sun low in the east as he pushed open the door. He had not slept well the night before, what little time he had for it after returning from Mount Hermon. He longed for a cup of coffee to jump-start his heart before the imagery session.

He always thought it odd how he didn't feel at home in this particular building—too close to the undercover end of things, he guessed. The armed guard was all business as he examined Ya'acov's ID card and compared the photograph to the original with an uncomfortable amount of care. Apparently satisfied, he checked Ya'acov's name off the list of those attending the live imagery session. He pressed a button, and Ya'acov pushed through the electric-lock door.

Dozens of officers milled around or conferred in small groups. They were there to see real-time pictures from a United States Air Force satellite, provided as part of the military cooperation between the two countries.

David Kruger waved at Ya'acov from near the center of the semicircular row of chairs. "Interesting report you turned in," David said as Ya'acov slid into the next seat.

"It was more interesting watching it happen. Four hundred tanks plus assorted nastiness converging on Qatanah ought to make us a little uncomfortable."

"They did announce an armored exercise."

"The colonel knows my position on that."

"Yes, and I'm inclined to agree with you. However, this is not something most of our leaders want to believe."

"Which could be dangerous for the nation."

"Perhaps. Let's see what happens. What do you make of the Phantom we lost yesterday?"

"A Phantom on a test flight surprised a terrorist weapons run north of Jericho. We splashed the cargo plane, but one of the terrorists shot our fighter down with a ground-to-air missile. The terrorists in the truck got away. Pilot got his knee busted up, but the backseater is okay."

"Who did it, and where are they?"

"Don't know. Could be the PRF, but it could as easily be the Popular Front for the Liberation of Palestine—General Command. The weapons are probably headed for Nablus, Ramallah, or Jericho." David's expression said he wanted more. "I think they went to Jericho."

"Okay. For your information, we're covering up the Phantom crash for now. We're reporting it as a training accident."

"Good. That'll make it easier on our snoops. Colonel?"

"Yes?" David replied warily.

"Northern Galilee is extremely thin in the armored department."

"You're speaking to the wrong officer. But the official position is that we have lots of threats besides Syria. And we don't want to break off our armored exercise in the Negev on mere rumor. We've invested a lot in that, and we don't want to waste it. And if something happens, the units in the south can get up north quickly."

"That won't do us any good if the Syrians are already in Galilee."

Ya'acov saw the signs. David had heard enough on the subject. Ya'acov glanced around the room. "Sure are a lot of heavies here this morning," he said without thinking.

"And one or two semi-heavies," David replied in a dry monotone.

"Sorry, sir. I didn't mean that the way it sounded."

"Your observation is correct. The Prime Minister is interested in the Syrian situation, even if he doesn't think they're going to do anything. If he's interested, you can bet the general officers will be too."

"Gentlemen," a short, balding lieutenant colonel announced, "we've established the downlink. We'll have the first live image in a few moments."

Ya'acov looked up at the huge video projection screen high on the wall in front of them. There were a few unconscious gasps as the first image flashed on the screen, tore up briefly, then steadied. The streets of Damascus crept slowly past as the satellite made its leisurely transit. The image jumped as a telephoto lens clicked into place.

"Look at that," Ya'acov whispered. "I never knew the detail was that good."

"It's every bit as good as the recon planes, and often a lot better."

The image shifted as the controller started panning the camera. The view drifted rapidly south following the major highway leading to Amman Jordan. When it reached Kissoue, it swept to the west until it came to Qatanah.

"There they are," Ya'acov said. "Looks like they're moving out again."

The controller held the camera on Qatanah as the Russian-made tanks rolled through the town and south down the road leading to Beit Jinn. At last the rapid panning stopped, with the view centered south of the town. The early arrivals were already in their assigned positions.

"Not quite as orderly as I would have expected," David commented absentmindedly. "And I don't see any camouflage nets yet. But these aren't exactly crack units either. So is it an armored exercise or not?"

"Perhaps it's a cultural exchange, Colonel."

"This is not a laughing matter."

"With all due respect, Colonel, the authorities are the ones not taking this seriously."

David looked at his young officer for an uncomfortable amount of time. Finally he turned back to the screen. "I'm afraid I have to agree with you."

19

HIDING THE EVIDENCE

Moshe glanced at the gold lettering on the door, then went in. Yitzhak Yadin looked momentarily startled, then quickly finished his phone conversation and hung up. "Don't you ever knock?" he asked.

"Usually not," Moshe confessed. "It's not something that occurs to me. What progress have you made on the veil?"

Yitzhak looked down at the top of his immaculately organized desktop. "I was about to call you. I'm afraid I have some bad news. We had a fire in the storeroom. The veil's been destroyed."

"What? How could that happen?"

"We're not sure. It started early this morning—I just got back from there. Apparently a bottle of isopropyl alcohol fell off a shelf and broke. Something set it off. The firemen are still checking."

"Anyone hurt?"

"No," Yitzhak replied quickly. "No one was there at the time. Jon worked until 2 in the morning. The fire started sometime after he locked up."

Moshe shook his head as he tried to control his growing anger. "This loss can't be measured, Yitzhak. I *trusted* you with the veil."

"It's not my fault. The storeroom was not the ideal laboratory, but it was all I had that was large enough."

"I do my job—I expect you to do yours."

"And I didn't?"

"You said it."

Yitzhak stood suddenly, placing his balled fists on the desktop. "This is *my* office! I'll thank you to get out of it!"

"I'm on my way."

"Wait," Yitzhak said as Moshe reached the door. "There's something else—something Jon discovered before he quit last night. The veil was not torn. On closer examination, he found the material was simply rotted."

"Rotted? How do you explain that? I saw the veil myself. The material was in very good condition."

"The portion you saw was. But both sections were rotted in the middle. We suspect some water collected in the bottom of the boxes—perhaps condensation, who knows. Anyhow, that's what we found."

"You're sure about this?"

"Absolutely. I saw the damage myself."

"You said it was torn."

Yitzhak scowled at his visitor. "We all make mistakes, don't we?"

"I'll say."

Yitzhak looked down at his neat desk. "You really must excuse me. I have a lot of work to do."

Moshe choked back what he wanted to say and left.

◆

Michael watched as Moshe trudged across the black and white tiles. "What's happened?" he asked.

"Where are Anne and Mars? I only want to tell this once."

"They're down in the *geniza*. And we have a guest."

"Great. So who is it?"

"Zuba Rosenberg."

Moshe's dark scowl lightened a little. "How is the old goat?"

"Interesting, as always."

Moshe paused, looking down at the ground, the glimmer of a smile fading. "He's family as far as I'm concerned. Let's go on down."

◆

Zuba turned around at the sound of Moshe's footsteps as he entered the *geniza* with Michael.

"Moshe, my friend, how are you? As if I had to ask. Such a find! I am so happy for you."

"It is rather nice," Moshe said with a forced smile.

"Nice? You find all this and it's only nice? I should have nice like this. All this and the Temple veil as well—torn in two like the Bible says. Anne and Mars were telling me about it when you came in."

Moshe's smile evaporated.

"What's wrong?" Anne asked.

"We've had a setback."

"What is it?" Anne persisted.

"There was a fire last night at the Museum. The veil was destroyed."

"No!" Zuba cried out. "Not that!"

"Unfortunately. And there's more. Yitzhak told me the veil panels were not torn—he said it was only rot."

Zuba pursed his lips, his eyes flashing. "There's rot here all right, but it's not in the veil," he said evenly.

Moshe avoided his indignant gaze.

"What do you mean?" Mars asked.

"Moshe knows what I mean. I'm familiar with Dr. Yitzhak Yadin. The destruction of the veil was no accident. I believe he did it on purpose."

"But why?" Mars asked, puzzled.

"Because it confirms the biblical story. The New Testament says that on the day Jesus died, the Temple veil was torn in two from top to bottom—demonstrating that the way to God is now wide-open because of Jesus. I suspect that Yadin destroyed the veil, then lied about what he had found."

"That's preposterous," Mars blustered. "Who cares about what the Bible says anyway?"

"Mars, please," Anne said, concern filling her eyes.

Mars set his jaw, keeping silent with obvious difficulty.

"I think Zuba is right," Moshe said in a small voice.

Anne looked at him in surprise. She looked into his dark brown eyes trying to fathom the deep feelings she sensed, feelings that were kindred to her own disturbing thoughts. Was the same thing pursuing them both? Was it a struggle between the truth and those who oppose the truth? If the Bible was right about the torn veil, and she now knew that it was, then what about the central person in the New Testament? She shivered. She could not think of this now.

◆

A brief knock sounded on the door. Ya'acov Isaacson looked up from his report, thought briefly about removing his feet from his desk, then decided not to. "Come in," he said.

Ari Jacovy came in quickly and closed the door. "Ah, the privileges of rank," he said as he eased into a chair.

"Well, *Lieutenant* Jacovy, what brings you my way? Someone throw something nasty in your sandbox?"

"My, aren't we in a good mood. No, I was only curious about what the Syrians are up to. The boss has me assigned to other things right now, and I needed a break before I die of boredom."

"Of course, what I'm doing is technically none of your business, going by Intelligence rules."

"Oh, I know that. But you're never strict about rules."

"Hmm. Flattery will get you nowhere. But it so happens I need to bounce something off someone. So I guess this is your lucky day."

"I'm all ears."

Ya'acov threw the report on his desk and crossed his arms over his chest. His smile of friendly banter faded as he thought about the cold facts, trying to decide if they were a threat to his country. "You've heard about the armored exercises the Syrians are having?"

"Yes. Announced beforehand and being carried out as they have in the past. Nothing unusual."

"That's what the senior officers are saying," Ya'acov agreed. "Is that what you think?"

"I don't know enough to say."

"Right. You don't have a need to know. For your information, the Syrians are conducting armored exercises. A reinforced tank division converged on Qatanah. The next day they traveled to Beit Jinn where they are now. They aren't using camouflage netting, and their formations are ill conceived. Each day they break into two groups and hold exercises for most of the day and then return to Beit Jinn. The exercises are very poorly done—almost like they don't matter."

"The Syrians don't have the best army in the world."

"That what our senior officers keep saying, but it's a dangerous assumption. Man for man, we have the best military machine in this part of the world, but the Syrians still have a formidable army. If nothing else, they sure have the numbers."

"So what are they planning?"

"They're planning to invade us through Golan."

Ari leaned back in his chair and looked up at the ceiling. "What about all our defenses?"

"You know history as well as I do. If they're really determined, they can get through. They probably know about most of our traps and where the artillery is. And now would be a particularly good time for them to try, since most of our armor is in the Negev for desert warfare exercises. As for the rest of the armor, we do have other enemies besides Syria. Basically, our senior officers won't even consider the possibility of invasion."

"That's a pretty dark picture you're painting."

"But I think it's right."

Ari lowered his eyes until he met Ya'acov's unwavering gaze. "You could very well be," he said at last.

◆

"You called for me?" Abdul Suleiman asked as he entered the room.

"I did," Avraham confirmed. "I have a plan. I want you to take the Eldan truck and convert it into a bomb on wheels. Rig it with a timer, but make it so we can substitute radio control if I want to."

Abdul's face remained passive. He wanted to know what Avraham meant to do, but he knew better than to ask. "I will get on it right away."

"See that you do.

◆

Lieutenant Aziz Massour looked straight up from the tank commander's cupola of his T-72 tank as if he could see the satellite that was passing overhead. The sun was low in the west, allowing only a little more
than an hour's daylight.

Not an engine was turning as each tank crew in the massive
encampment monitored the tactical radio net. The special work details
were huddling under camouflage nets waiting for the same thing the
tankers were. When the command came, although expected, it was still
a surprise.

"Scimitar," sounded loudly in his earphones.

The driver hit the starter before Aziz could give the command. The
lieutenant made a note to take this breach of discipline up with the man,
but what mattered now was to stay with the company and get on the
road. There could be no delays.

The two tank platoons in front moved out, a fine cloud of dust fanning out behind them. Aziz barked the order, and his driver started out.
Satisfied, Aziz turned around and was relieved to see the other tanks in
his platoon following.

Outside Beit Jinn, the armored column turned southeast onto a
road that was little more than a path. This was the part of the plan that
scared Aziz. He was sure the Israelis were unaware of the unpaved
road, but all this would be for nothing if one of the tanks threw a track
on the rough terrain. If that happened, the cat would be stuck with its
paw in the bird cage when the next satellite flew over. He marveled at
the excellent job his driver was doing despite the dust cloud that all but
made the tank in front of them invisible.

The special work details were out even before the last tank had
pulled out. They began frantically assembling tank mockups out of prefabricated sheet metal, complete with propane burners to simulate the
heat from the engines. Close up they were obviously fake, but from
overhead they would be quite convincing.

◆

Aziz smiled as they topped the ridge. Below them was the main highway leading from Damascus to Quneitra. The lead tanks slowed, then
pulled carefully off the narrow road and into the positions that had

been prepared when the secret road had been cut. The tank column was several hundred feet from the Damascus Highway, sheltered in the narrow valley between two ridges. As soon as each tank stopped, the entire crew was out setting up the camouflage nets.

Aziz watched critically as his driver pulled the ponderous T-72 into their narrow space. The tank ground to a stop, lurching on its suspension. The driver shut down the diesel immediately. Aziz climbed out of the turret, followed by the rest of the crew. Quickly they began setting up their camouflage net. As if on cue, the sun kissed the hills to the west. The rest of the column would park in the gathering twilight.

◆

Ya'acov thought of heading for his quarters without waiting for the latest imagery report. It had been a long day, and there wasn't really anything else for him to do. But he had the nagging feeling that something would happen the moment he left. His door opened unexpectedly, and Colonel Kruger relieved him of his decision.

"You're here late, Colonel," Ya'acov said.

"I was about to say the same thing."

"I thought I'd look at the next imagery report before I head out."

David was normally hard to read, a form of self-control he cultivated very carefully. But now he looked troubled. "That's why *I'm* still here," he admitted.

Ya'acov arched his eyebrows in surprise. "Well, sir, we should both know in a few minutes."

◆

It was almost exactly two minutes later that a short rap sounded.

"Come in," Ya'acov replied.

A sergeant looked in. "I have your imagery report, Captain," he said. He laid the folder on Ya'acov's desk and extended the clipboard. Ya'acov signed for the report and waited for the sergeant to leave. He then eagerly broke the seal and pulled out two typewritten pages and a single photograph.

"Would you like to see it, sir?" Ya'acov asked.

"No," David replied, waving it away. "This is your project."

Ya'acov quickly scanned the pages, lingering on the photograph. He looked up with a sheepish shrug. "We needn't have waited. No change from the pass made just before sundown. They're all bedded down for the night. You can even see which tanks are running their engines to recharge batteries."

David nodded. "So now we can both call it a day."

"I guess so, sir," Ya'acov agreed.

20

THE SEARCH

"What's supposed to be in this one?" Anne asked as she pried the lid off the wooden box.

"According to Moshe's list, knives."

"Knives?"

"I asked him about that. They were used to slit the throats of the sacrificial animals or to cut the sacrifices up."

"How gruesome."

"Yeah. Apparently the Temple was a regular slaughterhouse."

Anne looked inside cautiously. She reached in and pulled out a long knife with a wide blade. She turned it from side to side. "The blade is discolored," she said. "Do you suppose . . ."

"Blood?" Mars asked. "Could be. I suppose we could get the Museum to check."

Moshe walked into the *geniza* as Anne was replacing the knife. "I'm not sure I'll ever send anything to the Museum again," he grumbled.

"As careless as they were, I don't think I would either," Mars said, taking up the offense.

"It wasn't carelessness," Moshe said. "At least I don't think it was."

"So you're siding with Zuba," Anne said. "Yitzhak destroyed the veil because it supports the New Testament story."

"You're close."

"What do you mean close?" Mars asked, a puzzled expression on his face. "Either Yitzhak did it on purpose or he didn't."

"He didn't," Moshe replied.

"You're saying it was an accident? I don't understand. You said he did it on purpose."

Moshe almost smiled. "You didn't hear me. Or you heard what you wanted to hear. I said it wasn't carelessness. I didn't say he destroyed the veil on purpose."

Anne laughed suddenly.

"What's so funny?" Mars demanded.

"Your universities really should emphasize English more," Moshe observed.

"I'm afraid I have to agree with you," Anne said.

"Will someone *please* explain what's going on?" Mars pleaded.

"Should we?" Moshe asked.

"He won't let us have a moment's peace until we do," Anne replied. "I believe you are suggesting the veil has not been destroyed."

"There you have it, as the British would say."

Mars looked from one to the other. "I *still* don't understand."

"Yitzhak, for all his crustiness, reveres ancient artifacts as much as we do. He is, after all, a museum curator, although he much prefers his official title—Director of Antiquities. Impressive, is it not? It would go too much against the grain for him to actually destroy the veil. Hiding it and *saying* it was destroyed has the same effect."

"Are you sure?" Mars asked.

"Fairly."

"Why don't we go get it?"

"It's not that simple, unfortunately. I have no idea where Yitzhak hid it. And if we start sniffing around, he probably *will* destroy it, ancient artifact or not."

"So what do we do?" Anne asked.

"I'm working on it," Moshe replied after a short pause. "I think I know where the weak link is, but . . ."

"But what?" Anne asked, noticing Moshe's puzzled expression.

"Something Zuba said as I was walking him to his car. We've all seen the veil. How was something that heavy torn? How could it happen?"

"Maybe the priests did it?" Mars suggested.

"Remember the original report said torn, not cut. The difficulty of tearing it aside, why would priests do something that would confirm the New Testament story?"

Mars looked puzzled for a moment, but this quickly turned to irritation.

Anne looked at Moshe, wondering at the quiet introspection of her friend and colleague.

◆

Moshe looked around quickly as he entered Dan Adov's *Jerusalem Post* office. "It's been a long time since I've seen your office. Where's your typewriter?"

"I told you—we don't use them anymore. That terminal on my desk is hooked into our mainframe. I write all my stories on it. Saves a lot of time."

"If you say so," Moshe grumbled as he looked suspiciously at the green screen and the detached keyboard.

"But I'm sure you didn't drop by to see my terminal."

Moshe sat down in a side chair in front of Dan's desk. He smiled at the clutter that was so similar to his own office. But the smile soon faded as he remembered why he had come. "No. I need your help in getting something back that belongs to me."

Dan looked puzzled for a few moments before his expression cleared. "Oh," he said.

"What's this 'oh'? I didn't even tell you what it was."

"You don't have to. You've only lost one thing recently, as far as I know. So the veil wasn't destroyed after all."

"That's what I suspect. I think Yitzhak's hidden it, and I want to get it back before he *does* destroy it."

"And how may this humble reporter help you? And what's in it for me?"

"You're about as humble as Herod the Great. As usual, you get the story. And it should be quite juicy, stacked on top of everything that's happened."

"You've got a point there. I'll assume your suspicions are correct. So how can I help?"

Moshe extended a piece of paper with a number on it. "Call Yitzhak right now. You got this tip that the veil wasn't destroyed. Ask for his comments."

"Just like that? You want me to ask the fox if he ate the chickens?"

"Trust me."

Dan looked doubtful but reached for his phone. He punched the number and waited while it rang. A woman's voice answered. "This is Dan Adov with the *Jerusalem Post*. May I speak with Dr. Yadin? Yes, I'll hold."

Dan covered the mouthpiece. "He's very busy today."

"I'm sure," Moshe grumbled.

Dan motioned Moshe to be quiet. "Dr. Yadin, this is Dan Adov with the *Jerusalem Post*. One of my sources has told me that the Temple veil was not destroyed—that it's been hidden. Could I have your comment? Our readers will want to know what the Director of Antiquities has to say about this."

Dan listened to the answer, his head nodding unconsciously as each point was made. "Oh, I assure you I believe my source to be quite reliable. The story will be in the morning edition."

The phone clicked dead suddenly. Dan replaced the handset. "*That* certainly struck a nerve. He said the report was preposterous. The veil was destroyed. He asked if I was going to print an obviously false story."

"You gave him the right answer on that," Moshe said with a smile.

"Except we aren't printing any story."

"Don't be too sure. Meet me here at 7 o'clock, and I'll give you part two of your story."

◆

Moshe and Dan approached a side entrance to the Israel Museum under the harsh security lighting. Moshe produced a key and opened the door. The two men went inside. Immediately a small speaker started squawking.

"Excuse me," Moshe said as he ducked around a corner. Dan could hear a series of electronic beeps. The speaker fell silent.

"Had to turn off the alarm system."

"I won't ask how you knew how to do that," Dan said.

"Thank you. Now all we have to do is wait for the good Dr. Yadin."

Moshe and Dan stationed themselves in a side hallway off the corridor leading to the parking lot where Yitzhak had his reserved space. A little after midnight a key rattled in the lock. Moshe and Dan ducked quickly into an alcove. The door opened. They heard rapid footsteps, then a series of beeps as the alarm was reset. Moments later Yitzhak swept past, muttering about the guards who hadn't armed the security system properly. They waited until the director's footsteps faded, then hurried into the corridor.

"He's taken a side hallway," Dan said in a whisper. "Come on or we'll lose him."

They rushed to the first intersection and looked around the corner. Yitzhak was nowhere in sight. At the next intersection they heard faint sounds coming from the right. They tried to be as quiet as possible, stopping often to listen. The elusive footsteps were always just a short ways ahead. They passed gallery after gallery, each silent and sinister in the partial lighting. Then the sounds stopped.

"He's there," Moshe said.

"Where?"

"I don't know, but we'd better find him in a hurry."

They stopped at the next intersection. Moshe looked down one corridor and Dan the other. The archaeologist began to doubt the wisdom of trapping Yitzhak.

"This is no good," Dan said. "This place is a maze. We'll never find him in time."

Moshe looked at a glass case protecting a display of first-century coins. He took off a shoe and threw it through the glass. Instantly an alarm started clanging.

"You go that way," Moshe commanded as he picked up his shoe.

Dan hurried down the indicated corridor as Moshe hobbled back to the nearest side passage. Moshe whirled about as he heard a sound off to his left. A dark figure bolted out into the unlit passageway. The man hesitated, then ran for the opposite end of the hall.

"Over here, Dan!" Moshe shouted as he hurried toward the door the man had exited. Moshe walked in as Dan arrived.

"What about Yitzhak?"

"This is what I came for," Moshe said. There on the floor of the vacant gallery was the veil and something else—a can of kerosene with the lid off. Moshe bent down and put the cap back on. "Looks like we got here barely in time."

A clatter echoed in the corridor.

"Ready to talk to the security people?"

"A lot more than Yitzhak will be." Moshe smiled as the guard entered with his gun drawn.

◆

The public reaction to Dan Adov's story surprised even him. Yitzhak Yadin had resigned immediately, which had relieved the Museum's directors of any further accusations. But what caught the public's attention more than anything else was the veil—even more than it had when first discovered. And the one the media always wanted to interview was Anne.

"If you want, I'll tell him you're too tired," Mars whispered to Anne.

She looked up at him from the couch. At first she was tempted to agree. It had been a hard day at the site, and the hostel had been filled with reporters when they returned.

"No, thank you," Anne said with a weak smile. "This looks like the last one."

"Unless some more bozos come in."

"Let's hope not," she said as she got up.

The reporter told her his name, but it didn't register. The cameraman flipped on his light, almost blinding Anne.

"How do you feel now that the veil has been recovered?" the reporter asked, sticking the mike in her face.

Anne's head spun as she fought back exhaustion. "A very great tragedy was avoided. It would have been a terrible loss to the world if the veil had been destroyed."

"Christians are claiming that the veil's tear proves that the Bible is right, that it proves Jesus Christ was God's Son. What do you say about that?"

"They are welcome to their opinions, of course," Anne answered cautiously. "However, all we really know about the veil is that it hung in Herod's Temple. It is in remarkable shape for so ancient an artifact. And both panels are in two pieces for some reason."

"And you have no opinion on how this happened?"

"We will continue to investigate. But as of now, we don't know how it happened."

"The Jews are claiming that the tear in the veil is a hoax, that it was done on purpose to give credence to what they call the lies in the New Testament."

"It would be just as unscientific to comment on that as it would be to comment on the Christian claims."

"One further question—it's no secret that Orthodox Jews want to tear down the Dome of the Rock and rebuild the Temple. The Arab world is saying, rather forcefully, that the veil itself is a hoax, that it was fabricated as a clarion call to destroy the Dome of the Rock. Do you think there's any truth in this?"

Anne gave the reporter her best withering stare. Mars almost laughed as he saw the man's shocked expression.

"That's absurd!" she snapped.

The reporter regained his composure and ended the interview. The bright light clicked off. The cameraman lifted the camera off his shoulder.

"Who did you say you were with?" Anne asked, still in a daze.

"CNN," the man answered with a wry smile. "That little segment is going to be seen all around the world."

Anne watched the reporter as he followed his cameraman out of the hostel. At the door they passed a familiar bulky shape that turned out to be Zuba Rosenberg. She smiled as he made his ponderous way over.

"May I join you?" he asked as Mars returned.

Anne waved toward three easy chairs in a corner. "Please do. I'm glad to see a friendly face." She glanced at Mars. "In addition to Mars, of course."

Zuba waited for them to sit, then eased into the remaining chair with audible relief. "It has been a long day."

"It has," Anne agreed, "and I'm glad it's almost over. Are you leading a tour?"

He shook his head. "I'm between right now. I pick up a new group at Ben Gurion tomorrow." The genuine smile took them both in, but Anne saw the tension that overlaid it. "I wanted to talk with you back when we had that scare about the veil being destroyed, only I didn't have the chance."

"Why?" Mars asked suspiciously.

"I saw the look in Anne's eyes. Have you two considered that if the Bible is right about the Temple veil, it makes sense that it's right about Jesus Christ?"

"That's preposterous!" Mars snapped.

"Why?" Zuba asked, locking eyes with him. "If the Bible is right on such a small detail, why wouldn't it be right about more important things—actually the *most* important thing?"

Mars looked down. "Well, maybe they were careful about the details so they could sell the supernatural stuff."

"Maybe? We are talking science, Mars. I say we are dealing with a truthful book, and what it says is vitally important. It's a matter of life and death." He turned toward Anne. "I know this speaks to you. Why not search it out for yourself? Read the Bible and see if these things are so."

"Leave her alone!" Mars said, his voice rising.

"Mars, please." She saw the look of concern in Zuba's eyes. "Zuba, I appreciate what you are trying to do. But I need time to sort this out."

"Of course," he said as he stood. "Shalom. I will pray for you both."

Anne watched as he left the hostel.

◆

Less than an hour later the reporter's boast became reality as the interview was seen everywhere CNN was carried.

Avraham and his men watched the news report. He watched Anne as she talked about the veil. The unfairness of it all came down on the PRF chief. The Dome of the Rock had been nearly blown up, followed by an attack on the Jews' precious Yad Vashem. But all the world cared about was this stupid veil.

Avraham studied Anne's close-up. He wanted to remember this face.

21

HOSTAGE!

Outwardly, Majid Jaha looked as impassive as he always did. He looked under the rear bumper of the truck. The axle was almost resting on the rubber overload bumpers, and the tires were much flatter than normal. His expression did not change, but he continued to stare at the axle.

"Have you got the plan memorized?" Abdul asked once again.

Majid nodded.

"Tell me."

The man recited his task in his usual monotone. He was to drive the truck to Hadassah Hospital on Mount Scopus and park it at the delivery dock. There he would arm it, walk to the Central Bus Station, and catch a bus back to Jericho.

"Once you start the timer, how long do you have?" Abdul asked.

"Five minutes."

"Five minutes," Abdul agreed. "Seems short, but you'll have plenty of time to get away. Now remember—don't run. You're only walking down to East Jerusalem. There's nothing to connect you with the bomb. Don't worry when it goes off. It's a surprise to you. You don't know anything about it. Keep walking toward the bus station. Understand?"

"Yes."

Abdul glanced toward Avraham. There was a barely perceptible nod.

"Very good," Abdul said with a sigh. He didn't know if he was happy with this mission or not. But it was not his job to be happy about it.

Majid climbed into the cab. The engine started at once. Majid backed the truck out carefully, then drove slowly away. Abdul watched until he was out of sight.

◆

Majid almost smiled as he turned northward at the Mount of Olives. It was, indeed, going as smoothly as Abdul had said it would. He made each turn with calm assurance as he made his serpentine way up the side of Mount Scopus. He downshifted smoothly and made a cautious right turn onto Aharon Katzir. Up ahead was the British Military Cemetery, and beyond that was the towering structure of Hadassah Hospital. Almost there.

Majid started his left turn just beyond the cemetery. Out of the corner of his eye he saw a large pothole near the center of the intersection. He broadened the turn to try to clear it, then cranked the wheel hard to avoid the right curb. The springs groaned ominously as the load shifted to the right. The left rear tire fell into the hole. The sharp edge ruptured the sidewall, causing it to blow with a report like a rifle shot.

Majid pushed in the clutch and let the truck bump and wobble to a stop. He let a rare curse escape his lips as he looked through the windshield at the hospital not more than a hundred yards away. Close, but not close enough. He thought about arming the bomb and walking away. While this would cause an explosion, it would not accomplish the mission. But driving the truck on the flat was about the least stealthy thing he could do.

Gritting his teeth, he let out the clutch and promptly stalled the engine. He started it again and gave it more throttle. The truck lurched off, the ruined tire making a horrible flopping noise as the wheel rim scraped along the pavement, sending sparks flying. Majid tried to ignore the jarring ride as he concentrated on his slowly approaching destination. Each lurch reminded him of the hundreds of pounds of high explosives sitting in the back, all wired to the timer in the glove compartment. The distance decreased with agonizing slowness—from one hundred yards to seventy-five and down to fifty, without a soldier or policeman in sight. No one cared, it seemed, that the hospital's destruction was at hand.

He crept past the front of the hospital and beside a wing that seemed to go on forever. He looked out the side as the hospital's windows went by one by one. He pushed in the clutch when he arrived at the center of the wing. He set the emergency brake and switched off the engine, pocketing the keys. With a calmness he did not think possible, he opened the glove compartment. There was the timer, the small hand set at exactly five minutes. He pressed the big red button, and the second hand began its deadly countdown. Majid got out of the truck and glanced right and left. Not a soul. A tentative smile came to his lips as he started walking toward the Central Bus Station. The bomb would, he knew, level that wing of the hospital when it went off.

◆

Ari Jacovy tried to retain a professional sense of detachment as he drove up the slopes of Mount Scopus. He had been ordered to question the Phantom pilot now that the doctors at Hadassah had given their permission. The aviator had already been debriefed by the IAF, so it wasn't likely there was anything new for Intelligence. But orders were orders.

Ari turned onto Aharon Katzir. A sole pedestrian was walking toward him facing the traffic. The man appeared startled as the officer drove past. Ari glanced in the rearview mirror. The man stared at the retreating car for a few moments, then turned and continued his journey.

Ari turned left and followed the drive around to the back of Hadassah Hospital. Up ahead he saw a beat-up truck parked in the road. A quick glance revealed the cause: flat tire. He looked inside as he drove past. There was no one around. Apparently the driver was off getting help. Judging from the general condition of the truck, the tires were undoubtedly in bad shape also.

A frown crossed Ari's face. He slowed to a stop and looked back. After a brief hesitation, he put his car in reverse and backed up. He got out and looked the truck over. He noticed that the front tires looked almost new, in stark contrast to the devastated condition of the body.

Ari walked around to the back and tried the door. It was locked, which was not surprising. He returned to the cab. The driver's door opened easily. He climbed up into the cab and looked back. The cab was cut off from the back by a steel panel. He placed his hands on the steering wheel as he thought about going around to the back and forcing the rear door. Ari looked at the glove compartment. He reached over and turned the knob. The door opened downward. Ari scooted over a little in the seat and looked in. He almost lost control of himself when he saw the timer. The second hand was sweeping toward zero—only seconds away. Knowing he had no time for the proper way to do it, he grabbed the timer and pulled it out. A pair of wires dangled from the case. Ari wrapped the loose wires around his right hand and pulled hard. A muted click sounded inside the timer as the second hand hit zero. Ari staggered out of the truck and promptly threw up.

◆

Majid knew there would be trouble when he got back to Jericho. Although he had no watch, he knew at least five minutes had gone by before he got to the bus station. And yet there was no explosion. There was no way he could have missed it. What had gone wrong?

He bought his ticket and brooded as he waited for his bus. All the way back to Jericho he wondered what he would say to Abdul—or worse yet, to Avraham. Abdul, at least, could be reasoned with. But what bothered Majid most was that he would have to answer their questions. And talking was something Majid hated to do.

◆

Ya'acov swung his feet off his desk as Ari entered his office. His friend was very pale, and there were telltale spots on his shirt. Ya'acov waved him to a chair. "So what are the PRF up to now?" he asked.

"Did you hear?"

"Abandoned truck parked at Hadassah with enough explosives to level the place. Where have I heard something like that before?"

"Looks like it. And probably tied into that Syrian MU-2 we splashed."

Ya'acov only nodded.

"So, what do the heavies make of it?" Ari asked.

Ya'acov's smile was strained. "You are free to ask them, Lieutenant Jacovy."

"Oh no, sir. You're senior."

"Thank you. It so happens, I know. The colonel and I had a long talk about it after your report. He's surprisingly calm, but he's about the only senior officer who is. The PM, I was told, went through the roof and hasn't come down yet. There are some ugly rumors floating around."

"Is this 'get tough on terrorists' or something else?"

"Don't know exactly. The PM wants the PRF nailed, that's for sure. And his definite preference is dead. But some of the heavies are beginning to talk about Syria."

"Seriously?"

"Not enough to cancel our armored exercises in the Negev. They keep harping on the point that we can send tanks north in a matter of hours—and the fact that we have other countries to be concerned about. But at least they're talking about it."

Ari glanced at the map behind Ya'acov's desk. "Okay, so the Syrian threat's on the back burner. If the PM tells us to get the PRF, where do we look?"

"Before we shot the Mooney down I wouldn't have had a clue. Assuming the weapons were for them, they're probably in Ramallah, Nablus, or Jericho."

"Sounds logical. So which one is it?"

Ya'acov glanced back at his map. His eyes went immediately to Jerusalem, then traced the short distance to the Jordan River. "Jericho," he said.

◆

Majid pushed the door open and walked in. He could see nothing until his eyes adjusted from the brilliant sunlight to the gloom inside, gloom that mirrored how he felt.

"What happened?" Abdul asked before Avraham could speak. He and Avraham already knew of the failure from contacts in Jerusalem. What they didn't know was why.

"I do not know," the big man answered, truly as puzzled as they were.

"What did you do?"

"I did as you said. I drove to Hadassah. I set the timer. I walked to the terminal and came back here."

"Then why didn't it go off?" Avraham thundered.

"I do not know."

"It didn't go off because you didn't do it right!"

Majid hung his head.

"Did you hear me?" Avraham demanded.

"Yes."

"Either you didn't do it right or the detonator failed." Avraham looked around at Abdul, his eyes glowing.

"There was nothing wrong with the bomb. Someone found it and disarmed it."

"In five minutes?"

"There's no other explanation. I personally checked the bomb. It was working when it left here, and Majid is most reliable. Someone found it."

Majid glanced toward Abdul in appreciation.

"This is too much!" Avraham shouted. "I am surrounded by incompetents! All of you!"

He went into his private room and slammed the door.

Abdul sighed in relief. But he knew *Avraham's* timer had been turned on. And when it went off, they would have to do something. Abdul ran a hand through his hair as he wondered what it would be.

◆

Abdul glanced at his wristwatch. It was a little after 2 o'clock in the morning. He opened the door and called to Mustapha. A brief groan came from the cot where the man was sleeping.

"Avraham wants to see us," Abdul added.

Mustapha rolled out of bed. Still groggy with sleep, he pulled on his pants while Abdul waited impatiently.

"Come on. He wants to see us now, not in an hour."

Mustapha skipped his shirt and shoes and followed Abdul to Avraham's room. Abdul knocked.

"Come in," was the irritated reply.

They entered and at Avraham's invitation sat in the offered chairs. Avraham's large head turned slowly toward Abdul.

"How would you evaluate our operations?" he asked with deceptive calmness.

Abdul took a deep breath. He knew he was on thin ice. "Much of what you want to achieve has been done."

"Oh? Please explain."

"I have *never* seen the Jews as stirred up as they are right now, and the bombing attempt on Hadassah will make it even hotter, even though it failed. They know what *almost* happened. In this state they could very well do something rash, and that would bring the whole Arab world crashing in on them.

"On the other side, all Muslims are enraged because of what they think are Jewish plots to desecrate holy sites, especially the Dome of the Rock. And the Arab countries are showing surprising solidarity. It looks like Syria could be ready to act. If there is a war, it is possible we could annihilate the Jews and take *all* of Palestine. We are, it seems to me, poised on the brink of achieving your plans."

Avraham rocked back and forth in his chair as he thought about what Abdul had said.

"Perhaps," he said, deep in thought. "But maybe we need a little something extra—something to push things over the edge."

"What do you have in mind?" Abdul asked cautiously.

"A kidnapping."

"Who?"

"The woman on the archaeological dig."

"Anne McAdams?" Abdul asked.

"You know her name, I see. With all the exposure she's had on television lately, the public will remember her, too. The perfect victim."

Avraham looked intently at Abdul.

"Yes, I believe she is," Abdul said finally.

◆

Abdul tried to convince himself he did not look conspicuous in his western-style clothing. He checked the car carefully to make sure it did not have an alarm system. He looked around quickly, then opened the door and slid in behind the wheel. One swift blow from the hammer broke the steering lock. Abdul ducked his head under the dashboard. A few moments later the starter engaged, and the engine roared to life. Abdul checked traffic carefully, then drove to the Central Bus Station, where Avraham and Mustapha were waiting, looking reasonably western in their Israeli trousers and shirts.

Avraham climbed into the front seat, while Mustapha threw the beat-up suitcase in the back and climbed in after it. He opened it carefully and removed two Uzis and placed them in the front seat between Abdul and Avraham. He pulled a third one out for himself. He rotated the submachine gun in his hand, admiring its simple deadliness.

"Put it down," Abdul ordered, watching him in the rearview mirror.

Mustapha glared at Abdul but set the gun down on the seat. Abdul drove slowly past the Old City walls as if they were on a sight-seeing trip. He rounded the northwest corner, drove past the New Gate, and turned left toward David's Tower. He turned left again at Jaffa Gate, and they were inside the Old City and heading toward the Wailing Wall.

"There it is," Avraham said, recognizing the site from the television reports. "I only see two guards. The woman must be down in the secret room."

Mustapha leaned over the front seat and looked out in horror. "What'll we do about the guards?"

"Shut up, you old woman," Avraham thundered.

Abdul pulled up behind a battered, blue Volkswagen bus and looked back at Mustapha. "As far as the guards know, we're only a group of reporters. When we get out, put your gun in the front seat and get behind the wheel. Be careful of the wires under the dash."

Abdul turned to Avraham. "Are you ready?"

Avraham nodded.

Avraham pushed his Uzi toward Abdul. "Carry this for me," he said. He wiped his sweaty palms on his pants.

◆

Moshe pointed to the appropriate box near the center of the *geniza*.

"What's in this one?" Mars asked as he started working on the lid.

"Flesh hooks," Moshe answered.

"What?"

"Flesh hooks. Used in the Temple sacrifices."

"How nice."

"You asked."

Mars shot a quick glance at Anne, who was smiling. "What's so funny?" he inquired, trying unsuccessfully to keep a straight face.

"You are."

"I fail to see the humor."

Moshe held up a finger. "Now, children, play nice."

"Hmm," Mars grumbled.

"That's better," Moshe said, rubbing his hands in satisfaction. "My reputation as a *yenta* will suffer if you two get in a fight."

"*Yenta*?" Anne asked. "I thought *yentas* were female."

"What's a *yenta*?" Mars asked.

Moshe and Anne looked at him in surprise.

"A *yenta* is a matchmaker," Anne explained.

Mars's complexion grew noticeably pink.

Moshe clasped his hands and looked up. "A match made in heaven. True? Of course true."

Michael stood framed in the door to the *geniza*. "If I could interrupt with some business . . . Did you bring the Polaroid camera down here?"

Moshe thought for a moment. "No. It's still up in the bus."

"Thanks," Michael said and promptly disappeared.

◆

Avraham opened the door and got out. Abdul watched as he walked up the street past the Volkswagen bus. Abdul looked over at the guards. Good. They were just watching the "reporter" approach. Abdul quietly opened his door a little. Right on cue, Avraham clutched his chest and fell to the ground. The guards hesitated, then began moving toward the "victim."

Abdul sprang silently from the car and moved swiftly past the left side of the bus, staying low to keep the guards from seeing him. He paused at the front of the bus and looked cautiously around. Both guards were bending over Avraham. Abdul rushed forward almost soundlessly. One man heard something and started to look around. Abdul brought his Uzi down in a violent chopping motion, crushing the man's temple and killing him instantly. Abdul repeated the stroke on the second guard, killing him just as quickly. Neither man made a sound.

Abdul retrieved the other Uzi from his waistband and handed it to Avraham. Without a word they started toward the stairs leading to the *geniza*. While they were still fifty feet away, a head suddenly appeared in the opening. Avraham cursed.

Michael's head jerked around to locate the sound. He watched in horror as Avraham's Uzi came up.

"Don't fire," Abdul whispered urgently.

Michael turned and dashed down the stairs like a rabbit fleeing back into his hole.

"Come on," Abdul urged. "This is the only way out of there." They raced down the ancient stone steps.

◆

"Terrorists!" Michael screamed as he ran through the door. "They're coming down here! They've got guns!"

Moshe hesitated only a moment. He glanced around at Anne and Mars. "Get to the back!" he commanded. "You too, Michael!"

With a speed that surprised even himself, Moshe rushed over to the electrical breakout box for the emergency generator. With vicious tugs he started jerking the extension cords for the lights. One by one the large work lights blinked out, gradually turning the *geniza* dark. Moshe yanked the last plug out and watched as the vast room faded quickly to black as the quartz bulb dimmed.

Ghostly afterimages danced in his vision as he felt his way toward the back of the *geniza*. He ran squarely into a box and went sprawling over it, landing in a painful heap. He scrabbled around until he was facing toward the door.

The dim light coming through the door was partially occluded as a body eclipsed it. Moshe longed for a gun as he saw the sharp silhouette of the Uzi in the man's hand. The man entered, slowly tracing the heavy power cable from the generator. A second man followed the first, stopping inside the door.

Moshe could no longer see the first man, although the noise he was making was echoing loudly off the walls. Moshe felt about for anything that could be used as a weapon. All he could find was the rough edge of a sealed box.

A work light snapped on, suddenly bathing the room in a blinding glare. Moshe looked down the row of boxes he was behind. The light was about twenty feet away. He started crawling frantically toward it, oblivious of the rough limestone tearing at his hands and knees. A burst of flame erupted to his left. Moshe fell on his face, box splinters raining down on him as the Uzi found its mark just above him. He gasped as something red-hot seared his right calf. He scrabbled toward the light, wincing at the pain in his leg. He hit the tripod stand heavily and brought it down. The light went out as the bulb shattered.

Moshe listened. He could hear the man scrambling around for another light cable. Moshe knew he would never be able to reach the next light. He shifted his weight and bumped into something solid. He felt around and grasped the object. He didn't know what it was, but it was metal and quite heavy. Moshe struggled to his feet, ignoring the pain in his leg. He drew back his arm and threw the object as hard as he could, then waited for it to miss and hit the floor. Instead he heard a dull thud followed by the sound of two metallic objects hitting the floor. One of the terrorists crumpled to the floor with a moan. Moshe had new hope, though he knew the second man was still there.

A loud crash sounded at the back of the *geniza*. Moshe could hear someone crawling frantically across the floor somewhere behind him. Another crash signaled the demise of another light. That left only one, but that was on the far side of the room. Even as the thought entered Moshe's mind, the light clicked on.

Moshe's head spun around. The second man had his Uzi leveled and was glancing down at his companion. The man on the ground was groaning and holding his head. Moshe saw the look in Mars's eyes and willed his American friend not to move. Moshe's stomach went ice-cold. Mars bolted for the remaining light, jumping over rows of boxes like a high hurdler.

Anne's hand went to her chest. Her scream followed him across the room. "No! No! Mars! Get down!"

Avraham jerked his Uzi around and pulled the trigger. The trail of lead followed Mars and caught up with him, one slug ripping through his right elbow. He screamed and spun to the right, slamming to the floor and sliding into a box about ten feet from the light. A bright red stain spread slowly across his shirt.

Anne ran to him, completely forgetting about the gunmen. Avraham followed her with his gun but did not fire. She knelt beside Mars. Anne tried to see if he was still alive, but tears blurred her vision. She wiped them roughly away and felt his pulse. It was beating. He groaned.

"Mars . . . Where are you hurt?" Anne asked, daring to breathe again.

"My arm. Feels like it's on fire. Can't move it."

Avraham aimed at a box a few feet away and squeezed off a short burst.

"You are lucky to be alive," he growled. "All of you. Do as I say and you'll stay that way. Dr. McAdams, move away from him."

"I will not!" she shot back at him.

"You will do as I say or I *will* kill your friend!"

Anne hesitated. Avraham raised the Uzi and pointed it at Mars's head. She got up reluctantly and walked over to where Moshe and Michael were. Avraham glanced back quickly. Abdul was standing now, although quite unsteady on his feet.

"Now," Avraham said, "Dr. McAdams, you will come with us."

Moshe stepped in front of her, wincing at the pain in his leg. "What do you want? Why are you here?"

"I'll only say this once!" Avraham thundered. "Either Dr. McAdams comes with us *now* or everyone here dies. Which will it be?"

Anne glanced at Mars. She knew at that moment how much she loved him, how she longed for this not to be happening.

"I'll go," she said softly. She started walking toward the gold menorah standing at the side of the room.

"Where do you think you're going?" Avraham demanded.

"To get my purse!" Anne's expression cut into him like a knife. Avraham watched as she walked to the menorah and picked her purse up from its base. She turned and glared at him.

Avraham waved the Uzi toward the door.

She walked out with Avraham behind her. Abdul guarded their retreat. He waited until he was sure that Avraham and Anne would be almost to the car before he ran to catch up.

Moshe started to run from the room but collapsed as he took his first step. "My leg!"

Michael looked up in concern. "Are you okay?"

"I'm fine. You take care of Mars."

Michael looked back at Mars. "Where are you hurt?"

"It's my right arm. Feels like it's been ripped off."

"Can you get up on one of these boxes so I can see?"

"Don't know."

Mars rolled onto his left side, crying out in pain. He staggered to his feet only to lose his balance. He sat heavily on a box as Michael grabbed him to keep him from falling off.

"Can you sit up by yourself?" Michael asked.

"Yeah. I think so."

Michael took his hands away cautiously. He quickly unbuttoned Mars's shirt. He grimaced as he looked at the ragged, bloody mess where his friend's right arm was. He pulled out a heavy work knife and carefully cut the sleeve away at the shoulder. Then he worked the knife slowly down the sleeve and lifted the soggy mass away. Michael whistled as he saw the wound.

"How bad is it?" Mars asked, afraid to look.

"It's messy, but you won't die from it."

Michael hurriedly took off his own shirt.

"I'll take that," Moshe said as he limped over. "Go get us some help." Moshe took the impromptu compress and clamped it on Mars's elbow causing him to cry out in pain. "I'm sorry, my friend."

Michael stood up, uncertain what he should do. Moshe nodded toward the door. Michael left as quietly as he could, then broke into a run.

The reality of it all suddenly hit Mars. Tears streamed down his face, and he bowed his head as he sobbed.

Moshe released his grip on the compress for a moment, then reap-
plied it. "Sorry, Mars. I have to keep pressure on it."

Mars shook his head. "They've got her," he cried. "They've got my
Anne."

22

AN IMPOSSIBLE
RANSOM

The *geniza* was in almost total chaos. Regular IDF soldiers were interspersed with border policemen, standing around with their automatic weapons and nothing to do. One white-coated ambulance attendant was bending over Mars, while two others struggled to bring the wheeled stretcher through the maze of boxes. Moshe was trying to shoo away a fourth paramedic so he could talk with a young IDF lieutenant. The attendant was insistent.

"Hold on," Moshe grumbled. "I have to tell the lieutenant what happened."

Michael looked around in time to see Ya'acov Isaacson come through the doorway.

"More company," he observed.

Moshe half-turned and watched as Ya'acov came toward him as if drawn by a magnet. "Dr. Stein." It was more of a statement than a question.

"Have we met?" Moshe asked.

"No, sir. I'm Captain Ya'acov Isaacson with Military Intelligence. We're usually well-informed." Ya'acov looked quickly around the room until he came to Michael. "And you are Michael Shapiro, I believe. Mr. Marsh Enderly is being attended to, and Dr. D. Anne McAdams has been abducted."

The man *was* well-informed. However, Moshe couldn't help but note that one fact was apparently unknown even to Military Intelligence. "That is substantially complete," Moshe agreed.

"What part is not?" Ya'acov asked.

"The D."

"We will have that before the day is out."

Ya'acov glanced at the attendant working on Mars. "Is he stable?"

The attendant looked up as if he didn't understand the question.

"Is Mr. Enderly in stable condition?" Ya'acov repeated.

The attendant let his stethoscope fall against his chest. "Yes. The wound is quite painful, I'm sure, but not life-threatening."

"Good." Ya'acov turned to the regular IDF officer. "Lieutenant, you and your troops are relieved."

"But, sir . . ."

"That's an order, Lieutenant, and make sure standard security procedures are carried out."

"Yes, sir." The lieutenant wasn't happy, but he gave the order, and his troops started for the doorway. The border policemen hesitated, then gathered that the Intelligence officer meant them too.

Ya'acov looked at those remaining. "This incident is covered by national security. No one may discuss what you have seen or heard here. And, Mr. Enderly, as a guest in this country, this applies to you as well. Does everyone understand?"

He was greeted with the silence of agreement.

"Very well. I need everyone to leave except Dr. Stein, Mr. Shapiro, and Mr. Enderly."

"But Mr. Enderly needs medical attention," the attendant protested.

"You said the patient is stable. Please leave the room at once and wait at the top of the steps. I won't be long."

Ya'acov waited until the footsteps faded away. He pulled a small notebook from his pocket and clicked his ballpoint pen. In ten minutes he had the complete story.

He looked at Mars as he returned the notebook to his pocket. "I apologize for the delay in getting you packed off to Hadassah Hospital. I assure you this is critically important or we would never do such a thing. Now . . ."

"Who's taken her?" Mars demanded.

Ya'acov was momentarily startled. He looked sympathetically at the American but was well aware of how far he could go. "We don't know for sure."

"Who do you *think* did it?"

"I'm not allowed to say. As I said, this involves national security."

"So what are you going to do to save her?"

Ya'acov sighed. "You're talking to the wrong person."

"Do I need to go to my Embassy?"

"You could," Ya'acov said. But his tone offered no encouragement.

"As in lots of luck?" Mars pressed.

Ya'acov turned to Moshe. "Thank you for your cooperation. I'll send the ambulance attendants down on my way out."

Moshe nodded.

◆

Mars gritted his teeth as the ambulance made its way up the side of Mount Scopus to Hadassah Hospital, each bump feeling like a red-hot lance from his elbow to his brain.

Once at the hospital, the emergency crew X-rayed him and rushed him into the operating room. He was quickly under, even while the orthopedic surgeon was studying the dripping X-rays.

◆

He knew he was asleep, but he didn't want to be. Why couldn't he open his eyes? He tried again, very hard. They wouldn't open. He could hear sounds, but it was too much trouble to try and figure out what they were.

Maybe if he tried one eye . . . Mars struggled and managed to open his left eye a crack. It closed as quickly. The drowsiness seemed to weigh a ton.

"So you did survive," said a familiar voice. It was Moshe.

"Hmmph . . ."

"And you have retained your eloquence."

He was already asleep again.

♦

Mars walked through the gate and up the steps, passing through the scales and onto the Haram esh-Sharif. He looked to the right. There was the silver dome sitting atop the El Aqsa Mosque. And disappearing inside was Anne. He hurried after her, his feet flying over the ancient pavement.

He stopped inside. In a moment he saw her. He ran toward her. A foot darted out and tripped him. He fell forward unable to catch himself. He landed on his right side, screaming at the pain.

"Hold on," someone nearby said.

Mars was breathing heavily. It had been a dream, but the pain was real. "It hurts!"

"I know it does. I pressed the button for the nurse."

Mars tried to focus his eyes. A bearded figure was standing over him, his features hidden in the dim lighting. "Moshe?"

"I'm here."

The nurse rushed in.

"He's in pain," Moshe said.

"I'll be right back," the nurse said.

Much to Mars's surprise, she did come right back. She rubbed a patch of skin on his left upper arm. Then came a prick.

"You'll feel better in a moment."

"Thank you," he slurred.

She left them.

"How are you?"

"Like I've been run over by a truck."

"It's not quite that bad. Your elbow got busted up pretty bad. But you're lucky. Dr. Meir Kohn is Israel's best orthopedic surgeon. He says you should heal completely. You'll probably be able to predict the weather, but you should regain full use of the arm."

"Dr. Kohn just happened to be available?"

"Er, yes."

"As arranged by Dr. Stein?"

"I do happen to be acquainted with the man."

Mars was silent for a few moments. "Thanks, Moshe. I appreciate it."

"You are welcome, my friend."

Again an awkward silence.

"Moshe?"

Moshe knew what was coming. "Yes?"

"Is there any news about Anne?"

Moshe's silence told him the answer. "No," he said finally. "I assure you, I'm taking this up with everyone I know, officially and otherwise."

Mars knew this meant a lot. But it didn't relieve the hurt. The terror of not knowing . . . "Do her folks know?"

"Yes. Bob and Florence knew something was wrong the moment I told them who I was. She has such nice parents. There wasn't much I could tell them, except that we're doing everything we can to get her back. That sounds so inadequate."

"How did they take it?"

"They're strong people. Look at Anne."

Mars felt tears coming to his eyes. He wished he *could* look at Anne.

"They'll be coming as soon as they can," Moshe said. "They don't have passports, so they may have to wrestle with your State Department a little. Oh, I also called your dad."

"I'm surprised you were able to reach him." Mars almost choked as his throat constricted.

Moshe looked at Mars, wondering what was at the bottom of this particular war between the generations. "Your dad's coming," he said.

"What?"

"Your dad will arrive in Tel Aviv day after tomorrow, and that's about as quick as one can do it. He seems to be a rather resourceful man."

"You could say that."

"I believe I did."

Mars searched for something else to talk about. "What's this thing?" he asked, nodding at his right arm stuck out in front of his face.

"You look like an albino turtle. The doc put a cast around your chest and attached it to the arm cast. You won't be moving that for a while."

"When can I get out of here?"

"Getting restless, are we? Dr. Kohn said he might let you out day after tomorrow, if you're a good boy."

"And if I'm not?"

"Have you ever been?"

"That's answering a question with a question."

"It is?"

◆

Mars clicked through the TV channels in sheer boredom as he waited for the pain pill to take effect. Israeli daytime television wasn't any better than the American variety, he decided. He paused as the Dome of the Rock flashed on the screen. He punched up the sound.

". . . the abduction of Dr. Anne McAdams took a sinister twist earlier today when a videotape was delivered to the CNN bureau in Tel Aviv."

Mars jerked upright as Anne's picture flashed on the screen. She was sitting on a chair in a nearly bare room. The camera zoomed in on her face. Her face was wet as if she had been crying. Mars ached as he watched, longing to be able to do something. The picture cut back to the reporter.

"A note with the video identified the terrorist group as the Palestinian Revolutionary Force. The group is demanding that Israel withdraw from the entire West Bank and Jerusalem or accept responsibility for the death of Dr. McAdams."

Mars didn't hear anything else. He watched through his tears as the reporter concluded and CNN continued its relentless recitation of the current world woes.

◆

Moshe had no problem finding Joe Enderly. In fact, the elder Enderly found him. "Dr. Stein?"

Moshe turned to find himself looking at a middle-aged man of average height. Looking closely, he could see the family resemblance. But he also could see that the two Enderlys were quite different.

"Mr. Enderly," Moshe said, giving the man a firm handshake, which was returned.

"Please call me Joe."

"And I am Moshe. Welcome to Israel." He paused. "I wish it could have been under better circumstances. Your son will be fine. But . . ."

"Yes, I've heard about Anne McAdams. I'm sorry. Did I understand from your phone call that Ms. McAdams is more than a colleague to Mars?"

"Yes, I'm afraid that is the way of it. He has not discussed this with you?"

"No. My son thinks I want to run his life. He also thinks I don't care what happens to him. I had no idea. How's Mars taking it?"

"Badly."

Moshe led the way to his bus.

◆

Moshe stood in the doorway as father and son said their hellos. Moshe could see the conflicting emotions in Mars's eyes. The young man was obviously glad to see his father and was flattered that he had dropped everything to come be with him. But suspicion was there also.

"Moshe," Mars called.

"I am here. There's no hiding this bulk."

Mars smiled in spite of his concern. "I think I need some assistance from the resourceful Dr. Stein."

"Oh? I thought you young Americans could do anything."

"I tried. But Dr. Kohn won't let me out of here."

"I'm sure it's for your own good."

"But I've *got* to get out. I have to do something about Anne."

Moshe remained silent.

"Can you help me?" Mars insisted.

"I did discuss your situation with Dr. Kohn. You can get out, but you'll have to sign yourself out against advice."

"What's that mean?"

"It means you are refusing your doctor's advice and are therefore responsible for anything that happens."

"Fine. What do I do?"

"I took the liberty of having the form prepared at the nurses' station. All you have to do is sign it."

"And we're out of here?"

"Yes."

Joe Enderly looked at Moshe in concern. Moshe only shrugged.

♦

Joe Enderly saw his opening and drove the Eldan GMC Safari out into the Jerusalem traffic.

"You approve of the choice?" he asked, glancing at Moshe.

"It's very nice," Moshe said. "Perhaps I could have gotten you a better deal, but . . ."

"My Dallas travel agent arranged it for me, along with everything else."

"Then I'm sure it was the right thing to do."

Joe looked into the rearview mirror. Mars was squirming around looking for a way to get comfortable. "You okay back there?"

"Yeah. Real peachy. If I could figure a way to get out of this plaster maiden, it'd be wonderful."

"What's our first stop?" Joe asked Moshe.

"Police Ministry," Moshe said with a sigh.

"You don't sound hopeful."

"We'll see. Let's say my contacts have not been very encouraging. The military is not even a possibility. Things are very tense right now."

They found the Police Ministry offices easily. Joe dropped Moshe and Mars off and parked the truck. Together they entered the building and were greeted by an attractive receptionist.

"Shalom," Moshe said with a big smile. "I am Dr. Moshe Stein from the Hebrew University. We would like to see Mr. Mayer."

"The Minister?" she asked in surprise.

"I believe Mr. Ronnie Mayer is the Police Minister. Yes."

"Do you have an appointment, Dr. Stein?"

"No, we don't. But we're here on the Anne McAdams abduction case—you've heard of it, I'm sure."

"Yes, just a minute," she said. She picked up her console phone and punched an extension. "There's a Dr. Moshe Stein here with two other gentlemen to see the Minister about the McAdams abduction. Yes, I know they don't have an appointment." She looked up at Moshe as she listened to what the government official had to say. "Yes, I'll tell him.

Good-bye." She put the handset down. "I'm afraid Mr. Mayer can't see you right now."

"When *can* he see us?" Moshe demanded.

"I don't know." She looked up in relief as a young man pushed through the electric-lock door leading to the back offices.

"Dr. Stein, my name is Menachem Susser, one of Mr. Mayer's assistants. Can I help you?"

"I hope so. We're here to see what's being done to rescue Dr. Anne McAdams from the terrorists."

A pained look came across Menachem's smooth, professional features. "Would you gentlemen come back to my office? I'm sure we would be more comfortable there."

Moshe looked as if he doubted that but followed the man through the electric door. Menachem led them through a series of turns, then stood by a door and ushered them into a moderate-sized office. He pulled the door shut after Mars ambled in, then took his place behind the desk. "Now, gentlemen, what can the Police Ministry do for you?"

"Terrorists have abducted Dr. Anne McAdams, one of my colleagues. We would like to know what is being done to get her back," Moshe explained.

Menachem looked at Mars. "You must be Mars Enderly. And who is the third gentleman?"

"Joe Enderly," Mars's dad volunteered. "I'm Mars's father."

"Gentlemen, I assure you the Police Ministry is trying very hard to find these terrorists. We regret what happened very much and are doing all we can to catch those responsible."

"What's being done?" Moshe asked.

"I'm afraid I can't discuss current police work."

"Some friends of mine who will remain nameless tell me very little is being done right now. Something about political sensitivity and a higher priority agenda."

"I can't comment on that."

"When can we see Mr. Mayer?"

Menachem looked at Moshe for a few moments. "You can't. At least not right now."

"Should my friends go to the American Embassy then?"

"They certainly have that right." Menachem was definitely not encouraging.

"If you would show us out," Moshe growled, glaring at the man.

◆

Ambassador Jonathan Feldman looked out over his expansive, mahogany desk at a picture of the current occupant of 1600 Pennsylvania Avenue. Next to it was a picture of the President shaking hands with Ambassador Feldman with the White House Rose Garden in the background.

It was a pleasant day, Jonathan reflected. There were no pressing duties for the ambassador to perform. He had finished his morning danish, and the cup of coffee served in Embassy china was perfect. A folded *Wall Street Journal* lay beside the tray. All his investments were performing well. It was starting out to be, all in all, an exceptional day.

The intercom button flashed on his massive electronic phone set, accompanied by a muted cybernetic chirp. Jonathan sighed as he pressed the button.

"Yes?" he said.

"Sorry to bother you, Mr. Ambassador." His secretary's voice rose and faded as the phone's automatic gain control tried to maintain an even level. "Mr. Joe Enderly and two other gentlemen are here to see you."

Jonathan's mind shifted into high gear as he ran the name through his memory. *Got it. Joseph Enderly—owner of Dallas Heuristics, a company specializing in artificial intelligence software used mainly in the defense industry, including Israel Aircraft Industries. A multimillionaire. A contributor to the President's last campaign. So what did he want?*

"Please show them in," he said.

Jonathan hurried around his desk even as the door opened. Moshe received his official greeting, followed by Joe Enderly. Mars and the ambassador had difficulty in negotiating a left-handed handshake.

"Please make yourselves comfortable," Jonathan said, waving his hand toward three huge chairs arranged around his desk. The three men sank into the luxurious cushions as the ambassador made his way around to his position of power. "Now, Mr. Enderly, what can I do for you?"

Joe paused as he gathered his thoughts. How much help *could* he expect from his government, he wondered. "We are here to ask for your help in saving Dr. Anne McAdams."

The ambassador's sour expression signaled the end of his idyllic day. "That, indeed, is a tragic case. And I sympathize with you. We were horrified when we heard about it."

"Can you tell us what is being done to get her back?"

"I contacted Prime Minister Beker right after it happened. He assures me Israel is doing everything in its power to bring the Palestinian Revolutionary Force to justice."

"Yes," Joe said quickly, almost interrupting. "We had a talk with one of the Police Minister's assistants. He said essentially the same thing you're saying."

"Well, that's what we want, isn't it?"

"Not exactly. What we'd like is Anne McAdams back safe and sound. The Israelis keep talking about nailing the PRF. I suspect Anne's safety takes a backseat to that."

Moshe could not help a grunt of agreement. Jonathan glanced at him warily.

"This is one of the problems of living in a democracy," Jonathan said, warming to his subject. "There are limits to what can be done in situations like this because we are not totalitarian states. But these very limits are what give us our freedom—it's the price we pay."

"Let me restate my question," Joe said, being very careful to disguise his irritation.

"By all means," Jonathan replied, hiding behind his best smile.

"What will the State Department do to get Anne McAdams back?"

"Precisely what the Embassy is already doing. I am in constant contact with the Prime Minister's office about many things that affect Americans. I have already discussed Ms. McAdams's case with Prime Minister Beker, and I will continue to follow up on it. I assure you. I will leave no stone unturned. Now, is there anything else I can do for you gentlemen?"

Joe held back what he wanted to say. He had not achieved success in business by making enemies in high places. "No, Mr. Ambassador. We appreciate your help and your time."

"It's my pleasure." The ambassador stood up. The interview was over.

◆

It was very quiet in the trailer. Ya'acov leaned back in the borrowed swivel chair, a little surprised that David had allowed him to use a UAV again. Ya'acov, unable to sleep, had called his boss at 5 in the morning. David had listened to Ya'acov's concerns, even though the younger man had been forced to admit he wasn't sure anything was wrong. Apparently the colonel trusted his judgment more than he realized.

Ya'acov absentmindedly pulled a Butterfinger candy bar out of his uniform pocket and unwrapped it. He looked down in dismay as the melted chocolate covered his right hand. He paused for only a moment, then started eating the candy, ignoring the mess he was getting on his mouth. The two sergeants pretended to be unaware of what was happening. Avi Barak waited until Ya'acov had wiped his hands and mouth with his handkerchief.

"The bird'll be there in a few minutes, Captain. What are we looking for?"

"If I knew that, I wouldn't be here," Ya'acov said. "Those tanks we followed into Qatanah have moved down to Beit Jinn for exercises. I want to check on them."

"The captain is expecting something else?"

"That's a roger on your last."

"We should know soon." Avi trained the camera forward and zoomed the lens out. "Got a lot of early-morning glare, but I think we'll be able to see okay. There's Beit Jinn. Those things on the ground sure look like tanks." Avi zoomed in as the UAV approached.

"Don't see much activity," Ya'acov observed.

"It's early yet, Captain. Looks normal to me. Let's flip on the FLIR and look at the infrared." The screen broke up for a moment, then steadied as random hot spots stood out among the cooler surroundings. "They're beginning to start engines. About half are running, I'd say. Either they're getting ready to move out or they're charging batteries."

Ya'acov glanced at his watch. "Hmm, if I remember the schedule correctly, there's a satellite overhead about now."

Avi snorted. "They probably know about the satellite, sir, but they don't know about us—I can guarantee that. We're all but invisible. Ready to turn around and come home?"

Ya'acov continued to stare at the screen.

"Sir?" Avi prompted.

"No, Sergeant. Let's hang around for a little while. The satellite will be over the horizon in a few minutes. Flip back to video and zoom in as tight as you can. Pan around the tanks. Look for anything out of the ordinary."

Avi glanced at Yehuda Tennenbaum, who only shrugged as if to acknowledge that the officers get to call the shots. "Yes, sir."

A few minutes later a movement caught Ya'acov's eye. "Where did that guy come from?" he asked.

"The one walking away from that tank?" Avi responded. "I would guess he climbed out of it. Probably has to go take a leak."

"Look! There's another one. He came out from under the tank, not off of it. And there's another."

Soon the screen was full of soldiers walking away from the tanks.

"Sergeant Tennenbaum," Ya'acov called.

"Yes, sir?"

"Can you make a low pass over the encampment?"

"How low would you like to go?"

"Just be sure to bring the bird back."

"Hold tight." Yehuda throttled back and pushed the joystick forward. The video picture tilted as the UAV started losing altitude. The small aircraft spiraled down quickly until it was five hundred feet above the ground, southwest of the encampment. The rolling hills swept slowly past as the UAV approached its goal.

"Should be over that hill," Avi announced.

The encampment slowly came into view. Avi zoomed in as they approached, panning the camera from side to side.

"Hold on the side of that tank," Ya'acov ordered. "That doesn't look right."

Avi centered the camera on the tank and held it there. "I agree, sir, but I can't put my finger on it."

Suddenly a crack appeared and widened as a whole section of the tank's track swung up into the air. Moments later a soldier came through the opening.

"Those are decoys," Ya'acov said softly, as if the man on the ground might hear him. "Sergeant, cover as much of the encampment as you can in one pass, then get that bird back here."

Ya'acov's blood ran cold as he thought of the implications of what he had just seen. President Darousha was going to a lot of trouble to make Israel think his tank division was still in Beit Jinn. But where were the real tanks? Of one thing he was quite sure—they had not retired to the north.

"I need a secure phone," Ya'acov said with a calmness that surprised him.

"That radio telephone on the table in the corner has a scrambler, sir."

Ya'acov got up heavily and walked to the little alcove with its tiny table. The phone looked like a regular civilian model.

"Don't worry, sir," Avi said with a smile. "Despite what it looks like, it is secure. Works like a regular phone. When you want to go on scrambler, push the red button."

Ya'acov punched in David Kruger's office phone. It rang twice.

"Hello," David answered.

"On scrambler," Ya'acov said, pressing the red button.

The earphone screamed and warbled for a few seconds as the two units tried to find each other in their electronic jungle. Finally they synced in.

"Can you hear me, sir?" Ya'acov asked.

"About as well as these blasted things ever do. What's up?"

"Real badness. The peace-loving Syrians have flown the coop."

"What? The last satellite pass showed them still there—the right heat signatures and everything. And that was less than an hour ago. They couldn't have pulled out that fast."

"They've been gone for some time. What you saw were decoys. We did a low-level pass after the satellite was over the horizon and saw men crawling out from under the things. My guess is that they've got burners under there to fool our infrared gear."

"Do you know where the tanks are now?"

"No, sir. We're in the process of bringing the bird back. I'll bring the video and telemetry tapes back with me. Sir?"

"Yes?"

"We need armor in Galilee real bad."

"Get back here with those tapes."

"On my way, sir."

♦

Ya'acov looked up as David Kruger entered his office and sat down heavily.

"How did the briefing go, sir?" Ya'acov asked, knowing the answer wasn't good.

David leaned back in the chair and stared at the ceiling. He closed his eyes for a moment, then looked at Ya'acov.

"Your bombshell landed right after another one. I thought for a moment they were going to kill the messenger. The IAF has grounded all our Apache helicopters. The one that crashed the other day was caused by a gearbox failure. None of 'em fly, short of a national emergency, until all the gearboxes are checked."

"So, scratch one of our most potent anti-tank platforms."

"That's a roger. We still have the older Cobras—not as effective, but better than nothing. As for *your* news, the Syrians' latest ruse has the high command upset, but they can't decide what it means."

"What it means is obvious."

"To be fair, Syria does have other enemies. Or they could be doing this just to bug us."

"Or they could be about to invade."

"Or that. And that's what some of the generals are thinking. But there's no consensus."

"Are they going to do *anything*?" Ya'acov asked.

"Yes. They're sending a tank company into northern Galilee along Highway 91."

"One company? Eleven tanks? What about the armored exercises in the Negev?"

"The exercises will continue for now. They don't want to call them to a halt only to be embarrassed by a false alarm."

"It'll be a whole lot more embarrassing if the Syrians invade Galilee."

David couldn't argue that.

♦

Anne looked around the room for what seemed like the millionth time. It was still the same. She had no idea where she was. They had forced her to lie facedown on the floorboards during the ride to the safe-house.

They had not harmed her, which had been a surprise. In fact, no one had said anything to her since her arrival. One of her captors had video-taped her, but that was all. It was as if there was nothing else they needed from her.

The room was clean and spartan. There was a cot, a table with a lamp, and a chair. Meals were brought regularly—lamb and vegetables mostly.

But she had nothing to do, and that was really bothering her. She had plenty of time to think, but her thoughts kept coming back to the same thing: she loved Mars. And she missed him very much.

She looked at her purse on the table. They hadn't taken anything, although they had looked through it thoroughly. Probably looking for ladies' pistols or cans of Mace, she thought. She had never favored either.

She opened the clasp and looked inside. Her eyes ran over the familiar items: lipstick, comb, a pair of sunglasses in their case, chewing gum, a small package of Kleenex, her wallet, a bottle of Advil, and something else—the gift from Zuba Rosenberg. She ran her fingers over the textured cover as she looked at the gold lettering. "New Testament and Psalms," it said.

She felt a strong urge to pull the Bible out but a reluctance at the same time. Finally she took it out and cradled it with her left hand as her thumb opened it. The book fell open to the first Psalm. She looked down, and her eyes leapt to the opening verses:

Blessed is the man who does not walk in the counsel of the wicked or stand in the way of sinners or sit in the seat of mockers. But his delight is in the law of the LORD, and on his law he meditates day and night.

She closed the Bible and looked at it as if it had intruded on her private self. She slowly put it back in her purse.

♦

Captain Yossi Goldman clamped his mouth shut against the dust and grit as his tank brought up the rear of the 1st Platoon. Ordinarily the company's tanks would have been riding on transporters. But all those were in the Negev. All he had were the eleven Merkava Mark-3 tanks.

Since they were under radio silence, he was depending on Lieutenant Ehud Serlin to make all the right turns. Ehud was the 3rd Platoon leader, and it was his tank that Yossi could see whenever the company topped a rise.

He tried to get comfortable in his command cupola. But that wasn't possible in a Merkava tank doing thirty miles an hour.

23

LAST RESORT

The stunning view before them was lost on Mars. He, his dad, and Moshe were looking out over horizontal Jewish tombstones on the lower slopes of the Mount of Olives. Down the hill was the Kidron Valley, and up the far terraced slope was the wall of the Old City. Roughly in the middle of that wall were the two sealed-up portals of the Golden Gate. Moshe told the Enderlys that the Jews buried on Olivet were waiting for the Messiah. Mars didn't feel like arguing with him about that.

The three turned at the sound of someone laboring down the path behind them.

"You must be Joe Enderly," Ya'acov said as he extended his hand. He nodded to Moshe and Mars. "You are a most resourceful man," he added in admiration. "Dallas Heuristics and Israel Aircraft Industries carry a lot of clout, it seems."

"I guess that's a compliment. Thank you."

Ya'acov nodded. "So, I have a little briefing for you. It will be short, and this is all there will be. Please do not take any notes. And no tape recorders. All clear?"

Ya'acov waited until all three had said, "Yes."

"Very well. We are virtually sure that Anne McAdams is being held by a group called the Palestinian Revolutionary Force, or PRF for short. This group tried to bomb the Dome of the Rock, they very nearly blew up Yad Vashem along with a lot of Israeli and foreign dignitaries, and they tried to level Hadassah Hospital with a truck bomb. That one we barely defused in time. Not very nice people.

"Most recently they killed two guards at Dr. Stein's dig in the Old City, wounded the two of you, and abducted Anne McAdams. A video-tape of Anne was delivered to CNN, which they broadcast."

Ya'acov paused and looked at Mars. He knew what Anne meant to him. He cleared his throat and continued. "The note stated that Israel must abandon the West Bank and Jerusalem or Anne will be killed. The only other thing I can tell you is that we are doing everything we can to find the PRF and bring them to justice." Ya'acov turned and started walking away.

"What about Anne?" Mars demanded, his face contorted by his anguish. "Doesn't *anybody* care about Anne? All I hear is, you want to get the PRF. Don't people matter?"

Ya'acov stopped in his tracks. He turned and looked at Mars. "Believe it or not, I do care. I hate it when things like this happen. Now, you didn't hear this from me, but the government is concerned with what it regards as more important things than rescuing Anne McAdams. And there's nothing you or I can do about it." The look in Mars's eyes tore at Ya'acov's soul. "I'm truly sorry," he added.

♦

Moshe opened the door and brought Dan Adov into his apartment. "Come in, come in. I'm glad you could come over."

"What's this about?" Dan asked, looking past Moshe to his two guests.

"In a minute. Mars you know. The other gentleman is Joe Enderly, Mars's father."

Dan and Joe shook hands, while Mars gave the reporter an awk-ward wave with his left hand.

"Seats," Moshe commanded.

Moshe filled Dan in on the day's events.

"Wow!" Dan said when he had heard it all. "Why didn't you just storm the Prime Minister's office?"

"I thought about it," Moshe grumbled.

"So now you're going to have a go at the press, is that it?"

"Sort of."

"Well, I'll help in any way I can, but I really don't see what I can do. Seems to me you've tried everything."

"Almost."

"What's been left out?" Dan asked suspiciously.

"Do you have contacts with any free-lance military experts?" Moshe asked.

Dan whistled. "Of the kind I think you mean?"

"That's the only kind that can help us."

Dan leaned back and closed his eyes. "Someone does come to mind. The guy's name is Wolf Meisel. He was a colonel in the IDF until he was dismissed for condoning brutality in his command. He has no full-time employment but manages to live pretty high on the hog nonetheless. He's been involved in advising certain groups in Central and South America. You know—military hardware, training. He's been very close to government prosecution more than once but somehow has managed to avoid it. How, I don't know. Shady character, but he knows what he's doing. His IDF units were very effective, though unprincipled."

"You know what we want to do?" Joe asked.

"I can guess. Commando raid on the PRF."

"What do you think?"

Dan looked at Mars, then back at Joe. "If there were *any* other way, I'd say forget it. This is not the kind of guy you want your daughter to marry."

"But there is no other way."

"No, I don't think there is."

"So, can you arrange a meeting for us?"

"Don't know. I'll sure give it a try."

◆

It was hours after Anne had glanced at Psalm 1 and had returned the Bible to her purse. But the book had not remained there long. She didn't know if it was curiosity, boredom, or something else, but something compelled her to pull it out again. She began again at Psalm 1 and could not put the book down. She now turned a page and saw Psalm 150. The eyes of a scholar traced carefully over each verse:

> *Praise the* LORD. *Praise God in his sanctuary; praise him in his mighty heavens. Praise him for his acts of power; praise him for his surpassing greatness. Praise him with the sounding of the trumpet, praise him with the harp and lyre, praise him with tambourine and dancing, praise him with the strings and flute, praise him with the clash of cymbals, praise him with resounding cymbals. Let everything that has breath praise the* LORD. *Praise the* LORD.

She slowly closed the Bible and placed it on the table. The last Psalm seemed to her a fitting conclusion, like the loud cymbals it spoke of.

She pondered the range of human emotions she had read about: thanksgiving, trust, joy, anger, utter despair, hope. But one thing was for sure: the psalmists were convinced they were speaking to the God who could do anything. But then, what could be expected of primitive people?

The door opened, and a guard brought in her dinner on a crude, earthenware plate. He glanced at the Bible and swept it angrily off the table before he set the plate down. Anne got up, went around the table, and picked up the book. The guard ripped it out of her hands.

"Stop! Give that back!" she screamed.

The guard stalked toward the door. A black shadow blocked the way. Abdul glared at the guard. "What's going on?"

"He took my Bible," Anne accused.

Abdul looked at the guard in contempt. He extended his hand, and the guard dropped the book into it. Abdul dropped the Bible on the table and left without another word.

Anne reached for the plate, then stopped. One of the pages in the Bible had been bent over. She picked it up and opened it. She unfolded the page and found herself looking at a passage in Luke's Gospel. Her eyes seemed drawn to the 33rd verse of chapter 23. She slowly read Luke's account of the Crucifixion and continued until she came to verse 45.

... for the sun stopped shining. And the curtain of the temple was torn in two.

Slowly she closed the book. In her mind's eye she saw the immensely heavy veil hanging in Herod's Temple—the very veil she had seen with her own eyes. The veil that was indeed in two pieces, just as this passage said. Ninety feet of the heaviest fabric she had ever seen had been torn in two. But by what or by whom?

There was a strange stirring within her. She remembered a heart-to-heart talk with her mother on a Christmas break during her graduate studies. She had intended it as gentle instruction to explain why a modern scientist could not believe in God, certainly not as defined by the Bible. She could still remember how respectfully her mother had listened to her eldest daughter. Those deep brown eyes had gazed at her so lovingly as Anne had concluded, "Mother, if you need God to help you through life, that's fine. But I can't believe in fairy tales."

A wry smile came to Anne's lips in spite of her circumstances. Her mother's reply had caught her completely off guard, and she had never been able to forget it. "You'll come around, honey. I've already prayed to the Lord, and I have my assurance."

Emotion rolled over Anne like a wave. Tears streamed down her face as she felt a majestic presence overshadowing her. Suddenly all the things her mother had told her all through the years made sense. And with her own eyes she had verified the historical accuracy of the torn Temple veil. If the Bible were true ...

"Yes," she whispered, knowing the One she spoke to understood perfectly. In that moment she knew she had settled something with God. Yes. She did indeed believe that Jesus was the Son of God. And yes, she did receive her salvation from Him—the One who died for her—her Savior from sin and its penalty.

All thoughts of dinner were gone. She grabbed a tissue from her purse and daubed at her eyes. She flipped back to the Gospel of Matthew and started reading what she had never read before:

A record of the genealogy of Jesus Christ the son of David, the son of Abraham ...

◆

Wolf Meisel had been cautious at first but warmed quickly to the offer Dan Adov had relayed to him. He agreed to meet the Enderlys in Joe's room at the American Colony Hotel but had insisted that the Americans be alone. All this Dan had faithfully relayed to Joe Enderly.

Mars looked at his watch. "What do you want to bet he doesn't show?"

Joe consulted his Rolex. "He's still got almost ten minutes."

"Why does he want to see us alone? I'd like for Moshe to be here."

"I would too, but Mr. Meisel was quite adamant, according to Dan. I don't see that we had any option."

Joe looked at his son, his heart going out to him. He wished Mars could see that he really did care about him and what he did—and who he loved. "Mars?"

"Yes, Dad?"

"When you were in New York, you said you'd call me—let me know how you were doing."

Mars looked down at the floor. "I thought you were saying that because it was the right thing to do. And . . ."

Joe sighed. He knew how to finish what Mars had left unsaid. "And you didn't want me telling you how to live your life."

Mars's emotions went from embarrassment to rebellion. "If you must know, yes—I didn't want you telling me how I should do it."

Joe looked at his son as he sifted through all the things he wanted to say but didn't know how. "I know I've made mistakes, son. But you've misjudged me on one thing. At one time I *did* want you to come into the business so you could take it over one day. But I eventually got the message. I know you want to be an archaeologist. Now that I know that, that's what I want for you too. I want to see you succeed in what *you* want to do."

Joe paused, and a twinkle came to his eye. "I see you looking at me suspiciously, and I guess I really don't blame you. But I'm telling you the truth. I love you, son."

This flustered Mars.

"Oh, and one more thing," Joe added. Mars looked up. "I am also *very* interested in the affairs of your heart."

Joe almost regretted saying the last. He didn't want to cause Mars any more grief, but he did want his son to know how he felt.

Mars grew very red, but this quickly disappeared as a fresh wave of anguish swept over him. He looked up at his dad. Had he misjudged him?

He struggled for something to say but was saved by a discreet knock on the door.

Joe got up and opened the door.

"Mr. Enderly?" the tall stranger asked.

"Yes."

"You are expecting me. May I come in?"

Joe let the man in and quickly closed the door.

"No formalities please," the man said. "Perhaps we could sit at the table." He pointed to a worktable in the corner of the room.

Joe hesitated at this brusque introduction but walked to the table, where Mars joined him. The man's appearance matched his style—all business. He was tall, with the leanness associated with exercise instructors. He had cold, brown eyes and brown hair beginning to thin on top. His lined face said that he had spent many a day at the mercy of the desert wind and sun.

"Gentlemen, this needs to be short because there is much to do and not much time. I am Colonel Wolf Meisel. Dan Adov has filled me in on what you know, and I have taken the liberty of checking some of my sources. Anne McAdams has been abducted by the Palestinian Revolutionary Force. We don't know a lot about these terrorists except they are relatively new on the scene. Their leader is a man named Avraham Abbas, and his second-in-command is or was Abdul Suleiman."

"Is or was?" Joe asked in confusion.

"Please, Mr. Enderly. This will go quicker without interruptions. Abdul Suleiman was our prisoner until some idiot let him out. The day after he got out we chased someone who was almost certainly the man, but before we caught him, he jumped off a cliff. We searched the base of the cliff later but found no sign of him. He either crawled off and died somewhere or he escaped.

"Now, the Israeli government will not help you because they're more interested in getting the PRF—and they have more politically sensitive things to deal with. Your State Department is not in any position to help you either. The note with the videotape said the PRF would kill Anne unless Israel withdraws from the West Bank. And that is a death sentence, if they mean it."

Wolf paused as he looked each of the Enderlys in the eye. "And I assure you, they mean it."

"But that's ridiculous!" Mars shouted. "They know there's no way Israel will do that!"

"Hold your voice down," Wolf said through gritted teeth. "Yes, they do know that. That's not the point. The PRF wants to stir the pot of hate between Jews and Arabs. Anne happens to be a handy pawn."

"A pawn?" Mars said incredulously. "Anne is just a pawn? She's a human being!"

"Yes, yes, yes," Wolf shot back in irritation. "And you love her. I know all this. And that's why I'm here. There is no one in Israel who can save her except myself. I know what you're up against, I have the connections, and I have the military experience. I can do it, but it must be done quickly—there's no time to waste. My price is two hundred thousand American dollars, half in advance, plus all expenses."

Mars's mouth fell open. "You want how much?"

Joe held his hand up. "I agree to the price. I've taken the liberty of setting up fifty thousand dollars in advance." He pushed an envelope toward Wolf. "Inside you will find an account made out in your name, plus a five thousand dollar cash advance for expenses. I'm sure you will recognize the name of the bank. Stop by their Tel Aviv office, and they will make the final arrangements for you. The balance will be deposited in that account upon successful completion of the job. Any extra expenses will be covered in cash. Do you require anything else?"

Wolf looked through the envelope. "My contacts at Israel Aircraft Industries were right. You are a man of action."

"So let's get started. When will we hear from you?"

"I have a lot to do. I will call you tomorrow."

"Very well. We'll be here."

Wolf got up and was out the door as swiftly as his namesake. Mars looked at his father, seeing something he had not seen before. "Dad?"

"Yes, Mars?"

"Thank you. I really appreciate it."

"You're welcome, Mars. After all, we're talking about my son and, I presume, my future daughter-in-law."

This brought a fresh pang of worry. "Do you really think he can do it?" Mars asked.

"He knows his stuff. I don't care for the man, but I think he's probably the only chance we've got. We'll have to wait and see. Hang in there. This is just another gut-wrenching dilemma that life has thrown at us. We have to be brave—for Anne."

Mars nodded.

◆

Captain Yossi Goldman watched in satisfaction as his executive officer, Lieutenant Ehud Serlin, led the 3rd Platoon tanks off the road and into a field covered with tall grass and wild flowers and strewn with dark basalt boulders, each Merkava ducking down into a prepared pit with the turret base at ground level. The 2nd Platoon peeled off precisely and took up its position. That left the 1st Platoon with the company commander. The lead tank in the 1st Platoon turned off the road, followed the 2nd Platoon a short distance, then veered abruptly right. The four tanks in the 1st Platoon arrived at their positions at exactly the same time. Yossi sighed with relief as the sixty-two-ton Merkava tank ground to a stop. The driver shut the diesel down.

Yossi hit the intercom button. "Get the camouflage up!"

Hatches banged open as the driver, gunner, and loader climbed out of their holes and ran back to retrieve the camouflage netting. Quickly they had the poles up and were stringing the net over the tank.

Yossi eased himself out of his cupola, then stepped carefully off the turret onto armored decking above the right track. He walked forward until he could slide off the front fender to the ground. He stretched and tried to get the kinks out of his back, to no avail. He struggled up the pit's slope and started walking stiffly toward the 3rd Platoon's position, angling toward the front to view the deployment. A moment later he saw Ehud walking toward him, examining the same thing. *Good man*, Yossi thought, grateful he had this experienced lieutenant.

"Nice job," Yossi said, returning his executive officer's salute.

"Fairly nice," Ehud agreed. "The 2nd was a little sloppy, but I'll take care of that as soon as we're all camped down."

"Very well," Yossi acknowledged. He had not noticed any problem with the 2nd Platoon, but he would let Ehud worry about that.

"Captain, any changes on where you want the artillery and the TOW teams when they get here?" Ehud asked. He fully understood the importance of the artillery and of the Tube-launched, Optically-tracked, Wire-guided antitank missiles.

"No. We will execute the current plan—the artillery in their emplacements to our rear and the TOWs with us."

Ehud scanned the tank and TOW team emplacements. "Captain?"

"Yes?" Yossi answered, fairly sure of what was to follow.

"Any idea of what's going on?"

Yossi smiled. "You mean, what is one lonely tank company and a little artillery doing this close to Golan?"

"Yes, sir. My rear's feeling kinda breezy."

Yossi surveyed his tanks again. "Mine too. All I can tell you is that the orders came right from the top. We were simply told to get here as soon as possible and await further orders."

"Captain, if the Syrians come through that pass . . ."

Yossi looked at his second-in-command. "We will do our duty, Ehud."

Ehud looked toward the road leading to Syria. "Yes, sir."

24

FIREFIGHT IN JERICHO

B e out front at 8," the voice had said. Then the line went dead.
Joe and Mars were standing outside the American Colony Hotel
trying to look like they were enjoying the beautiful view. At exactly 8
o'clock a Chevrolet station wagon drove up and stopped. The driver
glanced at them briefly, then directed his gaze through the windshield
as if he had lost interest. Joe opened the back door for Mars and helped
him in. He closed the door and got in beside the driver.

"Did Wolf send you?" Joe asked.

The driver shifted into drive and pulled into traffic without saying
a word. After fifteen minutes of twisting and turning through the
smaller streets of West Jerusalem, they pulled up outside a small two-
story stone building. The driver continued to look straight ahead as Joe
and Mars got out. He then drove off, leaving them outside a weather-
beaten black door that looked as if it dated from the Crusades. Joe tried
the latch and found that it opened easily.

It was a dark, musty building. Light streamed out of an open door
in the back. Inside the room was Wolf Meisel at the head of a scarred
wooden table.

"Close the door," Wolf ordered.

Joe complied as Mars took one of the two vacant chairs. Joe joined
him and looked at Wolf expectantly.

"I've located where they are holding Anne McAdams."

"Where?" Mars demanded, hope springing up suddenly.

"In Jericho."

Joe held up a hand before Mars could speak again. "How did you find this out?"

"I'm afraid my sources must remain confidential."

"I'm paying for this operation," Joe reminded Wolf.

Wolf stared at Joe for a few moments. Neither man flinched. "Then I'm sure you understand that what I say is not to be repeated."

Joe nodded.

"Very well," Wolf continued. "I still have contacts in the military. They aren't sure where the PRF are but suspect they have relocated to Jericho. Using paid informants, I have identified their principal safe-house."

"How sure are you?" Joe asked.

"As sure as you can be in this business. Two men identified the place independently. I've had the house under surveillance since early this morning. Something clandestine is going on in there."

"So what are your plans?"

"Not to put too fine a point on it, I plan to take eight men and storm the house at dusk."

"What about Anne?" Mars asked. "She'll be killed."

"Not if it's done right," Wolf replied with obvious irritation. "Your dad was in the SEALS. He can explain it to you."

"Your sources *are* good," Joe remarked.

Wolf nodded.

"I want to be there," Mars demanded.

"Absolutely not!" Wolf grumbled. "The last thing in the world I need is a banged-up play-soldier mucking things up."

Mars glared at Wolf indignantly. He turned to see his father grinning at him in spite of the situation. "I'm sorry, Mars. He's right."

"Gentlemen, it is my plan to return Anne McAdams to you this evening at the American Colony Hotel. Now, if you will excuse me, I have much to do."

The taciturn driver drove Joe and Mars back to the hotel.

◆

With the hood up, it looked as if the car was about to eat the man. He looked up from the car's engine as two men emerged from the building across the street, got into a waiting station wagon, and were driven off. The "problem" with the engine resolved, the man closed the hood and walked to the corner where he knew there was a pay phone.

He inserted a phone card and punched in the number. The other end answered on the first ring. "It's as you suspected, sir," the man said. "Texas One and Texas Two have just had a meeting with Colonel M. Looks like something's on."

The phone went dead.

◆

Ya'acov's phone rang again right after he put it down. He picked it up. "Hello."

"Ya'acov—in my office, right now." David Kruger hung up.

Ya'acov felt the familiar ice-cold sensation start in his stomach and spread outwards. He was partway down the hall when he heard a familiar voice behind him.

"What's the hurry?" Ya'acov turned to see Ari Jacovy rush up.

"The colonel wants to see me. What's up? Make it quick."

"Sounds like things are starting to happen, and here I am stuck off in a corner writing reports."

Ya'acov managed a weak smile. "That's a very sad story, Lieutenant. But it so happens I'm going to need some help. I'll ask the colonel when I see him."

"I appreciate it," Ari said.

Ya'acov nodded, then rushed off. He knocked on David's door and heard a muttered reply that he took to be an invitation. He pushed the door open. David waved him to a chair. "Update," he demanded.

"Nothing up north. The weather around Hermon has us grounded. As soon as it clears, we'll launch a UAV over Syria to look for the tanks. On another subject, it appears that Joe Enderly, Mars's father, has been quite busy. One of our informants reports a meeting of the two Enderlys with none other than Wolf Meisel. I'm convinced Wolf's been hired to get Anne McAdams back, since they can't get our government or their Embassy to help."

"That's politics," David warned.

"Yes, sir, I know. Anyhow, this may help us. I intend to keep tabs on Mr. Meisel. He could help us locate the PRF."

"Okay," David agreed. "That's hot, but I still want the search for the Syrian tanks underway ASAP."

"As soon as the weather clears, sir. Oh, and one other thing—I'd like to have Lieutenant Jacovy assigned to me until this is over."

"Done," David said.

Ya'acov stood to go.

"Let's tread gently," David suggested.

"Yes, sir."

◆

Ya'acov looked up as his friend Ari entered without knocking.

"You sent for me, Captain?"

"Per your request, you've been assigned to me."

"So, what do we do?"

"We're going to try and find the Syrian tanks as soon as the weather around Golan improves. Meanwhile, I need you to head up something for me. It seems Joe Enderly has hired Wolf Meisel to try and get Anne McAdams back."

"Wow," Ari remarked. "Colonel Nasty himself. Well, he should be effective."

"My thoughts exactly. I want you to keep Meisel under surveillance. Maybe he can dig the PRF out for us. If it were me, I'd expect a move toward Jericho—commando stuff."

"What resources can I have?"

"Tell me what you need. Anything reasonable will be approved, I'm sure. But hold on a minute."

Ya'acov picked up his phone and punched in a number. "Communications?" he said into the mouthpiece. "This is Captain Isaacson. Patch me through to Sergeant Yehuda Tennenbaum."

A few moments later the sergeant came to the phone.

"On scrambler," Ya'acov said. "Can you hear me? Good. I'm going to put this on the speaker. Lieutenant Ari Jacovy is here with me."

Ya'acov pressed a button and hung up the handset. "How's the weather?"

"A little better, Captain, but we still can't launch. I'll call you as soon as it starts clearing. Will you be coming up here, sir?"

"As soon as I can. But you've got your instructions in case I'm late."

"Yes, sir. You can count on us."

"Good. One other thing. Is there a UAV base near Jerusalem? It would be a great help to Lieutenant Jacovy."

"As a matter of fact, there is. We should be able to provide whatever you want. The weather down your way is much better."

"Thank you, Sergeant."

Ya'acov pressed a button to terminate the call. He looked at Ari for a few moments as a thousand details raced through his mind. He jotted some names and numbers down for Ari.

"Keep tabs on Meisel. I'll probably be here until we can operate UAVs out of the Hermon base. If I'm not here, call Communications. Anything else you need?"

"Not a thing." Ari left, grateful for something useful and interesting to do.

◆

Abdul Suleiman tried to hide his irritation. It was another one of Avraham's spur-of-the-moment decisions, and it was throwing all of Abdul's plans into total disarray. They had been in Jericho too long, Avraham had said.

Abdul glanced at his watch. It was 1:07 in the afternoon. He gave the order for the men to start loading the new truck Avraham had acquired. The explosives and weapons would go in it, buried under crates of oranges. Some of the "workers" would travel on top of this load, while the others would travel in one of the two cars. Avraham, Abdul, and the American woman would be in the other. It would be up to Abdul to arrange for a new safe-house once they arrived at Ramallah.

◆

The sun was almost touching the Judean hills as Wolf Meisel drove the truck through the narrow roads of Jericho. He and his men aroused no interest among the Arab populace. Their robes and white, checkered *keffiehs* were quite authentic, and Wolf drove with proper Arab abandon. He consulted his hand-drawn map on the seat beside him as he navigated toward their destination.

A white-robed man stepped suddenly from a narrow alley pulling a donkey laden with a large sack of flour. Wolf was almost too late in looking up from the map. He saw the man out of the corner of his eye and immediately jammed on the brakes and cut the wheel sharply. This threw his men off their feet as the truck slewed to the right and screeched to a stop inches from the startled man. Wolf leaned out the window and gave the man a thorough dressing down in Arabic. The man set his jaw and glowered up at the driver. Wolf put the truck in reverse and backed up a little. He made a sweeping hand motion indicating the man should proceed first. The man resumed his unhurried journey and disappeared into the alley on the opposite side of the street. Wolf shook his head and drove off.

They were close now, one street over from the safe-house. Wolf noted the checkpoint and turned left onto a street barely wide enough for the truck. He slowed to a crawl as the foot traffic got up on the curb so the truck could pass. Wolf felt his heart rate increase as he neared the next intersection. They were one block away from their destination. The plan was to stop immediately after turning the corner so his men could take up their positions. Then Wolf would drive slowly toward the house. His commandos would blow the door with a small plastic explosive, toss in tear gas, and storm the house.

Wolf turned the corner and felt his heart leap into his throat. A truck was pulled up beside the safe-house facing this way, completely blocking the road. Men were loading crates and boxes. Two cars were in front of the truck, facing the same direction. Wolf stopped and looked at the Palestinian guards watching the operation. He looked back through the rear window. Good. His men saw what was happening.

Wolf knew he should cancel the mission, but that would mean admitting defeat—and the probable loss of a hundred and fifty thousand dollars unless he could stage another rescue attempt, which he knew was unlikely.

◆

Anne looked up as the lock clicked and the door banged open. The guard Anne had nicknamed Grumpy looked in and trained his fierce scowl on her. *Now what*, she wondered. She marked her place in the Gospel of John, closed her Bible, and placed it on the table. She watched the man warily, knowing something was required of her but having no idea what, since Grumpy didn't speak English.

"A gracious good evening to you," Anne said with a chipper smile. "And what can I do for your ugliness?"

The man growled something Anne couldn't understand and advanced on her with his rifle at the ready. She started pulling the Bible toward herself, intending to put it in her purse. The man slammed his rifle butt down on the book's cover, an evil gleam in his eyes. Anne jerked her hand away in fear. The man picked up the Bible with a filthy hand and looked at the gold lettering on the cover. Not understanding it, he threw the book into a corner, the leaves fluttering like a wounded bird. The man stepped to the side and pointed to the door. *That was clear enough*, she thought. *Time to go.*

A rapid burst of Arabic caused the man to whirl around. Abdul Suleiman was framed in the door looking like a parent about to discipline his child. Abdul waited. The man walked slowly to the corner and picked up the Bible. He then returned to the table and threw it down. Abdul spoke again. The man glowered as he picked up the book and handed it to Anne. She accepted it and put it in her purse. Abdul left them alone.

Grumpy bowed slightly and again indicated Anne was to leave the room. Anne clutched her purse and did as she was told.

She squinted and held her hand up against the red rays of the sunset that streamed in through the open door. Now she could see what the commotion had been. The house was almost bare. The terrorists were moving somewhere and apparently intended taking her with them.

Avraham and Abdul were at the door watching a truck being loaded. Abdul glanced to the left at the cars and past them to the guards and the street beyond. He stiffened suddenly. A truck much like theirs, parked at the corner, was pointing toward them. A man was in the driver's seat, and there were some men in back. As he watched, the men started jumping down from the rear of the truck. In ones and twos, they drifted slowly down the street toward the safe-house. They had nothing in their hands, but Abdul knew those billowing robes could cover almost anything.

Abdul motioned Avraham to silence as he reached over and grabbed an AK-47 that was propped against the wall next to the door. Staying in the shadow of the doorway, he braced the gun barrel against the inside door frame and took careful aim. The rifle went off with a booming crash as Abdul squeezed off a single shot.

The truck's windshield starred right in the face of the driver. The bullet drilled a neat hole in Wolf's forehead above his right eye, traveled through his brain, and blew a hole out the back large enough to hold a grapefruit. He was clinically dead even as his head rocked back with the terrible impact. A moment later he slumped over the wheel. His right leg spasmed, flooring the accelerator as his left foot fell off the clutch. The rear tires spun, churning up a cloud of blue smoke as the truck lurched forward. The rear wheels slewed sideways until the right rear fender slammed into a parked car.

The collision threw the rear back to the left. The truck screamed down the narrow street in first gear. The guards and loaders started running back to the safe-house. The truck sideswiped the lead PRF car and veered suddenly toward the house. It hit the corner dead center and knocked the stone wall down. A corner of the flat roof came down with a blinding spray of dust and rock shards, arresting the truck's career in an instant.

Abdul shouted to the men, ordering them outside to fight. He took a quick look out the door, then dashed to the other side of the street, ducking down behind a car. He looked up the street. Halfway to the corner he saw a thin, dark line inside one of the doorways. It grew slightly wider, and a head appeared above it. Abdul threw himself on the car's hood, leveled the AK-47, and squeezed the trigger. The rifle jumped in his hands as the long burst tore its way through the door frame. The man screamed and tumbled into the street.

Rapid footsteps sounded further up the street. Abdul scanned the houses quickly, then saw two men running stooped over, trying to hide behind the cars. Abdul brought his rifle up and got off a quick burst. One of the men sprawled on the sidewalk as the other passed behind a car. Once he got on the other side he straightened up and ran for his life. Abdul smiled as he slowly brought the gun up. He pulled the trigger, but the gun only clicked. The magazine was empty.

A shout came from a side-alley. Abdul looked over in time to see one of his men riddle two more of the attackers with a burst that emptied his magazine. *How many more does that leave?* Abdul wondered. But it didn't matter, he realized. At least one had gotten away.

He ran back to Avraham. "We must leave at once," he told him. Abdul expected a tongue-lashing from Avraham, but all he got was a glowering nod. Avraham ordered all the men except Abdul into the truck and told them to back down the street and head for Ramallah. He then gave Abdul a quick command. Abdul grabbed two Uzis and a canvas bag of loaded clips and propelled Anne out the door. Avraham ran on ahead to the undamaged Ford Escort. He jumped behind the wheel and cranked the engine as Abdul threw open the rear door, pushed Anne inside, and climbed in beside her. He forced her to lie on the floor as he hunched over the front seat. Avraham spun the car around and started following the truck. At the corner they parted ways as Avraham turned toward the north.

◆

Ya'acov looked at Ari as they listened to the speakerphone connection to the UAV base near Jerusalem. "What are they doing now?" he asked.

"Looks like it's all over, sir," the payload operator said. "It was a spectacular firefight while it lasted. You want me to bring the bird back?"

"Where are the vehicles?" Ya'acov asked.

"The truck is headed out of Jericho to the northwest, probably heading for Ramallah. The car is headed north—looks like they're going to take Highway 90."

Ari watched Ya'acov. He could tell his friend was working hard on something.

"Sir?" came the speakerphone.

"Yes?" Ya'acov replied absentmindedly.

"Do you want us to bring the bird back?"

Again Ya'acov hesitated. "How much longer can it stay up?"

"A little more than an hour and still have enough reserve to get back. Longer if it's expendable."

"Follow the car as long as you can."

It was the sergeant's turn to pause. "Yes, sir," he said finally.

Ya'acov pressed the mute button. "While they're doing that, call the duty desk and get some of our troops to intercept the truck. Then set up some roadblocks to stop the car."

"Assets are kinda thin," Ari observed.

"Do the best you can. I've got to run. There's an Apache helicopter waiting to take me up to Hermon. I'll call you once we lift off. Any questions?" His expression told the lieutenant there had better not be any.

"No, sir," Ari said. He looked concerned at the mention of the Apache but decided it was none of his business.

Ya'acov rushed out, moving more quickly than Ari had seen him move in a long time.

◆

Moshe sat across from Mars and Joe as they waited for news from Wolf Meisel. A single rap sounded. Mars jumped up, ran to the door, and swung it open. His expectant expression changed to shock followed by puzzlement.

"May I come in?" Ya'acov asked.

"Yes," Mars said, standing aside. "Please do."

Ya'acov closed the door and stood next to it. "Please sit back down." Mars joined his father on the couch.

"This has got to be quick. First of all, is it understood that I have not been here tonight?"

Mars looked at Joe questioningly.

"We understand," Joe said. "We won't say a word."

"That includes me," Moshe added.

"Good. I'm trusting all of you because this could get me court-martialed." He paused a moment, then plunged on. "You were expecting Mr. Wolf Meisel. He, in all likelihood, will not be returning. We observed him and his men engage in a firefight in Jericho a short time ago with a group we presume to be the PRF."

Ya'acov paused as he saw the anguish building in Mars's eyes. "I'm sorry to say, it went very badly."

"Was Anne . . . ?" Mars could not finish the question.

"We think she survived the attack. A truck and a car left the house after the fight. Three people were seen getting in the car, and we believe one of them was Anne."

"So they still have her?" Mars asked.

"We think so. When I left, they were heading north from Jericho."

"Where do you think they're going?" Joe asked.

Ya'acov considered this before answering. He had already said more than enough to land himself in prison for a long time. "You didn't hear this from me, and I definitely can't tell you my reasoning, but I would guess that Mr. Avraham Abbas is heading for Syria as fast as his little chariot can take him."

"By what route?" Mars asked.

Ya'acov had to smile at the directness of the question. "Dr. Stein is relatively familiar with Israel's geography."

Ya'acov turned and was out the door before anyone could ask another question.

◆

Anne clutched her purse as she huddled in the corner made by the seat and the back door, as far from Abdul as she could get. She tried to ignore the way Avraham was driving and was grateful she couldn't see much, as far down as she was sitting.

The reddish tinge of sunset was gone now, replaced by a dark blue that was almost black. There would be no moon tonight, but the stars were out, brilliant points of white light.

Avraham sat hunched over the wheel, driving the little Escort as hard as it would go. Fortunately the traffic was light and the highway was straighter than most in Israel, since it followed the lower Jordan River valley. Abdul divided his time between watching where Avraham was going and keeping an eye on Anne.

The small towns and crossroads flashed past, then disappeared, as if the white glow of the headlights had brought them into being.

Avraham slowed as they approached a Y intersection just past the town of Massu'a. He took the branch to the right, staying on Highway 90 as it angled closer to the Jordan River. Up ahead was the intersection with Highway 55, which on the left wound through the hills to Nablus while the right continued into Jordan.

Abdul leaned forward and said something to Avraham in Arabic. The other nodded, taking his foot off the accelerator and killing the lights. He cursed and stood on the brakes as the road disappeared from sight completely. In a few minutes his eyes adapted well enough for him to see. He put the car in drive and continued cautiously up the hill. When they topped it, he saw Abdul's advice had been correct. There, less than a mile away, were the obvious signs of an IDF roadblock. Red taillights were backed up on this side of the Highway 55 intersection, while white headlights were backed up on the other.

Avraham turned the car around, taking care not to drive into the ditch. He drove back over the hill and continued several miles before he dared to turn the lights on again.

He stopped when they arrived again at the Y intersection. He turned to the right and started up the secondary road, climbing steadily as they went into the hills. After the road curved back around to the northeast he turned the lights off again. He half-expected to see another roadblock as they intersected with Highway 55 further to the west. But it was clear.

Avraham turned left and flipped on the lights again. He continued driving through the hills toward Nablus, following the winding road until they came to Regional Road 588. He conferred briefly with Abdul. Nodding in agreement, Avraham turned onto 588 and continued toward the north at a much slower rate over the narrow road.

25

DESPERATE FLIGHT

"So, what route will this Avraham Abbas take?" Mars asked Moshe.

"I don't know," Moshe replied.

"But Captain Isaacson said you knew."

"No, he didn't. He said I knew Israel's geography. However, if you want to know where Abbas will leave Israel, I think I can help."

"Okay, where?"

"If they drive out, they'll have to take the Damascus Highway, either near Quneitra or a little bit north of there. There are about three different ways to get to the highway. If they try to walk out, it will still be somewhere near that highway."

"I have to go up there!" Mars demanded.

"There's nothing we can do," Moshe said with a sigh.

"But I have to try! Anne means more to me than anything in this world. And nobody cares what happens to her except me."

"That's not exactly true," Joe reminded Mars.

Mars looked down, acknowledging the truth of that. "Dad, I have to go!"

Joe looked at his son, then over at Moshe. "Can you drive us there?" he asked.

"Yes," he answered with resignation.

Mars looked up in gratitude. Moshe turned for the door.

◆

Ya'acov looked at the sinister, dark shape of the Apache AH-64A attack helicopter as the ground crew finished refueling it under the glare of work lights. It was spare and angular, sitting there under the umbrella of its massive four-bladed rotor. It looked like a huge, ugly insect, and Ya'acov was not at all sure he wanted to ride in it. The recent accident was not the only reason, but it would do for a start.

"Handsome, isn't it?" Lieutenant Joel Rabinovich said.

Ya'acov glanced at the IAF pilot to see if he was kidding. He wasn't.

"I think deadly comes closer," Ya'acov replied.

Joel scanned his craft and laughed. "In my book deadly is handsome."

"If you say so," Ya'acov said, smiling in spite of his concern. "When do we leave?"

Joel heard the apprehension in the Intelligence officer's voice. "As soon as the ground crew fills the tanks. Something wrong, sir?" The IAF officer knew what it was, but like most aviators, he delighted in the danger of his trade.

"I thought the Apaches were grounded."

"This is the only one that isn't. Did you hear about the crash in the Negev?"

"Yes. Sounded pretty bad."

"Yeah. I knew the crew. Ruined their whole day."

Ya'acov knew this meant they were killed. "So why isn't this one grounded?"

"All Apaches are grounded until their transmissions are inspected. This one was in the shop for a transmission replacement when the accident happened. Since the transmission is new, this one is exempt."

"But the replacement transmission is the same type as in the other Apaches, right?"

"That's a roger. But the requirement's been met. A new transmission qualifies as inspected."

"How nice," Ya'acov grumbled. He looked the helicopter over under the harsh work lights. "How are you armed?"

"We've got a pretty good sting. We're carrying eight laser-guided

Hellfire antitank missiles and twelve hundred rounds for the thirty-millimeter cannon. But we could carry up to sixteen missiles if the mission called for serious tank killing."

"What you've got sounds lethal enough to me."

"It's a moot point. Without a copilot/gunner, we're not about to engage anything. Looks like we're all fueled up. Ready to go?"

"Yes," Ya'acov said, which was exactly the opposite of how he felt.

Joel helped Ya'acov up into a seat that was below and in front of the pilot's and got him all cinched up in his harness. "Sir, please don't touch anything. We don't want to start a war by accidentally shooting off all our ordinance."

Ya'acov managed a grin. "Not to worry, Lieutenant. I shan't touch a thing. Oh, but there is one more matter."

"What's that, sir?"

"I need to have secure communications on this channel." He handed the pilot a slip of paper.

"No problem. I'll set it up as soon as we lift off." He showed Ya'acov how to work the intercom and how to switch to the radio. "You'll hear over the intercom when I've got 'em."

Ya'acov nodded.

Joel closed Ya'acov's door, climbed into the aft cockpit, and strapped himself in. The crew chief nodded when the pilot glanced at him. Joel hit the starter on the left engine and watched the RPM build. As soon as the turbine caught, he started cranking the right engine. The twin engines quickly whined up the audible scale. Just short of 100 percent, Joel pulled up firmly on the collective and pressed forward on the stick. The Apache leapt up into the darkness over Jerusalem and transitioned into forward flight. The expertness of the maneuver was lost on the Intelligence officer.

Ya'acov listened in on the intercom as Joel established a secure link on the VHF radio. "You're talking to Communications now, sir," the pilot advised him.

"Thanks," Ya'acov said over the intercom, then switched to the radio. In less than a minute he was patched through to Ari. "What's happening?" Ya'acov asked.

Ari's irritation was obvious even over the radio. "We got the truck on Highway 3 as it was heading for Ramallah. But we missed Abbas."

Ya'acov didn't know how he felt about that. He knew what would certainly happen to Anne if they trapped the PRF leader. "How?" Ya'acov asked.

"We lost contact with the UAV while Abbas was still on Highway 90, several miles from a roadblock. Up to that point I thought we had him. I was about to order a patrol south on 90 when the UAV flipped out."

"Did we lose it?"

"No. It went on autopilot as soon we lost the link. It flew back to base on its own and parachuted in. I understand the wizards are in a real flap trying to find out what went wrong with it."

"Okay. Set up a roadblock further north. Send a complete report to Colonel Kruger. Also, tell him I'm on my way to the UAV base near Hermon. I'll contact you from there."

"Yes, sir."

Ya'acov looked through the canopy as they flew rapidly toward Galilee. It was quite dark outside. The lights of towns and villages crept past, providing the only visual clue of their progress.

Joel's voice broke through his reverie. "Captain, Sergeant Yehuda Tennenbaum is calling you."

Ya'acov switched to the radio. "What's up, Sergeant?"

"We launched the bird a few minutes ago. Per your instructions, we've given it an original heading to take it out over Quneitra. Where to from there?"

Ya'acov flipped to intercom. "How long till we get there?"

"About fifteen minutes."

Ya'acov switched back to the radio. "I'll be there in about fifteen minutes. Go about ten miles past Quneitra on the Damascus Highway, then start searching to the north. I'll see you when I get there."

"Yes, sir." The sergeant signed off.

◆

The drive up to Ramallah on Highway 60 had not been bad. Unfortunately, this lulled Joe and Mars into thinking the rest of the trip would be as easy. Despite the fact that 60 became a smaller road that twisted and turned through the mountains, Moshe kept pressing the big GMC Safari as hard as he dared.

Mars looked out the windows in concern as they started through a series of hairpin turns south of Nablus.

"Are you sure this is the most direct way?" he asked from the backseat.

"It's not the most direct. Highway 90's the most direct, but we'd probably run into roadblocks on it. Trust me."

"Do we have a choice?" Mars muttered.

◆

Ya'acov started unbuckling his harness while Joel was making his approach to the UAV control trailer. He threw open the door as soon as the Apache settled down on its stubby landing gear. He ducked his head and ran for the trailer. He wrenched the door open and hurried in. Sergeant Avi Barak was looking back at him.

"Find anything yet?" Ya'acov asked.

"No, sir. You sure those Syrians didn't go somewhere else?"

"They're within striking distance of Galilee right now—you can bet on it!"

Ya'acov brought up a chair and sat down. Avi pushed the map toward him and traced the search pattern.

Ya'acov pointed to a spot half the distance back toward Quneitra. "I think you're too far east. Come back to about here."

"There aren't any roads there, sir," Avi said as he relayed the coordinates to Sergeant Yehuda Tennenbaum. The screen whirled as the UAV came around. A few minutes later the pilot reported they had reached the desired coordinates.

Ya'acov peered at the screen. "Turn north and get a little lower if you can." The image on the screen spun, then tilted as the small plane lost altitude.

"You think they might have cut a secret road through to the highway?" Avi asked.

"We'll see." Ya'acov saw a depression off to the right. "Come right a little and follow that valley."

A quick turn and the UAV was faithfully following the contour of the valley.

"Now let's switch to infrared," Ya'acov ordered. The screen broke up, then steadied as the FLIR camera started sending its heat picture. The image looked even stranger than the light-intensified one as the warmer ground bloomed over the cooler surroundings.

"Whoa, look at that," Avi said, pointing to a spot near the top of the screen that was slightly warmer than its surroundings. It grew steadily brighter as they watched. Even as it was shining bright, a few other glowing objects appeared up ahead, all lined up in the valley. "Captain, I think we've found your tanks."

Ya'acov felt his mouth go dry. "Are they getting ready to move out?"

"Don't think so, sir. My guess is some of them are charging batteries."

"I need the secure line!"

"It hasn't moved," Avi said.

Ya'acov hurried to the phone and punched in David's office phone number. David picked it up on the first ring. "On scrambler," Ya'acov said, pressing the red button. He waited for the units to synchronize. "Colonel, this is Ya'acov! We've found the Syrian tanks. They're hidden on a secret road immediately off the Damascus Highway! We need armor up in Galilee, and we need it bad!"

"I'll take care of it on this end," David said with a calmness that surprised Ya'acov. "But we're going to need some close-in Intelligence work, and you're it. Get Lieutenant Rabinovich to fly you to the tank company west of Quneitra. Stay as close to the action as you can, and keep me informed. Any questions?"

"No, sir."

"Okay, get to it."

Avi and Yehuda watched with concern as Ya'acov ran out of the trailer. "I sure hope the Syrians don't turn this way when they break through," Avi muttered.

◆

Lieutenant Aziz Massour looked at the trail as the runner went by. The reinforced armored division was under strict radio silence. So in the age of laser range-finders and thermal sights, the order to move out was being given on foot.

Aziz switched to intercom and told the driver to start his engine. The 780-horsepower diesel cranked for a few seconds, then rumbled to life, settling down in an uneven idle. Aziz couldn't see the lead tanks, but he knew from their sounds that they were moving. It wouldn't be long now. A moment later the tank in front lurched off. Aziz's driver let out the clutch and braked the right track, maneuvering them out of their tight parking slot. The massive T-72 tank moved out and pivoted back to the left onto the narrow roadway. The driver accelerated quickly, afraid of letting the tank ahead get out of sight. It was a dark night, and it would be all too easy to ram another tank or run off the road and lose a track.

Aziz was not a man given to reflection. But this mission did cause him to think. He had been a little boy the last time Syria had done battle with the Israelis. He vowed this one would go better.

◆

Joel began the engine-start sequence the moment he saw Ya'acov leave the trailer.

Ya'acov ran to the helicopter and climbed awkwardly into the front cockpit.

"Need help getting strapped in, sir?" Joel asked.

"No, I think I can do it. Do you know where our tank company is?"

"Yes, sir. They're the only tanks we have up here. That our next stop?"

"Right. And set me up a secure channel to Intelligence Communications in Jerusalem as soon as we're airborne."

"We're airborne now, sir." Joel pulled up firmly on the collective, and the Apache shot into the air toward the dark Golan Heights.

A few moments later Joel came back on the intercom. "I've got Communications on the line. The set's already on scramble."

Ya'acov flipped the switch Joel had shown him. He checked in with David Kruger, then lapsed into silence as the attack helicopter ate up the distance to the Golan Heights.

Ya'acov saw Joel put on his night vision goggles as they approached the Israeli tanks. The pilot banked suddenly. Ya'acov looked out but couldn't see anything. They touched down gently. Joel cut the engines.

"Here you are," he said, taking the goggles off. "And we have company." Joel pointed to an ancient Bell Huey sitting next to them.

Ya'acov glanced at the other helicopter without any real interest. "Where are the tanks?" he asked as he got out of his harness.

Joel pointed off to the right. "Go in that direction. You'll run right into them."

"Thanks. Would you get on the horn and tell them I'm coming? I don't know the password, and I'd just as soon not get ventilated."

"Can't have that, Captain. I'll let 'em know you're on the way."

Ya'acov waited until Joel told him the tankers were expecting him. He then walked into the night with the uncomfortable knowledge that he was approaching dozens of men who could quickly terminate his life in a variety of grisly ways. He had been walking for about a minute when he heard rather than saw the sentry.

"Halt!" the man commanded out of the darkness.

Ya'acov did as he was told.

"Who goes there?" the man asked.

"Captain Ya'acov Isaacson, and don't bother asking for the password. I don't know it."

Ya'acov heard the click as the soldier's gun went back on safety. In a moment he saw a dark shape detach itself from its darker background and come toward him.

"Right this way, Captain," the man said. "Captain Goldman is expecting you."

The man started off at a brisk pace that Ya'acov found difficult to match. He tripped on an unseen rock and almost fell. The soldier heard and slacked his pace a little, but not as much as Ya'acov would have liked. The Intelligence officer concentrated on picking his feet up and staying directly behind the soldier.

"Captain Isaacson?" came a voice from ahead.

"I wish I could see as well as you night-owls can," Ya'acov said with some irritation.

"I could make some typical comment about Intelligence, but you probably wouldn't appreciate it."

Ya'acov stopped. He was fairly sure who the unseen man was. Did he really have a problem with the Intelligence branch? Many regular IDF soldiers did.

"I'm Yossi Goldman," the man said. Ya'acov reached for where he suspected the man's hand was and shook it. "And not to worry. I'm not one of the Intelligence baiters."

"I guess I'm glad to hear that. So, what do you make of the situation?"

Yossi paused a long time before answering. "It's grim. I mean, *really* grim. We have eleven tanks, twelve artillery, and eight TOW antitank teams to hold off over four hundred Syrian T-72s plus artillery and assorted modern nastiness. '73 was bad, but not *this* bad. If they decide to break through, there's no way we can hold 'em off until our tanks get here from the Negev. Looks like the heavies goofed, big-time."

"What about the Air Force?" Ya'acov asked.

"No help there, at least not at first. They'll be too busy knocking out missile sites and antiaircraft artillery—that and slugging it out with the Syrian MiGs for air superiority. On top of that, all the Apaches are down, except the one you're in, and we can't count on the Cobra gunships either. They don't have FLIR gear, and the weather guessers say we're in for heavy-duty fog in the morning. Oh, and one more thing you might want to put in your report . . ."

"What's that?" Ya'acov asked, dreading the answer.

"I don't think any of us are going to be alive this time tomorrow. The heavies better decide what they plan to do with four hundred Syrian tanks loose in Galilee, with more to follow."

Ya'acov didn't know what to say. The silence drew out. "I wish you the best," he said finally, regretting how hollow it must sound. "I have to get back."

"Would you like a guide?" Yossi asked.

"Thanks. I probably wouldn't make it otherwise."

◆

Avraham had fumed as Abdul helped him navigate around the IDF roadblock. Now they encountered light traffic as they traveled north on Regional Road 588. They followed its twisting course, veering right at the Y intersection with local Road 5799. This road carried them east toward the Jordan River valley again. Several miles further on they turned north again on Regional Road 458. Abdul began to breathe easier when he saw the intersection with Highway 90 up ahead.

Avraham turned onto the highway and accelerated quickly. He glanced back at Abdul. "How are we doing?"

"Not bad. If we don't have any more trouble, we should be at the border in an hour or so."

Anne felt her stomach knot up. She watched the headlights of the southbound cars, each one taunting her with the illusion of safety so close, yet so far away. The Ford Escort hurtled on into the night, taking her ever closer to Syria, and farther from Mars and happiness. Tears began to well up in her eyes to drop unseen on her blouse.

Anne looked up suddenly in alarm. The car had entered a curve that was growing progressively tighter. Avraham cursed and took his foot off the accelerator. The tires screeched in protest as Avraham maintained control by the slimmest of margins. Abdul tensed but remained motionless, his fate controlled by the one he served.

Anne leaned to the side a little and looked out the windshield into the black night. Then she dropped her gaze to the instrument panel. She watched Avraham as he made quick corrections to the steering wheel. He turned the wheel as they entered a tight left turn. Anne watched the right-hand ditch as the headlights illuminated it. It dropped off abruptly, leaving a narrow shoulder littered by rocks and boulders.

Abdul saw a sudden movement out of the corner of his eye. Instinctively he reached toward Anne, but he was not quite quick enough. Anne lunged over the front seat and grabbed the steering wheel, pulling it to the right as hard as she could. Avraham tried to counter the move but was too late. The Escort swept over the shoulder and became airborne over the deep ditch. They landed with a heavy crash. Rocks pounded the underside of the car as Avraham wrenched the wheel, trying to get the car under control. The Ford slued sideways as it rushed toward a large basalt boulder directly in its path. Anne watched in fascinated horror as the right-front fender plowed into the boulder.

The car bounded into the air and started a sickening roll to the right. The Escort landed on its top, shattering all the windows, peppering the occupants with pea-sized granules of tempered glass. Anne collided repeatedly with Abdul and the front seat as they rattled around unrestrained by seat belts. She lost track of how many times the car rolled, but the horrible grinding and pounding seemed to go on forever.

Finally it was over. The Escort had come to a stop upside-down. The only sounds were the pinging of the hot engine and the sound of some liquid pouring out on the ground. Anne was sprawled on the roof of the car with Abdul beside her. She couldn't see Avraham since she was facing backwards toward the hole where the rear window had been. She brought her hand up to wipe her nose. It came away wet.

Anne shivered as she started crawling toward the opening. The small glass shards ground cruelly into her hands and knees as she struggled toward freedom. She flattened out as she came to the window frame, feeling through the opening with her hands. The rock-strewn ditch was only a few inches below her. She started wriggling through. Up above, a car roared by unseen, its headlight sweeping over the deep ditch but not illuminating the car at the bottom. Anne brought her knees up to the window. A rough hand grabbed her left ankle as she started through with her right leg. She cried out in surprise as she struggled against the restraint. The hand only gripped harder, sending pain shooting to her brain. Anne rolled on her side and kicked out with her free leg, connecting with a meaty crunch. The hand let go. She scrambled forward and rolled out of the car.

Anne lay on her back, the rocks gouging her cruelly. She knew she had to get up and run, but a thousand pains rebelled against such an action. She forced herself to move. Her vision exploded in countless stars as she struggled to her feet. She stood for a few moments, swaying uncertainly as dizziness tried to overcome her. She looked around at the dark, indistinct shapes until she realized she was facing away from the road. She spun around and took one step forward, running into a wall of flesh. Strong arms encircled her, shook her like a rag doll, and threw her back to the ground.

Anne looked up. Although all she could see was a towering black shape, she knew it was Avraham. Slowly he raised his right arm from his side. The starlight glinted dully off the Uzi's barrel. Up the gun came, pointing directly at her head.

A scrabbling noise sounded behind them. Abdul said something quickly in Arabic as he struggled to his feet. The gun barrel did not waver. Anne shot an arrow prayer to her Lord, expecting to see death each passing moment. Avraham slowly lowered the gun and clicked on the safety.

"You have no idea how close you came," he said. Although his voice was low, Anne had never in her life heard such hatred directed toward another human being.

◆

"I'm glad that's past," Moshe said as he guided the Safari around the twisting curves north of Nablus.

"What's that?" Mars asked.

"Nablus. Not exactly the best place to have an accident or flat tire."

"Arab town?"

Moshe hesitated. "Yes," he said finally.

"How are we doing?" Joe asked.

"Not bad. We're a little over twenty miles south of the Sea of Galilee. We're probably a couple of hours from Golan."

Moshe's concentration was riveted on the road as it twisted and turned on the way toward Jenin. Mars's thoughts went ahead of them, wondering where Anne was and if she was all right.

26

ALL ROADS
LEAD TO SYRIA

I won't do it!" Anne said defiantly.
"You will or I'll shoot you and use your dead body instead!"
Avraham brought his Uzi up level with her heart. Abdul said something in Arabic. Avraham ignored him and flicked the safety off with a final-sounding click.

Anne knew he meant it. "Stop! I'll do it!"

Avraham seemed almost disappointed as he slowly lowered the submachine gun. He nodded toward the roadway above them. Anne struggled up the steep slope with Avraham and Abdul following close behind. At the top, Avraham looked up and down the road. They were on the crest of a hill and could see quite some distance in both directions. The traffic was light. Here and there were the headlights and taillights of cars traveling on the sea of blackness.

Avraham judged that a northbound car would be next to pass. He motioned with his gun. Anne lay down on the shoulder while Abdul arranged her convincingly. The two men disappeared behind a huge boulder to wait. The oncoming car slowed as it came around the curve, then slowed further as the headlights swept across Anne. After a moment's hesitation the car picked up speed again, rushed past, and was gone. Avraham stalked out into the middle of the road and shook his fist at the retreating car.

Turning, he saw that a southbound car was approaching. Avraham pointed, and Abdul moved Anne north of the great boulder and re-positioned her. Again the two men waited behind the rock. This car also slowed but did not stop. Avraham cursed and kicked a rock into the road.

He looked up and down the road. The next car would be northbound, and after that, it might be quite some time until another came along. Avraham gave an order to Abdul in Arabic. The other hesitated, then led Anne south of the boulder. When she started to lie down on the shoulder, he gripped her arm and led her into the northbound lane. She looked up at him in horror.

"Don't say anything," he hissed as he saw her open her mouth. "He will shoot you if you refuse. Lie still and don't move."

Anne glanced back at Avraham. He had his Uzi out and pointed at her. She lay down on the rough surface, mindless of the pain in her lacerated hands and knees. Abdul took one final look, then ran back to Avraham. The men ducked behind the boulder.

Anne listened. At first all she could hear was the thundering of her pulse. Then she heard the engine noise. It started out as a faint humming sound that came and went with the light breeze that tugged at her hair. Gradually it grew louder. She could hear the car decelerate as it entered curves, only to pick up speed coming out. The car had a distinctive squeal as if something were wrong with the brakes. Anne had no idea how many curves came before the one where she lay, but she counted three as she listened, not daring to turn her head to look. She looked straight ahead toward the outside of the curve.

In a few moments she saw what she dreaded. The headlights of the approaching car were beginning to shine on the tops of the bushes lining the road. She could hear the car clearly now. Moments later the engine throttled back and the brakes squealed briefly as the car entered the curve. Would the driver see her in time, she wondered. The light from the headlights grew brighter and began to sweep around the curve, closer and closer to where she lay. The sound from the motor seemed almost deafening as it maintained the car's rapid pace. Anne knew the driver would never see her in time. He was too close! The squeal of tire rubber almost gave her heart failure. It seemed to last forever as the car ground its relentless way toward her. Every moment she expected to have the front wheels maul her, ending her life in a brief flash of agony.

Then it was over. Silence except for a strange noise she finally recognized as an idling engine. She opened her eyes. She was looking at the right-front wheel, not two feet from her head. She shuddered involuntarily. She heard a door open and someone get out. Shoes crunched on the pavement as the driver hurried to the front of the car. He bent down and said something in Hebrew. Behind her she heard footsteps running toward them. She thought about shouting a warning, but it was too late. A burst of automatic gunfire cut the man down even as he started turning around.

Avraham shouted to Abdul as they raced toward the car. Abdul ran for the passenger side, while Avraham made for the open driver's door. Inside, a terrified woman struggled to release her shoulder harness so she could slip over to the steering wheel. Finally it was loose, and she grabbed the wheel to pull herself over. Avraham skidded to a stop as she reached for the door handle. He pulled the trigger on his Uzi only feet from her face. Abdul wrenched the passenger-side door open, grabbed the woman's ankles, and pulled her out of the car, smearing the seat with blood as he did so. He dragged her body to the bottom of the ditch, then returned for the man.

Anne looked up at Avraham in horror. "Get in the back!" he ordered, pointing the submachine gun at her. She crawled to her feet and did as he said. Abdul climbed up from the ditch and into the backseat beside her. Avraham slid under the wheel and jerked the door shut. He slammed the Volvo's gear selector into drive and drove off.

◆

The horror spun around and around in Anne's mind like a bizarre carousel from hell, one that ran faster and faster, threatening to throw her off, smashing her against an unfair world. She had no idea what the two terrorists intended doing with her, although she knew she had come very close to leaving this life. And two people she had never met were lying dead beside the road, their only crime being that they had something the terrorists wanted.

But just when the carousel seemed about to self-destruct, something happened. She felt a peace she could not understand. This was baffling. She knew there was absolutely no reason for optimism. Anne dwelt on these things as the Volvo made the turn at the Sea of Galilee and continued up its east coast.

♦

"We're getting close now," Moshe announced as he slacked off some from his white-knuckled pace.

"Where are we?" Mars asked.

"We just turned onto Highway 91, the main road leading to Quneitra."

"How much longer?"

"Not long, but I imagine we'll run into an IDF roadblock pretty soon."

As if in confirmation of Moshe's prediction, the Safari topped a rise, revealing a line of red taillights on the road ahead. Moshe watched as most of the eastbound cars made a U turn to return the way they had come. The few that went through, he guessed, were on government business. Moshe rolled down his window as his turn came.

"Shalom," Moshe said to the soldier.

"Shalom," the soldier replied mechanically. "The road is closed. You will have to turn around."

"I am Dr. Moshe Stein of the Hebrew University. My colleagues and I are on our way to a dig near Har Odem."

"I'm sorry, Dr. Stein," the soldier said, not sounding one bit sorry. "Government vehicles *only* beyond this point."

Moshe looked at the man in irritation. "How long will the road be closed?" he asked finally.

"I don't know. Now, I must ask you to turn around. You're blocking the other cars in line."

"Can we pull off and wait?" Moshe asked.

The soldier looked at Moshe as if he were crazy. "You can if you wish. I wouldn't recommend it."

"Why?"

"I can't say."

Moshe shrugged and pulled off the road under the watchful eye of the IDF guards. "I guess we wait and see," he said.

"What's going on?" Joe asked.

"Hard to say," Moshe replied. "My guess is, we're expecting some nastiness from the Syrians."

"How far are we from the border?" Mars asked.

"Oh, several miles I guess."

Mars leaned back in the seat.

◆

"Turn here," Abdul advised as he strained to see the map, using the glove-box light.

Avraham turned right on Regional Road 888 at the northern end of the Sea of Galilee. "How much further?"

"A little less than ten miles to Highway 91. From there it's another ten or so to Quneitra."

Avraham grunted as he guided the agile car through the curves. He drove in silence until they were less than a mile from the highway. The Volvo topped a hill. Ahead was the unwanted sight of taillights at another IDF roadblock. Avraham swore and stood on the brakes. He quickly turned off the car's lights and made a U turn, scraping the right fender in his haste. He hurried back over the hill, then slowed to a crawl as he looked to the right and left, trying to see into the inky shadows.

"There," Abdul said, pointing at an indistinct shape in the murk. Avraham turned off the road carefully and followed the rutted dirt track until they were out of sight. He shut off the engine and turned in the seat.

"What's going on?" Avraham demanded, his tone sounding as if Abdul were responsible.

"If we were close to Jericho, I'd say they were looking for us. But this close to the border, I don't know."

"What about other crossings?"

"The same, probably."

Avraham cursed again, his hands drumming on the steering wheel. With all his experience with Avraham, Abdul had no idea what his leader was thinking. He only knew the man was very close to a violent outburst. Abdul's blood ran cold as he remembered what he had seen Avraham do in similar moods. He remained silent, hoping this would pass quickly.

"Abdul!"

"Yes?"

"Get up to the top of the hill and keep an eye on the Jews."

Avraham turned in the front seat as Abdul opened the door and got out. "And you," he said as he brought his Uzi to bear on Anne, "you make one sound and you're dead."

Abdul trudged off in the darkness, hoping Anne had the good sense to do as Avraham said.

27

SYRIAN TANKS ON THE GOLAN HEIGHTS

All night westerly winds pushed moisture-laden air from the Mediterranean Sea, overlaying the entire area of Galilee and the Golan Heights. Gradually the temperature dropped until it reached dew point shortly after midnight. The fog started as wispy tendrils in the low areas. Then it became heavier as it spread out of the bottoms and onto higher ground, reaching even the passes through Golan. It reached maximum density in the hours before dawn—a fog that would have done London proud.

The scream of incoming artillery shells surprised Captain Yossi Goldman even though he had been expecting it. Large-caliber rounds exploded all around them, shaking the heavy Merkava tanks and pelting them with shrapnel and rocks. He knew the Syrians did not know where the Israelis were and were only carrying out standard Soviet armored tactics: artillery barrages precede the assault by tanks and infantry. He knew a direct hit was unlikely and only hoped he would not lose his antenna.

Yossi glanced down. His gunner was peering up at him anxiously. "It won't be long now," he told the man.

◆

Lieutenant Aziz Massour looked down into the crowded interior of his T-72 tank. At his order, the driver let out the clutch and struggled with the braking laterals to steer. Aziz let out an apprehensive sigh, glad they were finally going into action, but wondering what the outcome would be.

The operational plan was not complicated, but the dense fog had thrown one kink into it—there would be no close air support until the fog lifted. But the armored and mechanized infantry brigades would start out as planned, with the leading tank company responsible for clearing any minefields. Aziz had missed that honor, being in the 1st Platoon of the second company in line. He looked backward quickly before facing forward again. The tanks were almost on top of each other to maintain contact in the swirling fog. He hoped the tanks in front would not stop suddenly.

Aziz tried to reassure himself as the tank column continued to push through the unrelenting fog. So far the operation was going exactly as the command staff had predicted. Even the weather was cooperating. Although the dense fog made tank driving hazardous, it would also keep the Israeli fighter-bombers on the ground during the initial invasion. Of course, the weather grounded the Syrian aircraft as well.

The column was traveling more slowly now as they followed the curving road west of Quneitra. Aziz knew he would not breathe easier until they were on the plain where they could spread out below the Golan Heights.

◆

Captain Yossi Goldman peered through the infrared sight. What he saw made his blood run cold. His experience in previous tank battles had taught him that courage and fear were not mutually exclusive. He had no trouble seeing the Syrian battle column as it crested the ridge—their radiated heat was better than any searchlight. And while Yossi's tankers could see the Syrians, the reverse was not true. The Israelis were hull-down in their pits and were camouflaged and were monitoring the radio net with all nonessential equipment shut off. The guns were laid on the mountain road ready for instant action.

Yossi hit the radio transmit button. "Execute!" All eleven Merkava tanks started engines at the same time. Yossi's gunner made a slight correction to the hundred-and-twenty-millimeter main gun and fired, causing fire and smoke to blossom around their tank, baptizing them all in the stench of cordite. A few seconds later the shell penetrated the lead Syrian tank and exploded. The tank's internal stores of ammunition went off, showering the trailing tanks with chunks of shrapnel like a metallic hailstorm. The rest of the Israeli tanks held their fire. Yossi smiled at their discipline. One shot. One tank destroyed. Best of all, the Syrian advance was temporarily stopped.

◆

Joel Rabinovich initiated the engine-start sequence the moment the first round was fired. He and Ya'acov had not actually seen the impact, but the fog had brightened briefly, followed immediately by the concussion.

Ya'acov switched to transmit. "Balloon's gone up!" he shouted.

"What can you see?" David asked in Jerusalem.

"Not a blasted thing! We're covered by the worst fog I've ever seen! We heard the execute order over the tactical net and we saw the flash. That's all."

"Are you airborne?"

Ya'acov felt his stomach churn nervously. "Not yet. Lieutenant Rabinovich is winding up his eggbeater now."

Joel smiled in anticipation as he heard his name. "I presumed you wanted to observe from upstairs. We're a sitting duck down here."

"Proceed," Ya'acov confirmed. Then he keyed the transmit again. "We'll be airborne in a moment, Colonel."

"Keep me informed!"

The lightly loaded Apache leapt into the air, depending completely on its electronic eyes and ears for survival. Ya'acov felt completely cut off as the helicopter tore through the endless sea of gray. The mist was changing in color as dawn approached, but it grew no less dense.

◆

Abdul shivered as the early-morning chill settled into his bones. He was dripping wet and cramped with inactivity as he waited behind a boulder less than fifty feet from the IDF roadblock. He had watched them from the ridge until the fog had forced him to come closer.

The moment he heard the tank gun followed by the explosion he knew what it was, even though the sound was weakened by the clinging fog. Moments later he heard shouted orders at the roadblock. The sound of pounding feet echoed, seeming to come from every direction. Vehicle doors opened and slammed shut. Tailgates clanged down, followed by the heavy tread of booted feet on metal. The Jews were pulling out like the cowards they were. He ran forward until he could barely see the shadowy outlines of the vehicles. One by one they turned and drove off to the west on Highway 91. Abdul ran back to the ridge.

"The roadblock is gone," Abdul reported as he got into the backseat with Anne. "I am sure you heard the tank blast. Something's up."

Avraham grunted as he started the car and backed carefully out of their hiding place. He turned north on the highway and drove as fast as he dared, keeping a close eye on the white center line. Reaching Highway 91, he turned right toward Syria.

Anne looked out at the clammy grayness that seemed almost solid, though it was growing lighter by the minute. She was glad the dark night was over but was not sure the fog was much better.

Once again her thoughts drifted back to Mars. She had not known it was possible to miss someone as much as she missed him. Memories of the sweet times they had had in Jerusalem returned with a power that surprised her. Why, she wondered, had she not cherished their relationship more while she had it. And now . . .

She closed her eyes and prayed silently. *O God, please help me. Bring Mars and me back together, please.*

◆

Joel aimed the forward-looking infrared up the road to Quneitra. He looked past the burning tank and saw a line of Russian-made T-72s extending over the ridge. They were blocked for the moment, but the pilot knew that wouldn't last long. Joel made a one-eighty and flew toward the west.

"What was that?" Ya'acov asked, seeing a fleeting image on the FLIR display.

"Don't know," Joel said. "Let's go around again for another look."

He brought the gunship around in a high-speed pirouette that lost Ya'acov's stomach before it was done. The heat source spun back onto the display as the pilot rolled out on an easterly heading.

"Looks like a car," Joel said. "All by himself, too. Don't see any other vehicle on the road. Suppose he's lost?"

Ya'acov looked at the display. The car was driving up the road toward Quneitra, heading directly for the Syrian tanks.

"No," Ya'acov said slowly. "I think our PRF chieftain has surfaced, heading for Syria no matter what."

"Sir?" Joel asked in confusion.

"Unfinished Intelligence business. But we've got more important things to do. Swing back around where we can watch the Syrian column."

"Yes, sir."

◆

Moshe rolled the window down as the soldier came running up. "Turn around and drive west!" the man ordered.

"What's wrong?" Moshe asked.

"Syrian tanks are breaking through Golan!" the man said before he realized he was not supposed to tell. "Get out! Now!" He turned and ran off without waiting for an answer.

Moshe could hear the sounds of starting engines as he started the Safari. He turned the big GMC around and started driving west.

"Stop!" Mars shouted. "We can't leave now! What about Anne?"

"Patience," Moshe said softly as he scanned the shoulder as they drove along.

"You can stuff your patience! Let me out."

"Trust me, Mars. Now keep quiet and let me concentrate!"

Mars sat back in the seat, an angry scowl settling on his face.

A half-mile down the road Moshe jammed on the brakes, causing the Safari to slide sideways on the slick highway. He jerked the gear selector into reverse and spun the wheels as he backed up. Mars and Joe looked out the right side. There was a slight depression leading up to the road.

"There," Moshe said triumphantly. He turned off the road and drove up the dry wadi at a bone-jarring rate that threatened to blow a tire or put a hole in the oil pan. When the dry riverbed made an abrupt right-angle turn, Moshe followed it, killed the engine, and shut off the lights.

"This is the way to one of my digs. I was hoping I could find it before our IDF friends caught up with us."

The fog grew lighter to the south as the IDF vehicles roared past.

"Moshe?" Mars said, leaning forward.

"Yes?"

"I'm sorry."

"Mars, it may surprise you, but I understand."

Mars sat back slowly. He remembered Moshe's own loss in northern Galilee.

Fifteen minutes later Moshe turned east on Highway 91. He rolled his window down as they crept cautiously toward the border through the unrelenting fog. A sinister quietness hung over them as they approached what the IDF troops were retreating from.

◆

Avraham pressed harder on the accelerator as the Volvo started up a steep hill. In a few minutes the oppressive grayness up ahead started to break up. Avraham slowed the car and rolled down his window. A muffled clanking noise echoed around them, growing louder by the moment.

"Tanks!" Abdul said. "And they're close!"

Avraham turned and looked at Abdul. "What . . ."

"Turn around!" Abdul interrupted. "If we stay here, we'll be run down!"

"We'll do no such thing!" Avraham thundered, pounding the steering wheel. "Get out!"

The PRF leader threw open the door and stepped to the pavement. Up ahead the clanking noise seemed almost on top of them. Abdul emerged on the far side of the car dragging Anne ruthlessly by the arm.

"Run for it!" Abdul shouted over the din. He stepped down into the ditch beside the highway and started up the steep far side, with Anne struggling to keep her footing. Avraham paused for a moment, then ran to join the other two.

They got behind a large boulder and turned back toward the road. The screaming sound of tearing metal echoed dully as the lead tank rammed the Volvo off the road, hidden behind the veil of fog. A moment later they heard the whistling sound of an incoming shell.

"Duck!" Abdul shouted.

The three threw themselves to the ground behind the boulder. The grayness erupted in a flash of light accompanied by a blast that seemed to shove them against the sharp rocks. A moment later a far greater explosion flattened them again, raining jagged pieces of metal all around them. When the deadly rain stopped, they stood and looked down toward the road. Flames raged upwards like an immense blow-torch, burning away the fog immediately around the wreck. Through the swirling fog they could see the lead tank burning furiously. The Volvo, off the rear quarter of the tank, was also burning. Behind the pyre was the Syrian column, temporarily blocked.

28

THE BATTLE BEGINS

They got another one," Joel Rabinovich said as he glanced at the FLIR display. "Looks like the road is blocked again."

Ya'acov looked at the display sourly. "So it's two for David and zero for Goliath. But there's no way we can keep it up." Ya'acov relayed the information to David Kruger in Jerusalem as the pilot brought the helicopter around to head west again.

"That's interesting," Joel said a minute later.

"What?" Ya'acov asked.

"Got a heat source coming toward us on the ground."

"What is it?"

"Looks like a car. Has to be some lost civilian. There aren't going to be any military vehicles out by themselves."

Ya'acov looked at the FLIR display as if it might tell him who was down there.

"Want to go down and look?" Joel asked.

Ya'acov paused before answering. He was tempted to do just that. "No," he said finally. "Let's see if we can get above this soup."

"You're the boss."

The Apache gained altitude rapidly as Joel orbited in a large circle. They broke out suddenly into the clear morning air at sixty-one hundred feet. A sea of gray stretched below them almost as far as they could see, heaviest around Mount Hermon whose white head extended through the fog to the north. The fog dissipated rapidly to the north and east but remained heavy down the Jordan rift. To the west it reached almost to the coast, where the Mediterranean Sea glittered as it reflected the early-morning sun.

"MiGs to the east," Joel said. "Could be real trouble when this fog lifts."

A strident warbling sound erupted from their headsets. "Uh oh!" Joel shouted as Ya'acov was about to ask a question. "We've got to go now!"

Without any warning, the pilot threw the helicopter on its side and dove back into the fog in a sickening spiral. He ejected multiple flares during the almost uncontrolled descent as Ya'acov struggled to keep his stomach from rebelling. The Apache rolled level, then banked steeply in the opposite direction. The fog flashed white outside the cockpit, and the helicopter shook as if it would come apart, shrapnel pelting the bottom.

"What was that?" Ya'acov demanded as Joel continued to dive for the deck.

"Didn't you hear that warble in your headset a moment ago?"

"Yes. What was it?"

"Radar. They launched a missile at us. Fortunately our flares decoyed it away. I recommend we stay near the ground unless you're itching to push up daisies."

Ya'acov wiped his sweaty hands on his trousers. "Roger that! But there's something I'd like to take a look at."

"What's that?"

"See if that ground contact is still there."

Joel leveled out and turned to the west. "There he is," he said almost immediately. "Creeping along and headed straight for the border. If he keeps going on that road he'll run right into the Syrians."

Ya'acov's jaw set as he struggled with what he clearly knew his duty was.

"You'd think the jerk would know enough to turn around and head for safety," Joel grumbled.

"Yeah, you'd think so," Ya'acov grumbled. "Okay, flip on your landing lights and land in front of him."

"Sir?" Joel asked.

"You heard what I said, Lieutenant. I want you to land in the road."

"Yes, sir," Joel replied with obvious reluctance. "Okay if I wait until we're down to flip on the lights?"

"Yes," came the grim reply.

Joel brought the gunship around in a tight circle and landed in the middle of the highway. As soon as the wheels touched down, he flipped on the brilliant landing lights. The outside of the helicopter became almost white, like being inside a frosted light bulb.

"Don't shut down," Ya'acov ordered as he unstrapped. "I'll be back in a minute."

"Yes, sir," Joel replied.

Ya'acov opened the cockpit door and clambered down, keeping his head low as he ran out from under the rotor-blades. Then he slowed as the brilliance of the landing lights began to diminish. A little further on he saw the grill of a GMC Safari appear through the murk. Feeling strangely like a traffic cop, he walked to the driver's door and looked in the open window. "I could ask what you three are doing here, but I don't have time. You're heading right into a tank battle. Turn around and get away from here as fast as you can."

"No!" Mars shouted from the backseat.

"You *will* or I'll have the three of you arrested!"

"Anne's up here—I've got to find her!"

"You can't do *anything* in the middle of a tank battle!"

"Captain Isaacson?" Moshe interrupted.

"Yes," Ya'acov replied in irritation.

"It might be best for you to get back in your machine and let us be. If we were to be arrested, the questioning could get quite pointed. And you know where that could lead . . ." Moshe looked up at the officer as the latter thought it over. "Well?" Moshe prompted.

Ya'acov glowered at the archaeologist. "That's not fair."

"Not much in life is," Moshe agreed.

Ya'acov looked back toward the glow that indicated the waiting helicopter, then back inside the Safari. "Okay. The younger Mr. Enderly will come with me."

"What for?" Mars asked apprehensively.

"Come with me! You're not under arrest, if that's what you're thinking."

"Go on, Mars," Moshe urged.

Mars got out of the backseat and joined Ya'acov, who held up a hand. "Don't say a word when we get to the helicopter. Understand?"

"I'll be quiet," Mars agreed.

They walked back to the Apache and around to the front cockpit. Ya'acov opened the door and climbed up and into the seat. He then motioned for Mars to climb up and sit in his lap.

"Sir," Joel objected, "we can't take a civilian with us."

"This man has information vital to Intelligence, Lieutenant. I require his presence to perform my mission."

"But, Captain . . ."

"Lieutenant, are your operational orders clear enough for you?"

"Yes, sir."

Ya'acov buckled the harness over Mars and himself. "Very well. Get this helicopter airborne."

29

DELIVERANCE

Anne looked down at the ruined tank, the burning hulk still dissipating the fog in its immediate vicinity. The Syrian tanks were rumbling quickly past now on their way to the plain below, where the IDF tanks waited. She glanced around at her captors. They were both watching the tanks. She shifted her footing, dislodging a small pebble. Abdul turned toward her instantly, his hand moving instinctively to his Uzi.

◆

"Where to now?" Joel asked.

"The Syrian tank column."

Joel stayed low until they were close to the crossroads, then popped up long enough to image the road with the FLIR.

"Bad news," he said as they dropped back down. "They've broken through to the plain. The mine-clearing tanks are sweeping both sides of the road. I count four T-72 companies coming in behind the plows with BMP-1 armored personnel carriers behind them. And the road into Syria is solid armor."

"Tell our tank company while I update Jerusalem."

Joel waited until Ya'acov was finished with his longer message. "Sir, Captain Goldman is asking for spotting."

"Do it," Ya'acov agreed as he switched back to the tactical radio net.

Joel popped the Apache up two hundred feet and reported target coordinates to Yossi Goldman, then descended rapidly to hover just above the ground. The fog lightened momentarily as the Merkava tanks fired. The shock waves buffeted the helicopter. Joel made a spiral climbing turn and took a quick look up the highway.

Joel keyed his mike. "Bravo four one, this is Dragonfly. You hit two tanks, but there are at least four companies deployed, and it looks like they're ready to cut loose."

The sky to the east flashed repeatedly. Moments later the armor-piercing and anti-personnel rounds erupted in deadly blossoms among the dug-in Merkavas.

Yossi Goldman's voice was tense but controlled. "Dragonfly, this is Bravo four one. We're moving. You got any sting on that bird?"

"Don't have any gunner," Joel replied.

The roar of Yossi's tank came clearly over the radio. "This is it. As soon as we're repositioned, we make our stand and I turn the artillery and TOW teams loose. But don't expect much."

Before Joel could reply, a Syrian tank fired, destroying the tank immediately to the right of Yossi's. The company commander's shot missed the enemy, and the Syrian's return fire blew up the tank on Yossi's left. On the commander's order, the remaining Merkavas roared out of their positions and pivoted to the right, forming a column heading south. A Syrian shell hit Yossi's tank at the base of the turret, blowing it off and killing everyone instantly. The following Merkava slowed to get around the burning derelict and received a killing shot as well. Lieutenant Ehud Serlin, now in command of the tank company, laid his thermal sight on the nearest Syrian, bringing the Merkava's gun into approximate aim. The gunner took over, sighted on the tank, and fired. The round penetrated the enemy tank commander's hatch. A fireball erupted above the T-72, followed immediately by a sheet of flame.

"It's about time!" Ya'acov shouted as he watched the carnage on the FLIR display.

"Captain," Joel said, spinning the helicopter back toward the highway, "our guys can't last more than a couple of minutes. Better warn the brass."

◆

Lieutenant Ehud Serlin looked through his infrared sight as his tank lurched to a stop. The Syrian tank companies advanced confidently, like they knew the battle was over. Nothing stood between them and their conquest of northern Galilee. Ehud knew that everyone in his tank company would be dead in a few minutes. His gunner looked up into the commander's cupola.

"Won't be long now," Ehud said.

The tactical net radio squawked to life unexpectedly. Ehud started to key his mike to ream out the one responsible for this breach of radio discipline when he stopped. It wasn't one of his tanks. It was a transmission from the lead armored brigade several hours to the south. The freak weather conditions were apparently channeling their radio transmissions far beyond the normal range. Ehud snorted, wishing they were actually as close as they sounded!

◆

"What was that?" Ya'acov asked.

"Sounds like the 7th Armored Brigade, sir," Joel replied.

"How far away are they?"

"Several hours at least. But with these weird atmospherics, sounds like they're right below us."

"Yeah, it sure does," Ya'acov said slowly. He looked down at the FLIR display. The rolling plain was crawling with Syrian tanks. In moments the eight surviving IDF tanks would be history and the Syrians would be sitting on northern Galilee. "Joel, put me on the armored tactical net! Oh, and what's the call sign for the acting company commander? Quick!"

"Bravo four two," the pilot replied, flipping a switch.

The Intelligence officer shut his eyes as he tried to concentrate on what to say. "Bravo four two, this is Dragonfly. Be advised that the lead elements of the 7th Armored Brigade are in sight traveling east on Highway 91 and require your guidance. Over."

Ya'acov held his breath during the brief pause. Would the officer understand?

"Roger, Dragonfly," came the reply at last.

Ya'acov thought he could hear hope in the officer's voice. Ehud flooded the tactical net with messages directing the supposedly present brigade toward their Syrian targets. The radio traffic far to the south ceased immediately.

Ya'acov looked at the FLIR display of the advancing Syrian tanks as he willed the southern commander to understand. The radio remained silent. He had almost decided the ploy was not going to work when the brigade commander began issuing orders to his tanks to take up firing positions on either side of the highway.

"Think it'll work?" Joel asked.

"If it doesn't, we've had it," Ya'acov replied. "We need maybe one more thing."

"What's that?"

In answer to Joel's question, all eight of Ehud's Merkava tanks opened fire on the Syrians, firing as rapidly as they could reload. Moments later the reserve Israeli artillery started rapid-firing. Ya'acov watched in fascination as the TOW missiles started tracing their brilliant white lines across the FLIR display.

"Look at that!" Ya'acov shouted, pounding Mars on the shoulders. "Must have splashed a dozen of 'em."

"This isn't going to convince them," Joel said. "We're not hitting hard enough."

"Can we engage?" Ya'acov demanded.

"No, sir! Not without my copilot/gunner."

"I didn't ask you that, Lieutenant. Can you fire the missiles by yourself?"

"It can be done, sir, but . . ."

"No buts—do it!"

Joel shook his head as he brought the gunship around. He checked the FLIR as he selected and armed a Hellfire missile. He selected the T-72 closest to the remaining Merkavas with his helmet designator and thumbed the switch to send the missile on its way. A brilliant lance of light shot forward into the fog and attenuated to a pulsating glow. A brilliant line traced its way over the FLIR display to the T-72. The tank erupted in a fountain of fire, becoming history and therefore of no further interest. The pilot designated the next tank and loosed the second missile. Moments later that T-72 was dead as well. Joel rolled the gunship on its side and dove for the deck.

"What was that for?" Mars demanded.

Joel almost smiled. "Don't want some ground pounder with a missile ruining our day."

"Quiet," Ya'acov ordered before he reported the situation to David.

Joel waited until Ya'acov finished his transmission. "What now?" he asked.

"Can you make a quick pass over the Syrian column without getting us shot down?"

"Roger that, Captain. You guys strapped in real tight?"

Mars looked around at Ya'acov apprehensively. The Intelligence officer could only shrug. "Let 'er rip," he said.

Joel opened the throttles wide and banked the helicopter around to the south. Then he pulled an almost vertical bank and headed diagonally for the highway and the rear of the lead armored companies. Another gut-wrenching turn, and they roared straight up the road, scant feet over the wrecked tanks. Moments later they swept over the long line of tanks rolling past the wrecks. He followed the column for more than a mile before making an abrupt right turn followed by a pull up over the ridge, staying in the rugged terrain until they were back at the crossroads again.

"What did you see, Captain?" Joel asked.

"A bunch of Syrians who need convincing."

"Roger that. Did you see that burned-out car?"

"What car?" Mars demanded.

"Yeah," Ya'acov said. "I saw it."

"What car?" Mars repeated.

"There's a burned-out car on the highway."

"Was it the car Anne was in?"

"There's no way of knowing," Ya'acov said, not sounding very convincing even to himself. "Lieutenant, let's go tank hunting! I want the Syrian commander to think the roof has caved in on him."

"Yes, sir!"

Joel cranked the twin turbines to 100 percent and headed for the highway to Quneitra. Approaching the burned-out Volvo he popped up and launched a Hellfire missile at a T-72 tank that was nearing one of the still-burning tanks. The missile penetrated the top of the turret and blew it off. Joel swerved sideways and dove for the ground as a warbling sound started in his headset.

"Hey, some guy down there doesn't like me doing that!"

A streak of blinding white light swept up from below, passing close enough for the aviators to see the missile's slim body. Joel flew to the east and popped up again, this time not quite as high. He quickly designated another T-72 further up the road and launched his missile. He watched as the white lance disappeared in the murk, only to blossom on the FLIR display a moment later.

"Further up the column!" Ya'acov ordered.

"Roger that!" Joel replied.

The Apache descended rapidly and pulled into a tight 180-degree turn, flying south at top speed. They screamed past the Quneitra road axis as Joel angled toward a ridge to the left. He turned east and followed the ridge tops as he worked his way around the Syrian tank column to the north.

Two miles later Joel turned north in a deep valley. "Look at that!" he exulted as he scanned the FLIR display. The valley led straight to the Quneitra highway just over five miles away. The pilot rolled the Apache on its side and descended until three tanks could barely be seen on the FLIR. He designated the first T-72 and fired the missile. Its hot exhaust flashed a brilliant white, then was lost in the fog. Joel watched the missile's flat arc in the FLIR display as it merged with the tank. The explosion blew the tank's turret into the air. Joel designated the next tank and sent the second missile on its way. Moments later that tank was also in ruins. Joel shifted to the last tank in line and fired. This missile passed behind the T-72's turret and exploded on a hilltop a half-mile further on.

"Hold fire!" Ya'acov ordered as he saw Joel lining up with the last Hellfire. "Further to the rear!"

Joel shook his head, irritated at having to let the lucky Syrian get away. He cranked the Apache's turbines and hopped the eastern ridge. The following valley was not as obliging as the previous had been. The pilot followed its twisting path for a while, then flew through a notch into the next valley to the east. This one offered a straight shot at the highway. Joel pulled the collective up to rise above an intervening hill.

A bright infrared source bloomed to the right as he designated his target. Joel cursed the unseen missile as he glanced at the ridge to the east, knowing they could never make it. He spun the Apache around in a sickening whirl and shoved the stick forward, willing the helicopter to escape the death that was hurtling toward them. He punched out flares every five seconds as he mentally calculated where the infrared missile should be. When he could wait no longer, he racked the Apache over on its side and headed east. The missile exploded in a brilliant flash where they had been the previous instant. Shrapnel peppered the helicopter, seeming to search for a vital spot.

"That almost ruined our day," Joel grumbled. "I vote we try another valley."

Ya'acov remained silent as Joel hopped the eastern ridge. This valley went straight for a few miles until it made a dog-leg turn that hid the Syrians.

"Want to try this one?" Joel asked. "We'll be right on top of 'em by the time we get to that bend."

Ya'acov did not want to go any further to the east. But he did not want to get them shot down either. "Nice choice you give me," Ya'acov replied sarcastically. "Let's check it out. I don't want to go any further into Syria."

"You're the boss," Joel replied as he started the Apache toward the bend.

A few minutes later they arrived. Joel stayed low as he peered cautiously up the short distance to the road. This leg of the valley ran almost due west, giving a very good view of the highway. What they saw was very far from ordered.

"Well, well, well," Joel said with glee. "Would you look at that. Seems like the peace-loving Syrians are advancing to the rear."

"It worked!" Ya'acov exulted.

"I've got one more missile."

"Let's urge them to hurry," Ya'acov said, agreeing with the pilot's suggestion.

Joel designated a target at random and fired. The missile flew straight to its target and blew it up. "Captain, the chain gun has twelve hundred rounds. You want to hose 'em down some?"

"Better not," Ya'acov replied. "Get us back to the crossroads so I can report this to Jerusalem."

Pouting like a child told he could not play with his toy, Joel spun the helicopter and retreated to the south before flying west out of Syrian territory.

30

SHOT
DOWN

Unable to believe what he was hearing, Avraham climbed cautiously down onto the road. It was true. The Syrian tanks were in full retreat. Soon the last one was lost in the fog to the east as it made best possible speed. All that was left were the funeral pyres that littered the highway amid the blasted-out shell holes. Avraham shook his head in disbelief as he clambered back to where Abdul was holding Anne.

"They're retreating," Avraham said in answer to Abdul's questioning look. The way he said it precluded any discussion.

"Come on," Avraham ordered.

"Where are we going?" Anne demanded.

"Same as before!" Avraham growled at her. "Damascus! Now move!"

The three descended to the roadway and started walking east.

◆

"What about the burned-out car?" Mars asked as the Apache orbited the survivors of the IDF tank company.

"What do you want to know about it?" Ya'acov asked, not wanting to volunteer information.

"Is it the one Anne was in?"

"Probably," the Intelligence officer replied. He didn't add that she was also probably dead.

"Fly back up there—I have to know."

"Captain, we can't do that," Joel interrupted.

Mars squirmed around and glared at the pilot. "Look! The most important person to me in the whole world is on that road! I have to know! If there's any chance she's alive, I have to try and save her! I have to!"

Ya'acov turned his head and peered out the side of the Plexiglas canopy.

Mars turned back to the Intelligence officer. "Captain Isaacson?"

"I heard you," Ya'acov replied through clenched teeth. "And the answer is no."

"You've got a stake in this too," Mars persisted. "We're already in the air. What would it hurt to just go look?"

Ya'acov tried to glare at the American but found that he couldn't. "Lieutenant, one more trip down the road please," he said finally.

"Captain, you *know* we're not supposed to do that!"

"And, Lieutenant, I'm telling you this *is* an Intelligence matter. Get this helicopter moving!"

Joel hid his irritation by making an especially uncomfortable 180-degree turn. Dropping down close to the road, he cranked the turbines up to 100 percent and started down the highway. Near the burned-out car he slowed. The heat from the nearby burning tank had dispersed the immediate fog. There were no bodies around the car. Whether any were in the car was impossible to tell.

"I don't see anything," Joel reported.

"Then she could still be alive," Mars said with a glimmer of hope.

"You saw the carnage we were in the middle of," Ya'acov noted.

"But she could still be alive," Mars persisted.

"Continue up the highway," Ya'acov ordered.

Joel transitioned to forward flight without voicing his objection. The Apache swept over the shattered T-72 tanks as the three men checked the vast graveyard for any sign of life.

◆

"Stop!" Avraham ordered. He half-turned, listening intently as he looked toward the west. He could see only about six feet before the rest of the world was lost in grayness. A faint whine seemed to come at them from all directions. Gradually it grew louder.

"It's a helicopter!" Avraham roared. "Get off the road!" He stood his ground and cocked his Uzi. He waited until the aircraft was almost on him. Then he sprayed the air with the submachine gun.

◆

"There are three people in the road ahead," Joel announced.

"Is it them?" Mars demanded.

"Who knows?" Joel replied. "Could be Syrian soldiers cut off from their unit."

He pulled back on the stick and started to turn. A Uzi slug penetrated the left engine cowling, severing a fuel line near the burner cans. Jet fuel under high pressure sprayed the outside of the turbine's combustion stage, erupting immediately into flames followed by an explosion that destroyed most of the engine controls.

Joel cursed as he saw the fire light come on. He cut the fuel and power to the engine and jabbed the fire extinguisher button. Nothing happened. He hit it again. The circuit was dead.

"Fire in the port engine!" the pilot announced. "Stand by for a crash landing! When we hit, get out and run for it!"

Joel slowed the Apache as much as he could, then let it drop like a brick onto the highway. The helicopter bounced hard on its landing gear, bounded a few feet back into the air, then settled with a crash. Turning the master switch off first, Joel threw his door open, jumped down, and ran forward to the front cockpit. He clambered up, wrenched the door open, and helped Mars and Ya'acov out.

"Head for the ditch!" he ordered, pointing to the side of the road.

They rolled into the ditch just as the Apache exploded. Sharp pieces of metal whizzed overhead and rained down nearby with sickening thuds. As soon as the impacts ceased, Joel looked up and pulled his nine-millimeter semi-automatic from his shoulder holster.

"Will they attack us?" Mars asked, louder than he intended.

"Probably not," Joel whispered. "But I sure wouldn't count on it."

"If it *is* the terrorists, what do you think they'll do?"

Ya'acov hesitated because he was sure he knew. "If it is them, they'll keep going. They're almost in Syria now. If they wait, our forces will pick them up."

"That's what I thought," Mars said. He jumped up and, before Ya'acov could stop him, started scrambling up the rock-strewn road, swinging his cast like some immense fiddler crab.

"Mars, come back here!" Ya'acov shouted halfheartedly. He knew there was no possibility he would. Mars disappeared into the thinning fog, the clatter of rocks the only indication of his progress.

Ya'acov looked back at Joel. The pilot was eyeing him with a curious expression. The Intelligence officer knew what he was thinking. This would indeed be difficult to explain to the brass. The young lieutenant was glad the captain was in charge.

"What now, Captain?" Joel asked.

Ya'acov looked toward the east as he pondered the question. "Lieutenant," he said finally, "give me your gun, then get back to the crossroads as quick as you can. Tell them we've located the PRF leaders and I'm trying to intercept them."

"But, Captain . . ."

"That's an order, Lieutenant. Give me the gun."

Joel reluctantly handed over the automatic and got to his feet. With one final look at Ya'acov, as if the latter might come to his senses, he turned around and started loping down the highway to the west.

Ya'acov looked up the road at the swirling fog. He started climbing up the way he had seen Mars go.

31

TOGETHER AGAIN

Mars heard pebbles clattering down the slope behind him, making strange hollow sounds in the fog. He felt an icy pang in the pit of his stomach as he looked back. He wondered briefly if it was Ya'acov but knew it was more likely a stray Syrian, and he was not prepared for that. He increased his pace on the steep road. But the faster he went, the more noise he made on the treacherous incline.

He stopped. Whoever was following was gaining. The sounds behind him were growing louder by the moment. In his hurry he did not see the slick rock until he landed on it with his left foot. His foot flew out from under him, and he landed heavily, knocking the wind out of him. Sharp rocks poked and jabbed him as he lay in the gray mist.

He knew he had to get up, but he couldn't—it hurt too much. He screwed his eyes shut against the pain. He thought of Anne somewhere up ahead. He gritted his teeth and rolled over on his side, jarring an injured elbow. Again his brain exploded with countless stars.

When Mars heard a scraping sound, he opened his eyes. There, towering over him, was a man he would learn was Avraham Abbas, head of the PRF. The man's Uzi was pointed right at Mars's heart.

"Mars!" Anne screamed when she saw who it was. She rushed over to him and knelt down before Abdul could stop her. "Oh, Mars, what are you doing here?"

Mars looked at her, tears coming to his eyes. She was alive. He wanted to say a thousand things, but what finally came out was, "I came for you."

Anne cried as she looked at the cast and his disheveled condition. "Dear, you shouldn't have." She kissed him gently.

"But I *had* to. I *love* you."

"I love you too, Mars, more than I can tell you." She kissed him again and held his hand in hers. He smiled. Her hand was warm and soft. She looked like a sweet little bird. In spite of all the danger around him, he glowed inside.

"Get up, you two!" Avraham growled. "Now I have two hostages, which I probably don't need anymore." The threat was clear enough. "Now get up or I'll make sure you two stay together forever."

Anne stood and helped Mars up. She glared at Avraham as she led Mars up the road to where Abdul was waiting.

◆

Ya'acov listened so hard it made his head spin. He had heard Mars's dramatic fall and the tearful reunion. That had been clear enough. He had also heard Avraham's marching orders. He waited a minute for them to get out of earshot, then started down the same road Mars had gone down. He stopped for a moment and listened. Nothing. He started walking toward the east, hoping he would hear them before he was heard.

◆

"You still shouldn't have done it," Anne whispered as she walked along, her right arm tucked through his left. She intended this to be a scolding, but she couldn't carry it off. She looked up in his face, tears in her eyes.

"Are you all right?" he asked, realizing after he said it how silly it must sound.

"Shut up!" Avraham ordered.

◆

Ya'acov paused for what seemed the hundredth time. Nothing yet. Even though the fog was thinning, it still seemed to cloak every sound. The Intelligence officer knew he would have to pick up his pace or he would never catch them. But if he did that, they might hear him.

He shrugged as he stepped out again, this time taking longer strides. He kept the automatic up as he looked for shapes to materialize in the featureless gray ahead of him. After a few more minutes he began to wonder if the terrorists had left the highway.

A flicker of movement caught the corner of his eye. Ya'acov's mind moved faster than his body could respond. Dread descended on him, and he knew he was in trouble before he could identify what it was. He started turning to the left. A dark shape was rushing toward him, and something hard hit his wrist, causing the automatic to go whirling away to clatter across the pavement. His wrist shot red-hot lances to his brain as he finally faced his attacker. Both men were shocked as they recognized each other. For the first time since the Dome of the Rock attack, Abdul had the IDF officer at his mercy. A cruel smile creased his face as he motioned for Ya'acov to start walking.

Abdul scooped up the nine-millimeter automatic and fell in line behind the Intelligence officer. Soon Avraham, Mars, and Anne appeared. Mars groaned when he saw Ya'acov. Nothing seemed to be going right.

◆

Joel arrived at the crossroads out of breath. The acrid smell of cordite hung heavily in the wet air. He stumbled across roads and fields skirting shell holes and burned-out tanks. He was looking for the tank company, but the units had apparently dispersed. The pilot cursed the fog as he searched for any sign of IDF troops.

He was about to turn to the south when he saw a dark shape a little further on. He walked cautiously forward and saw it was the IAF Bell Huey he had seen earlier. He rushed up to the aircraft and looked inside. The pilot was nowhere to be seen.

A thought crossed his mind, a thought that was normally incompatible with military discipline. But he knew Captain Isaacson expected help, and he hadn't been able to find any. And here was a helicopter he knew how to fly.

He opened the door and climbed in, hoping it was operational and not some dead bird. Flipping a series of switches, he was assured it was indeed alive. Moments later the turbine lit and started its RPM climb. He put on a headset, selected the appropriate frequency, and keyed the transmitter. Nothing. That explained the abandoned Huey—the radio was dead. Joel lifted off and was immediately on instruments without any of the high-tech imagery gear he had on the Apache. He ascended through the fog until he broke out.

The cloud deck was much lower now. The fog bank would burn off soon. Best of all, the sky was clear of fighters. Joel pushed the stick forward and made best possible speed toward where he estimated he had left Ya'acov. When he arrived, he brought the Huey to a hover and started descending into the thinning fog. He kept a constant watch to either side, wary of outcroppings that could wreck the rotor-blades. Finally the ground peeked through the murk. He had hit the highway dead center.

Joel started the Huey forward, guessing the terrorists had to be to the east. His eyes darted from side to side as he looked for them to appear out of the mist. There was a steep slope on either side of the road, but the one on the left gave way to an abrupt dropoff.

◆

A helicopter was approaching. Avraham turned his head to the side as he tried to determine where it was. "Watch them!" he ordered over his shoulder. Abdul motioned for Anne, Mars, and Ya'acov to walk toward the ditch.

The dragonfly-like shape appeared out of the fog as if it had materialized out of nothingness. Avraham started raising his Uzi as he looked at the startled expression on the pilot's face. Joel started pulling up and toward the dropoff as Avraham pulled the trigger. A jagged line of bullet holes stitched the Plexiglas canopy, just missing the pilot's head. The Huey disappeared into the fog.

Avraham continued to look west down the road as the sound of the Huey faded. He tried to follow the helicopter's course, but the echoes seemed to come from all directions. He wished the sounds would fade away, but they didn't. Avraham cursed the pilot's persistence.

Avraham caught a movement in his peripheral vision. He started turning to the right, toward the dropoff, as the helicopter came charging out of the fog. Slowly the gun came up. But the Huey's right landing skid hit Avraham full in the chest, throwing him to the ground. His head cracked solidly against the pavement, the impact pounding the air out of his lungs. The Uzi flew out of his hand and skittered into the ditch behind him.

Joel spun the helicopter on its axis, pointing it toward Abdul and his captives. The terrorist whipped his Uzi around and brought it up. Ya'acov grabbed Abdul's gun hand with both of his and tried to wrench it away. Abdul turned on the IDF officer, intense hatred coming to his eyes. Smoldering memories burst into flame as he saw his opportunity for revenge.

Joel hovered over the dropoff, the blast from the Huey's rotor-blades throwing grit in everyone's face and making it difficult to stand up.

"Get out of here!" Mars yelled to Anne over the roar of the heli-copter, pointing down the road to the west. She shook her head. "I'm not leaving you," she said simply, looking into his eyes. He couldn't hear what she said but knew what it was.

He looked past her. Avraham was struggling to his feet, shaking his head to try and clear it. He looked up and down the ditch. Mars followed his eyes. Both men saw the Uzi at the same time. Mars ran for the ditch, waving his ungainly cast like a shield, but Avraham got to the ditch first and reached down for the weapon. Mars plowed into him with all the grace of a freight train. Avraham dropped the Uzi as Mars rolled over and landed on top of him.

Mars glanced back toward Anne as Avraham struggled under him. Abdul almost had his Uzi in Ya'acov's face. Mars struggled to his feet, dodging a swipe from the still-groggy Avraham. The American ran toward Abdul without a thought of what he could do to help. Abdul heard him coming and looked around. Mars swung his cast around as if he were in a hammer toss, landing a blow on Abdul's temple that hurt Mars almost as much as it did the terrorist. Ya'acov wrenched the Uzi loose and brought it down on Abdul's head, knocking him out.

Ya'acov swung the submachine gun around toward Avraham only to find that Anne was in the line of fire. Avraham groped for his Uzi, found it, and ran for Anne. Before she could move, he grabbed her and jammed the gun into her neck.

"Drop the gun!" Avraham roared, trying to ignore how much his head was hurting. "Drop it or I'll kill her." Ya'acov tossed the Uzi into the ditch.

"Now order the pilot to land!" Avraham continued.

Ya'acov waved to Joel, motioning for him to set the helicopter down. The pilot hesitated, then flew to a clear spot and set the Huey down, cutting the switches.

"Drag Abdul over to the helicopter!" Avraham ordered.

"Stay here," Ya'acov whispered to Mars. He bent over Abdul's unconscious form and grabbed him under the armpits, then dragged him over to the helicopter. Avraham watched every movement, his gun barrel boring painfully into Anne's neck. Abdul groaned and reached for his head. He blinked away tears as he saw Avraham approaching holding Anne close to himself.

"Tell him to open the door!" Avraham shouted. Ya'acov motioned to Joel. The pilot crouched as he walked back to the side door. He opened it and looked down. Avraham waved him back to the cockpit.

Avraham grabbed Anne's arm in a painful grip. "Get in!" he ordered. Anne struggled to climb up into the helicopter, cutting her leg on the threshold. Avraham shoved her in and pulled himself up after her. The terrorist turned and motioned Ya'acov to help Abdul up. But Abdul was already struggling to his feet. Ya'acov guided him to the door, where the terrorist slumped over the threshold. Avraham bent down and held out his hand. When Anne looked over the broad back of the PRF chieftain, Ya'acov caught her eye. She nodded, then rushed forward with her hands outstretched. She hit Avraham from behind with a blow that was not very hard but was quite strategic. Avraham caromed into Abdul, causing both to tumble out of the Huey. The PRF leader landed painfully on his shoulder and wound up on his back, the Uzi sliding away across the pavement. Ya'acov ran for the gun. Avraham heard a sound and looked back to see Joel stoop at the door and jump to the pavement.

"Come on!" Avraham shouted to his accomplice when he saw he

could not get to the gun. He and Abdul ran to the edge of the road and jumped into the fog-enveloped dropoff. Ya'acov and Joel rushed to the edge and listened. The sound of falling rocks and pebbles continued for some time before stopping.

"I'm not about to go down there," Ya'acov admitted. "Get everybody aboard—move it!" Joel nodded and led them back to the helicopter.

◆

Only patchy remnants of fog remained when the Huey arrived back at the battleground. Joel flew straight to the GMC Safari that was waiting by the side of the road a few miles further on. The pilot set the helicopter down on the road and opened the side door to let Mars and Anne out.

When Joel returned to the pilot's seat, he looked over at Ya'acov sitting next to him.

"What now, Captain?" he asked.

"You say the radio on this beast doesn't work?"

"That it doesn't."

"Probably just as well. I need time to get my story together. Well, Lieutenant, how about a leisurely trip back to Jerusalem?"

"You've got it," Joel said, trying to sound lighthearted. He in no way envied the Intelligence officer.

◆

Moshe and Joe were out of the Safari even before the Huey landed. Mars and Anne rushed out from under the rotor-blades, with Mars doing his best to help with only one free arm. As far as Anne was concerned, he couldn't have done better. Moshe hugged Anne as he wiped tears from his eyes. Then he hugged Mars, as best he could around the cast.

"Mr. Enderly?" Anne asked, seeing Joe hanging back.

"Joe," he corrected as he opened his arms to hug her. Mars joined them both.

They all turned their backs to the Huey as it took off behind them. Mars turned around as the helicopter turned to the south. Ya'acov was looking out of the canopy. Mars and Anne waved as the helicopter picked up speed. The Intelligence officer waved back.

"You will have to tell us everything," Moshe said as he ushered them back to the Safari.

"We will," Mars agreed. "But there's something I have to do first."

"What's that?" Moshe asked, scratching his head.

Mars took Anne's hands and pulled her toward him. "Anne, will you marry me?"

Anne looked at him, her eyes shining. Yes, this was what she wanted with all her heart. Why had she not seen it from the beginning? she wondered. Why had it taken this?

"Yes," she whispered, crying as she spoke. "Oh, Mars, I love you so much. And I thought I'd never have a chance to tell you. I'll *never* forget your coming for me."

He drew her into his arms and kissed her. For a long time, neither was aware of anything else.

◆

Moshe excused himself once they were back at the American Colony Hotel. They had called Anne's parents from Zefat on the way back. Her parents had been overjoyed. Against all odds, it had come out the way Mars had wanted and Anne had prayed for.

Joe led the way up to his suite and called room service as Mars and Anne settled down on the sofa. Mars felt a twinge of pain as he slipped his uninjured arm around Anne. Joe picked an easy chair and sat down.

"Mars, I need to tell you something," Anne said.

"Why, sure, dear." Mars grinned as he said it. It didn't seem quite natural to say "dear"—yet. Joe smiled, and Anne blushed.

"Dearest Mars . . ." Anne started.

It was Mars's turn to blush.

"I'll get out if it'll help," Joe volunteered.

"No, stay," Anne insisted. "What I want to say is that I've changed."

Mars was instantly wary. "In what way?" he reluctantly asked.

"I've become a Christian," she said. She puzzled at how that sounded in her ears. Somehow she felt the announcement should have been more special. The look in Mars's eyes concerned her.

"How did this happen?" Mars asked, having a hard time hiding his disappointment.

"I read the Bible Zuba Rosenberg gave me."

"Great," Mars grumbled.

Anne looked down, trying to keep Mars from seeing how she felt about his reaction. "Mars, this is important to me."

"Okay."

Anne looked at him intently, but he avoided her eyes. Her heart ached with the love she felt for him. She longed for him to understand what she now knew.

"I was reading the Gospels. I came across this passage where the Temple veil was torn in two when Jesus was crucified. And then it struck me. The veil the Bible is talking about is the one we found. It was torn in two, and no one can explain how. It bothered Dr. Yadin so much that he tried to cover it up. Don't you see? The Bible is true. So what it says about Jesus Christ is also true."

Mars looked into her eyes. "I love you so much I can't stand it. But no . . . The Bible is only a collection of fairy tales. We *know* better. Anne, we're *scientists*."

Anne looked away. Two emotions raged inside her. She loved Mars. And because she did, she wanted him to understand the truth. This conversation hurt more than she could say. "Mars, I love you, dear. I only hope you'll discover what I've found."

Mars nestled his head next to hers. Once again he wondered how an otherwise intelligent person could believe in God. It just didn't make sense!

32

AND THE TWO
SHALL BE ONE FLESH

A hectic two weeks followed Anne's rescue. Nothing else would do for Anne but a wedding in Jerusalem. Mars favored a civil ceremony, but Anne insisted it had to be a church wedding conducted by a minister.

Not many relatives or friends could come or cared to visit a country with such a reputation for terrorism. But Robert and Florence McAdams, Anne's parents, never venturing outside Texas in their lives, packed up and flew to Israel. Flo delighted in the adventure and plunged into helping Anne plan the wedding. That it would be in the capital of a foreign country only added to the spice. Bob McAdams, though not as sanguine as his wife, knew his place was with his wife, and that *his* privilege would be that of giving away the bride.

Mars's first meeting with his future father-in-law proved interesting. Although the young man harbored no uncertainty of his love for Anne, he still stammered and found it hard to meet Mr. McAdams's steady gaze when he officially asked for her hand in marriage. Bob, previously coached by Flo, graciously gave his consent.

It took Flo only a little time to figure out how Middle Eastern bazaars worked. That behind her, she had a wonderful time planning the wedding details. Aided by the ever-present Moshe Stein, Flo stormed the Old City souks to find material for Anne's dress, locate a seamstress, and buy the countless things needed to make the event perfect. At first the McAdamses hesitated to impose on Dr. Stein, until it became abundantly clear that the archaeologist considered himself the *yenta*.

When Flo confided that she didn't know what to do about locating a church and minister, Moshe brought in Zuba Rosenberg. The Messianic Jew called in Reverend David Bridges, a retired Lutheran minister who happily arranged for the couple to use the small chapel in the Church of the Redeemer in the Old City. When the pastor suggested a meeting with Anne and Mars before the wedding, Flo was surprised but readily agreed.

At exactly 9 A.M., a week and a half before the wedding, David Bridges knocked on the McAdamses' door. Bob opened it and ushered the smiling minster in.

"Come in," Bob said as he closed the door. "I'm Bob McAdams, and this is my wife, Flo." He then waved toward the couch. "And the reason for your visit—my daughter Anne and her intended, Mars Enderly."

Mars and Anne got up and shook hands while Bob brought a chair for David. He sat and regarded them all with deep blue eyes set in a leathery, lined face, a face that had seen much history in seventy-two years of life on this earth.

"Would you care for some iced tea?" Flo asked. "We have that and some delicious cookies I found in the market."

The minister thanked her, and she rushed out to fetch the tray. She made her rounds, making sure everyone had everything they needed before placing the tray on the coffee table.

David sipped his tea and tested a cookie. "Excellent," he pronounced as he placed his glass on a coaster and quickly finished the cookie. "Thank you for agreeing to see me. I know you're wondering about that, so I'll get right to the point. In times past ministers did what we called premarital counseling, although I understand it's less common now." He shrugged his shoulders. "But I guess I'm old-fashioned."

"Oh, yes," Flo agreed. "I know what you're talking about. Some of our ministers do it, and some don't. It seems to be their choice."

David nodded. "It has a purpose, and I insisted on it when I was active in the ministry. But now I hardly ever conduct weddings." He smiled as he turned toward Mars and Anne. "You two can relax—this isn't going to be a regular premarital counseling session. We don't have enough time for that , and besides, the sessions are between the couple and the minister only."

Anne watched his face. Reverend Bridges had an engaging, genuine smile, but was there some tension there? "I appreciate your interest in us. I want the wedding to be perfect."

"And so do I. That's why I'm here. Now, Zuba and Moshe have told me a lot about you two. I have no doubt—talking to them and seeing you—that your love for each other is deep and genuine. But there is one question, as a minister, I feel I must ask."

Mars felt Anne's hand tense.

"What's that?" she asked.

"Zuba told me you are a Christian." He shifted his gaze to Mars. "Mars, do you share her faith in Jesus Christ?"

Silence descended on the room like a thing that could be felt. Mars struggled to maintain eye contact with the minister as his emotions fought a silent battle that surfaced only as a tight scowl. Finally he cleared his throat. "My beliefs are my own—they're private."

He felt Anne's hand start to tremble and looked at her in concern.

"I see," David replied. "I want you all to know I come as a friend. And *as* your friend, I feel it my obligation to warn you about how God feels about this."

"What are you talking about?" Mars demanded.

Reverend Bridges opened his Bible. "The Apostle Paul had this to say in Second Corinthians chapter 6, verse 14: 'Do not be yoked together with unbelievers.'" He paused when he saw the look of shock on both their faces. "He was advising the believers in the church at Corinth not to be closely associated with those who were not Christians. And the closest human relationship is marriage."

Mars squeezed Anne's hand. "Are you saying I'm not good enough for her?"

David sighed. "That's not the point at all, Mars. Nobody lives a perfect life—Christian or non-Christian. But the Christian lives his or her life for Christ, with the help of the Holy Spirit, whereas the non-Christian lives for self. This causes friction in a spiritually mixed marriage because the goals are different. Hence Paul's advice."

Anne looked up at this. "I've only read the Gospels and the

Psalms—I haven't read that passage. You said it was advice and not a command?"

David could see the hopeful look on her face. He closed the Bible. "Actually, it's a command, but many Christians do not take it seriously. Earlier in my career I would have refused to marry you. But let me ask you both a question: do you *really* love each other?"

"More than anything," Mars said in a rush. David knew the tears in his and Anne's eyes were real.

"He means more to me than anyone on earth," Anne blurted out as she broke down sobbing. David waited patiently as she tried to bring her emotions under control. "He was all I could think about after they kidnapped me—how much I loved him and how I'd never see him again. And then when he came after me . . ."

Mars shifted uncomfortably on the couch.

"I see," David said. "And I presume if I did not marry you, you would go elsewhere."

After a pause they both nodded.

"As I thought," the minister said. "In that case, though I am not perfectly at peace about it, I will marry you. And I will pray that God will bring about spiritual unity in your house."

His mission done, David stood and took his leave, suggesting that Mars and Anne visit the church and view the Old City from the bell tower. They both said they would like that.

In the days that followed, Mars, of course, wanted to monopolize Anne's time, and he became a little petulant on the occasions when she had wedding details to resolve. But he mostly got his way.

Before the final two weeks were over, the pair had seen almost everything that Israel had to offer. They talked at length about their future life together, the meshing of their careers, and the bigger question—did they want children? Anne settled that one rather quickly: they did, and fairly soon, as she felt her biological clock ticking on. Only one subject remained off-limits. Anne knew her new faith could not be mentioned.

Mars and Anne learned something almost all betrothed people experience. No matter how soon the wedding will be, it seems to take forever for *the* day to arrive, though it did indeed come.

Around 7:30 A.M., Mars met Anne at the American Colony Hotel.

He took her hand as they walked toward the Old City. They entered through the Damascus Gate and followed Bet Ha-Bad to the Gothic splendor of the German Lutheran Church of the Redeemer with its tall, thin bell tower. They knocked on the western door and waited while the caretaker made his leisurely way there. The elderly man let them in and showed them to the doorway of the tower. His duty done, he shuffled off.

"I'm not sure my short legs are up to this," Anne said as she peered upward at the turreted stairwell.

"You can do it," Mars encouraged her.

Both were panting when they mounted the 177th step and walked out to the eastern parapet.

Mars shielded his eyes from the sun's glare. "There's the Dome of the Rock."

But Anne was looking at something else. "Yes, and beyond that is the Mount of Olives. Somewhere out there, a long time ago, Judas betrayed Jesus."

"So it is written," Mars replied.

Anne looked over at him, wondering what he meant.

Mars pointed to the left. "Up there is the Mount Scopus campus of the Hebrew University."

"And Hadassah Hospital," Anne added.

Mars looked down at his repaired cast. "And Hadassah," he agreed.

They made a leisurely turn around the tower as the Old City sprawled below them. They viewed the Jewish Quarter to the south with its new and reconstructed houses, and the *geniza*. The Citadel of David was to the west and beyond that the King David Hotel.

"These places have given us fond memories," Mars admitted.

Anne smiled up at him. Mars held her hands as he looked into her eyes, trying to understand the complex emotions welling up inside him. At 1 o'clock that very day they would become Mr. and Mrs. Marsh Enderly. But that wasn't exactly right. A wry smile came to his lips, and Anne caught it in the warm morning light.

"What's so funny?" she asked, eyeing him warily.

"I was thinking about our married names," he admitted.

"Mr. and Mrs. Mars Enderly," she said with pleasure.

"Close."

"Oh, that's right. It has to be Marsh for official documents."

"No, actually it will be Mr. and Dr. Marsh Enderly," he said, maintaining his composure with difficulty.

She tried to level him with her high-beams but couldn't keep it up. "All right, *Mr.* Enderly. I happen to know someone who will have his Ph.D. soon enough. And if you ever introduce me that way . . ."

"You'll what?" he asked innocently.

"Just try it."

"Moshe was right," Mars said, wisely changing the subject. "I think this is the best view in the Old City."

"Mars, I think it's the most beautiful sight I've ever seen."

"I know of one prettier."

She smiled up at him. "You're a little prejudiced."

He answered her with a kiss, pulling her close. When they broke, both were gasping for breath.

"That's my reply," he said when he could speak.

They walked back to the American Colony Hotel hand in hand and oblivious of the bustle of early-morning traffic. Mars escorted his bride-to-be to her parents' door when a familiar voice sounded behind them.

"A match made in heaven," Moshe rumbled with obvious satisfaction. "True, of course true."

"It's kinda early," Mars observed. "Isn't a *yenta's* job ever done?"

Moshe glanced at his watch. "It will be around 1:30 this afternoon. Now, how are you two lovebirds doing this morning?"

"We're doing just fine," Anne answered for them.

"And we'll be doing even better after some breakfast," Mars added. "Care to join us?"

"Mars, dear?"

Mars looked at her warily. "Yes?"

"I'm having breakfast with Mother and Dad, and, then I have to start getting dressed. We discussed this earlier."

A frown crossed Mars's face as he remembered. "Oh, yeah, I remember. Look, couldn't we . . ."

"No, dear, we couldn't. I need time to get ready."

"But . . ."

Moshe put his arm on Mars's shoulder. "I think I am in need of nourishment. Please help me downstairs before I faint." He glanced at a smiling Anne. "I will take good care of him for you."

Mars gave in as gracefully as he could. Anne watched them as they disappeared around the corner.

◆

Mars looked at the doors he and Anne had entered only a few hours before.

"Very impressive church," Moshe said, pointing up at the bell tower. "And such a view."

"Yes, it is," Joe Enderly echoed.

Moshe waited a few moments for Mars to reply. "I think the younger Mr. Enderly has other things on his mind, not that I blame him. Shall we go in? I think we're expected."

Reverend Bridges was waiting for them at the small chapel's altar. He led them to a room off to the side and reminded Mars and his dad of their entry cue. The minister then ducked out as the organist started playing "Sheep May Safely Graze." About twenty minutes later the organ thundered the opening chords of Wagner's bridal march.

"That's us," Joe said, beaming at his son. He nodded toward the door.

Mars managed a strained smile.

"*La Chaim*," Moshe intoned as the two Enderlys walked into the sanctuary.

At the center of the altar they turned and faced the back of the chapel. Mars's mouth fell open as he watched his bride walking down the aisle. Anne seemed to be the focus of a spotlight as she glided forward on her father's arm, the silk folds of her dress rustling softly. They stopped before the altar. The minister asked who gave the bride.

"Her mother and I do," Bob replied. He smiled at Mars, then returned to his wife. Flo daubed at her eyes.

Mars tried to remember all the things he had been instructed to do. And he mostly succeeded. Finally, the bewildering ritual over, Reverend Bridges broke into a smile of pure enjoyment.

"You may now kiss your bride," he said.

Mars lifted Anne's veil and looked deeply into her eyes. His eyes

closed as their lips touched. He had not intended what he called a pro-
duction number, but it developed into one. Their hearts were one as the
background sounds faded away. Mars broke off when he heard a ner-
vous cough coming from somewhere near him. He cocked an eye at the
minister, who motioned for them to face the congregation.

Mars blushed as he and Anne turned as one.

Reverend Bridges held up his hands. "Ladies and gentlemen, it is
my very great honor to introduce to you Mr. and Mrs. Marsh Enderly."

The organist started playing *The Toccata Fifth Symphony* as the
Enderlys began their retreat. The magnificent chords rolled off the
walls as Anne walked beside her husband. She squeezed his arm.

"Dearest Mars," she whispered. "I love you so much!"

To be continued
in an upcoming sequel.

ACKNOWLEDGMENTS

I want to thank the people who helped make this book possible:
My wife, LaVerne, who besides encouraging and praying for me is also my first editor.

Dave Dickinson, who made sure I got the military facts right.

Mary Reid and Susan Osborn of *The Christian Communicator* who critiqued the manuscript.

Les Stobbe, my agent, who faithfully represented me and believed in what I was trying to do.

John and Jan Simon and Ken and Pat Maitz who provided valuable suggestions.

And the many people who prayed for me and the book.

My special thanks go to my friends in the Dallas Bible Study Fellowship classes and in Trinity Fellowship. I sincerely believe this book is an answer to their prayers.